# Waymaker

# Waymaker

Torion Oey

Cover illustration by Arsalan Ali

ISBN 979-8-9987682-3-1 (paperback)

*For you, who got in the way.*

## Chapter 1: Rebirth

*I'm going to die.*

"Simeon… I love you. I'm sorry."

His older brother sat in the corner of the sanitized room, facing the floor and only sparing sidelong glances. His mom stood over his bed while a doctor had one hand on her shoulder and the other hand on the ventilation machine. He couldn't see them; he was unconscious. He had been for several days. He had little cognitive capacity but he still somehow perceived their presence as well as his end.

"He's 14." His brother's voice cracked.

*That's right… it's my birthday.*

The doctor's hand on his mother's shoulder tightened. Her whole body heaved as she clung to the bedsheets. Time elapsed, filled quietly by her muffled sniffles and groans offset by the ventilator's patterned mimicry of inhaled air and something oddly resembling a heartbeat in place of an exhale. A moment came when only its sounds remained.

*…I'm going to die.*

His mother's eyes met his brother's. She gently placed a hand on his forehead. She moved it to his head. She then slowly brushed her other hand over the doctor's and nodded.

*Luke… Mom… I want… to…*

The machine turned off. Everyone stayed as the seconds passed. And then he passed.

*** 

He opened his eyes. He floated in a void of iridescent dust of blues and greens. The edges of his form blurred as it caught the dust blown against him by a gentle breeze. The infinite particles wavering about him seemed as an endless mist. At first he didn't feel the light tickling like sand until he saw his feet actually touching a translucent, reflective surface. Or perhaps the floor was only reflective.

"Hello, Simeon."

As the woman's voice resounded warmly in his ears he then perceived the sound of the dust being blown around. It resembled blades of grass shifting against one another, or a soundless beach whose rearranging dunes were all that made noise rather than the wind and the waves. When the woman spoke he found that he, too, had a voice as he replied. "Hello?"

"Hello."

He followed the direction of the sound and saw an empty space in the dust. It was a silhouette; a woman's form, a bit taller than him, standing upright and facing him. Unlike his form, in which he not only occupied space but appeared to be a distinct thing within the void and mist, she appeared to be no thing other than what the dust outlined. The outline lifted a hand and politely waved. "Hi," he said.

"I am a god."

"A god," he repeated. He thought nothing major about it; his thoughts were simple; but he thought maybe he should think something more about it. "Is there more than one?"

"I am the God of Desire." Her outline paced closer.

He considered the woman's outline and remembered certain emotions. *I have felt scared, intimidated, lust, and longing.* At the memory the emotions crashed inside him and he took a step back.

The woman's outline paused, a hand offered almost hesitantly out. "Is something wrong?"

"My memory," he said, "I remember… things. I died."

"You are dead," her voice affirmed. "But you are not gone. I can bring you back to life, if you want."

*I can live again?*

"The reason I am speaking to you here and now is because I noticed you had quite a few unmet desires. I think the only thing worse than wasted potential is wasted dreams, and I can't stand by when that happens."

"I want to live again," he said strongly.

Her outlined open hand drew closer. "Tell me, what more do you want? I can do something about aiding you in the direction you wish to live your new life."

He looked at the offered hand without moving. "I want to do what I enjoy."

The dust trailed around her outline as her arm withdrew and she placed her hands on her hips. "Could you be a bit more specific?"

"I didn't enjoy doing much in my past… life. The only highlights were the people I spent time with." Taking a step forward he offered his hand now. "I want to find things I really like to do, as well as enjoy them with others… and for others."

The god hummed. The sound reverberated clear and strong, peacefully as well as painfully. Her outline moved, her hand taking his. It felt more like he touched the smooth surface of sand than an actual thing. The dust around her outline became an endless rush as it streaked to the place they touched hands. The dust then began coating his form, growing and thickening. "Go, then, with my blessing. Live out what you want."

His vision dimmed and his form buzzed while the wind rose. The void and dust burned until new sensations and new colors replaced the peculiar world and he heard a baby's wailing.

## Chapter 2: The New World

"Just look at young Simon! He's practically a man already!"

Simon held his gaze on the pages of the book in front of him, surreptitiously aware of his parents praising him. Every time his name came up it piqued a dormant memory that refused to surface. But that mattered little to him now, having lived with it for 13 years. He turned the page, pretending to read while they pretended to talk to each other.

"We need to get him new clothes," his mother said in a businesslike manner. "His pants only cover up to his shins. And his hair, one of us needs to cut it before it gets too shaggy."

His father harrumphed agreement. "You're better with the scissors. I'll take care of prepping for his school," he added when she made an opposite sound of disagreement. "We're looking at the two local schools, yes?"

"No," Simon said.

His parents bashfully peered at him through the doorframe to his room from their spot by a sink. The house, a cottage by the eaves of their town's valley, contained three separate rooms between the three; one bedroom for them; a kitchen for all; and another bedroom for Simon. "We've told you we only have the money to provide transport from town," his father replied. "Funding for other schools would only be possible with another decade's worth of pay."

"*Unless* incoming students receive recommendations." He closed the book and stood up from his desk crammed by the foot of his bed.

"Only the competitive schools provide waivers for tuition. Only those who are at the top of entrance exams receive those."

"Which is why I want to compete! The tests are free, and I can get paid for internships!"

His parents looked at each other. His mother then spoke, saying, "We appreciate what you're trying to do for us."

"It's not impossible," he continued, leaving his room to stand by the entrance to the house in the kitchen. "I can get in, especially if I have magic—" He broke off, seeing their pained expressions.

"Even if you have magic, other students would have had years of training."

*That's true, there are terrible odds of me being among the best without years of experience let alone any.* "I still want to try." He held their gaze. "The worst that would happen is I'm rejected and we've lost money on travel costs."

"Field work isn't bad," his father said lightly.

"It's not bad, but I don't want to have a life depending on the..." Another inscrutable memory pricked his mind. *Depending on what?* He shook his head and continued. "...the whim of others! I want to make my own path."

His father rocked back on his heels, considering Simon. The townsfolk generally held adventurers and knights in high regard for keeping the peace, but in their boonies they also shared a fear that such peace was precarious. The population wasn't large enough to hold its own guild, and their own direct line of communication to the knights was through the company of four stationed there. "I never liked the idea of becoming a knight... I like the idea even less of you becoming one."

"I don't want to be a knight, I want to be an adventurer!"

His father laughed. "I can't fault you for having dreams. But adventurers live on the whim of others the most; without townsfolk like us requesting jobs, they have nothing to do."

"Father, that's not entirely true! They explore—"

"Dungeons?" His mother folded her arms over her teal and purple bodice. "Those are designed to kill adventurers. They're ridiculous death traps, full of unknown creatures and darkness, there's no reason—"

"There's no known reason! That's a reason!" Simon insisted. "But I wouldn't think of trying exploring anything now! Just—you know—please, let me see if I can do magic. No one here can afford a way to test who has magic, but the school's tests let you do it for free!"

His father huffed. "And here we figured our 'covert' talk would be able to convince you." Giving Simon a shrewd look, he asked, "Is this what you really want?"

"It is. It's what I desire…" Simon trailed off, some form of yet another memory powdering his thoughts with a sense of déjà vu. *Déjà vu? That's not Brullian… What is that? What language is that?*

"Very well. We can cover travel expenses. But you must return when—if you don't make it."

"If you do," his mother added, "Send a letter. Send three letters; you have to include everything that happens."

Simon beamed at them before leaping the short distance the kitchen provided to hug them both. "I will!"

*** 

A week's travel alone by horse (the cheapest option next to a shared wagon) saw Simon to the theocratic city of Narumont. He stabled Fado beside The Grizzled Ghoul—an exceedingly cheap inn for room and board partly thanks to its vaguely blasphemous name—and headed down the cobbled street toward cleaner, more impressive streets and buildings. *And my new school* he thought hopefully while eyeing outdoor signs that hung above doorways. The signs were made of real metal, a material far too pricy to waste for anything other than tools back home. *What if the metalworkers messed up the lettering for the shops?*

He turned a corner and continued down a thoroughfare with more bustle happening between commoners. He could tell they were commoners even if they wore much more fashionable (and clean) clothes that held traces of religious symbolization; each outfit displayed deeper monochromatic blue, green, and purple colors; and each consisted of rounded lapels or collars encircling necklines, most sporting a pin or several pins representing one of the High Clerics who were basically the royalty of Narumont. His clothes were thankfully new, no longer ill-fitted and covered him respectably from head-to-toe. Still, he felt like he stood out with the plain tan trousers and untucked forest-green tunic that fell a ways below his waistline. *Mom said I'd grow into it.* In the distance he saw the end of the more packed buildings where space opened up on expansive lawns marking the campus grounds. Surrounded by the lawns was the enormous single-building school: Verlangen Seminary. He picked up his pace.

The bustle of commoners transformed into stalled traffic of students. They wore smart-looking sapphire blue suede jackets with four buttons (a button for each of the High Clerics as he recalled); the color of the fuzzy leather came from the breed of cattle native to the land who fed primarily on blueberries. *Anthocyanin* Simon recalled when studying the school's customs. *The rare pigmentation mirrored by the cross-bred chamelions' skin and fur makes it expensive. If I do well, I can get a uniform for free…* He eyed the neat black, unwrinkled cuffed trousers that each student wore and shivered at the thought of how much just the uniforms could cost.

He was forced to stop by the end of what he guessed was a line leading down the thoroughfare to an orientation station atop a lawn. Some other students pressed closer behind him. He turned in a circle, noticing the confused and mildly distasteful looks they gave him. "Hi," he said softly before facing forward. From what he could tell he was among the youngest there. *Most are probably returning students. They check everyone for their magic before health inspections and then the tests…*

Simon lost himself in his thoughts and the time seemed to jump as he blinked and noticed the front of the line had disappeared and he was looking at a pair of faculty members sitting at the station looking back at him.

"Hello," the one on the right, a woman with spectacles atop a hooked nose, said. "Please place your hand in the bowl so we may gauge your magical ability."

*The bowl.* His gaze fell to the large clay bowl resting on the center of the rectangle table before him. The bowl held holy water, the kind he knew could detect the magic in people. Slowly, he pulled the cuff of his tunic further up his forearm. He then lowered his right palm until it lay flat against the bowl's basin.

The water bubbled fervently. It remained cool to his touch.

The hook-nosed woman's mouth formed an 'o' before she gestured for him to remove his hand. Behind him came murmurs from several other students.

"No way!"

"It's bubbling so much!"

"Is he secretly royalty?"

"An illegitimate kid?"

Adjusting her glasses, the hook-nosed woman said, "Please follow me." She stood up from the station and guided him deeper onto the school grounds away from the majority of other students toward a similar station, this under a canopy. There another pair of faculty members waited, leaning far back into their portable chairs with their heads lolling, seemingly daydreaming. The woman coughed to announce their presence and the two sat forward immediately.

"Yes!" said one of the men. He straightened his sleek blue jacket that lacked the fuzzy outer layer the students' uniforms had. His eyes blearily met the woman's and he stood up swiftly, knocking back his seat and almost knocking over the table. "Pheona! Are we divining this student?" He gave Simon a once-over. "Is this a new student?"

"I've not taken the tests yet," Simon said.

"You haven't?"

"Hush, Stephen," the woman, Pheona, said. "Bring out a crystal."

"Uh, right," the second man said. Though they each wore the same kind of jackets belonging to faculty they seemed to treat Pheona with more respect than a simple coworker. He scrambled to procure a crystal from a black box resting under the table. He used a teal silk handkerchief to handle the crystal before offering it to Simon.

Simon's heart had been beating faster since discovering the holy water had reacted to him, and he could hardly believe he was being given a divining crystal already. *The information about the entrance tests said divining would only happen after students passed.* Chills lanced down his back at the thought he'd been accepted as he shakily reached out to touch the crystal.

The moment his fingers touched the crystal the three faculty members leaned in expectantly. Simon and the others looked at the crystal for a long moment.

"Nothing's happening," Pheona said, confused.

"I see something," the man holding the crystal said.

"You do?" Stephen asked.

Pheona sighed. "Spit it out, Hane!"

Hane winced before pointing at Simon's hand. "The surface of the crystal touching his skin is changing color."

Stephen pressed closer to peer directly through the crystal while Pheona rounded the table to do the same on Hane's other side. They stayed like that for some time.

"…What do you see?" Simon asked worriedly.

Pheona straightened and adjusted her glasses. "It's faint, but the crystal's coloring is very slowly changing. Remove your hand."

Simon let go and let his arm fall to his side. Where he had been touching the very surface of the crystal retained a sort of faint blue like an artist's watercolor paint. It barely extended deeper into the crystal towards the core, maybe several millimeters beneath the surface. *I didn't read anything about a divining crystal not fully turning some sort of color.*

"That's odd. The holy water bubbled like it'd been over a piping hot stove when he put his hand in," Pheona muttered.

"Really?" Stephen reappraised Simon more slowly. "What's your name?"

"Simon," Simon answered.

"How long have you practiced magic?"

"I… haven't practiced. I never had a teacher."

Stephen looked at Pheona. "That could explain somewhat."

Pheona shook her head. "The color is blue, meaning he has an affinity for water magic. I want to measure his actual output… Give me that." She snatched the crystal and its entirety washed over in a starkly opaque copper red.

Pocketing the crystal, she beckoned Simon to follow her to yet another station, this one without a canopy and being used by several other students. "You're aware of the materials we use for our magic tests, correct?"

Simon nodded and said, "The holy water detects whether a person possesses magic. The crystal divines a person's affinity. And the blessed ink measures the person's magic power numerically."

Pheona continued straight on without looking back, apparently satisfied with the answer. Ahead of them two students were being led away by a faculty member while the last student was dipping her forefinger in an ink bottle. Pheona and Simon reached the table just as the student pressed her same finger onto a large sheet of paper spread across the table. Simon observed as the splotch of ink left by her finger moved to form the number 1505. The student smiled and nodded at the remaining faculty member before racing after the other two being led to the school building.

"Who's this?" the sitting faculty member asked Pheona, taking a quill and dabbing it in the bottle in preparation to write.

"Simon," Pheona said.

The faculty member's hand swished, copying the name down swiftly and elegantly underneath the last girl's name. "You may go ahead," the man said, returning the quill to a dry cloth and sitting back.

Simon dipped his own finger into the ink bottle. He waited for the largest globs to fall back into the bottle so he didn't drip anywhere else before moving his hand to press his finger down beside his name. He waited a moment before lifting his finger.

Pheona peered across the table as the ink shifted on the page. She narrowed her eyes and snatched the paper up before Simon could see what the number finalized as.

"That's unruly," the other faculty member commented, smirking at Pheona. "Is the reason you're escorting him around because he's promising?"

Pheona looked up from the page. "It says your magic power is 10. That's practically useless."

## Chapter 3: Limits

"That doesn't seem right," Desire commented, a frown heard in her voice. Her silhouette, ever-accompanied and framed by dust, peered down through the translucent-reflective floor. "How could he have such meager magic power?"

"Pardon me," a clear, clipped voice intoned.

The dust picked up into a flurry and the invisible hands of Desire's form clenched. "Terminus!"

The God of Boundaries padded from the shadows on the outskirts of the void. Dust barraged his plain features that resembled an everyman who held a desk job; the part of his face from beneath his nose to where his chin and neck connected was covered in a stubble that outlined his mouth which was set in a line; his black irises remained fixed on Desire as he walked, seemingly unperturbed by the dust storm. He casually put his hands in the pockets of his slacks and let his unbuttoned blazer sift freely in the wind as he stopped to stand a few feet away.

"What are you doing here?"

Terminus tilted his head as he side-eyed the shimmering movement beneath their feet. "You meddled with something of mine."

Desire sighed and the wind settled, the dust following shortly after. "Simon you mean? He's not yours. Anyway, how did you—"

"I told him," came a ragged whisper. Another form detached from the void and slinked toward Terminus. The third god's form resembled a woman with a prominent hunch in her back that kept her head permanently level with her shoulders. She staggered until she halted beside the taller god and leered up at Desire. Her eyelashes were like brittle nails that shuttered her pale, yellowing eyes.

The surrounding dust stilled almost to a full stop. "Sticking your nose in my business again, Doubt?"

"Don't blame her," Terminus said sternly. "If I wasn't made aware, you would've created a being too powerful for its own good."

"I only gave him a blessing," Desire hummed, placing her hands on her hips.

"And I only gave him a limiter," he replied.

"A *limiter!?*" Desire cried incredulously. "The world he was born into has humans with 100 magic power at the *least*! He has 10!"

The God of Doubt cooed, her face looking to be the only thing pleased about her while her hunch and the rest of her body tremulously shifted around.

"As unnerving as ever," Desire scoffed.

Terminus cleared his throat. "Great things require great restrictions. He still has your blessing. The next time you think about pulling something like this, tell me in advance. Maybe we could come to more of an agreement." He gave Desire a long look before turning and pacing away.

"That's all?" Desire muttered to herself. "Buzzkills."

Doubt cooed again, the lines around her mouth expanding as she smiled and turned from Desire.

"He's going to be all right, no thanks to you!" Desire called.

Terminus melded with the void without a word. Doubt slowly hobbled away, her grin remaining despite facing away from the God of Desire. "I doubt it," she whispered, and faded into the black.

*** 

Simon blearily followed a group of students being led to the final test by Hane, one of the two faculty members who had manned the divining station. After being let down by the scope of his magic power Pheona had abruptly left him to take the written exams with the others. His hopes of doing well were riddled through. *I don't think I'm going to get a better score than the average. Probably below average.* The only questions he knew he got right had to do with the magic tests themselves and the items used for the tests.

He internally groaned and let his head fall back to stare at the reddening sky while he walked. The thrill of testing positively for magic followed by the disappointment of his meager magic power replayed in his mind. *I should've known it from the divining crystal. They're kept stored, untouched and out of direct sunlight to prevent the coalescence of magic until needed for use. I had such little effect on it!*

"Hey," a girl's voice interrupted his thoughts.

He faced forward and glanced around warily. A light tugging on one of his sleeves drew his attention to the girl who spoke walking on his left. "Hi," Simon said awkwardly. None of the other students had talked directly to him up to that point.

"You were ahead of me in the first line," she said matter-of-factly. She looked to be half a foot taller than Simon with crisp ivory hair that fell in waves around her face.

Simon blinked, feeling a mix of embarrassment. *With all the extravagant clothes I hardly noticed some of the other students' features.* "I'm Simon."

"I'm Avril."

"Oh, like April." Simon glanced at some of the other students who snickered and glanced their way.

"I saw the holy water react to you," she continued, unbothered by the other students. "I wanted to know what your magic power was."

"Oh, that…" Simon grappled with the strong urge to lie and the guilt of lying. "I'd rather not say."

"You don't have to be modest," Avril said. She read the pained expression on his face and added, "You also don't have to tell me, if that's what you prefer. What about your type of magic?"

Simon's face relaxed. "I have an affinity for water."

"Like the High Clerics?" Avril's voice lifted excitedly as her head fully faced him. "Is that why Pheona guided you away? Water is considered the divine element of Goddess Toive! Only a few have an affinity for it, which is why they're considered blessed. Do you have your crystal? I want to see the pretty blue!"

"Uh—" Simon faltered. *They didn't give me the crystal. Did other students get to keep theirs? If so, why didn't they...* The answer came to him immediately. *There wasn't enough magic to fully use the crystal so Pheona took it to probably throw away.*

"Hey, what's wrong?" Avril asked worriedly when Simon became crestfallen. "Did you forget it somewhere?"

"Y-yeah."

The group around them halted, bringing their attention to Professor Hane who pointed at a row of containers each holding a type of material. "This will be your field test!" Hane called. "We've set up training dummies for you to use your respective magic on. If you have an affinity for multiple types make sure to use each of them on the dummies. We'll start with students in the front."

Simon glanced around at where he and Avril stood. They were pretty much in the back, and those standing on their sides moved to press closer to the front. Avril hung back with him.

"Don't worry about what the other students think," she said. "They don't have high expectations for country folk."

Simon tugged at the hem of his oversized tunic. "Are you…?"

Avril shook her head. "I've lived in Narumont my whole life. I've dreamed of going to Verlangen Seminary almost as long."

Simon nodded as the students inched forward, trying his best not to focus too much on the ongoing performances. His focus on trying not to focus on his limited ability caused him to ask, "What is your magic power?"

She smiled at him. "2090."

The blood drained from Simon's face as he mentally quantified what that meant. *She could probably go all day casting low-tier magic continuously, and maybe a few hours with middle-tier magic. Meanwhile I...* "Is that the highest magic for the incoming students?"

"It's higher than most students currently attending as well," she said.

Simon nodded less certainly this time. *She's friendly, though I wouldn't describe her as humble.*

They both came to the front where Hane waited. The faculty member watched as the remaining students moved to the boxes, making marks with a quill on a paper pressed into a clipboard. Once the final student ahead of them finished pulverizing one of the dummies with metal chains (the chains had torn off two of the makeshift limbs while the wooden body was bent and ruptured where they dug in), Hane eyed Simon first.

Simon moved in response despite his growing doubt. *There's no way I can harm a dummy. I don't know any basic magic.* He stepped up to the box containing ten or so gallons of water. From what he saw, none of the other students had made use of the water. He heard whispers from the other students. *I don't know what they're saying, but I can guess.*

He breathed in and focused. *I need to attack the dummy with water somehow. I can try the same body movements others did.* Putting his left foot back and leaning forward on his right, he extended his right arm straight out at the dummy. He clenched his teeth, mentally urging the water to move.

Nothing happened.

Simon lowered his arm before reextending it, bracing it now with his left hand.

A breeze across the lawn stirred the water's surface and it remained otherwise unmoved.

Now the students were talking louder.

"He's from the boonies, so whatever he could do must've been impressive to the locals," one laughed.

"I heard there are hopefuls like him every year."

"He should go home."

Simon dropped his arms, feeling the fear cloud his thoughts. *I can't do this—not on their level. Nowhere near their level. Maybe if I—* He knelt and stuck his hands into the water. *Nothing. It's not holy water.*

"What's he doing?"

"This is embarrassing."

*I can't even make water move on my own. What's the use of an affinity if I have no magic power?* Simon clenched his hands and willed the water to do *something*.

Slowly, a brief rise of bubbles puttered at the surface before the water stilled.

Simon blinked. *That was something. Maybe more?* His skin remained cool while the gentle tickling of air pockets uncoiled from the cracks in his fists and rose. A slew of bubbles emitted a steady sound.

"Well, looks like he's not useless."

"At least he can boil water?"

"The water isn't steaming, though. I don't know what he's doing."

Simon relaxed his hands and the bubbles ceased. *It's something, but it's not enough. I can't do anymore.*

He turned and walked away from the field test back towards the students, letting the water chill his forearms and hands while it dripped and dried away. Avril gave him a thin smile as he passed.

"Don't worry," she said calmly. "I know some of the faculty. I can talk with them and see what I can do to put a good word in, given your affinity."

Simon straightened a bit. "You will?"

Avril nodded, her ivory hair waving gently around her smiling face. "I'll try."

*She's really kind. But could she save me? I don't know what she could possibly do to convince the school to admit me.* His cheeks still burned from embarrassment but also gratitude that she would go out of her way to do that.

He turned to watch how she did, hoping she could dazzle everyone into forgetting what just happened. She promptly positioned herself in front of a dummy that had no container. She swished her arm and torrential wind made a series of incisions across the dummy, splintering the wood.

The students ooh-ed and clapped when the wind subsided. She then swished her other arm and a segment of the ground jutted out to impale the dummy through its torso. The dummy's upper body detached and fell to the ground.

"That's everyone!" Hane called before the cheers went wild. "Return to the front of the seminary grounds tomorrow morning where the results of the exams will be posted."

Simon breathed a sigh of relief and dread. *The only options are my written scores being exceptional, which...* He shook his head and watched Avril return to the body of students with a proud smile. *No, those scores are not at all going to be exceptional. I'd hoped to possibly get admitted into the scribe tract if I didn't have magic. But no, my only hope now is Avril.*

***

The sky became engulfed in shadows as the night grew late. Simon had remained by the end of the thoroughfare, watching the people move around storefronts and sightsee the nearby magic school's campus. Avril mentioned returning to tell him what she could after talking privately with a faculty member. Simon didn't have a clock on him, but his own sense of time told him something like an hour had passed.

*Maybe I should look for her. Fado will be getting restless in the stable.* Simon started walking, following the way Avril had gone down a side street. He came to the next thoroughfare over, this one less wide and crowded. *Where would they have met? An inn would be my best bet to look.*

He guessed from the mingling of salt and bitter smells which way to go while gauging the directions of the swelling of sounds and laughter. He passed by window after window, taking a moment to peer through and see if she was inside any of the buildings. After losing track of how far he'd gone he saw a head of white hair sitting within an inn. He went through the open door and blinked to adjust his eyes to the brighter atmosphere.

The room was moderately occupied, its barest tables still housing one or two patrons. The log furniture and sidings along the walls made the room feel quaint but felt a touch like it was trying too hard to fit into a countryside theme. He looked over at Avril who was talking to a school staff member—Stephen—at a two-person table.

*Should I approach them or wait more?* Simon stepped closer hesitantly. Deciding against interrupting, he sat at one of the larger square tables that one other patron occupied. The patron paid him no mind, continuing to divvy up some coins atop the table by a trio of empty mugs.

"…the last test Simon showed what he could do."

Simon perked up upon overhearing the conversation between the two.

"I told you, even though we're related I'm not supposed to discuss other students' scores."

"I'm not talking about scores. Anyway, he said he had an affinity for water—"

"I *know*. I was administering the divining tests."

"—and when he went to do the field test he failed completely!"

*What?*

Avril went on. "The worst of the other students at least managed to put a dent or two in their dummies, but he didn't so much as touch one! All he could do was cause the water to bubble a bit and then he gave up! I couldn't have asked for a better opening act before I went."

Stephen remained quiet while listening to the girl talk.

"He thinks I went to talk to you to see if I could recommend the school to admit him, but he has no potential. I only talked to him in case he actually was impressive."

"He's waiting for you?" Stephen asked.

"Probably not anymore. He'll go back to wherever he came from, if not tonight then after the results tomorrow."

Stephen sighed. "That's not very nice."

Avril let out a forced laugh before turning to look out the window. "You know as well as I do 'nice' isn't a familial trait."

The patron opposite Simon finally met his gaze. "Do you need something?"

Simon dumbly shook his head, got up from the table, and walked out the door.

## Chapter 4: Remembering the Old World

*Just check the board. Just check the board. Then you can leave.* Simon murmured the thought to himself under his breath while the students crowded around the front of the campus grounds. It was the start of the following day and the entrance exam results posted on the bulletin setup listed the names of students who had been admitted in black ink while everyone else wouldn't see their name.

"S, s, s," Simon muttered, jostling and being jostled as the other students tried to pinpoint their names. "S… S…" He froze. There were three names starting with 'S.'

*Sawyer.*

*Sheena.*

*Sinom.*

Simon blinked, re-reading the last name of the S's. "What," he breathed. *Sinom? SINOM?*

Disgruntled sounds of the student ahead alerted Simon to the fact he was accidentally gripping the student's shoulder. He quickly let go and nonchalantly stared at the name again while the male student turned his head and looked around to find who'd grabbed him. *Did they misspell my name? Is it a spelling mistake? Is there someone actually named Sinom?*

Simon remained rooted in place as his thoughts warred with each other. He stayed there for some time, unaware as the crowd of students changed and the sun climbed higher. He may have stayed there indefinitely if not for the hand that grabbed his and yanked him through the crowd toward the side street he'd taken the night before.

He almost tripped as his legs moved rapidly to stay beneath him. The bespectacled face of a hooded Pheona turned momentarily to look back at him as she dragged him off the thoroughfare. When they were alone on the side street she let go of his hand and faced him.

Simon was about to ask what she was doing when she forcefully pressed a book into his stomach. "Wh-*oof*!" Simon gripped the sleek teal bindings and wrenched it off him.

Pheona let go and took a step back.

"What are you doing?" he finally was able to ask. "And what is this?" He turned the book over to the front cover and saw there the same blank sleek bindings.

"It's a tome," she said hastily. "There is no one named Sinom. I made your name an anagram, figuring you'd be confused and stick around the exam results for me to find you."

"But… Why?"

"Because you didn't pass the exams," Pheona said plainly. "You didn't pass."

Simon felt it unnecessary for her to say it twice, but it did somehow register clearer the second time. "I—then what's this for?"

"The holy water does not lie," she said. "You still have magic. Even if it's a tenth of the power that the lowest-tier mages have."

*Even the lowest mages have a magic power of at least 100?* Simon opened the tome to the first page and saw a faint curving line form a circle before his eyes. "Something appeared," Simon said in surprise.

Pheona took a step away, her back remaining just within the shadow of the buildings before the next thoroughfare. "Every mage has a tome and every tome is unique to the mage. The school provides unbound tomes to every incoming student who possesses magic."

"I don't get it," Simon said, turning to the next page and reading a short passage already there. It was a spell on summoning and dismissing the tome. The number 10 was written beside the spell's name *Koota / Poista*. "…It takes 10 *sakti*—that's magic power, right? 10 to either summon or dismiss my tome? That's all I have!"

Pheona let out a short breath. "It might seem useless now. Maybe it is. You have to figure out for yourself what you can do with your magic. If you do, you may be able to return to attempt the exams next year. The more you do with magic, the more defined the first page of your tome will become. The image that forms there is meant to be a symbol of your power. Right now it's a faint circle that looks to be no more than a centimeter wide. A circle resembles flow and is rather fitting for one with a water affinity. You'll know if you're capable when that image becomes fuller and more intricate." She glanced over his shoulder and made a shooing motion. "I can't stay longer. Best of luck."

Simon blankly watched her speed off around the corner. He looked back down at the spell. *A tome of magic... My magic.* He flipped to the next page and saw that it was blank. He flipped a few more pages and then quickly through the rest of it, making certain everything else was blank except the first two pages. *Great. So far I know how to summon and dismiss this thing.*

He closed the tome and considered what to do next. *I didn't pass. But I might be able to next year... I just need to become more capable.* He smiled thinly to himself. *'Just.' She said the way to track that is with the image on the first page, and to progress I have to use magic. Right now I can only cast one spell. If more spells appear in my tome but I don't have the remaining power to summon it... Well, I only have one spell to use right now anyway.* He shrugged and held the tome in both of his hands in front of him. "*Poista.*"

The tome vanished, his hands pushing slightly into the empty space from the residual tension of holding it up. He blinked a few times, surprised that it had worked so easily. *I thought I'd give it a try before having to really study the 'how-to' of the spell. It worked out, I guess. Now I just have to remember 'koota' to bring it back when I have more magic to use. How long will it take to regain? How will I know I've regained it?*

He turned around to take a look at the students continuing to scour the results board for their name. *I was counting on passing to be able to stay at the school, but I only have enough money to return home. I guess…*

Chatter from the thoroughfare behind him caught his ears.

"…guild members are holding a meeting. Apparently there's a major job that needs to be done outside the city."

"You don't mean the dungeon?"

"Probably. I only heard there were monsters widening their territory."

*A dungeon.* Simon heard his mother's words of warning about exploring such places echo in his head. But between staying idle and casting roughly one spell a day (or more if he were lucky) and finding a treasure that could increase his power, the choice was easy. *But between living safely and probably dying, the choice is also easy.*

Simon patted the pockets of his trousers, feeling the loose coins. *I can go home and hope my magic can increase day by day. Or I can stay and see about other opportunities. Do I go? Do I stay?*

His stomach growled and suddenly his mind was made up. *I'll eat here and then check out this guild.*

He stepped into the thoroughfare to follow the pedestrians as they chatted. They wore different clothes than the other more religious attires; fitted pants and tunics something like what Simon wore but of stronger material. *Adventurers?*

"The dungeon still hasn't been explored fully, right?"

"Yeah, yeah. Adventurers complain all the time that they've not found much treasure, so the best of it is probably still there waiting."

They turned down another side street, Simon following several paces behind. They went quiet in the less populated area before ducking down an alley. Simon blinked, curious about their sudden flighty behavior. He stepped up to the mouth of the alley to peer down and was pulled off his feet.

His body flew in an arc over one of the men gripping Simon's arms. The man slammed Simon onto the pavement. A *crunch* echoed and his vision blurred and sharpened as pain lanced across his back.

Simon weakly took in air to replace all that had been knocked out of him. The two men stood over him and prodded the sides of his body with their feet, feeling around for money. One of the men's boots touched the coin pouch in his trouser pocket and emitted a jingling sound.

"Doesn't sound like much," the burlier man who had swung Simon through the air commented.

"What do you expect from hopefuls looking for easy money?" the tall but otherwise nondescript man said.

Simon barely understood what was happening while the majority of his attention was on the pain. *Something is broken. They intentionally spoke up about a dungeon to lure me here?* Simon winced as the tall man clawed a hand to wrench the money from his pocket.

"Well, I was certainly expecting more than this," the tall man commented as he appraised the contents of the money pouch.

"He probably traveled from some poor country town. Come on, let's head back and see what other failed or hopeful students might have on them."

Simon gasped as the air finally came back to him. He strained his left arm to try touching the area on his back that had hit the ground. The pain lanced across his body and he quickly relaxed. *I can't move right now.*

His eyes followed the men as they walked around him and left the alley and out of sight. He could hear the murmur of people nearby passing the alley, but none were stopping to take notice. Or, if they did, they simply left him alone.

Simon continued sucking in breaths, each intake straining the bones and muscles near his lower spine. *What am I doing here? I don't want to be here. I need help. I want to…*

Just then a different kind of pain seared its way across his scalp. He recoiled as memories flooded him, the involuntary movement causing another jolt of physical pain to radiate from his lower back. *I want to… I wanted to stand. I want to move. But I couldn't. Now I can't. I was in a hospital. Hospital? It wasn't an infirmary like in this world. My mother and brother were in that world. Brother?*

*That world? Earth. The god brought me here after I died.*
*How did I die? I was unconscious for the final days of my*
*life. I heard the doctor mention asphyxiation. Before the*
*hospital… I was walking near a man-hole and fell in…*
*someone pushed me… the sewage gas caused it. How long*
*was I in the hospital? A week. Maybe more or less. My*
*brain wasn't working afterwards. I forgot how to move and*
*breathe. I wanted to…*

"Hey."

Simon blinked, focusing on the pair of green eyes
staring directly down at him. The woman wore a nun's
attire, but unlike the black and white he knew from his
previous life it was the same water colors as the other
commoners around the city. More hot sensations coursed
through his brain as the memories of people, places, and
things from his previous world hit him.

"Can you move?"

Simon's sight grew darker and a wave of tiredness
fell over him. He fell asleep.

## Chapter 5: The Waymaker Guild

*I want to move.*

Simon woke up in a heavily blanketed bed and immediately rose to sit upright. He patted the spot on his chest where crisp late-afternoon light filtered through horizontal blinds across him and his bed and splashed the floor. He moved his hand to feel around his throat, the memory of soreness causing him to check. *I felt a weight on my chest and throat and couldn't move… No, that was before when I was Simeon. That other world—was it real? What was on top of me?* His body shuddered and he blinked rapidly, feeling like he was going to cry but the tears remained behind his eyes. *I also couldn't move recently. My back is—* Simon's hand moved to feel around his back where the pain had been. *My back is fine?*

"Your back is fine," came a female voice.

Simon turned his head to a seated figure at his bedside. He recognized the same luminous green eyes peering back at him but now through a plain cherrywood mask carved in the style of a horse fitted over the rest of her face. She still wore the blue-green nun attire.

"I healed it. I take it someone did that to you? Did you provoke them?"

"What? No, I—" Simon restrained himself, feeling the mix of anger, desperation, and fear from being made immobile again bubbling into his voice. *She helped me. Breathe.* "Two men walked by me talking about a guild meeting to explore a dungeon."

Her eyes blinked. "Where were you?"

"I was by Verlangen Seminary."

"You're a student," she said.

"No. I didn't pass the entrance exams." Simon felt his spirits decline. *Being nothing more than entertainment for the other students, failing the exams, Avril betraying me, getting my back apparently broken, losing my money... And all this after dying in a previous life. A* previous *life. It's unbelievable, but for some reason it's what I believe. For now, unless my mind was broken alongside my back.* "I might just be destined to fail and die," he muttered.

The woman laughed loudly, startling him. "I haven't seen anyone this hopeless in a while! What's your name?"

He lowered his eyelids, remaining quiet.

"So you're a failed student! You come from out of town?"

Simon nodded, uncertain of how he felt about the woman's cheerful attitude.

"You came all this way to not get in, huh? That's a bummer. Too bad about getting mugged as well."

"Are you not from Narumont?" Simon asked, wondering at her style of language being more like the people in the countryside.

"I was abandoned here as a baby," she replied, tilting her head down to gaze at the light cast on the floor slowly inching its way to her feet. " 'Could say I'm more acquainted with the ruffians than the well-to-do folk here."

*Really?* Simon gave a slow look at her clothes.

"Don't be surprised. Everyone here worships Goddess Toive. She is the power behind our magic, supposedly." The woman's eyes returned to Simon. "Though you didn't make the cut into Verlangen. Do you not have magic?"

Simon suppressed a sigh. "I have some."

"Oh?"

"Why are you wearing a mask?" Simon asked, remembering her fair and pretty face before he passed out.

The woman shrugged. "I own it, might as well use it."

"Where am I?"

"The guild those two men mentioned."

Simon moved the covers off him and placed his feet on the ground to fully face her. "This is the guild? Why'd you bring me here?"

"I'm the guild master," she said.

Simon waited a beat to process what she said. "You're the guild master," he repeated. "Wait, you heard those men, so wh—"

"Never mind why or what I was doing." Coins chinked dully in her hand when she procured a money pouch. *His* money pouch. She tossed it the short distance to him, where it lightly bounced off his stomach and landed on his lap.

Simon shuddered and his eyes fluttered rapidly while he hyperventilated.

"Whoa, easy there, kid. Breathe. What's your affinity?"

*There's still something I can't remember. Why am I reacting like this?* He took some time to control his breathing, the writhing in his chest quelling somewhat. "Why do you want to know?" Simon finally asked.

The woman gripped Simon's shoulders and stood. Simon's body lifted off the ground and bed and he let out a cry of surprise. "Tell me and I'll put you down."

"H-hey! Okay! It's water!"

The woman let go and he landed on his feet. "Good. I was right to bring you here."

Simon rubbed his shoulders, feeling the dull ache left by her fingers digging into the skin. He sidestepped her and backed up to the door.

"What's up?" she asked, her horse mask facing him as she turned.

"You're strong," he said breathily. His fingers wrapped around the doorknob.

"Are you leaving?" she asked.

Simon didn't respond. He opened the door and stepped backwards out of it. The woman didn't move. He took another step back.

"If you're going to leave, the exit's on the ground floor." She made a twirling gesture, directing him to go ahead and turn around.

Simon paused, glancing around at the vacant hall that looked to have a series of similar bedrooms but whose doors were closed. "Who are you?"

The woman turned her seat around and sat back down. "Masaka."

*Sounds Japanese* Simon thought, recalling another memory from Earth. "Do you know the Goddess Toive?"

"That's a strange question," Masaka said. "It's not like I know her personally. No one does. It's not in the nature of a god to be buddies with anyone. 'Course, I don't know what the nature of a god is in the first place." She chuckled to herself.

*A god, meaning there are more?* Simon suspected she knew more than she was letting on. He squared away the possibility of other people being reborn like him and asked, "What did you mean you were right to bring me here?"

"My affinity is the body. I can heal and alter people, as well as sense fluctuations in them. I've sensed a strange power from you since I saw you lying in the alley."

"How is it strange?" Simon asked.

"You tell me. You were tested by Verlangen Seminary, weren't you?"

Simon bit his tongue. "My magic power is 10."

A few seconds passed before Masaka laughed even louder than before. "Kid, you're crazy! You thought you'd get accepted into Verlangen with that amount of magic?"

"I didn't *know* that's all I had," Simon said with annoyance.

"C'mon, that's not all, right?"

"Right now all I can do is summon and dismiss my tome."

Masaka hushed herself. "You have a tome?"

"I—yes, I—"

Masaka streaked from her chair and pushed Simon against a wall by a banister leading downstairs, her horse mask inches from his face. "Show me!"

"I can't! Not right now," Simon added when she let out a hiss. "I need to regain my sakti."

"What're you talking about, your sakti's fine!" Masaka's eyes drew closer and the front of her mask touched his nose. "Summon it!"

"Fine, I'll try! *Koota!*" The tome appeared with the sound of a puff of air next to their faces.

Masaka snatched it before it fell and she threw open the bindings. "There's not much here. Still, getting your hands on a tome is something. What'd you do, steal it?"

"No! One of the faculty members gave it to me."

She quickly appraised the first two pages and shut it to hand back to him. Her eyes widened when their eyes met again. "Whoa. You said your magic power was only 10, right?"

"Yeah. Why?"

"That spell to summon your tome costs that amount of sakti but you don't look to have lost any of it. What's your name, kid?"

The door opposite the stairwell opened and a brown-haired girl whose face somewhat resembled a chipmunk in an appealing way halted before barreling into them. Her nose twitched while her dark eyes appraised the situation. "Masaka! What are you doing? Who is this?"

*She's maybe two or three years older than me.* Simon glanced between the two, waiting for the guild master to let him go. She didn't. "I'm Simon."

Finally Masaka let him go. "This kid was banged up by some thugs so I took him here," she said lazily in the girl's direction. "What are *you* doing? Everyone should've cleared out when the call to raid the dungeon went out."

"I'm… not ready for a dungeon yet, I don't think." The girl noticed Simon edging closer to the stairway. "Hey, watch—!"

Simon's heel went too far past the edge of the first stairstep and he fell backward. Twisting his body and letting go of the tome, he managed to brace himself on his side rather than his back as he tumbled the rest of the way down. His momentum when he hit the ground floor was stopped by a table. A lit candlestick toppled and fell. Grimacing from the bruises echoing around his stomach, ribs, and hips, he unthinkingly caught the candlestick. He heard the sound of his fingers singing before the pain of the hot wax coating his skin burned through the shock.

"OW!" He let go of the candlestick and blew out the flame when it hit the ground while nursing his right hand.

Masaka took the stairs slowly while the girl meekly waited. "Kid, you're a magnet for trouble aren't you?"

*No, just everything since I've arrived in this city has sucked* he thought to himself, borrowing the sentiment from his past life. "Water!" he said urgently. "Where is it?"

Masaka, continuing to loaf down the stairs, pointed at a counter with a birch bowl already full.

Simon picked himself off the floor and hurried to stick his hand in the water. Its coolness eased some of the stinging, and he quickly got to work removing the wax stubbornly sticking to his hand. The water bubbled, surprising him at first, but he ignored it as he scrubbed despite the pain on his raw skin.

"Is he a mage?" the girl asked when Masaka stopped at the bottom of the stairs to watch Simon from afar.

"He's injury-prone," Masaka commented. "Healing is wasted on me. He's been hurt more in a day than I have in a month." Her eyelids drooped as her green eyes bore into him through her mask. "You can stop scrubbing. That's holy water, if you didn't notice. It'll heal you on its own."

Simon exasperatedly faced her while keeping his right hand in the bowl. "What do you want from me?"

Masaka glanced at the tome lying open on the floor where it had fallen. "Before you were robbed you were looking to see about the dungeon, weren't you?"

"So what?"

"No one would explore a dungeon unless they wanted something. What do you want?"

"I want to be left alone." *I want to get stronger! To not get robbed, to not rely on self-interested backstabbers, to not die… to live my life!*

"You're telling me, kid. How about I help you? Join this guild and do some guild work and I'll leave you alone."

*Join the guild?* Her *guild?* "Guilds cost money, don't they?"

"Our jobs cover that. I'll keep the debt low and throw in one of our empty rooms as a deal if you agree to one of the posted jobs now."

Simon thought about it. "Why should I instead of leaving right now?"

Masaka chuckled. "Even without my magic I consider myself a good judge of people. You came to this city on your own, which tells me you've got initiative. I'm talking about the stuff adventurers live and breathe."

"And look where it got me."

"Exactly!" Masaka crooned. "You took a path that got you worse for wear. An adventurer doesn't expect success for every choice they make, though they do hope. And among adventurers, the Waymaker Guild is a home for those who brazenly go their own path."

*The Waymaker Guild?* Simon hadn't heard of it, but he also hadn't been studying the various guilds in Narumont. His annoyance had ebbed at some point, either thanks to the soothing holy water or something Masaka said. "What are the rules of the guild?" he asked.

Masaka pointed a hand at him triumphantly. "A Waymaker only ever has one rule: never back down from what you want."

## Chapter 6: Bubbles

*Alone. At last…* Simon sat on the same bed he'd woken up in earlier that afternoon. The window remained shuttered but the night outside was dim enough that no light needed to be blocked. The seat Masaka had sat on remained by his bedside; the only other furnishing aside from the bed and chair was a flat desk next to his head when he lay down. The setup reminded him of his own bedroom. *Not my bedroom, the one I have now. My old one.* In his past life the bedside chair was almost always occupied by… someone in the morning, usually as a means of playfully waking him up. He frowned, blinking quickly. *Is it possible to miss someone I never knew? Who was it that woke me up?*

The memory of medical tables surfaced and he glanced over. He blinked away the image of a ventilator that momentarily replaced the desk. *Strange how I remember that, and not…* Then the figures of his mother and brother sprang to mind. *My former mother. And I don't have siblings now.* He turned onto his side to face away from the chair and door and look through the shutters. The neighboring building's lights were off, and the nearest lampposts were at the far end of the street out of sight. Only a screen of black filled his vision. *I can't picture their faces. Would it be possible to return to that world? It had no magic like this one. Do I want to?*

He rolled over again to face the door. A pang gripped his heart at the empty chair by his bed. *They also stayed by my bedside while I was unconscious. I can't remember their faces. Why can't I remember them?*

A phantom weight pressed down on his stomach and slowly shifted up to his chest and neck. Sitting up, Simon tugged distractedly at a sleeve of his shirt. *Alone.*

He stood and went to the door, opening it quietly. The hall was empty. None of the adventurers would be back for some time. Masaka mentioned dungeons taking days or even weeks to explore. Aside from her and that other girl, he wouldn't be running into anyone. He lightly padded to and down the stairs. The lounge expanded back from the stairs towards the street he had seen outside his window. A series of candles remained lit and flickering atop the five round tables occupying the space. *Someone's still awake.* Several stools rested upside down atop each table respectively, giving off the impression of a tavern after hours rather than a guild. By the wall of the stairs he saw the same birch bowl, again full with holy water, resting atop the counter. He went to it and knelt, opening a cupboard beneath the countertop. A stack of bowls of the same material and design rested within, as well as a few translucent pitchers of some kind of dark liquid. He took one of the bowls, closed the cupboard, and filled it in the nearby sink.

Simon then carefully balanced the bowl so as not to spill as he walked to the exit. The door was thankfully one that only needed pushing to open, and he shouldered his way through to step onto the dark cobbled street.

The outside air was chilly. The quiet murmur of crowds could not be heard from the corner of the city in which the Waymaker Guild resided. *Odd that there was more noise near the Grizzled Ghoul. Or maybe it's not odd.* He counted his luck for being able to get a better night's sleep, and mentally noted to send another letter to his family after completing the "job" Masaka would assign him later. Earlier on his way to return Fado to a stable he'd sent a letter off with a mail carrier, leaving out that little detail of taking on something as part of an adventurer's guild; he had come clean about his entrance exams, however. *They'll be sure to send something encouraging back, as well as persuade and remind me about the benefits of farming that they want me to take on.* Simon turned to a patch of lawn wedged between the guild house and an adjacent building. Its edges touched the street and spread back to end at another of the guild house's walls. A garden table and a pair of wrought iron chairs with decorative floral backings rested in the center of the space, the lawn nestled between the three walls.

Simon took the bowl to the table and put it down. He glanced up to make sure no windows faced the little alcove. *I can practice in peace here.*

"*Koota*," he said, and his tome appeared on the table next to the bowl. Flipping it open, he turned to the third page which remained blank. *I will get stronger. I can't just have one spell.* He sat on one of the chairs and submerged both his hands in the bowl.

*Remember what I did during the final practical test… I did something.*

He concentrated, clenching his hands. The tickling of bubbles snaking their way out, around, and up his hands gave rise to a mild feeling of joy. *It's working!* He continued to concentrate while wondering what exactly he did that caused the magic to work. *The water isn't getting warmer. I don't get it, but it's working.*

He glanced at the page. Still, no spell appeared. *If this isn't its own spell, then I must only be forcing out whatever magic I have left to make bubbles. If I just used up my apparent capacity of magic to summon the tome, these dregs won't last long.* He remained fixed in his seat, watching the stream of bubbles gently patter the water's surface.

***

The front door of the guild slamming caused him to jump out of the chair and break his concentration. He looked up at the street and noticed dawn had broken and the morning light would soon fall onto the cobblestones.

"There you are!" Masaka rounded the corner and put her hands on her hips. "You've been out here all night?" Her bright green eyes peering through her horse mask darted from the bowl, to his wrinkled fingers, to his face. "Good! You've been practicing. You'll need it for the job."

*My first job as an adventurer.* Though country life had gotten him used to early hours, he'd never once pulled an all-nighter (another phrase borrowed from his past-life memories). Oddly, he didn't feel tired. He shook his hands to wave away the water that clung to them before brushing the rest off on his pants. "What is the job?"

Masaka thrust a ratty sheet of paper out for him to read.

"*Black chamelion fur wanted: kill 10 and bring to Jen's General Store. Reward: 10 gold.*" He looked up at Masaka. "The chamelions around here are all blue," he said.

"They change color based on their surroundings and food," Masaka said, pointing to the bottom of the paper at tiny scrawling.

Simon narrowed his eyes. *Located in Rivermouth Dungeon.* "This says they're in a dungeon."

"That's right," Masaka said.

"I'm not prepared for a dungeon."

"No one is," she replied. "But, you've got a point. I'm sending Kairi with you."

"I don't—I mean, I won't be any use." He pointed back at the bowl. "Chamelions are territorial, aren't they? I can't cast any spells other than summoning my tome."

"Right," she said sarcastically. She handed him the page as she went by to stand beside the table. "Looks like you've got another spell."

"I do?" He rushed over and stared at the third page. Sure enough, new writing detailed a spell. "*Bubble.*" A single large bubble spontaneously materialized at the bottom of the bowl and popped when it reached the surface. *I didn't touch the water to cause that! But…* "Are you serious? That's it?"

"Looks like it costs 10 'sakti' as well," Masaka added, rapping a knuckle over the spell's listed magic power required. "Look at you! You've been at it all night and still have the energy to cast something! In fact," she bent around either side of him, looking his body up and down. "You don't look depleted of sakti in the least."

"Why is that? If I can use magic this much, why did I get measured with only 10 magic power?"

"Probably because that's the limit of the amount you can use," she said. "I've heard some people having curses like that; they can only cast spells that cost a fixed amount of sakti. From what I can tell, you don't have any curse on you. But you're stuck at the most basic of low-tier spells."

"So *why?*" he asked again, frustrated.

"Your sakti regeneration must be incredible," she answered simply. "Have you tried summoning and dismissing your tome quickly?"

Simon shook his head. He looked down at the tome. *"Poista."* The tome vanished. *"Koota."* The tome reappeared, open on the same page. *"Poista."* It vanished.

"Ooh," Masaka said with intrigue. "Let's see what happens... Keep doing that."

*"Koota. Poista. Koota."*

***

The afternoon arrived and Simon and Masaka were still outside the guild house.

*"Koota!"*

"Yay!"

*"Poista!"*

"Yay!"

"*Koota!*"

"Yay!"

With every spell he cast Masaka gave a loud cheer. They ignored the growing crowd of people watching them curiously.

"*Poista!*"

"Yay!"

A man shook his head and walked off. "Best leave them. Waymakers are unruly, even among adventurers."

"*Koota!*"

"Yay!"

Three women wandering by hurried quicker upon seeing the guild master jump and throw a fist into the air with her cheering. "She's wearing the horse mask again," one commented with disdain.

"*Poista!*"

"Yay!"

The door to the guild house banged open, halting Simon's spellcasting. The girl from the other day rounded the corner looking flushed, her previously well-kept brunette hair now disheveled.

"What is going on?" she asked with a hint of frustration. "I've been waiting to go on the job but no one came by the lounge! Then I heard you cheering, and—"

"Simon's practicing!" Masaka said happily.

"*Koota!*" The tome appeared.

"I see that," Kairi said, her frustration ebbing.

Masaka grabbed the tome and flipped the page. "Ooh! There's another spell!"

"Really?" Simon made a move to take the tome from her but Masaka shifted away. Letting go of the annoyance as quickly as it came, he peered over her shoulder. The fourth page displayed the spell:

*Bubbles 10*

*Creates a short stream of bubbles from an available water source.*

"How is this useful?" Simon asked dejectedly.

"What did you say?" Masaka's horse mask faced him, her cheerful tone completely absent and now flat. She shut the book, the *thump* causing the pedestrians lingering on the street to flee as if sensing danger. Kairi retreated to the corner of the guild house.

Simon, uncertain now, shrank back. "How—"

Masaka dropped the tome. She picked Simon up by his shoulders and pressed him into the back wall of the tiny garden.

Simon let out a cry of surprise. "What—?"

"Shh. I'm going to tell you a story." Her voice remained unnervingly low and neutral. "Once there was a girl who was abandoned in a foreign city as a baby. She was raised at an orphanage. There she learned about magic and the Goddess Toive. When she was old enough to go places on her own, she ran away. The city was welcoming and cruel at the same time. People were equally willing to give leftovers or beatings to the girl when she asked for food. She learned on her own about the magic she could use and was able to recover from the worst scrapes. She went back to the people who beat her up, and she beat them up. Then she found people wandering around like her and so she made a guild. The end." She dropped Simon and walked back to the front of the guild house.

Simon landed, wobbling slightly.

"You're going to go to the dungeon with Kairi now," Masaka called back to him over her shoulder before disappearing around the corner. The sound of the door slamming indicated she'd gone back inside.

Simon looked down at the paper detailing the job still in his hand. *What was that about?*

Kairi warily looked at him then beckoned for him to follow. "Come on. I know the way."

## Chapter 7: The Lonely Boy

"What's with Masaka?" Simon stepped over an upturned tree root while Kairi took the lead.

"You upset her," Kairi said softly. She guided him through the forest to the east of Narumont. They'd been walking in complete silence since leaving the guild house. "You can only do what you can do when you can do it."

Simon glanced up from the ground at her. "What?"

"That's something Masaka says a lot." They arrived at a clearing but Kairi didn't pause to rest before remerging into the forest of thin trees. Their gray-brown bark had scrapes; something like claw marks where the bark was more of a salmon color.

"What does that mean?" Simon asked. He passed a few trees with more salmon-colored bark protruding from the trunks and inhaled a faint cinnamon kind of smell.

"A lot of things." She breathed out slowly, taking a moment to carefully observe the area before turning left. "You've only just found out you're blessed with a water affinity."

"Yeah." Simon considered the words again. "You're saying I want to do something I can't right now? Why would that upset her? Isn't that following the guild's rule?"

"No." Kairi stopped walking and faced him. "You were complaining. Complaining is another way of giving up." She looked around carefully again. "We're close to the dungeon now."

"I wasn't complaining. I—"

"You were," she interrupted him. "And I get it. You've got a strange limit to what you can do with magic even though you have an affinity for water. But you have an affinity for *water*. Including you, there are only five people I know who have that, and four of them are the High Clerics of Narumont. What you can do with water, no one but they can do that. Even if it's just making some bubbles." She started off again toward the growing sound of trickling water.

Simon let the older girl's words sink in. *I've been focusing too much on what I can't do. I let it get in the way.* His face reddened as he continued to follow her. *They've given me a room in their guild and all I've done in return is hurt myself and—ugh, complain. They must think I'm an ungrateful brat.*

"Did you seriously stay up all night practicing magic?" she asked.

"Oh. I… yeah."

They came across the river and Kairi led the way opposite the direction of the water's flow. She gave him a hasty look back without saying anything more.

*I don't know what I can do to help in a dungeon, though* he thought worriedly. *I don't know Kairi. She probably can take on a few chamelions on her own. I think.* His gaze dropped to her hands clenched tightly at her sides. He wondered about the decision to send just the two of them to this dungeon while the rest of the guild went to the Narumont dungeon. Just as he wondered this, the mouth of the river appeared in the distance around a bend. The water streamed out from within a hulking cavern, a makeshift moss-and-rock walkway following it inside. *That's the dungeon?*

The river's mouth expanded into a large body and then thinned to return to the stream they walked by. The progression of the water reminded him of a digestive system, from the esophagus leading from the dungeon entrance to the stomach-like lake before traveling on. A single chamelion grazed in the low grass beside the stream leaving the mouth of the cave. Its fur was black all the way from its short snout to its tufted tail; its massive cat-like legs had two pairs of toes facing opposing directions with respective dagger-length claws sticking out of each toe. They caught the light with an eerie blackness as well.

"We're supposed to kill that?" Simon said, his voice weak. *Either of its paired toes looks like it could fit around my neck.*

"Rivermouth Dungeon has more of them," Kairi said quietly, halting and staying still while watching.

The chamelion looked to have noticed them even from a distance though only continued to move its head up and down to lap up some water. Its tail flicked back and forth as if set to a slow rhythm.

"Stay here," she whispered.

Simon nodded. "Okay. But what should I do?"

"Whatever you can." She shuddered, then took off, sprinting incredibly fast along the lakeside, heading straight at the creature.

Its tail flicked once more before becoming taut as it lifted its head and bared fangs around the same size as its claws. It backed up while squaring its shoulders at Kairi in a sort of intimidation posture.

Simon gaped as Kairi continued running without slowing. *I'd sooner run away.*

Kairi's arm snaked out as she closed the gap between her and the chamelion while it reared back to bring its powerful paws down on her. She jabbed at its chest with a knife-hand, but her hand didn't make contact. She quickly changed directions and dodged to the side out of the way of its descending claws.

The chamelion growled in pain as a tint of red glistened across its chest. It backed up toward the cave, then turned and ran to a nearby tree.

*She hurt it?* Simon continued to watch Kairi closely. She kept near the beast, jabbing her hand out twice more at its retreating back but missing. Except, two more spots of blood dotted its fur as its claws powerfully dug into a hickory tree. *She's not touching it, but somehow she's hurting it... What kind of magic is she using?*

While remaining attached to the tree, the chamelion launched its rear claws back, pummeling Kairi.

Her hair fanned around her face as she fell on her back. She was up the next moment, running a hand down her torso. She seemed to find no injuries. Kairi darted past the creature, ran a circle around the tree, and leapt into the air. She continued to pump her legs and she rose as if her feet were catching invisible footholds. She circled around up and up, running on air.

*Her affinity is air? It must be.* Simon crouched and padded along the side of the stream, watching the chamelion's back legs thrust out again at Kairi who barely jumped out of the way. *I didn't know the air could be like a weapon that could be sharpened. Or hardened? That must be how she protected herself.*

She leapt back when the chamelion tore some of the vertical bark from the tree to hurl at Kairi. Most of it scattered around her though a clump knocked into her left leg, possibly bruising it. She began favoring her right as she moved around the tree in the air, keeping out of the chamelion's reach.

*She's wearing it down, but I need to help somehow. What can I do?* Simon looked around frantically for something. *There's a river. I can make it bubble… which would be useless. There are trees, some sassafras and others hickory. Hickory…* His eyes caught unnatural patterns along the ground close to the dungeon. There were burnt patches as if someone had been camping there. None were recent. Around the patches were remnants of ash. *Ash and water…*

Simon crept toward the tree the chamelion still climbed around, its body almost fully wrapping around the entirety of the trunk. Kairi was no longer able to find a way to get closer as its focus remained on her and it seemed to know her movements now. He stopped as close as he dared without being directly underneath should the chamelion decide to jump down. Breathing in, he pointed at the chamelion and chanted the spell. *"Bubbles! Bubbles! Bubbles! Bubbles!"*

Kairi froze to stand in the open air. The chamelion's eyes pinpointed Simon standing beside a nearby tree. It growled menacingly.

Simon chanted faster. *"Bubbles-bubbles-bubbles-bubbles-bubbles!"*

Its growl became a moan. Its grip weakened around the hickory tree and it painstakingly crawled down the trunk. Its body heaved and it vomited.

Kairi snapped back into action and let herself drop down through the air. She sliced a hand across the back of the chamelion's neck.

It let out a low half-groan half-howl and its body crashed to the ground.

Kairi slowed her momentum back on the ground, her feet kicking up stray leaves and dirt. She looked back and forth from the unmoving body of the creature to Simon, piecing together what he'd done. "You made it sick from the water it ingested," she commented, brushing her hands together. They shook slightly, likely from adrenaline. "How did you know to do that?"

Simon stood up fully from his awkward crouch. "Is… it really dead?"

She glanced back at its body that remained lying still by the hickory tree. "I cut through its neck deep enough."

Simon grimaced. "My family does farmwork," he said. "We make our own lye and sometimes use it to improve the quality of soil." His mind drifted to his parents likely tilling the fields at that moment before the spring planting. *I'm glad to no longer be forced to wake up in the early morning. I still stayed up all night…*

"Lye is used for soap," Kairi said, bringing his focus back.

"Yeah… yes. I figured I could force the lye to concentrate in the water in its stomach…" He grimaced again as he pictured it. "I don't think I can take doing this nine more times."

"I'll admit this is a rough first job. It's not at all like my first job."

"What was your first job?"

Her cheeks reddened and she shook her head. She focused her attention on the entrance to the dungeon.

He took the hint. "How are we supposed to carry even one of these back to the city?"

Kairi picked out a satchel from one of her pockets and she offered it to Simon. He took its opening uncertainly. Kairi, still holding the other end of the satchel, raced away. The satchel expanded wide and opened up from their hands to the ground as if it were elastic. She moved to run toward the chamelion and Simon did the same.

Together they swept the entirety of the chamelion's body into the satchel.

"Let go!" she called.

He did. The satchel's opening snapped back to her, closing and shrinking back to a size that fit her pocket.

"Masaka gave this to me before we left. It is one of Lenard's—he's another member of our guild and uses containment magic."

Simon nodded, then shook his head in wonder. "That's an unusual affinity. Does everyone in the guild have weird affinities like body or containment?"

"A lot of the Waymakers do," Kairi said shortly. She stopped making eye contact, acting suddenly shy. "Let's finish this so we can head back."

*Did I say something?* He let it go for now, the thought of nine more chamelions lurking in the dark of the cavern sending a shiver down his back.

As if his thoughts conjured it, something materialized from the darkness of the cave. It was a humanoid shape whose form didn't touch the ground. Its lower body ended with tatters like a ripped sheet. It had no legs and silently floated out of the dark.

Kairi's body tensed and she backed up, bumping into Simon.

Simon apologized, then gasped when his voice wavered in and out. At the same time the sound of the flowing river also cut in and out, unsteadily quieting, returning to a normal volume, then getting more quiet. It took him another moment to realize Kairi was speaking to him.

"—shadow wraith—touches kill any—nothing will—away—" The floating tattered figure sifted through the air. Kairi spun, her face filled with fear as she pushed him forcefully. She shouted, soundless, but Simon clearly read her mouth. *RUN.*

A sharp wrinkling sound cut through the now-silent riverside and the thing—the shadow wraith—moved impossibly fast to hover just ahead of him by another tree. The tree's lowest branch obscured the wraith's face. The rest of the wraith, now in direct sunlight, seemed to filter out the light like a canopy of leaves. It was dizzying to look at. Its tattered form held no holes, but the sun still shone through it and was masked by it at the same time. On either side of its form falling from where shoulders would be were two limbs, each ending with three straight claws instead of hands. Finally the wraith's head ducked under the branch as it floated forward toward him; what looked like eyes was a blackness emptier than the void he remembered when speaking with the God of Desire.

Simon felt Kairi's fingernails digging into his wrist trying to pull him back. He let her pull him while stooping to grab a fistful of loose dirt. He threw it at the wraith now several feet away from him.

The dirt lightly powdered around and through the wraith's face. *It didn't connect?*

The wraith flitted forward and swiped its claws.

"—ction!" a voice called from somewhere.

The wraith's hand went straight through Simon. Coldness expanded from the line it rent through his torso. His heart stopped and his arms numbly relaxed. The sensation of going in and out of water was replaced by a sharp, sinking one. Kairi's touch on his wrist disappeared as he collapsed to the ground and the world went black.

*All was silent and dark where he was. His thoughts were all that accompanied him:*

*I'm cold. I was cold when I died. I was lying in the bed of the hospital and I was still cold.*

*His vision came back and he saw a hospital room. There in the corner in a seat was his brother. Though he'd never seen the hospital room, had never been conscious to perceive it, he felt like he knew it exactly. "Luke," he said weakly.*

*A choke came beside him and he turned his head to the woman gripping the doctor's shoulder.*

*Simeon's heart clenched. "M-mom?"*

*His mother's face was set in a frown as she blinked furiously. "Simeon, thank God you're awake!" Her mouth wrestled to remain shut while her bright blue eyes failed to hold in tears.*

*The sound of a switch flipping echoed through the room. The doctor's arm fell from the ventilation machine to hang lifelessly at his side. Simeon collapsed back into the bed, his eyes closing and his body no longer moving.*

*"Simeon! SIMEON!"*

*Though his body was no longer available to him, he remained conscious and impossibly seeing and hearing everything. 'Mom!' he thought desperately. 'Luke! I can't breathe! I can't move!'*

*Luke put his head in his hands and his shoulders heaved uncontrollably.*

*'Mom, I want to move! I want to wake up!'*

*There was nothing he could do. His life was failing.*

*"I love you!" his mother cried. He'd never heard her sound so weak. So hopeless.*

*'I don't want to go away!' Simeon couldn't move. 'I don't want to go away!' Simeon couldn't speak. 'I don't want to go away from you!'*

*His brother and mother remained there by his bedside.*

*'I want to tell you—' But he couldn't. When he passed, he didn't. But when he passed, he wanted.*

*His brother and mother remained by his bedside.*

*His thoughts raced with the memories of them. His mother woke him up every morning. He couldn't remember a morning she hadn't woken him up. His brother would stick his head over the bunkbed on top to grin down at him as he slowly regained consciousness. Some days Luke would wake first and watch him in a seat on the ground facing him. He longed for that, even if it was weird. Other days Luke grew impatient holding the silly face and poked him awake before his mother could call his name. He longed for that too. And his mother would wake him up every day. Every day she'd call his name. And he would wake up.*

*"Simeon!"*

*But he wouldn't wake up this time.*

*His brother and mother remained by his bedside.*

*'I want to tell you that I love you, too! I want to tell you that I know you're there! I want to tell you that I hate this, and I don't want you to cry, and I don't want to go, and I want to wake up, and I want to see you there!'*

*He didn't wake up.*

*'I want…'*

*He left them. He had left them. They were gone, and he was gone. How long had it been? Thirteen years… The bedside he knew had been empty for thirteen years. He lived in a cottage in a village. His parents didn't wake him up. He loved them, but they weren't there in the mornings. They're farmers. How long had he longed for those mornings to see people he would never see? He didn't know he had missed them until he remembered. It pained him. And the weight on his chest that kept him there was back. It moved up his body.*

*His brother and mother were gone.*

*He was alone with the echoes of their voices and faces.*

"Simon!"

Simon woke up.

His heartbeat was racing, his breathing was unsteady, and his clothes were damp with sweat. He swiped a hand across his face to make sure there was feeling there. *I'm awake.*

He looked around. He was lying in his bed back in the guild house, morning light filtering through the shutters. Kairi sat in the chair by his bed while Masaka stood by the headboard. Her bare face looked down at him, her eyebrows raised with worry over the luminous green eyes.

"Simon!" she said warmly. "You're up!"

A light, wet tickling accompanied by a smacking sound touched his chin. He looked down at the wide, eager eyes of a scruffy white terrier dog curled below his collarbone. The weight on his chest shifted as the dog pawed its way closer to lick him again. *Bear. I forgot all about Bear. He wasn't there when I—I left him.* A guttural cry escaped him. He clutched the sheets and brought his knees to his head as tears fell freely down his face. The dog playfully rolled off him to the side of the bed.

"Simon!" Masaka hesitantly reached for his shoulder, then placed her hand over his forehead.

He wailed, shaking his head and digging it into his knees.

"I'm sorry," Masaka said, moving her hand back.

He grabbed her hand and clutched it to his head. Masaka briefly tensed before relaxing and staying still. He continued to cry until he couldn't. At some point Kairi had brought in a platter with water, some bread, and a handkerchief. Once his chest was still, he let go of Masaka and gathered himself. He looked at the handkerchief Kairi offered and numbly took it to wipe his face.

"I didn't think a shadow wraith of all things would be at the entrance," Masaka said. "I followed you in case you needed help. I'm glad I did." She took a handful of the bedsheets wetted with stray tears and remnant sweat. "I can wash these. I'm sorry."

Simon froze, looking from her hand that held his sheets then to her face. She stood by his bedside, and Kairi watched worriedly from the chair. *Luke and Mom are gone.* He felt more tears slowly trail down his face.

"Simon?" Kairi said. "What's wrong?"

He sighed, and felt something in his chest finally release. "Nothing. I'm glad you're here."

## Chapter 8: A New Job

Simon spent the rest of the morning in bed. Every now and then Masaka would come in and out of his room to check on him, along with Scrubby the terrier dog. She brought in water bowls and fresh handkerchiefs she used to dab at his skin. She'd healed his body from the worst of the injury with her peculiar magic but still needed to apply holy water to undo whatever had happened. He hesitated to ask her at first about the shadow wraith; remnants of coldness and numbness wavered across his body in patches. "What happened?" he asked finally when the door opened and she walked in with a fresh bowl of holy water. A low murmuring of noise echoed up from the first floor, a sign some other adventurers had returned from their own dungeon excursion. The door closed, cutting off the murmurs.

"Shadow wraiths have a strange effect on the world around them," Masaka said, seemingly reading his thoughts of what he meant to ask. "They mute sounds—make you feel like you're going in and out of water." She took the old handkerchief he had kept hold of from him and dipped a new one into the water bowl to then dab at his forearms.

"The other neat thing about them is when they touch something alive the alive thing spontaneously dies."

Simon shivered and Masaka moved the cloth to wipe at his neck. "I'm not dead," he stated.

"I cast a protection spell before it touched you," she said. "Didn't prevent all of the necrosis, though."

"Necrosis?" he repeated, worried.

"Hey," Masaka said seriously with a frown. "Are you doubting my ability?"

"N-no…"

Masaka took the cloth away to rest on the lid of the birch bowl and placed the bowl down on the floor. Her features softened. "I really didn't intend such a catastrophic event. Creatures like those wraiths remain as far from outdoors as they can get. Light is hard on them, as is the open air. It went back into the cave as quickly as it came out, but… I'm sorry."

Simon nodded, then shook his head. "You don't have to keep saying you're sorry."

She tilted her head. "Really? Regardless of what I intended, I did put you in real danger."

"I think chamelions are dangerous," he said. "But Kairi told me about something you say. Doing stuff when you can, or something. I guess I sort of get it."

Masaka smirked. "Awfully mature for your age, huh? What did it feel like?"

Simon blinked. She sounded almost giddy. "Being touched by the shadow wraith?"

"Yeah!"

Simon thought about it. "Do you know what the touch of shadow feels like?"

She shook her head. "It feels colder when I'm in the shade."

"No, it's like…" Simon shivered, thinking about the dream he had while unconscious. "Like shadow, shadow. Some intellectuals from my hometown described it as a burning hotness and others described it as some frigid cold. It's really neither, not really a physical feeling at all. It's numbness. Absolute numbness. No hurt, no pain, and no emotional feelings like joy or fear. It's no feeling whatsoever."

Masaka cupped her head in a hand, looking at him slowly. "Nngh," she muttered finally, shivering herself. "Sounds sucky. Luckily my magic is pretty much the antithesis to shadow wraiths. But there are other ways to handle them. There are ways to heal the body other than my body magic as well. You know about the High Clerics, don't you?"

Simon nodded.

"Yeah. Each of those four uses water magic like you and can heal people like nobody else. If you manage to learn to use your own magic, you could be on their level."

Simon shook his head doubtfully. "The level of magic I can cast is basically useless." A dark look passed over Masaka's face and Simon remembered what Kairi had told him about complaining.

"Maybe you're right," Masaka said, surprising him. She picked up the bowl again and placed it beside him on the mattress over the sheets. "I heard from Kairi you caused a chamelion to throw up. You used the bubble spell?"

"*Bubbles*," Simon said, nodding at the water as the surface bubbled for three seconds before subsiding.

"Hmm," Masaka commented. "You *are* weak."

Simon was thinking it, but it still hurt to hear. His body sagged a bit while he lay there.

"You're weak in mind and magic. No one I've known has been as weak as you. I doubt no one I'll ever know will be as weak. What's with the face?" she asked. Her arm shot out and she flicked his chin.

"Ow!" Simon dumbly rubbed at the stinging.

"I said you're weak, not useless. You're like that birch bowl. Take a look at yourself. Give yourself some credit. After all, you learned two spells in a day, and put one of them to practical use. It took me months to do something like that." She turned and walked to the door, putting a hand on the knob before opening it. "You can only do what you can do when you can do it." And with that, she left. Scrubby let out a quick whine and launched off the bed to chase after her, clearing the door just before it shut.

Simon absently rubbed his chin. "Was that meant to cheer me up?" he asked himself. He eyed the bowl and sat himself up, his back leaning against the wall. Placing the bowl in his lap, he hovered his hands over the water's surface. His eyes flicked to a flat fold in the bedsheets. "*Koota.*"

His tome appeared atop the fold, already opened to the page that displayed his *Bubbles* spell. The next empty page looked oddly appealing rather than a representation of his limits. *I suppose I'll try my magic some more.*

***

"All right, get out of the bed," Masaka ordered, shoving his door open and letting it slam back and closed on her horse mask that was again covering her face. Her footsteps trailed back down the hall towards the stairs where the murmurs had grown loud enough to trickle through his door.

Simon withdrew his hands from the bowl and wiped them as dry as he could on the handkerchief damp from the holy water. The numb spots cropping up randomly across his skin had stopped at some point and he no longer worried his body would give out if he stood. Careful not to tip over the water bowl on his bed as he got up, he experimentally shifted his weight from his right foot to his left foot before fully standing.

He held his arms out wide to keep balanced. Once he was comfortable, he let his arms fall and he appraised his clothes. *I haven't changed in three days… I must smell awful.*

*Wait… Could I use magic to clean myself?* He looked back at the water bowl, considering how much dirt and whatnot now left the once holy water no-longer-holy. *I don't know for sure whether the bubbles I made in that beast's stomach upset its stomach on its own. If I actually managed to gather whatever lye there was together, I could… I could…* Simon searched for the thought that tickled familiarly at his brain while he walked to the door and opened it. The murmurs grew and he fully got the idea of just how many adventurers the Waymaker Guild had. He peered over the landing's banister that overlooked a portion of the floor below and saw clusters of four-to-five people standing, sitting, and leaning along the counter that stretched from the foot of the stairs by the back wall. *Theoretically*, Simon remembered and slowly walked to the stairs. *I could theoretically separate dirt and grime from myself with water. I'd like to try whenever there's a chance to take a bath.*

Simon descended the stairs slowly, warily eyeing the colorful characters of the adventurers that loitered around the lounge. He stepped over a man lying lengthwise along the bottom step, the man prone and apparently asleep despite how uncomfortable it must've been with his nose pressing into the wood boards of the floor. Some of the adventurers gave Simon a glance but didn't look back. He decided to stand by the counter and wait there for whatever Masaka had called him out for.

There was a creak and one of the round tables fell onto its side atop a frail man's bare stomach. The man was giggling wildly while a woman stood balanced atop the other edge of the table. She seemed to be intentionally pressing the weight down on the man's worryingly outlined ribs. "Pain, pain, pain!" she was saying with rising excitement, her mouth contorted in a sort of grin. Scrubby let out accompanying yips while darting between the sea of feet.

The man cackled, apparently not bothered at all by the weight that should have crushed his twiggy body. He began thrumming his hands on the sideways tabletop, creating a general rhythm. Meanwhile, everyone else seemed to be either entertained by them or entertaining themselves with talk about… Simon shifted his focus to pick out just what they talked about.

"—the Basted Basilisk should have something succulent."

"It's a terribly dry day, isn't it?"

"…pain, pain, PAIN, PAIN!"

"Keep it down, Perish! I SAID SHUT IT!"

"You have to buy me a new sword."

Simon turned to the boy who looked his age but with more childish features who had spoken to him. "Huh?" Simon asked, unsure where the boy had come from.

"Barto broke mine and he refused to buy me a new one," the boy said, pointing to the cackling twiggy man under the table. "Masaka said you're new, and new people have to listen to veterans."

"I don't have any money."

The boy's face remained blank. His dull grey eyes blinked once. "Oh."

Simon faced the room when Perish, apparently the woman standing on top of the toppled table, began half-screaming and half-singing the word 'pain.'

"PERISH, SHUT UP!"

A mug flew through the air and clocked the back of her head. Her only reaction was to go silent while her head remained frozen in the position it'd been knocked.

"Ahem."

Simon turned again and found the boy had disappeared and it was now Masaka standing beside him.

"A*hem!*" she repeated a little louder. Only the few leaning along the counter near Simon turned to stop their chatter and face her. The man lying prone on the floor by the stairs also turned his head to look blearily up at her.

"HEY!" she finally shouted.

A strange pressure radiated from her and Simon felt his body grow weak. He had enough strength to remain standing, though he could sense the full force of whatever she was doing was being sent across the rest of the lounge.

Perish lost her balance and toppled off the table and the man's cackling grew weak and his arms limply thudded on the ground, no longer able to tap out a beat. Everyone else's bodies sagged and their murmuring silenced.

Simon weakly clenched his fists, testing the strength he had left. It felt like he couldn't so much as keep a coin grasped in his hand, his fingers too loose. *This is body magic?*

"Well?" The pressure eased from Masaka as she looked around at everyone's faces through the holes in her horse mask expectantly.

"We made it to the tenth floor of the dungeon," came a gruff voice from a burly man on Simon's other side.

"And?" Masaka waited. "Don't tell me everyone gave up again. Even you, Dulon?"

The burly man hesitated. "The pressure is too great to go past that floor."

"Did anyone bring back items to sell?" Masaka asked, her voice now monotone. She looked down at the prone man. "Lenard."

The man gingerly procured a misshapen rock from his pants pocket and rolled it along the floor to bump against her shoes.

Masaka stooped to pick it up. She then threw it on the floor hard. The rock shattered and a small pile of gold coins clinked together as they settled. "Hm. This looks like it'll be enough to buy Frisk a new sword."

"Good," came the boy's voice Simon recognized from before, though he couldn't pinpoint where the boy was.

Masaka turned to look at Simon. "Kid. You're going to help us reach the 11<sup>th</sup> floor."

Everyone's strength returned to their bodies and the adventurers along the guild lounge stood upright (all except Lenard). "Who's he?" Dulon asked. His muscles seemed to expand along his arms and Simon edged away to stand a bit closer to Masaka.

"A new Waymaker," Masaka said. "Simon, these are the others in the guild. Not all of them are currently here, but you'll be acquainted with them soon enough."

"What's on the 11<sup>th</sup> floor?" Simon asked. "What's on the 10<sup>th</sup> floor?"

Masaka momentarily adjusted the horse mask on her face. "Water. A lot of water."

Simon avoided her eyes. *I can't tell her that I'm weak. She knows already.* "I didn't complete the last job."

"I know. I'm going to send you back to the Rivermotuh Dungeon tomorrow. We'll be returning to the Narumont Dungeon at the end of the month."

*What?* "You think I can do something by then?" he asked.

"Kid, you can only do what you can do when you can do it. Don't decide what you can do now will be all you can do later."

*Right, right.* Still, Simon was uneasy she was tasking him with going further into this dungeon. *One that no one else in the guild can apparently go further into.* His mind finally processed the idea of returning to the Rivermouth Dungeon so soon and he paled.

"If that's all for now, I'm going to do some gambling!" Barto, the twiggy man, moved to the small pile of coins then halted. "Hold on—where'd the money go?"

Simon hadn't noticed himself that the pile had disappeared.

Barto growled. "Frisk! Curse that sneaky brat, I'm going to make his toilet soft so he falls in it!"

Masaka made no move to discipline the man.

*I suppose Waymakers really hold true to their individual desires,* Simon thought. *Even if they're as lame as messing with someone's toilet.*

"Kid," Masaka said, addressing only him now. "Kairi will be taking the days off with everyone else. I'll be sending you back tomorrow with Perish."

Simon blinked and his eyes cut to the older woman who now progressed to the door leading outside. "Her?" Simon asked dubiously.

"She behaves like a flamboyant drunk but is one of your seniors. You won't have to worry about the shadow wraith with her."

Nodding as the warmth of blood returned to the surface of his skin, Simon then quickly turned his head back to the guild master. "You're not going to come?"

"Nope. I'm taking the time off myself." She walked away a few paces, then turned. "I suppose what you really want is to get stronger, right? You wanted to get into Verlangen. The thing is, education is wasted on people who don't know enough to see its usefulness or see the usefulness of themselves. I can see about arranging for you to be admitted there… if you can reach the 11th floor." She left off there, walking to the front door with the other guildmates and exiting the building.

"Why does she keep calling me 'kid'?" he mumbled to himself.

"Because you're weak," Dulon said gruffly. He and Lenard remained in the lounge while everyone else filtered outside. "She sees you as a kid, which you are. 'Course, she also sees your potential. Whatever that is, she thinks you can help us out in the dungeon." Dulon looked Simon up and down and rolled his eyes.

*I guess I don't blame anyone for doubting me when I doubt myself.* He looked around, remembering Masaka had said Kairi would be taking the rest of the month off as well. He didn't see her during that brief meeting. *Of everyone I know here, she's the least intimidating.* He stepped back over Lenard, who'd returned to lying face-down with eyes shut, and climbed up the stairs. He reached the second floor landing and moved to the door Kairi had come out of when he first arrived. Lightly, he knocked. There was no sound inside. "Kairi?"

Silence. Then: "What is it?"

"Um." He could tell by her voice she wasn't entirely happy. Uncertain what it was (and whether he should pry), he asked, "Does the guild have a bath?"

"…There's a door in the stairwell. Follow the tunnel and at the end of it is the bath."

He didn't remember seeing a handle or any sort of door on the stairs, but nodded anyway. "Thanks."

## Chapter 9: His First Dungeon

Simon found the door to the bath. His fingers caught upon a barely perceptible wooden groove along the side of the stairs. He pressed it and the wood swung back on a hinge. *There really is a tunnel* he thought upon seeing a dark stretch straight ahead before ending at a lit area a ways away. He padded inside and let the door swing shut behind him. *I don't have a change of clothes. I'll have to figure out a way to wash these.*

He stepped into the warmly lit space. It was small, though larger than he was used to. It reached about as far and wide as his cottage back home. One single-person limestone pool held calm water in a corner, while another wider limestone pool occupied the majority of the area. Its water gave off steam that rose to the thatch ceiling. A bamboo bench sat in the corner opposite the smaller pool. Simon took off his clothes and folded them messily atop the bench before stepping fully into the large pool.

The water immediately warmed his skin through. The pool was thankfully only deep enough to come up to his chin when he fully relaxed in a sitting position. *It's not holy water, but it is relaxing.*

The door at the far end of the tunnel echoed when it opened and he turned. *Dulon told me there were scheduled bath times. Please don't be one of the girls that walked in...* The figure of a tall man wearing only a yellow towel wrapped around his waist entered into the bath house.

Simon relaxed a fraction, but remained tense. He noticed an array of faint scars across the man's torso, some wrapping around his sides and shoulders. *Are those whip scars?*

The man paused, only for a second, before slipping himself into the water comfortably away from Simon on one end of the large pool.

*I didn't see him in the lounge earlier.* Simon averted his eyes and focused on what he went there to do. *I don't have soap. Will Bubbles work?*

"Who are you?" the man asked.

Simon looked over, seeing that the man's hair was now slick from water and fell in large, stuck strands down his face to his nose and down to the top of his neck in the back. "I'm Simon," he said. "What's your name?"

The man rearranged his hair to stick to the sides of his face as he cupped more water to lightly release over his head. "Procel."

Simon expected the man to say more, but he didn't. Procel continued to methodically drip water over his hair and then bring some up to his face, no longer paying attention to Simon.

Refocusing, Simon cupped his hands just under the water's surface. "*Bubbles,*" he muttered. A quiet pattering of bubbles cropped up from his hands to the surface. It lasted a few seconds before stopping. "*Bubbles.*" *I wish I didn't have to repeat the spell over and over again. Come to think of it, not all of the students applying to Verlangen Seminary spoke a spell name out loud during the final test. Avril didn't...* "*Koota,*" Simon said, and the tome appeared on the floor behind his head already open to the *Bubbles* spell. He turned and read over the details. *Nothing written about silently casting spells. That must mean it's something I can't do...*

"You have a tome," Procel commented. He leaned his back against the pool's smooth stone siding. A part in his hair revealed his left eye peering back at Simon.

"Um, y-yes. Don't you?"

Water fell away as he lifted a hand and a deep, dark blue tome appeared between his grasped fingers. He let it go to thud lightly on the outside edge of the pool behind him.

"Oh," Simon said. "People seem interested whenever I have mine out."

"Who's people?"

"The guild master."

Procel stopped staring as he looked ahead and closed his eyes. "Masaka doesn't have a tome."

"Oh," Simon said again. *The staff woman from Verlangen said all mages had one.* He opened his mouth to ask about Masaka before remembering the story she'd told him about growing up.

"Everyone else here has a tome," Procel continued after seconds of silence. "She's fascinated by them since they instantaneously lay out what a mage learns. It's something she had to commit here." He pointed at his head before letting his hand submerge beneath the water.

"Why did you sound surprised by my tome?"

"You're young," Procel replied.

Simon cut himself off before he said 'Oh' again. "You summoned your tome without speaking. Can anyone do that?"

The water sloshed as Procel shifted his position to sit facing Simon. His eyes opened slowly and he nodded.

Simon blinked, wondering at the man's ceremonious movement. He realized Procel was prompting him to try it. Simon looked at his own tome and focused. *I want it to… disappear!*

The tome remained.

Simon shut his eyes and thought the same thing but more forcefully. When he thought of it disappearing he opened his eyes. The tome remained.

"You're new to magic," Procel said. He sat directly beside Simon, somehow closing the distance without disturbing the water for Simon to notice.

Simon flinched and warily eyed Procel while the man lifted Simon's tome and flipped it open to the first page.

Procel stared at the first page with the miniscule image of a circle for some time. He then briefly lifted the other two pages to skim the spells there before closing the tome. "So you're a water mage." Something in his tone came across like Simon's affinity wasn't what interested him.

"I want to be able to do magic without saying the spell every time," Simon said.

Procel nodded slowly, putting the tome back on the pool's edge.

"…But you said what's in the tome shows all that a mage can do. So it's something I can't do?"

"The tome shows what a mage learns. What you can do is another matter and may not be in the tome yet."

*You can only do what you can do when you can do it.* Masaka's voice resonated in his head. "So… I can do magic without speaking, I just have to learn how to."

"Yep." Procel waded back until he was a comfortable distance and he returned to resting his eyes while soaking in the water.

*That's… helpful?* Simon wasn't sure what to think of the man, but at least now he didn't feel stuck. "What about you?"

"What about me?"

"What kind of magic can you do?"

Procel remained silent for half a minute. Then: "I'm a summoner." He stood up and stepped out of the pool, his tome disappearing at his feet. After drying himself off he clicked his tongue and hesitated at the tunnel. "Perish is waiting for you." He exited the pool room silently, leaving Simon alone again.

"…Ah!" Simon rocketed from the pool to grab his towel and clothes, calling the dismissal spell for his tome as he went. He dressed quickly and almost dislocated his shoulder as he rushed into the tunnel. Grimacing at the ache blossoming down his chest and back, he pushed open the entrance door and found the lounge empty save for the woman Perish.

"Let's go, newbie," she said, and moved to the door.

"Already? Masaka said we'd leave tomorrow! I—I only just left my room today."

Perish lowered her eyebrows as she turned back to appraise him. "That means you're refreshed and ready, then."

Simon couldn't exactly argue, but more so he didn't want to argue. Not after being allowed to rest there several days without finishing the job he was given. He followed her meekly while checking around for Procel who somehow disappeared. *How did he know Perish was waiting for me?* Simon shook his head to get rid of the unnerving thought. *Maybe he acted like he didn't know me at first. Forget that, I have to prepare myself for Rivermouth Dungeon... again.*

***

"Ten black chamelions," Perish mused before folding the job listing into fourths and stuffing it into a pocket folded neatly into her muted blue bouffant gown. She and Simon stood side by side at the mouth of the dungeon, its dark interior stretching on beyond eyesight. "You got one with Kairi earlier, so we just need nine more."

Simon eyed the wide skirt of her dress for what was far from the first time. "Do you normally wear that kind of thing when exploring a dungeon?"

Perish answered while moving into the cave, Simon following behind. "I wear what I want. Floofy is fun." She continued to step further into the darkness of the cave without slowing.

Simon squinted as the diminishing light became barely perceptible reflections off the uneven ground and walls. The accompanying noise of the river paralleling their path softened as the path bent away into its own cave, and the sounds soon became faint echoes. He blinked, starting to lose track of the frills of her dress just ahead of him. Fragmented sounds of drops *plock*ed and echoed on rock. Only their footfalls were continuous. A tremor ran down his back as he envisioned the shadow wraith hovering somewhere in the dark. *Masaka said I didn't have to worry with Perish here. But...*

A soft humming sounded ahead of him and he stopped short, getting into a guarded crouch. His ears took another second to recognize the source of the humming coming from Perish. The sound was unlike her somewhat deeper voice, light and harmonious.

Simon blinked, imagining the dim silhouette of her walking on in her fancy dress down the cave. *Wait... I'm not imagining it.* Her form was coming into focus and becoming illuminated by a soft blue light.

Her humming loudened when she turned slightly and parted her lips to let her voice carry more fully. Her dark eyes reflected the strange light that blazed alive along her dress; they silently encouraged Simon to continue on.

*This is song magic?* Simon straightened and moved to fall back in step shortly behind her. The frills of her gown glowed without any discernable source, like an extravagant lampshade. He now not only respected the dress choice but also welcomed it.

Perish continued to sing a wordless tune. The tune seemed to have traces of some of the country songs Simon knew growing up but with less of an upbeat rhythm and lingering, almost melancholic notes. What previously was disjointed droplets of water hitting the ground seemed to be woven into the rhythm her voice created. The watery blue light that enveloped her form reached far up the curving tunnel and found an opening where manmade carvings marked the end of the natural cave.

Simon squared his shoulders as they stepped into a broad and tall chamber much like the interior of a chapel building. Unlit sconces rested on the front sides of rounded pillars meshed with the flat walls. The walls stretched on a ways before angling to rejoin directly ahead of them where some sort of altar rested. Simon gazed in awe at the blue-tinted chamber. Beyond the partial pillars and the single altar, the room was otherwise empty. *I don't see any way further. Is this the end of the dungeon? Where are the chamelions? And the—*

Perish's voice quieted back to humming when she closed her lips. The light along her dress dimmed somewhat but remained enough to illuminate the majority of the room. "*There's movement in a hidden corridor,*" she sang softly and then hushed her voice. The light in her dress remained. "There." She pointed to a spot between the middle columns on the right side of the room.

As if opening at her gesture, a rectangle piece in the wall twice Simon's height slid away. When it was large enough, a group of five chamelions stampeded into the chamber and turned their progress toward them both at the entrance.

"Uh," Simon said worriedly. *I already can't do much, but there's no nearby water source for me to do anything.* He shifted between standing by Perish and shrinking away. The woman's upright and unflinching posture gave him confidence while the oncoming animals the size of wagons gave him doubt.

"I can take care of them," Perish's voice rose above the thudding and scraping of chamelion feet and claws. She looked sideways at him. "But then why are you here?"

Simon's face whitened and he clenched his hands. *I have to do something!* "*Koota!*" His tome appeared opened in his right hand to the page detailing his Bubbles spell. The stampede was almost upon them.

"*A—*" Perish drew the vowel out and it echoed onto itself until the frequency of the note made Simon dizzy. The chamelions' progress became stuck, several of their legs suspended in the air while their grounded legs tried to dig and push themselves forward. "*—bout-face!*"

The chamelions whipped around in unison and their charge became confused as they ran back to the center of the chamber.

While Perish was half-humming and half-singing something more, Simon's eyes searched the room for anything. *Anything,* he thought. *I can't use fluids in people or animals unless they recently drank.* The opened corridor the chamelions came through held the only possibility of something useful. *No,* Simon realized, *there's something else I can use.*

Simon spun, shutting his tome, and raced up the dimly lit pathway they had come from.

"Running away?" Perish asked, somehow finding the time to fit the question into her singing.

Simon didn't bother explaining, using as much of the little light as he could to search for the small glints of droplets that were coming from the cave ceiling. *I heard them all over... There!* Simon's free hand clawed out and caught a drop just beside him.

He brought himself to a halt and kept his hand in the air where the droplet had fallen, waiting for more. Several seconds went by before another droplet wetted his palm. *This is something. But not nearly enough. I need more, somehow.*

Perish's song wavered down the path.

*She can handle it... but then why am I here?*

Another droplet splashed his hand.

*I need more!* His head swiveled, already knowing the futility of racing desperately to catch every droplet that fell. *More... More?* He looked down at his hand. *Can I make more?*

He was aware that the magic he used to make bubbles didn't involve heat and so had to be working with the particles already there. *But am I manipulating the water to create pockets of air? Or am I removing the water to then leave air which then makes the bubbles?*

Another droplet landed in his palm.

*Do I need to think this hard about it? It's magic, isn't it? If I really have an affinity for water, I can just do things with water!* He curled his fingers closed over the shallow wetness centered in his hand and ran back toward Perish.

Her voice was rising as the chamelions regrouped and tore toward her. She glanced back at him and smiled slightly. "I thought you were frozen in fear back there," she again squeezed into her wordless song.

Instead of stopping, Simon ran straight ahead of her toward two chamelions baring their fangs ready to devour him.

"Hey, wait—!"

Simon threw his arm out and opened his hand. A cup's worth of water splashed the bottom teeth of a chamelion before its jaw closed around his arm.

*"Stop!"*

Simon gritted his teeth and clenched his eyes shut. He felt the points of the teeth touch his arm but not puncture the skin. Perish's song had stopped. He opened his eyes. The chamelions were frozen completely in place. The beady yellow eyes of the one whose mouth enclosed Simon's arm stared at him hungrily. Simon carefully removed his arm and backed away, laughing lightly.

Perish reached out and slapped his back hard. "Are you crazy? What was that?"

Simon composed himself and shivered. "I splashed it with water," he said. He couldn't keep the giddiness out of his voice.

"Yeah, I saw that!" Perish snapped. "Was that all you planned to do? Did you think about what would happen after you'd give a chamelion mouthwash?"

"Yes." Simon held her stern gaze. "I'd either get eaten or be saved by you."

Perish's eyes flashed and she defiantly forced a smile down. "That's it? You were planning on me saving you?"

"This is all I can do right now," Simon said, looking down at his hand. The remaining film of water that stuck to his hand had reformed somewhat into another shallow puddle.

Perish *hmph*-ed and faced the frozen chamelions. "I'll take 90% of the reward."

Simon blinked. *I was only doing this job to take care of my debt.*

Perish let out a shriek and the bodies of the chamelions crumpled to the floor and remained unmoving.

Simon shivered again. *She… killed them.* He let the water he had been gathering in his hand fall away before dumbly pulling out the bag Kairi had used for the first chamelion that held Lenard's containment magic. *She pretty much did all the work, but she's leaving me with one of the gold coins. She's scary, but maybe she's nicer than I thought.*

Simon remembered the tome in his right hand. He dropped the container and quickly flipped it open to the fifth page. On the opposite page of his Bubbles spell was… more writing!

*Swell 10*

*Adds a fraction of the water from an available water source to the water source.*

Simon re-read the brief but rousing spell three times before turning the page. To his excitement, there was one more spell scrawled on the sixth page.

*Creation 10*

*Creates water.*

## Chapter 10: The Girl of Doubt

A knock resounded on her door. "Kairi."

*Masaka.* She shifted her legs off the canopy bed, its frames adorned with long sheets of cloth that gently rippled from the displaced air as she moved between them. She momentarily paused, her fingers wrapping slowly around the knob. She knew that the guild master knew she was in there thanks to her affinity. *Why couldn't I have a better affinity?*

Kairi opened the door and flinched when she saw Masaka's plain face looking back at her from where she stood by the banister nearby the guild stairway.

"Gee, am I that ugly?" Masaka dropped her smile as soon as she made it, beckoning Kairi to follow her down the stairs.

She didn't bother to protest, but asked, "Where are we going?"

"Doesn't it bother you?"

She lowered her eyebrows and waited until they made it down the stairs to ask the inevitable follow-up question. "What?"

"Simon's out facing a dungeon and he's only been here for—" Masaka abruptly stopped, glancing up at a wall with notches symbolizing the numbers of a clock. "—75 hours."

Kairi took in a quick breath before continuing to follow the guild master. "You said you can't read my thoughts and emotions."

"I can't," Masaka affirmed.

*You can just sense physiological signs that can help you guess.* Kairi let her feet guide her out of the guild house and along the street after Masaka. "You know I'm not the competitive type."

"You're the self-critical type." Masaka's blank face turned briefly back as if to pin the words good and well to the girl.

Kairi wanted to protest. She settled for clenching her hands as they walked.

"You can only do what you can do when you can do it," Masaka went on. "It's not your fault you could not handle a shadow wraith. It's my fault for putting you in a situation you could not handle."

*I could have*— No. She had reimagined how the encounter could have gone. Even hypothetically, no outcomes turned out well. Escape would not have been possible; she couldn't carry them both even with a strong wind, not with the shadow wraith's speed. Nothing would have worked out without Masaka's support. "I wish I had a better affinity." She cringed as she said it. Moments passed without Masaka turning back around. *Right after I lecture Simon about complaining, I go and say that.*

"As a Waymaker, it's essential to be able to define what you want."

Kairi widened her eyes. She'd expected to be chastised, but Masaka just kept walking.

"It's one thing to want something different for yourself, and it's another thing to want something different about yourself. Some things you can't change." Masaka raised a hand to look down at. She opened and closed it a few times before dropping it back to her side. "The Goddess knows I've tried."

Kairi almost didn't hear her as the guild master led them along another rural street traveling outside Narumont. She found it hard to believe Masaka would want to change her affinity. *What* would *she want to change?* "Where are we going?" she asked again.

"Right over here." Masaka took several long paces off the road across the start of a pasture and stopped walking, turning finally to face Kairi. A breeze ruffled the blades of grass around them, gently flapping the folds in Masaka's nun habit.

Kairi stopped a few steps away, looking around at the open space. "Why?"

"Simon is weak. He's already well aware of his limits. You, on the other hand…"

Kairi frowned. "I'm not?"

Masaka shook her head, concealing her hands beneath her robe. "I don't believe you're aware of your limits. At all."

*This sure has made me feel better.* Kairi folded her arms. "Why don't you tell me about my limits, then?"

Masaka withdrew a hand holding her horse mask. She brought it up and settled it over her face. Her shadowed green eyes faintly glittered between the openings. "No. You're going to show me."

Masaka brought her hands together sharply. A sound like a thunderclap echoed across the field. Faraway cattle let out sounds of worry as they fled further away towards stables.

Kairi shuddered, feeling the atmosphere, her own body, change. *She's serious.*

A hiss of breath passed between Masaka's lips as she drew her hand, now a fist, back.

Kairi glanced from the telegraphed punch to the narrow space between them.

"If I touch you, you're done." The fist hurtled towards her like a river.

Unable to brace her body to move out of the way or block, she did the only thing she could think to do and let her legs give out.

Masaka's punch sifted through the loose hair that was too slow to follow Kairi downward.

Kairi caught herself on the palms of her hands hard. She looked up to see the horse mask angled toward her, the glint behind the eyeholes still faintly visible.

"That's one punch. You have nine to go." Masaka brought her fist above her head.

Kairi had no time to let out anything more than an unsteady garble. She dug the nails of one hand into the loose dirt and gripped the grass as best she could, and with the other hand she palmed the air. She barely forced herself to twist out of the way with enough torque.

Masaka's fist slammed the ground and the earth buckled. Clumps of dirt flung upward and broke apart in a shower that fell across both of them. "Eight."

Kairi unsteadily pushed herself onto her feet. She turned and ran sideways along the grass lining the road. The flapping clothes alerted her that the guild master was in close pursuit. Before she turned to look back, Masaka's face slid into view.

Wide-eyed, she stared at the rapidity of Masaka's body matching her own speed being carried with the help of wind. Masaka brought her arm back.

Pulling her own arm back, she gathered the air to a single point in front of her fist and swung it to meet Masaka's own fist.

The force of the strike broke the formulated blade of air, the pressure all at once rebounding around her hand, arm, and entire form and ripping her away on a sharp gust. She managed to get her bearings midair and regathered another layer of air to land on before she fell onto the other side of the road.

Masaka remained standing on her own side of the road, though she also had her fist cocked back.

*She couldn't punch me from there, could she?* On her next breath Masaka cleared the road and the horse mask was in her face. Purely out of instinct she brought both of her arms up, layering them with several sharp pressure points of air to counter the descending fist while simultaneously bolstering the air beneath her feet.

Three separate sounds like explosions occurred in succession, Kairi's mind racing to process it all as she felt the wind knock out of her: her blades of air broke again, loudly releasing the pressure back towards her; the air underneath her feet had broken, unable to suspend her against the force of Masaka's fist alongside the rebounded air; and her body slammed into the ground.

Masaka landed a second later, the hem of her robe brushing Kairi's arm as she lay coughing, struggling to refill her lungs.

*She didn't touch me… yet! Think! I need air. What would Simon do?* Her eyebrows lowered at the thought as she continued to cough. *He manipulated water inside a chamelion's—*

Her eyes lit up as she saw Masaka starting to raise her fist once again. All at once the air expanded in her lungs without her consciously breathing and her coughing ceased. At the same moment Masaka's fist came down.

Another explosive sound erupted as a crater formed under Masaka, caving in part of the road.

Kairi, kicking out of the way on a gust of wind, twirled into a standing position with another push of air clear of the danger. "Five," Kairi said.

Masaka straightened and looked slightly up at Kairi from the depressed earth. She silently raised her fist.

This time Kairi didn't wait for the guild master to spring into action. She ran along the road, plumes of air pressing on her back and aiding her to take three strides-worth of distance with just one. Still, and again, Masaka slid back into view, able to keep up with her.

Kairi's feet slipped out from under her and she fell backward. Her fall continued into a long, unnatural slide that never touched the ground. Above her another explosive *boom* resounded.

*Even when she isn't punching anything it sounds nasty.* Kairi grimaced and manipulated the air to pick her back up, her feet returning to the road in a sprint.

Masaka hadn't slowed down, but her tone changed. "You fell on purpose."

"Four."

Masaka blinked, her eyes glinting as they fell to Kairi's mouth that kept closed after the girl spoke. "I see!" In a sudden spurt of movement, she jumped ahead of Kairi and brought her arm back.

Kairi leapt high, a sharp updraft carrying her above the guild master whose swing struck nothing but made another resounding impact. She noted with annoyance the grass in the same direction of Masaka's swing frantically quiver under the wave of pressure. *It's like she can also control the air.* "Thr—"

Masaka also leapt into the air, clearing Kairi and traveling beyond the height of a two-story building.

*Why would she do that? She has no footing anymore...* Kairi let herself land on a pocket of air several feet above the ground and watched Masaka start to fall, rubbing part of her cheek. She frowned as she heard Masaka laughing on her way down past her, and even continue as she landed, sending up a cloud of dirt on the road.

"Almost!" Masaka said, taking the horse mask off her face and grinning up at Kairi. "You almost got to zero!"

"What?" Kairi brought her hand away from her face and spotted thin dots of red. *My cheek is cut? When did it—?*

"No need to stay up there. I said if I touched you you'd be done."

Kairi let the air lower her back to the ground. She landed, then eyed Masaka rubbing one of her pinky nails. "You used your nail?"

"Particulars," Masaka said dismissively. "More importantly, you discovered a new ability!"

Kairi sighed, then nodded as she began to naturally breathe.

"I thought it was odd when you stopped coughing. But look at you! You're not even panting!" Masaka, though not apparently tired, was breathing with some exertion.

"Y…yeah." Kairi folded her arms and felt her face warm slightly.

"I have an idea!" Masaka stowed her mask back somewhere in the folds of her robe and patted Kairi's shoulder. "Do me next!"

Kairi was forced to unfold her arms as Masaka pulled her back along the road toward the crater. "Huh?"

"Test my limits next! Control my air and let's see how long I can last!"

Kairi shook her head. "No! I mean, you know I can't control the air in someone else!" *It would only be to the miniscule extent Simon did it.* She felt annoyed again at comparing herself to him, but to some degree less than before.

"Control the air around me and prevent me from breathing!" Masaka instructed, stopping them at the center of the crater.

*You could just hold your breath* Kairi thought, shaking her head again. But, grateful for the guild master's help with her own breakthrough, she obliged.

## Chapter 11: The Young Knight

"Hey kid! I heard you learned some new spells yesterday?"

"Yeah!" Simon nodded happily and spun his tome atop one of the tables in the lounge of the guild. Masaka flipped the page with the two new entries back and forth, taking even more time and showing more excitement than Simon did when he read them. When he and Perish returned to Narumont, Perish incessantly sung and caused civilians to gawk at them on their way to the guild house. Simon had pretended to not be with her as she led a wagon carrying two of the chamelion bodies (she'd insisted on displaying at least a few despite Lenard's convenient containment bag). He figured she just wanted the attention. Meanwhile he was just glad his first job was complete.

"Well, well, well! Look at you, you can do more now!"

"He's going to need to progress five times faster than he currently is," Dulon murmured from his own table near the stairs. He and Lenard were the only other members there, Lenard lying prone once again at the bottom step with his head facing Simon and Masaka's table. "If we're to get past the 10th floor," the burly man added when Masaka gave him a sour frown.

"I wanted to ask about that," Simon said. "Dungeons are a thing only talked about as unknown and dangerous where I'm from. I've heard they hold mystical objects or treasures, but my parents and most of the adults say they're myths to keep people optimistic about them. Do they really hold treasures?"

"Depends on what you find valuable," Masaka replied. "Dungeons are pretty much storerooms, only more elaborate and well-guarded."

"There wasn't any treasure in the Rivermouth Dungeon."

Masaka flipped further back in his tome to reread the Bubble and Bubbles spells. "You brought back the black fur of the chamelions there, which was worth something to the one who posted the job. Besides the creatures that live there, Rivermouth has been thoroughly explored so anything like a 'mystical object' would've been taken or moved."

Simon quirked his head. "What did you mean by storerooms?"

"Think about it, kid," she said. "Dungeons aren't naturally occurring structures in the ground. Someone built them. Someone powerful enough, and with things they want protected."

"So… they store these things in what we call dungeons." Simon watched as Masaka turned the page back to the inner binding.

"Ooh!" Masaka exclaimed. "The circle symbol here! It's gotten bigger!"

Simon nodded. Though it wasn't much, the previously centimeter-wide circle had expanded to be about twice the size of the width of his thumb. So, about two centimeters by his estimate. "I still have a ways to go." Masaka handed him back his tome and he spoke "*Poista*" to dismiss it.

"It's impressive you've done this much in a few days," Lenard said from his spot on the floor. His voice came out flat and somewhat nasally, maybe from the strain of being in his position.

"Yeah," Simon said, realizing it'd only been a few days since he learned he had magic and now he could do four different water spells. He wanted to ask what Lenard was doing on the ground, but he still had more questions about the dungeons. "So, the Narumont Dungeon we're going to at the end of the month, who built that one?"

"The High Clerics," Masaka said.

"The—*what!?*" Simon clenched his mouth to keep it from falling open. "But—if it's a storeroom, then it's theirs!"

"Right," Masaka said.

"Then we're not exploring dungeons, are we? Adventurers—we're *stealing!*"

"Right," Masaka said.

"And trespassing," Dulon added.

Simon gave him a long look. His mind returned to his initial decision to visit the guild and explore dungeons. *I don't know if this is for me.*

"No one who ventures into a dungeon commits any crimes," Masaka said. "They're still open to the public. It's just up to the dungeon's owner what they decide to do with anyone who goes in. If they wanted to rely on the law, they'd keep their valuables in their homes."

"The High Clerics let people go in, then?"

"Unless they decide to defend the dungeon themselves, they do." Masaka waved her hand through the air dismissively. "Dungeon owners are confident in their protections so they don't usually guard them themselves. The High Clerics especially. If anything, dungeons are like a challenge that, should anyone best it, they deserve whatever's waiting there for them, by the owner's honor."

"Oh—kay." *If the dungeon owners think that way, I guess I'm okay with it.*

"With your first job complete, you're free to do whatever until we need you next." Masaka lifted her head slightly to look down her nose at him, the kind of look his mother would give when about to teach him something.

Simon nodded, stopping her from saying what he knew she was going to say. *You can only do what you can do when you can do it.* "I'll continue practicing with the little I can do," he told her. *Now that I can do spells silently and create my own water… I can test my magic out much more.*

*** 

Simon took the following day to get a real look at the city of Narumont. With his days off, it was the first thing he could think to do after sending his parents a letter with some of his earnings from the completed job to compensate for his trip fare. *There must be a place, hopefully somewhere nice, to practice magic.*

He steered clear of the thoroughfares he knew that held the majority of shops between the guild building and the Grizzled Ghoul where he first stayed. Instead he followed the narrower, crisscrossing cobblestone paths between residences. Narumont truly was a city as he imagined them to be. *Or is that how the old me imagined them to be?* He knew little of fantasy in his old life—the concept of magic there was what was common here and what people in his town referred to as fantasy here was the kind of technology that was common there. *Old-fashioned,* he surmised to be what his old-life self considered the city. An abundance of stonework whose level of detail indicated the wealth and status of the residents, little metal used and scarce use of glass for windows except for the shops and second floors.

Rounding a corner, he found a pretty street with a row of blossoming trees on either side. Small patches of lawns lay in front of the houses behind each tree. He looked up from the flat walls of the first floor to their second floors. *The guild building doesn't have windows on the first floor either, but my room does. Is it to protect from thieves?* His hometown had no such problem, but it also wasn't prosperous enough to have more than one floor. *Unless basements count.*

Simon rounded the following corner around the last tree of the pretty street and found a long, more bustling street that went past an imposing stone wall. He changed his pace to match those walking around him and eyed the top of the wall that rose a few feet above his head. Beyond it he could see the top of a grand duplex building. Commotion ahead brought his attention to where there was a gap in the wall and several people were peering through it into what was likely the big building's courtyard. He stopped on the opposite side of the street and gazed past them at what captured their interest.

Beyond the gap in the wall that held an iron gate were pairs of knights sparring all across the wide courtyard. More patches of grass were scattered across the inner grounds. The metal rings of their chainmail *chinked* with their movement, and their greaves *clanged* along the stone. Some fought bare-handed, others held broadaxes and broadswords.

Simon took his eyes away from the spectacle to listen to the other onlookers.

"They're not that great," a flat-faced man in plain traveler's clothes said.

"This isn't the adepts' training time," another man said, his voice thin and stature wiry.

*Knights,* Simon thought. *The men watching and those sparring are both knights. But the men are dressed like the scarce knights stationed back in my rural hometown.*

"Let us in on this!" the last man, stout and broad-shouldered, called across the way into the courtyard.

One of the knights sparring closest the iron gate stood fully upright and left his partner to peer through the bars. He tapped the gate with one of his gauntleted hands. "I guess the gate didn't make it clear to you three, this is a closed practice."

"C'mon," the stout man said, looking up at the much taller knight. "No true knight would turn down a challenge!"

The knight's sparring partner, who was between the two and about Simon's height, joined him at the gate. The partner was fully outfitted unlike the other knights, a heaume completely covering his head and face. He folded his arms. "No true knight would accept every challenge given."

Simon blinked while the three onlookers flinched in surprise at the knight's voice. *A woman?*

"What's a woman doing in the Narumont Knights?" the wiry man asked, his body hunching closer toward the gate.

"I'm not a woman," the knight replied. She raised her hands and, slightly struggling, pulled off her heaume to reveal a young and stern face. Her hair was a deep red cut in a bob whose longer strands were held close to her back by a red headband encircling her neck.

"Apologies, girl," the wiry man replied. "What's a girl doing with the Narumont Knights, then?"

"My name's Lumi," she stated, replacing her heaume over her head.

"If a girl can spar, we can, too!" The stout man grabbed a metal bar of the gate and yanked it open.

Simon gasped. *Did the knights not lock it?*

"Hey!" The tall knight protested but the stout man shouldered him out of the way. The wiry man acrobatically dodged around the knight's grasping hands to follow, and then the flat-faced man joined them as they moved to the center of the courtyard.

The girl knight's head turned to follow their progression without attempting to stop them.

"Excuse me."

She turned back to look at Simon approaching.

"Do you mind if I come in, too? I just want to watch."

She wordlessly shook her head and moved toward the three troublemakers. Simon chose to walk inside anyway, figuring sparring with a knight might be a good opportunity.

"What's this?" The captain of the knights was as tall as the first knight and as sturdy as the stout man who now stood before him. "You three again? I've told you to leave our practices alone."

"I want a chance to see what you're made of!" the stout man said.

"Give it up, Lenny." The wiry man placed a hand on the stout man's shoulder. "The captain's more on my level."

The stout man huffed, then laughed at the height joke. He turned in a circle to appraise the gathering knights slowly breaking away from their personal sparring. "Who wants to face me, then?"

Simon waited for the remaining knights to fully turn their attention to the circle of people before stepping behind and finding a line of sight of the three men.

"I will," the girl knight said.

"Lumi—"

"I *will*," Lumi said, cutting off the captain.

The stout man, Lenny, faced her and smirked. "Didn't you say a knight wouldn't take up any challenge?"

"You're not a challenge," Lumi's reply came coldly from behind her heaume. "You're a disturbance."

Lenny's smirk turned into a grimace. "*Brat.*" He snatched one of the encircling knight's broadaxes and got into a basic fighting stance.

Lumi drew a long, thin sword from a scabbard hung at her waist. Its width was no more than four centimeters, about the size of two of her fingers. She rested the tip on the stone floor.

"Not strong enough to wield a broadsword, huh?"

Lumi silently lowered herself, bending her knees and bracing her back foot.

Lenny charged, holding his axe in both hands in front of him. He intended to wait for her to move to gauge how to swing.

Lumi remained motionless.

Lenny was a few feet away when he chose to commit to a swing. He let go of the axe with one hand and reared back.

*She looks like a fencer.* Simon watched both transfixed. *He's good,* was all he could think as Lenny used the momentum of swinging his arms ahead of him in sync with his feet.

The man pivoted his body, the axe spinning with him, and it came swiftly toward Lumi's left side. It wasn't intended to be piercing and more of a blow, but the strength of the man's swing and his added momentum looked to be enough to sweep cleanly through her arm and torso.

Lumi finally moved, the tip of her blade traveling faster than the eye could see. The base of her blade was all Simon registered as it, too, spun, except Lumi didn't use her full body to spin it and only deftly used her arms, wrists, and hands. She stepped back, her blade wagging a dance around Lenny's devastating blow that was just short of hitting her. Then it homed in on his arm that held the axe.

At the moment his swing was complete the tip of her blade nicked a spot on his arm that forced him to let go. The axe spun wildly through the air toward the observing knights. Those in its way cried out in fear and cowered without getting out of the way.

A long arm shot out and grabbed the broadaxe's small handle, stopping it abruptly before it impaled into a knight's chest. "You should be more careful, Lenny." The wiry man turned the axe over with mild interest before handing it off to the knight who had escaped death thanks to him.

Lenny gripped the source of trickling red along his right arm and shook his head. "Whatever, Fox." He walked off to the edge of the circle of knights and sat, casually pulling out some bindings to dress his wound as if it were usual.

"Fox!?" The name was murmured across the Narumont Knights.

"Wild Fox, the country knight?"

"He was said to have gone across the country's border... He took out the Order of Mosfilt on his own!"

"I heard he annihilated them..."

The knight captain cleared his throat loudly to silence them. "Good work, Lumi."

Fox, appearing to bask in his reputation, turned to Lumi. "Now you fight me."

Simon considered the man who looked to be not very threatening beyond his height. He held no weapon and no armor unlike Lumi who was fully outfitted. *Is he serious?*

In the moment he had the thought Fox had darted from the knights making up the circle and in a flash came beside Lumi. Lumi only had a moment to turn her head slightly before Fox's bare fist collided with the right side of her heaume.

The metal sang from the impact and her head jolted painfully. Her heaume flew off her head as her neck caused her head to rebound. Her hair being held by the red headband around her neck escaped and fluttered.

Though Simon wasn't too close he could see her glazed eyes telling the power of the single blow. *That's bad.*

Before Lumi's body could fall, Fox brought up a leg and did an upwards kick that connected with her torso. Her whole body spun while hovering in the air, her arms like a ragdoll.

The other knights looked on, either stunned or too scared to stop it. Only the knight captain looked to intervene. "Enough!" he shouted.

Fox didn't appear to listen, in another series of swift movements sending three more punches into Lumi's shoulders and stomach.

Lumi finally crashed to the ground. Her armor was dented with pieces of it either hanging or having been chipped clean off.

"I said stop!" The knight captain had his sword drawn and he advanced on Fox.

Fox turned, his animalistic grin making it clear he wasn't done. He took a step toward the captain then froze. A ball of water splashed over the back of his head and soaked his short black hair. His grin fell and he turned in confusion.

Simon quickly dropped the arm but Fox discerningly saw his movement.

"You threw water on me?" Fox muttered.

Simon took a step back, then planted his feet firmly on the ground. "He told you to st—" A startled breath was knocked out of his lungs as Fox's fist impacted with his stomach. *Wha—*

Too fast, Fox yanked Simon into the center of the circle and threw him to roll along the ground. Fox appeared above him in a flash, his fist raised to strike his head. *Too fast!*

"I SAID STOP!" The knight captain's sword streaked through the air and Fox leapt out of the way.

"Fox, I think that's enough," Lenny said warily. The flat-faced man was frowning but not making any move to join in himself.

Fox's breathing was abnormal as he lifted himself to his full height and set his eyes on the knight captain. "Not yet." Again, he moved too fast for anyone to fully react.

Simon could only stare as Fox kicked the knight captain's side and sent him crashing with the same force he'd done to the smaller Lumi. Fox faced Simon again and Simon's blood went cold. *I need to move!* "Stop," he said weakly, still regaining his breath.

"If you didn't want to fight, you should've stayed with the other knights," Fox said with a breathy voice. He stooped and again raised his fist, this time aiming at his stomach.

The pain following the blow streaked straight through his midsection and echoed up his spine. Simon brought his arms up much too slowly as Fox brought his fist up again. A metal boot clanked against Fox's head, jarring him and stilling his hand.

Simon glanced to the side to see Lumi, blood flowing from a cut on her cheek by her mouth, pulling off her other boot.

"You're not done either?" Fox whispered.

"K-*koota!*" Simon gripped the spine of his tome and swung it. Its cover whapped Fox's chin and caused him to move away from where Simon lay.

Fox rubbed his jaw and grinned again. His arm dropped and he crouched in a stance ready to run. "You too? A mage, no less! Then, let's have some fun."

"Hey." A hand clamped down on Fox's shoulder just as he kicked off the ground, his body awkwardly springing forward and then snapping back to be held firmly in place. Masaka's horse mask peered around his head. "You've hurt my kid."

Fox's eyes looked sideways at her wildly.

"Who—?"

Masaka's hand tightened on his shoulder and then he wasn't on the ground. He was in the sky, screaming flailing helplessly up and into a cloud.

## Chapter 12: Training

"It seems every time you're left alone you're battered," Masaka commented. Her hands hovered over Simon where he lay. His skin pricked with irritation from the effects of her healing until it finally settled and his face felt normal.

"Were you following me?" he asked.

She shrugged. "You do what you want, I'll do what I want."

*I'm not sure if stalking is something you can just do if you want,* Simon thought. He faced the girl who remained sitting, a nasty bruise along her own cheek. "I'm fine now, you should heal her."

Masaka glanced at the young knight and nodded. "Just a second." The ground buckled as she launched up into the air.

Simon looked up and saw Masaka barreling up into the sky to meet the body of the whirling Fox. She performed a snap kick that he, somehow, cushioned with both his arms. Still, the impact sent him flying even higher,

back through the same cloud and out of sight. Masaka fell
back down and landed hard.

"M-Masaka!" The knight captain rushed to stand
back up and made a swift hand motion from one of his
shoulders to another, something like a sign or salute. "What
are you doing here?"

"Keeping watch over my kid, here."

Simon's face reddened. "I'm not your kid!"

Masaka left him to kneel by Lumi. The girl,
unflinching and with eyes closed, let Masaka hover her
hand along her face and then body.

"Is he all right?" one of the encircling knights
asked, their heads turned skyward.

"Fox?" Masaka finished healing Lumi and stood
upright. "He's taken many beatings from me, he's fine. I'll
get him to cool off. Feel free to continue with your
practice." And then she was gone, her shadow disappearing
into the cloud far above.

The knight captain's gaze swept the courtyard
hastily, brushing the spot on his torso Fox had kicked. He
flinched when the sounds of thunderclaps echoed down

from above. "A-all right, we'll leave them to it. Get back to sparring!"

The knights rushed in response. Simon began to approach Lumi but the knight captain's hand clamped down around his wrist.

"Where are you going?"

"Uh," was all Simon said.

"You need to leave, along with them." He pointed at Lenny and the flat-faced man who were discreetly shuffling back toward the gate.

"C-can I practice here?"

The knight captain blinked at him. His mouth quirked slightly. "Masaka did call you her kid... I suppose I can extend a favor to the Waymaker Guild's master. Just..." He again brushed the place he'd been hit and said quietly, "Forget you saw all that happened here."

Simon picked up on the request to maintain the captain's honor and nodded.

"Lumi!" the knight captain barked, and Lumi hustled much in the manner as if given an order.

She quickly grabbed her heaume and stood at attention in front of them, her back straight and arms at her sides with the heaume under an arm. "Yes, sir!"

"I want you to spar with Masaka's kid, here."

"Sir!"

Simon's face reddened even more. "I'm not her kid," he muttered under his breath, but followed after Lumi who led the way to a vacant area of grass in the courtyard. When she faced him, her cold and calculating look sent a shiver down his body. He felt like she was observing prey. "Um, are you all right?"

"I've been beaten before," Lumi said. She replaced her heaume over her head, covering her face.

*Right, she's a knight... but she's young. I doubt she's been hurt that much.* Simon caught himself. *Then again, maybe my own experience isn't a good measure of how much others have endured.*

"Prepare yourself," Lumi said, brandishing her slim sword.

Simon eyed the tip of it as it rested down on the ground. *Fox is crazy, but she's pretty fast, too. What can I do against someone fast?*

Her wrist twisted, her blade turning in kind and upturning a pinch of dirt, and she rushed forward.

*Whoa, whoa, whoa!* Simon didn't expect such an aggressive attack with the way she'd waited for Lenny before. He brought his arms up to protect himself and stepped slightly away from her swing, but it wasn't nearly enough.

Her sword stopped just before slashing into his side. Her stern face remained unwavering.

"Could... Could we do that again, but you go a bit slower? Please?"

She wordlessly moved back to her original spot a ways back on the grass and turned to him again. "Prepare yourself," she repeated.

Her hand and sword made the same motions and she rushed at him.

*She's not going any slower! How do I get her to stop?* Simon's mind suddenly lit upon an answer to fending off quick and close combat. Only, he didn't have time to cast it as her sword returned an inch away from his stomach just above his hip bone.

"Um—"

"I will not go slower," Lumi said. "Doing so would make this teaching, rather than sparring. And that's no use to me." She returned to her spot and repeated her steps.

*What am I, then? A training dummy?* Simon clenched his hands and steeled himself. *Create.* His wordless spell took effect within his right hand, a trickle of water consolidating on his middle finger. His thoughts churned with another word, and the little water grew. *Swell. Swell.*

*Swell.*

*Swell.*

Lumi was in motion by the time his fist had been engulfed in a ball of water. Her eyes moved, slower than her body which had begun swinging her sword again. Then they registered Simon bringing his hand up to strike her sword.

His palm opened and grasped the blade.

Lumi flinched, the first sign of emotion from the young knight. But no blood or sickly sound of cut flesh came. Instead a light *crunch* resounded and her eyes widened.

Not water, but a thin ball of ice coated Simon's hand where her sword was embedded.

She tried to pull it back but Simon kept hold of the blade.

"*Frost*," Simon repeated over and over in a soft chant.

"Magic?" Lumi murmured with distaste while she struggled to free her sword. "That's unfair!"

Simon interrupted his chanting to say, "Using a sword against someone unarmed is unfair!"

Lumi finally let go of her sword and spun. Her foot arced out and kicked at the hilt hard. The force broke the sword free from the ice and its chunks fell to the ground.

Simon looked at his hand, bits of frost still clinging to his skin. It felt cold, but it didn't hurt or cause numbness. *Maybe it's because it's my own magic, or I'm keeping it from harming me.* He waved his hand around to try and rid himself of the clinging ice, but it didn't fall off. *I should've thought of that... Oh!* "Bubbles," he said. The frost sticking to his hand returned to liquid form to tickle with a weak series of bubbles before trickling down into the grass. Smiling, he wriggled his fingers. "That's now five spells I can do." He returned his attention to Lumi who had taken off her heaume and was watching him.

"Your magic involves water," she stated.

"Yeah."

She looked down at her sword with leftover chunks of ice around its midsection. "Remove this," she said, pointing. "I don't want to break it."

"R-right." He opened his hand and silently manipulated the frost to turn to bubbles and trickle away.

Lumi flourished her sword, a spray flecking Simon's shirt. "Why didn't you do that earlier?"

"Um." *She's way too serious. Typical of a knight, I guess. Maybe it wouldn't be bad to let her know.* "I didn't think of it before. Also, my magic power is weak."

She sheathed her sword. "What does 'weak' mean?"

Simon stifled a sigh and said, *"Koota."* The tome he'd summoned earlier teleported from the spot on the ground he'd left it at and into his hand. He opened it up and showed her.

She silently read the spells, then turned to the next few pages to read over those. "All these spells say they require 10 sakti. I've heard of versions of these spells but for other more common elements like earth and air, and they're basic. The lowest amount of magic for those were 100."

"Y-yeah. I can't cast spells that use more sakti... that is my capacity."

"You're working with spells with a fraction of the power of basic spells," she said.

Simon nodded. Wanting to change the topic from how weak he was, he asked, "Why did you become a knight?"

Lumi's mouth parted slightly. "My father was a knight."

Simon nodded again, awkwardly waiting for her to elaborate. She didn't. Thinking better of questioning what 'was' meant, he said, "You didn't ask about the tome."

Lumi glanced down at it. "I thought most magicians had them. If you have the same affinity as the High Clerics, it's natural for you to have one as well."

Simon pointed at the red hairband she wore. "Why do you have that around your neck rather than hair? Wouldn't that keep it down better?"

Lumi patted the top of her head where unsettled strands crisscrossed. "It tends to fall off when I practice."

"Oh. Why do you wear it at all?"

Lumi's closed frown returned and she handed him back the tome. "You said 10 sakti is your capacity, but you cast several of the spells here."

Simon didn't know how to explain the way his magic seemed to replenish instantly. But, he did know he'd cast a new spell. He turned to the seventh page opposite the sixth and read another new spell.

*Rime 10*

*Turns water from an available water source into frost.*

"Rime?"

"What's the matter?" Lumi asked.

"I—didn't know I could cast a spell without saying the spell name." *I guess variations of the name make it work? I can cast spells without speaking, so maybe just having the idea of the spell in mind is enough.* A smile played on his lips. *That means I could say something unusual that has the spell's meaning to me to throw off attackers.*

"All but your first spells are in the common tongue," Lumi said, interrupting his thoughts.

"Huh?"

"Koota and Poista. Those are eastern words for 'gather' and 'remove.' "

"Oh." Simon considered how she knew another language, but decided to ask her what the other spells would be called. "What about 'rime' or 'frost?' "

"Kuura," she said.

"*Kuura.*" The air around them chilled and something like a fog wafted into view. It was slight and only interrupted the clear air for a moment before dissipating. "It worked. Cool!"

Lumi looked at him slowly. "You can come back and train," she said after seconds of silence.

Simon searched her face for a hint of sarcasm but found nothing but her stern frown. "Really?"

She shrugged. "If you're really an adventurer in the Waymaker Guild, you can. I'll spar with you." She dipped her head slightly before walking back to the knight captain who paced between the other pairs continuing to spar.

It took Simon another few seconds to realize that was a sign of respect. *I think I will come back.* More series of crashes echoed from above. He looked up but couldn't see what Masaka and Fox were doing up in the sky, if they were still up there. *Fox didn't seem like he'd be done fighting for a while… I guess I'll leave Masaka to it.* He walked from the courtyard and continued on through the city.

## Chapter 13: Attrition

That night Simon heard from Masaka that the country knight 'Wild' Fox had his leave of absence reduced which required him to leave the city to go back on duty. She didn't discuss what sort of fight they had, but apparently the Narumont Knights considered it a favor and agreed to Simon visiting the knight academy when he could. During his following visits he got to learn the sorts of training knights underwent and their code of honor. For her part, Lumi was exemplary in following the code and was known more for her ethics than her youth among the knights.

"Where'd you get your sword?" Simon asked during one of their sparring sessions in the same courtyard.

Lumi swished her slim blade through the air and sheathed it to take off her heaume. Simon learned to ask frequent questions, as the girl would only yield when a topic interested her or if Simon yielded first. And, it was the rare chance for her to actually show her face when she responded. Her red bangs clung to her face from the light sweat she'd worked up while her hairband kept the longer strands in the back close to her neck. "This is a rapier. I picked it up on my first day at the academy."

The academy, Simon had learned, was what the knights referred to when speaking about the massive building and grounds that served as their quarters. "I thought it was a family heirloom," Simon said. "Or something. You're skilled with using it."

Lumi looked carefully at the other knights who were on break and sitting side-by-side in the shadow of the wall by the gate at the academy's entrance and exit. "It was a reward for fighting five knights."

Simon gaped at her. "You fought five knights on the first day you became a knight?"

She took her gaze off the resting knights and nodded in response.

"All at once?"

"No, one at a time," she said, a light smile flickering on her face for a moment. "They were new, too. But I wasn't exactly new."

*Her father was a knight.* Simon knew it wasn't a topic she'd discuss further, along with her hairband for whatever reason, so he continued to talk about the sword. "It doesn't seem like it would do well against other weapons or armor. Could another knight's broadsword break it in a single swing?"

"Possibly, if strong enough. It'd take a number of swings around the same spot upwards of the base of the blade away from its sturdiest part. But I don't use it for hard blocks, and rather at most for deflections either with the blade or protective hilt. A longsword would be narrowly more suitable for blocking, but that uses two hands. I like rapiers better for that reason."

"They're quick," Simon said. He sat down on the grass in the patch they stood on, hoping it'd signal for her that he was tired and she should take a break as well.

Her breathing got heavier as if she only just realized how long they'd been practicing and she slowly knelt down to sit.

"It's impressive you can overpower other knights. And you're my age."

"I'm 15."

Simon blushed and turned his head away from her and the sun. *She's roughly two years older than me, then.*

"I wouldn't say it's overpowering. It's more like a series of strikes that finds a weak point or weakens them." The volume of her voice rising slightly with excitement caused Simon to look back at her. "When I fight, I use attrition."

The word was new to Simon, and he shook his head in confusion.

"I use gradual and continuous attacks," she said.

Simon thought over all the times they'd sparred. At first it felt like she was just relentlessly going for finishing strikes, but that was only because he was weak and leaving himself open. *Not that I'm much stronger now*, he thought. Still, when he learned to guard himself better she continued to be relentless but not as quick to finish a session with one swing. The rime spell was very useful for dealing with her sword since it was less powerful than the other knights' weapons. *It takes all my focus to keep my spells up to her pace and keep myself guarded.* "Oh!" Simon said.

Lumi's eyes widened, startled by his outburst. "What is it?"

"You're saying attrition is the way you pace your attacks!"

"Right," Lumi said with a nod. "That way I'm not forced to block what I can't block."

"That's kind of like the way my magic works!"

Lumi raised her eyebrows.

"I don't use powerful attacks, because I can't," Simon said, his own excitement creeping into his voice. "But I use a number of spells to have them be capable of doing something useful long enough."

Lumi shifted, crossing her legs and uncrossing them. She settled for favoring one leg while leaning back onto her opposite arm that propped her up from the ground. "I don't really know what magic entails, but that sounds right."

"So far I've only managed to keep up guarding, but if I paced my spells the same way when attacking..."

"Strategic attrition requires persistence, but patience is also key," Lumi said. "Grinding too hard will wear yourself down before anything else can be done."

"I guess that's true," Simon said, reining in his excitement. "I still don't know what my limits are for how many spells I can cast."

"Really?" Lumi's eyes sparkled as she blinked at him. "You said your guild is scheduled to go into the Narumont dungeon in a few weeks. You should find out what that limit is."

"I know… But—" He cut himself off when Lumi stood up again.

"We should spar more." She gestured for him to get up. "Let's spar without stopping. No finishing blows, only continuous attacks. Let's see who tires out first."

Simon considered her, at first figuring it'd be easy given she wears all her armor. *But Lumi is truly relentless… She'll pass out before she stops attacking.* But, the challenge was appealing, and he really wanted to know what his limits were.

"Ready?" Lumi asked.

Simon nodded, and his thoughts snapped into gear as her sword danced toward him.

## Chapter 14: Infinity

"Today's the day!" Masaka's footsteps pounded each step of her descent as she imperiously swept a hand across the lounge. The place was packed with guild members, about the same as when Simon last saw them on their return from the Narumont Dungeon. "Now's the time!"

"Time to be disappointed," Dulon muttered, leaning his back against the counter.

"We're going back!" Perish muttered in an opposite, excited tone. She wore her same blue bouffant gown from the time she escorted Simon through the Rivermouth Dungeon.

Barto giggled, playfully whapping the back of Perish's hair to make it swing out and back. He caught the chair leg Perish immediately broke off from her own seat and swung at him.

Masaka's final step on the ground floor killed the song that had started from Perish's mouth along with the growing murmurs from the other members. Lenard, who, as ever, lay by the bottom step, flinched. "Before we begin our journey, we're going to have a ceremony to welcome our newest guild member."

"Ceremony?" Simon questioned. He turned to Kairi and Frisk, the only other two teens in the guild who sat at the table with him.

"Do we expect to really get to the 11th floor?" Barto said, his boastful voice tremoring with residual laughter from Perish's annoyance.

"Of course we will!" Perish declared. "We'll get the High Clerics' treasure, and all the other guilds will finally recognize us!"

"They already recognize us, Perish!" Masaka said.

Dulon huffed a dry laugh. "We're recognized for our *temerity*."

Masaka ignored him and nodded at the other woman with approval. "We will succeed!"

"Um," Simon tried again, "What ceremony?"

"I have another sword now," Frisk commented. "We're sure to make it through this time."

"If we do, I hope there's a treasure that amplifies magic," Kairi said.

"To the street!" Masaka cried. The guild members surged from the lounge out the single door.

Simon's anxiety spiked but he followed the crowd ahead of Masaka. The members pooled in a semicircle, allowing pedestrians to trickle by while giving the Waymakers concerned looks. Simon kept to the edge, waiting as Masaka moved to stand in the center of the semicircle and street.

"Who will volunteer to participate in the welcome ceremony?" Masaka called.

The uninvolved pedestrians fled from the street.

*Maybe they know what this is and are used to it,* Simon thought.

Dulon stepped forward and halfheartedly raised a hand. "I'll test the new member."

"Test!?" Simon wasn't fond of the idea of a ceremony, much less a test he had to take. *In front of everyone?*

Masaka pointed a finger at him and curled it twice to beckon him over. "Come on up, Simon! Our ceremony of skill and spirit is for you!"

"How thoughtful," Simon murmured and stepped tentatively up to face Dulon. *Someone could have bothered to let me know sooner.* He glanced at Kairi and Frisk. *Though Kairi is skilled with wind magic, I'm not sure how either of them could've completed this 'ceremony.' 'Test' must mean I have to fight him, which seems ridiculous. Do I have to win?*

Masaka stood off to the side between Simon and Dulon, her nun's attire bustling in a light breeze. She looked at them both seriously. The street was now vacant of other citizens. "Well, then, Dulon, you volunteered. You get to choose the task Simon must complete."

Simon gulped down a breath shakily. *He decides!?*

"Simon," Dulon said. "You will have to… make me fall."

Simon's head spun for a bit before he focused on the large man's shoulders and sturdy legs. "Huh?"

"The ceremony has begun!" Masaka announced, and she leapt away to the opposite side of the street from the semicircle of guild members.

*There's no way I can physically force him down,* Simon thought as Dulon advanced on him. *Unlike Lumi,*

*I'm not trained for physical combat.* He lightly stepped back, a maneuver he'd perfected with how quickly Lumi attacked him in sparring sessions. Dulon moved slower, either casually or cautiously, in any case giving Simon time to go through the steps in his head to cast *Creation* and *Rime* several times.

When Dulon saw the water take shape and crystallize around Simon's hand he advanced quicker. Simon felt the frost hone itself to three points as his repeated *Creation* spell tapered off. Dulon's fighting stance shifted and a fist came toward Simon's head.

Ducking, Simon brought his own ice-encased fist and punched the bigger man's stomach.

The three icicles that had formed makeshift brass knuckles (or ice knuckles, as Simon called them) chipped off and fell to the street floor.

Simon gaped at the miniscule cuts his ice had torn through Dulon's shirt but hadn't broken the bigger man's skin.

"That's cute, kid." Dulon brought both his arms up to slam them down atop Simon's back.

Simon escaped being squarely hit but was knocked over and to the side when he shifted out of the way and Dulon had adjusted his aim.

"I'll give you a hint: my magic is defensive." Dulon continued to pursue Simon who nimbly backpedaled the other way down the street. "That means you're not going to have an easy time harming me."

*Defensive magic...* Simon stopped backing up and rushed the man.

"Kid, did you not hear what I just said?" Dulon mocked, bringing his hands up in preparation.

Simon brought his same ice-encased hand back whose ice knuckles had reformed and threw a punch at Dulon's guard. The icicles broke off again harmlessly and fell to the ground.

"Such weak magic won't do anything to me!"

*Magic is a resource that is tapped into, like a well or a reservoir.* Simon dodged a lazy swing Dulon threw at him with a fist. *Usually magicians only need to tap it a few times for any given situation. Dulon is probably only using his magic right before I hit him to protect himself. In the current situation, I'm casting roughly six Creation spells and six Rime spells to make my ice knuckles work. So, I'm tapping into my magic 12 times while he is tapping into his magic once to negate mine.*

Simon shook his head while moving back from another of Dulon's fists. *I may have no apparent limit to how many times I can tap into my magic, but the rate I'm draining his is far too low.*

"Given up?" Dulon asked, advancing again while Simon kept space to continue thinking.

*He knows I'm barely an adolescent incapable of doing anything powerful enough to him.* "You might be the perfect person to try this on," Simon said softly.

Dulon bared his teeth in a frown while Masaka and a few members chuckled on the sidelines. "You thinking of 'trying' something like I'm an experiment? You brat!"

"*Kuura,*" Simon murmured, and his thoughts echoed the word to cast the spell several more times silently.

The air around Dulon cooled and misted over, and he stopped walking toward Simon in confusion. He turned in a circle and rubbed his arms, his body shivering slightly. "Neat trick," he growled. Dulon's body went still and he advanced at the same pace as before. "You should also know, my defensive magic protects from more than just blows."

Simon darted to the side to give himself the other large stretch of street to use to back up. "*Kuura*," he murmured, again echoing the spell in his mind.

The mist clung to Dulon's clothes and bits of frost formed on its outer fabric, though Dulon made no show of being cold or slowing down. His imposing figure marching amidst the small flurry while the rest of the air remained clear and sunny gave him an ominous sort of appearance.

"*Kuura*."

"You're wasting your time," Dulon said.

Simon glanced at the street and smiled. "You've already wasted yours."

Dulon growled. "What was that!?"

"*Rime*."

Dulon's next footsteps faltered and almost slid out from underneath him. The cobblestones that had slicked over glinted with a fine icy layer. Dulon grunted, regaining his balance before he completely fell. "Nice try, kid."

Simon backed up slowly, muttering the same word. *"Rime. Rime. Rime."*

Dulon's face was now set in a toothy frown as he carefully shifted his weight over the slick street. Meanwhile the frosty air continued to bite at him, and Simon, unimpeded by anything, kept out of the bigger man's range.

Simon skirted again around Dulon's reach to gain the better stretch of the street. Because his magic was so limited and weak it only kept to the area Dulon occupied. While Dulon progressed, where the ice had formed behind him had already melted in the regular afternoon air. *One benefit of bottom-tier spells*, Simon thought to himself.

"Fight me already, brat!" Dulon grunted, his breath visibly puffing in the chilled air around him.

*"Rime." Rime, rime, rime.* Chanting was now second nature to him, more thanks to Lumi's sparring sessions and his own private practice with water bowls. He never did find out the limits of his magic as his body had physically given out before then and Lumi had claimed another victory in her winning streak against him.

"This isn't going anywhere," Bartol murmured from the sidelines.

"It's amusing to see Dulon chase the kid," Perish mused.

"He's actually going to lose," Kairi murmured.

Simon half-listened to their chatter while backing up past them. Dulon's body had begun shaking slightly, but neither he nor Dulon let up. "*Rime.*"

Just as Simon had neared the last bit of the street Dulon fell to a knee, panting. All at once it seemed the energy left the man. Simon stopped chanting.

Slowly, the air around Dulon unmisted and the man could be seen shivering.

Masaka swept to the center of the street between them and nodded her approval. "This concludes the welcome ceremony! Congratulations, Simon, you've passed!"

Dulon gasped again, lifting his head to bask in the sunlight. "Geez, kid. That's some rotten magic you have."

"You should've gotten serious sooner," Frisk said, suddenly somehow standing in Dulon's sunlight.

"Get outta here, brat!" Dulon waved his arm but Frisk's form had somehow disappeared again. "Damn him... I'm going to clog his toilet when we get back..."

Simon scratched his cheek awkwardly. His battle of attrition had actually succeeded, but knowing Dulon hadn't taken him seriously made it seem like it wasn't really a win.

"Kid," Masaka said while pointing with three fingers, a signal that all the other guild members seemed to immediately understand and took to march ahead to one end of the street. Dulon unsteadily got to his feet, sighed, and followed shortly after them. "You figured Dulon's defensive magic would drain quicker if you constantly hit him with the cold. Nice work!"

"Thanks." Simon looked at the departing guild members. *Oh, right.* "*Koota.*" He'd made it a habit to check his tome every time he used magic, just to see whether a new spell had written itself in. He flipped it open, but found nothing new among his spells. He only noticed one difference when he flipped it back to the image on the first page. Another circle was etched right beside the first, their edges touching. "That's weird." He felt Masaka brushing up behind him to look over his shoulder.

"Infinity," she said with intrigue. "Either this means your magic involves math or that's a sign for your peculiar sakti regeneration rate."

"Am I really ready to help with this dungeon, though?" He expected to hear what seemed to be her motto. Really, he wanted to hear it. It was comforting.

Instead, Masaka shrugged. "You can try."

## Chapter 15: Overwhelming Power

Simon didn't notice they'd arrived until the other guild members started descending inside what looked like a fancy exterior of a mausoleum. "This is it?"

Masaka patted the wave-like stonework outlining the open double doors. "What were you expecting?"

Simon looked both ways at the normal, everyday street with civilians bustling by. It looked like any other street in Narumont, the only difference was the stout, square, ten-foot-by-ten-foot dungeon entrance that occupied the space where a normal building would be. "It's just here in the middle of the city?"

"Open for anyone to wander into!" Masaka confirmed. "Children are warned and kept away, 'course. Let's go down!" She led the way inside. Simple wide stairs descended for what looked like a hundred steps.

Simon kept pace with her. His eyes stayed on the floor so as not to accidentally fall. The shifting forms of the other guild members ahead were cast in artificial electric light emitted from bulbs that hung facing each other along the walls every five steps or so. "How large are each of the floors?" Simon asked.

"The first few are about the size of colosseums. Not really sure about the others. My guess is they're each as big as the city."

Simon felt his throat dry a bit. *Right. This isn't just an outing. This could take weeks.*

"We've already mapped the ways to the deeper floors all the way up to 10." There was a crinkling sound and Masaka handed him a tightly folded brown paper.

Simon unfolded it and tried to make sense of the map. The creases formed by the folds created a makeshift grid that segmented individual drawings of what looked to be the 10 floors. Whoever had drawn them did a pretty good job considering they had to squeeze the details of each floor in its entirety between the creases. Each floor had a relatively straightforward design from the first floor on; each was circular with hard lines defining an array of rooms. The lower floors progressively had fewer details, with open, blank, and unfinished space that the drawer had left. Though no doors were marked, a tiny path of arrows pointed a way from the entrance of each floor to the next floor.

Simon felt his feet getting precariously close to missing the upcoming steps and he quickly handed the map back to Masaka. "Are there places to rest?"

"You could rest anywhere," Masaka replied. "Except anywhere you're likely to be attacked, so I don't recommend it. We'll stop at a place on the third floor when we reach it. It has lesser creatures that you can get some practice with when you're on watch duty."

"Watch duty…" *Not an outing,* he reminded himself. The words of warning from his mother about dungeons came to mind. Ahead the guild members had reached the hundredth (or so) step and were moving on to the first floor. *If there is treasure here that can increase my magic, I have to find it.* He steeled himself and stepped onto the first floor.

***

"I've been thinking," Simon started to say. Electric lights flourished as the Waymakers continued down onto the third floor; rather than less extravagance, the interior of the dungeon seemed to get fancier. The previous hundred-or-so steps that seemed to mark every descent to a lower level signaled the visual transition. In addition to the better lighting, the walls were no longer plain stone and had been given additional details. Carved wave-like patterns decorated the stone, a warming aquamarine color, likely to symbolize the High Clerics who had designed it.

"It's good to think at your age," Masaka said. "Most adolescents should do it more."

Simon ignored her teasing. "Not everywhere on these floors has been explored, according to the maps."

Masaka tilted her head back and forth. "Well, they kind of have, but no one's gotten the details down to translate it into a map yet."

"But the lower floors… between five and ten, there's a lot more blank area."

"Sure, the lowest floors must have stuff left unexplored," Masaka agreed.

Ahead, Frisk appeared and poked his head around an adjacent corridor. So far many other Waymakers did the same, but none had found monsters, creatures, or whatever that warranted action. Simon wondered at the boy's ability to come and go undetected, but quickly returned to his more pressing thoughts. "I've only heard about the 10th floor, but it's apparently a big obstacle for everyone."

"Right."

"Could there be something on the previous floors, like the ninth, that could... I don't know, help get past the 10th floor?"

"I doubt it, but it's possible." Masaka looked ahead where a trio of the Waymakers had gathered defensively. It was Kairi, Bartol, and Dulon. Beyond them, something was detaching from the ground like it had melded itself to it. Its body quickly formed from the stone into the shape of a wolflike quadruped. "Stona!" she called, then said quietly for Simon to understand, "It looks to be a wolf breed."

Simon knew about several creatures that weren't like anything in his past life, and Stona were one of them. He'd expected the dungeon to have something different, more fitting to the water element, as well as constructs or traps made from water. But the stone creature that towered before the three leading Waymakers was neither and was simply a creature unto itself.

Dulon charged the beast with a shout, grabbing its attention. The stona dipped its head, its jaw opening and ready to snatch him up.

Bartol, the much leaner man, swept by Dulon, aided by a wind Kairi had whipped up. He set his palms flat against the stona's front left leg.

Simon watched in awe as the creature's sturdy leg gave out despite not looking to break or be even slightly hurt. He and the other Waymakers toward the middle and back of the group continued to watch, though all were being patient and not looking like they intended to jump in and help. "Should we do something?" Simon asked Masaka. "Kairi's wind probably won't do much to that thing."

"You'd be surprised," Masaka said. She folded her arms and looked on.

Kairi's hands became fists and four opaque 'claws' visibly formed in the air between her fingers. She sliced them across the creature's same leg. She rent four lines through it, causing the stona to emit a low scream.

Dulon intervened when its jagged jaw snapped towards Kairi. His hands caught the stona's mouth. The stona sharply closed its mouth on them.

Simon flinched. Except, Dulon didn't react in pain. The man's face was set in a mild manner between tense and relaxed, even as he was thrown off his feet by the stona rearing back and dragging his body with it.

The stona opened its mouth to let go, and Dulon soared up to the high ceiling. A cloud of debris engulfed him as he slammed into the stonework. The stona turned its attention to Bartol who had continued palming the creature's other legs and was making his way to its last.

"Look out!" Kairi called. She started running, her feet lifting off the ground and continuing to carry her up and around the creature on thin air.

The stona's lone good leg kicked the wall. The entire corridor shook violently and caused multiple Waymakers to fall over, including Bartol who fell dangerously close to where the creature could simply fall and crush him.

Kairi dove quickly and raked her windy claws against the leg that continued to thrash against the same wall and ground. Her magic was less effective on the stone that hadn't been touched by Bartol, and the most she made were light scratches on the stona's surface.

Dulon's shout caused the stona to lift its head up and watch as he fell from the crater in the ceiling he'd made on impact. Its mouth opened again, its neck angling to catch Dulon in its gaping jaw.

Simon watched in disbelief as Dulon folded his arms tightly to his chest and kept his legs straight as he plummeted. *It's like a diver's form* Simon thought, a memory of watching the Olympics surfacing in his mind.

Dulon plummeted straight down feet-first, and his legs collided with the bottom teeth and jaw. Instead of being caught, his body broke straight through. He landed hard on the dungeon floor with a resounding *boom*.

The stona let out another roar. Its movements stilled, its leg no longer creating an earthquake. Bartol and Kairi ran away from it. Its head lowered slowly and Dulon moved out from under it. The steady roar continued weaker until it was a growl as it lay its head on the floor. Its large left, stony eye steadily looked back at Dulon who stood right by it. Finally its equally stony eyelid lowered and the creature's form dispersed the same way it had formed, becoming one with the floor.

"Well, that's that," Masaka said. "Let's move on."

Simon felt something like guilt for the creature, but knew it wasn't really dead and would be reforming its broken pieces over some time before it could come back and terrorize the next adventurers that came by. The Waymakers continued on, Kairi, Bartol, and Dulon falling back for another trio to take the lead.

***

It took another two days to reach the tenth floor. The nights had been less tense than Simon thought they'd be, as the fancy lights adorning the floors seemed to reflect the outside sun as well and darkened and lit accordingly with time. Masaka also hadn't assigned him to watch duty as she'd changed her mind and felt it best he rested as much as he could before they faced…

"A waterfall?" Simon's words barely reached anyone before they were ripped away in the thunderous, continuous crashing sounds. The stairs ended at a semicircular platform that extended out enough to house the entirety of the Waymakers before ending and dropping off. On all sides of the platform, from the stairs leading up to the platform's end, water rushed down. He'd heard that they said it was too much water, but he found it hard to believe this was all they couldn't get across. "Has anyone… tried going through it?"

"They have," Masaka said. She nodded at Dulon, and Dulon reached a hand out. The moment his hand breached the water it wrenched his whole body down and he had to stop himself from hitting the floor.

"Geez," Simon murmured. Others kept a safe distance from the platform's edges. Simon's eyes swept over the platform, noting that while water surrounded it there didn't seem to be a speck of water touching it. He quickly tracked where Dulon touched the ground and saw the water that had clung to his fingers quickly recede off the edge of the platform to join the waterfall again. "It's magic."

Masaka patted his shoulder and moved to the right edge of the platform casually, her nose inches from the cascade. "Good you noticed. Whenever we've tried to disrupt the flow, the loose water immediately flows back to return."

"I've thrown a lead ball into the water and it was simply taken away," Dulon said.

"Why'd you do that?" Simon asked.

"To see if it'd hit anything on the other side."

Simon gazed for a moment at the waterfall. "No one knows how wide it is?"

Both Masaka and Dulon shook their heads. The other Waymakers began testing out the water for themselves: Perish sang an upbeat tune that dissipated quickly in the constant roar; Lenard pulled out a glass jug from a pocket that he tipped lightly into the water's path which promptly caused the jug to shatter; and Kairi attempted to buffet the waterfall with gusts of wind that made no more than momentary imprints in its surface.

Simon spotted Frisk edging toward the front edge of the platform with his sword raised. The boy swung it vertically through the waterfall and when it came out the top part of the blade was gone and left a jagged edge. Frisk turned on the spot with an awkward smile as the other Waymakers looked at him angrily. "I'll need a new sword," he said, and promptly vanished from sight.

"So, kid, what do you think?"

Simon turned back to Masaka. "Of the waterfall?"

"Yep. Think you can do anything with it?"

Simon thought. "Well, it seems pretty much impenetrable."

"Whoa. That's a pretty big word, kid."

Simon grimaced at the repeated pet name she'd given him. *There are other words I know from my previous life that I'd better not blurt out.* "I think it works like a spring."

"A spring?"

He'd avoided saying 'fountain' since no such structures were designed in either his hometown or Narumont, from what he'd seen of it so far. "The way the water is continuous makes me think it flows in a cycle, but with the help of some kind of magic. This is just a guess, but whatever gets swept up in it has to be deposited somewhere since it doesn't come back."

"We've considered that," Masaka said. "It's possible, but we can't know for sure. None of us are willing to jump in and test it out."

Simon shrugged. "Maybe wherever the water takes things is where the next floor will be. But I sort of doubt that since it's strong enough to destroy things that go into it." He hovered a hand as close as he dared to the nearest part of the waterfall. Natural waterfalls sprinkled and had droplets that went astray, but this one was perfectly uniform. "Everything about it seems to be saying that it's a test of strength."

"Explain for the slow ones here, kid," Masaka said.

Simon awkwardly glanced at the others close enough to listen in. "Well… I don't think it's really a test. Or, if it is, it's not meant for most people. The only way I see getting through or into the waterfall is either being as strong as it to withstand it, or having another strong enough force to stop it." *And this force… it's way too strong. I can cycle my magic, and if what Masaka and my tome says is accurate I can do it endlessly, but endlessly cycling the weakest spells won't do anything to an endless cycle of the most powerful spell.* He looked at Masaka, eyebrows raised. "This is overwhelming, especially for a newb— novice like me. I know you say all that stuff about what you can and can't do, but… Why did you think I could do anything about this?"

She smiled. "Sure, it wasn't likely you'd be able to do anything. But, those with an affinity for an element have a better grasp of it and can give insight that others might've not known." She cupped her mouth and called, "All right, everyone! We're heading back!"

"What?" Dulon frowned. "Already?"

Simon knew the words before she even spoke them.

"You can only do what you can do when you can do it. You heard Simon, we need to get stronger! So that's what we're going to do! Back to the ninth floor!" She whirled and snatched someone's arm out of the air. Simon had to blink a few times to recognize she'd caught Frisk while he was using his strange magic that cloaked himself. "You too, Frisky. Maybe we'll find more treasure to pay off your second broken sword."

## Chapter 16: Infinity Redux

Simon sat cross-legged on the tenth floor's platform letting the continuous cascade of the waterfall thrum through his ears. *It's been seven days since we arrived on the tenth floor. Nine days total in the dungeon.*

"We'll be staying another week before we head back to the surface," Masaka said loudly to make her voice heard. She stepped down onto the platform from the last of the steps leading back up to the ninth floor. "The other Waymakers are filling out more of the map. We've come full circle in finding the perimeter of that floor..."

Simon couldn't see the smile that played across her face, but he did hear her laugh lightly. He was a bit put off with being kept from watch duties every night, as well as being ordered by her to be alone on the tenth floor to puzzle things out.

"Speaking of circles," she said, "I've been giving the magical inscription in your tome some more thought. Circles have a very special meaning in the world of magic. Come to think of it, how old are you kid?"

Simon turned his head slightly to glance back at her. "Thirteen… and almost a half."

"Almost a half," she repeated, her smile continuing to play on her face. "Well, you're nearing the age for a formal education. Had you gotten into Verlangen Seminary, you'd learn early on that a circle is basically a sacred symbol. A circle represents a cycle, and the Goddess Toive who Narumont folk revere is believed to be the cause of this cycle. The flow of this cycle, of life, death, but more specifically energy, our magic, or 'sakti,' is through her. Or so it's believed."

*Toive*, Simon thought. *It couldn't be a coincidence I met a goddess before…*

"So, really that sort of symbol in a tome would indicate someone having the blessing of the Goddess."

*Blessing.* Simon's mind reeled, remembering the goddess—Desire's final words to him. *'Go, then, with my blessing.'* "What sort of blessing?"

"That's what I've been thinking about," Masaka said. She slowly stepped up beside where Simon sat as she talked. "Water is another thing considered sacred due to its relation with flows and the Goddess. If I were to guess, the

High Clerics who have affinities with water likely have a similar inscription of a circle or two in their own tomes. I've only really thought the relation between the Goddess and water was a way to prevent civil wars between our city and others in the country who follow other gods because... well, people generally like and respect water, regardless of religious meaning."

"Other gods…" Simon wasn't much a follower of religions, now or in his previous life, thanks to his country town's secluded and down-to-earth culture. He guessed it was the farm town's quiet and peaceful nature to not have to be intellectual or whatnot about life and everything.

"Yup, there're other gods. But I've no idea what the point is of competitively believing what god is more powerful or better than another god. The thing that strikes me more is magic, and more recently tomes as I've seen by those owned by other Waymakers including yours. Gods and whatever could be behind it, so maybe there's something to the beliefs."

*She has a fair bit of knowledge for someone I assumed hadn't had a formal education. That is, if that story she told about her past was true. I guess her nun's habit isn't just for show.*

Her eyes moved from watching Simon to appraise the waterfall. "Right. So, with all the connections from the symbol of a circle, to the Goddess and cycles and flows and water, I thought it meant something about the very nature of your magic."

"Like the way it quickly regenerates?"

"Yeah. There's another word that I personally use that really conveniently describes all this, and it's chakra. Which, interestingly, literally means 'wheel.' "

*Now* that's *a word I remember from my own world.* Simon's mind did another flip at the implications of the same words and concepts spanning his previous world and his current world. Thinking about it some more, it was too insane of a coincidence for English from his previous world to be what's known as Brullian or the common-speech in his current world. Even more, he could've very well ended up as an entirely different species, but here he was with humans. *Could it be the same world? Since magic is a thing, I doubt it. And the maps don't resemble any of the continents of Earth.*

"—Simon!"

Simon's head jerked. He'd unintentionally drowned her voice out (but he could blame it on the loudness of the waterfall). "Sorry, I didn't hear what you said."

Masaka shook her head. "I said your tome's symbol that's transformed into two interconnected circles which represent infinity may indicate a way to get through this waterfall."

It was Simon's turn to shake his head. "What was that about chakra?"

"Wheel. Magic. Sakti. Energy. Related words and synonyms. The point is that if the Goddess is in charge of the flow of magic, then being blessed might give *you* some of that power to be in charge of the flow of magic. At least, your own magic."

*It makes sense.* "But I thought about that—somewhat, already, too. I can cycle spells for however long, maybe forever, but they'll only ever be weak. It'd be like endlessly turning a force of ten droplets against a force of a million. The force of a million will remain the same while I manage to turn ten, twenty, thirty, or maybe even a hundred if I can turn them all in succession quickly enough."

"Then do it quickly," Masaka replied seriously.

"What?"

Masaka sighed. "This is why I don't teach things, people don't listen. Kid, infinity doesn't just represent a cycle. It represents an increase. Because your sakti is uniquely capped at a pathetic 10, that increase should mean it's related to your sakti regeneration."

Simon wanted to say something insulting to her but refrained. "It's… still only droplets, even if increased a bit quicker."

"You're bound by conventional thinking," Masaka said dryly. "A waterfall is made up of droplets. An ocean is made up of droplets. You don't change much of anything if you stick your hand in one and push against the flow of either once." Masaka's arm suddenly plunged into the cascade ahead of them.

"Wha—Masaka!"

She clenched her teeth but remained standing. Her eyes bore into his. "But if you stick two hands in…" She shoved her other arm into the waterfall and her knees buckled partway. She somehow forced herself to remain upright. "You'll make a bit more of a disturbance. And if you get more hands, well… What I'm saying, kid, is that you have more hands than I do to make something happen here."

She quickly brought her arms back and held them to her chest. The water had torn through the sleeves of her clothes and bruised the skin all over. All the water that'd been disturbed quickly retreated off the platform and back into the waterfall. "I'm fine, I'll recover in a bit. Think on this." Turning, she walked back off the platform and up the stairs.

*That sounded like an order,* Simon thought. *Think about… what, though? I guess I more or less get the point she was making about increasing the force…* He instantly saw what he got wrong. *My magic isn't about straightforward force. That's what everyone else's is like, including Masaka's. She can afford to apply brute force, and others can afford to increase the power of their spells with more effective or energy-costing spells.* "I'm not an ocean," he murmured. He glanced around, feeling slightly dumb for saying it out loud, but no one was around. He tentatively stood, flexing his fingers. "But I can change it… I'm the force behind the ocean."

\*\*\*

Simon dropped his hands and hunched over, panting. The waterfall surged ever on, erasing the mild buildup of water he'd managed to slow momentarily.

"Working hard, I see."

He straightened quickly and turned toward the elegantly dressed Perish. "Um—yes. What are you doing here, is something wrong?"

Perish smiled and waved her hand through the air, her blue gown billowing with her movement. "Nothing at all. I got done with my watch and wanted to see whether you had made any progress."

Simon lightly bit his lip. "I've practiced enough to change some of the flow of water and got a new 'movement' spell that affects water. But I'm not even close to stopping the water from falling." He felt annoyance build in his muscles when Perish folded her arms. "Why am I down here? Why is Masaka making only me practice with this waterfall instead of helping with exploring the dungeon? Why am I never on watch duty?" He frowned at Perish's amused expression. "And why do you really dress like that?"

"I told you. Floofy is fun."

"But *why* here in a dungeon!?"

She pursed her lips, seemingly as a means to stifle her smile. "It's what I want."

Simon knew he was letting his exasperation get the better of him, but he didn't care. "What does that even mean!?"

Perish hummed, the wavering note causing Simon's muscles to loosen. She quieted and said, "Everyone in the Waymaker Guild wants something. It's the one rule that binds us together as a guild. What I want..." She clutched at the folds of her gown and twirled. "...is to be recognized and lavished!"

Simon stared at her. "You... want to be famous?"

"Yes!" she cooed, her face drawn upwards in excitement. "Dungeons are wonderful treasure chests! If I don't find clothes, I still find items worth selling and buying what I want! And I get praised for the achievement of exploring a dungeon! Isn't it wonderful? Imagine how the crowds will look once we've found what's behind this waterfall!"

Simon nodded slowly, then shook his head. Her hum had eased his annoyance some, but he didn't think highly of her… *Vanity*, he recalled the word. "We're only staying for two more days and I'm not much closer to an answer here, so whatever… treasure you hoped for we won't likely see."

Perish finally became serious, letting go of her dress and relaxing her face. "Despite never getting a formal education, Masaka is an excellent teacher. Still, I suppose I can make up for what she was never taught." She beckoned Simon over. When Simon (reluctantly) stood beside her she said, "Summon your tome."

"*Koota.*" His tome appeared in his already grasping hands. He let Perish open it and point at the top of the pages where his spells' names were.

"You already know this, but the numbers here show the sakti a spell costs. *Koota*," she hummed, her own tome appearing in her hands. She opened it and held it next to his tome to compare the numbers. "See, my Song spells cost 100 sakti compared to yours which only cost 10. That number is the amount required to cast the spell, but you can pour in more sakti to cast an even more powerful spell."

Simon looked at her with confusion. "How does that help? I can't make anything more powerful when 10 is my max!"

"Shush and patience," Perish said. "That's only the strength of a spell. There's still more you can do in spellcasting without necessarily using more sakti."

Simon traded his frown for a half-open mouth. "There is? Why haven't I heard this before?"

"You've not been formally taught," she said, then added, "And you're still young. Such concepts may go over your head."

*Everyone thinks of me as a kid,* Simon thought bitterly, knowing it was irrational because he truly was a kid. *I still have memories from my old life. Technically I'm 26! But I can't just say that.* "What would go over my head?" he challenged, folding his arms.

Perish paused, looking him up and down as if assessing him. "What do you know about science?"

Simon froze. "That's… a weird question. What kind of science?"

"Good answer, but not the one I was looking for. Scientific science: what do you know about it?"

"Sci—what? Is there science that isn't scientific?"

Perish shook her head. "I knew this was probably too much for you."

"Hold on!" Simon sighed. *I think she's just asking about the method of science.* "You mean the structured study of the natural world?"

Perish's mouth opened and she closed her tome. "Huh… that was almost exactly the answer I was looking for. *Poista.*" Her tome disappeared and she gestured to his tome. "Magic is the opposite. It's unscientific phenomena capable of being performed by humans. It is conceptualized as spiritual force or energy that is gifted to humans by various gods. Magic is typically unique to the individual, but its learning and method is fairly linear in that the individual performs it very much the same way through his or her body and mind."

*Whoa, whoa!* Simon wasn't prepared for an impromptu course on magic. *Poista,* he thought, disappearing his own tome and focusing on what she said.

"Magic is measured by 'sakti,' the common term for spiritual force or energy that is what an individual has at his or her disposal at any given moment. An individual's sakti is naturally depleted when magic is used, and when an individual is tapped he or she will no longer be able to perform magic until enough sakti is recovered. Sakti naturally restores over time and its recovery may also be sped up by resting, eating, sleeping, and entertaining activities."

*Entertainment?* Simon considered asking her what that meant but she was already continuing on.

"Spells themselves, while unscientific and not well understood, work somewhat like technology—though technology is basic and only provides simple things like turning things on and off with electricity or water power or wind power. Magic more complexly creates, runs, or turns on-or-off phenomena of the world."

*Oh, that makes sense. Spells are like data and commands input into the world that create phenomena.* Simon unfolded his arms and scratched his head. *But the technology I'm thinking of is more advanced than this world. Her analogy is eerily fitting for a computer CPU. I can't tell her that, though. There isn't anything close to a computer here.*

"The most common and basic magic that magicians perform is through simply casting a spell of some type and degree of power that's dependent on the individual's sakti."

*Type and degree, the basics… I'll call that the 'data entry' for a spell, then.*

Perish's explanation slowed some as if to allow Simon more time to think. "The more complex magic that magicians perform is through spells that do more than the basic world-changing phenomena. An example of a basic spell for you is creating water out of thin air, your 'Creation' spell. An example of a complex spell for you is metaphysically moving water with your new movement spell one way and then another with a single spell rather than two. It's like telling water to go from A to B and then to C, without needing to cast the same spell twice."

*One spell doing multiple things with the same initial cost… Oh! That's like the 'command entry' for a spell, or making a spell 'smart.'* Simon turned his head to look at the waterfall.

"Are you with me so far?"

Simon turned back, realizing he must've looked like he was losing interest. "Um… 'Smart' spells… Those are what the High Clerics must've used to make this waterfall maintain its force and flow without actually being here, right?"

Perish blinked. "Wow. You catch on fast." She nodded at the waterfall. "Yes, this waterfall must be under a kind of self-sustaining spell. Its flow and force may go on indefinitely, and regardless of anything that interferes with the flow the waterfall will eventually correct itself to return to its original flow as the initial spell commanded without the High Clerics needing to cast another spell."

"That seems... way too powerful."

She nodded again. "Powerful, yes. But, like you said, smart as well. Something like this requires a lot of sakti, but it won't continue to drain a magician once it's cast, unlike repeatedly casting a spell to sustain the waterfall. And that, Simon, seems to be how you've been getting by so far. Am I right?"

For some reason he felt embarrassed. "It's all I can really do... At least, that's what I thought."

Perish's smile returned. "I'm not saying you're wrong. But wouldn't making a spell more complex be more... efficient?"

Simon pondered. *Smart spells...* His heart leapt. The sheer information dump she'd given him distracted from the very simple thing she was trying to get across.

*Complex spells with only the initial cost of sakti...*
Thoughts gathered from his conversations with Masaka
which in turn danced with the new ideas Perish had given
him. *One spell of little power, with the complexity to build
upon itself... with me as the battery.*

He turned and held his right hand out at the
waterfall. "*Move.*"

Perish looked on at the heavy cascade rushing by. A
blip in the stream much like a pebble changing the flow
appeared. The blip held, widening slightly. Perish clapped
her hands and twirled again excitedly. "Yes! You made one
simple spell do more than just one thing!"

The blip widened more quickly, becoming a
respectable foot-wide breach.

"Yes—whoa..." Perish's voice trailed off as the
breach became a sizable gap, and then the gap became a
cavity. She stared as, for the first time, the back of the
cavity opened up before her and the other side of the
waterfall came into view. The cavity became a gulf, and a
wide open space allowed for many to be able to move
through with water falling on either side.

Simon clenched his left hand and fully extended his right as if punching the air. The crashes momentarily silenced as the rest of the water bent in its progression. The bend sharpened until the flow reversed on itself and cascaded back upwards. Explosive noises came from above where the cycling water collided with the reversed water. Then, all at once, the water fell disarrayed and everywhere.

Perish and Simon covered their faces as it soaked everything before falling down off the platform and into a shadowed abyss below. The waterfall didn't return.

"Simon," Perish murmured. "You—"

A new roar deafened the area, followed by the beating of wings. Across the abyss where another platform jutted from the opposing wall with a similar opening marking the entry to the tenth floor came a vague swarm of flying creatures. They spooled out of the opening and expanded, and the roars became more numerous, belonging to each.

Perish's hands tightened and she half-sang, half-shrieked. The air vibrated, the sounds momentarily stilling the creatures midair. "Chimeras!" she yelled, grabbing Simon by the back of his shirt and violently tugging him back to the stairs. "Run!"

# Chapter 17: Kid

Simon took the first step up before his body was overcome by a wave of weariness. He sluggishly turned back to Perish as the waves of chimeras flew dangerously fast at her. *I can't leave her alone!* But his body wasn't working the way it was supposed to. He collapsed, weakly catching himself to lay in a semi-propped position on the second and third steps. *I guess I found my limit, finally.*

"Simon!" Perish said worriedly when she glanced back and saw him unmoving. The first of the chimeras closed in on her, their heads tenebrous in strange clouds of shadow. Their vague elongated jaws snapped toward her. She spun out of the way as two of them flew dangerously close, the strong clamping of their mouths indicating their power. She let out a discordant shriek. The rest of the horde that blotted out the entirety of the room as they converged on the tiny platform was momentarily stunned again.

The two that had gone past her tumbled directly at Simon. Time crawled as Simon stared at the creatures' leathery wings that they had folded forward so that the claws at the end of the limbs would latch onto him. Just as they sharply dug into his shirt Masaka barreled through the air and tackled them both to the platform in a sort of bearhug with both their necks tucked beneath her underarms.

Simon dumbly clutched the scraped but unbroken skin where the claws had touched. Shouts consumed the stairway as the rest of the Waymaker Guild charged around him and poured onto the platform to take up positions.

"What happened here?" Masaka called, punching both chimeras simultaneously before tossing their defeated bodies off the platform to give everyone more space. "And shorten it for me."

"There are ch-chimeras," Simon said.

Masaka nodded at the forms in the air writhing as they got back to their senses and flew nearer. "That's a bit too short, kid."

"He's tapped," Dulon muttered, his back to them as he rolled his shoulders in preparation for whichever chimera got within striking distance. "That much is clear. Whatever happened, his magic was used up."

Masaka turned to Perish who quietly hummed and nodded at Dulon's assessment. "So he broke the waterfall. Great!"

"I can't move," Simon said weakly. "Wh-what are these chimeras?"

Before Masaka could reply the chimeras began another assault. She shut her eyes, apparently focusing on something else. The Waymakers standing along the edge of the platform seemed to grow in size.

Simon blinked, their forms returning to normal before they appeared to regrow. *What is this? It's like an optical illusion where images seem to move without them actually moving.*

The creatures roared. Dulon roared back and launched himself into the air. He slammed into four of them before disappearing in the horde.

"Beasts," Masaka replied finally, opening her eyes and standing tall. She, too, appeared to be shifting in form but at the same time not. "These seem to be a special breed, like the black chamelions of Rivermouth Dungeon. Normal ones are a combination of animals, but these are more than avian. The shadows around their heads are like a shadow wraith's, which means they have magic. But unlike shadow wraiths, they don't seem to kill you at a simple touch." She said this last bit while observing the frayed parts of Simon's shirt.

Another line of chimeras was taken out by Dulon shooting through the air. He twisted his body around and launched again off a wall.

Simon looked on in awe while the other Waymakers flung their own types of magic at the horde. "He really was going easy on me before," he murmured.

"I'm providing everyone strength with my affinity right now," Masaka explained. "But yes, he was. Rest up, kid, we'll take it from here." She leapt the same way Dulon did with sheer strength and flew straight into the horde. Her body spun wildly and the chimeras unfortunate enough to be in her path or close were either knocked down or their wings and limbs got torn and they fell into the chasm.

Simon's body felt slightly less weak, but nowhere near up for fighting anything. He took her order to remain resting. *If I can't do anything, I'll assess the situation. What's happening and why is it happening?*

*The waterfall stopped,* was his first thought. *Obviously.*

Perish's song climbed in volume and a wave of chimeras approaching the platform stopped flapping their fleshy wings and tumbled down. Beside her Lenard was pulling out knife after knife from a seemingly endless supply in a bag on his back and throwing them. Some sunk into the bodies of chimeras while an equal amount missed.

"They're quick," Lenard said with an annoyed tone.

"Here." Frisk appeared and tapped the next knife with two of his fingers. "Try now."

Lenard smiled and threw it. The moment it left his hand it disappeared, and then reappeared the moment it sunk into the chimera he'd aimed at. "They can't dodge what they can't see. Thank you, Frisk. Do that again."

Frisk shrugged and continued to tap the knives Lenard produced and threw.

Simon watched on while thinking. *Now the chimeras are attacking. The sound of the waterfall stopping could've been enough to summon the chimeras, but I wouldn't put it past the dungeon to have some sort of signal that caused them to attack. Maybe the waterfall was a*

*barrier keeping them inside in addition to blocking anyone*
*from moving on to the tenth floor.*

Kairi's hands swirled in a pattern, and wind mimicked the motion on a larger scale in a pack of the chimeras. They tumbled from the air, but quickly regained balance and homed in on her.

"Get back!" Bartol pulled Kairi from the edge and swept his hand out at their grasping claws. The claws harmlessly compressed against his skin before rebounding. "Soft!" he remarked almost like a taunt.

Perish's song climbed again and a pack of chimeras' bodies jerked as if something had hit them. They fell down into the chasm the next moment.

"My magic's *still* too weak?" Kairi clenched and unclenched her hands. "Fine. I'll do what I can."

Simon eyed her slowly as she stayed back from the front lines of the platform and tossed out single bolts of air. The bolts effectively pierced a chimera's body or wing like Lenard's knives. *Dungeon monsters seem to exist as guardians*, he continued to think. *Sort of. Dungeons are their homes and they breed there. That's probably how so many of them got here, without adventurers or other monsters interfering with their space behind the waterfall.* Simon felt his body's strength return a bit as excitement and hope kindled in his stomach. *Without any adventurers being past the waterfall, there must be treasures here!*

He half-smiled at Perish who continued to sing. *She must be happy.* His smile quickly fell as guilt for not helping in the fight flooded his body. *Why am I acting like I know anything? I'm just lying here helplessly while they do all the work. What right do I have to any treasure?*

Enough chimeras had fallen that the horde was thinning out. Simon was afraid at first their number would be overwhelming, but Perish's singing immobilized them infrequently to stop any sudden charges. Their main way of attacking was straightforward as they couldn't fight well if angling their body or using their back half of their bodies to attack due to each tapering off into a serpentine tail. Masaka and Dulon acrobatically soared between walls, continuing to take out lines of chimeras on their own without need for a floor.

Soon the various cries of the fallen chimeras dissipated as the last few fell below the platform into the dark. Masaka and Dulon landed back on the platform, their eyes sweeping the air and opposite platform.

"That's the last of them," Masaka said.

Another roar that shook the entirety of the room came up from the depths in reply. Tendrils the size of arms shot up. They wriggled around wildly before touching upon a wall or platform and began following either as if searching by touch.

"What the hell is this now?" Dulon barked, kicking a tendril that wriggled close to him. The tendril made no sign of pain, and instead reacted by wrapping around his foot and hauling him into the air. It then swung Dulon back down and his body crashed loudly against the platform. Cracks appeared, but the platform remained firm.

"Dulon!" Masaka called. She raced toward his unmoving body while several more tendrils found their way to Lenard, Bartol, and Perish.

Each Waymaker that was touched began struggling against the tendril, which in turn caused the tendril to yank them off the platform and slam them back down the same way Dulon had been.

Masaka buckled, falling onto a hand and knee.

*What's happening?* Simon's mind raced to make sense of the new creatures while assessing if everyone was alive. *Masaka's body magic must've protected them, but it's also affecting her. Dulon's moving a bit now, and the others are groaning. But these tentacle things are going to kill them if—*

"Everyone run!" Masaka called. She pushed herself onto her feet and faced the chasm of the room. The Waymakers moved away from the cracking stonework of the platform that was no longer firm from the tendrils' impacts on it.

"But Masaka—!"

"Escape now!" she ordered.

Dulon grunted and found his feet. He stumbled to the stairs and made a grab for Simon.

"I'll get up, you're in no shape to carry me!" Simon told him.

He hesitated only for a moment, then continued on up while mutually propping up Lenard who looked to have suffered the worst of the impact as he was limping. Bartol seemed relatively unharmed, his softening magic likely helping. Kairi and Frisk helped Perish along, and the last of the Waymakers withdrew.

Simon's breathing grew heavier and longer. His body was still weak, but he knew he had to get up. He breathed in. *Masaka's still here. Maybe she's better fighting without having to supply everyone with her body magic.* He breathed out. *But there are too many tentacles for her to take care of on her own.*

Masaka batted at two tentacles that drew close to her. Rather than immediately latching back onto her, the tendrils were thrown back and collided with the walls.

*Her blows are effective, but—*

Another roar shook the room and a long head of a creature no larger than a human's rose from the chasm, supported by a wriggling neck like the other tendrils but slightly larger in size.

"Hey!" Perish called some ways up the stairs, apparently having noticed Simon wasn't with her. "Get up here!"

Simon weakly got onto his knees, feeling tremors in the muscles of his body. The slight effort was enough to tell him he hadn't recovered fully. He waved at Perish. "I'm coming!" He looked back at Masaka, her pose stalwart as she faced the eerily human head atop a snake's body. Its skin, including the head, was scaled and one color like moss. The scales meshed around its face forming a muted nose, cheeks, mouth, chin, and skull. Energy returned to his body, enough from the primal instinct to run from this thing.

Its mouth opened and the roar shook the room again. Masaka got into a low stance and slammed her hands together. Her clap was equally deafening, seemingly shocking the creature to cut off its roar and peer closer at her. The scales formed around the eyes drew back and revealed the eyes themselves.

Simon had expected slits, but its eyes were also humanlike. They were ovular with deep brown irises haloing large black pupils.

The creature's scaled mouth opened. Instead of the same roar the surrounding tendrils surged from nearly every direction at Masaka.

Masaka's body moved inhumanly fast, her hands and feet snapping out in consecutive hits that pummeled the creature's simultaneous attack.

Its mouth remained hanging open while the tendrils appeared to regroup. Crashes from below sounded and dozens more tendrils shot up from the chasm. Their scales were slick, and the crashes below indicated that wherever the waterfall had gone that that was where they came from.

Masaka backed up from the cracking edge of the platform that finally started to crumble away. From Simon's vantage point he saw a waterline rising with the other tendrils, filling the darkness of the chasm until it held at a level just before the edge of the platform.

*I need to run.* Simon knew he had to. He looked up at the others' retreating forms now halfway up the stairs to the ninth floor. *There's no way I can help here.* He pushed himself up into a kneeling position.

The creature's tendrils shot again toward Masaka. She was able to deflect most of them, but she couldn't move fast enough to block them all. Two pummeled her left shoulder and lower abdomen.

Somehow, she kept herself standing while the impact caused her to slide back several feet almost within Simon's reach. From this distance he could hear her breathing. It was ragged.

*She's pushing herself beyond her limits.* Simon could tell she wouldn't hold out long. Not after already giving everyone else her own support. *But I'll only slow her down. Worse, I'd sooner get her killed.*

"This is bad," she muttered to herself. "It's formed into one body, but with so many parts it'll reform again even if I damage it en*ough*." Her last word spiked, pain appearing to finally hit her.

Two more of the creature's tendrils slammed against her stomach and she coughed up blood. At the same time, she somehow managed to grab other tendrils and crush them in her grip.

Simon wanted to help. *I want to. I want to… But I can't.*

"Simon." Masaka's voice cut through his thoughts like a mountain piercing a cloud layer. "I could use your help."

For a moment the creature's writhing in the waters and the cracking of the room's stonework fell away. He stared at her. He thought she hadn't been aware he was still there. *She called me by my name.* She remained facing forward. *She didn't even look back once. Does she have that much confidence in me?* New energy flooded his body.

Chunks of the walls crumbled into the churning water after Masaka swatted another series of tendrils back. She continued to nimbly duck and weave around the tendrils as they attacked. She didn't even wait for his response.

*Has she always had this much confidence in me?*

The creature bellowed and the majority of its tendrils attacked in unison again. Simon stood up.

*It's all I can do, but since she's done so much already... I'll just have to do it again.* He reached his hand out and spoke. "*Consuming Rime.*"

Masaka traded blows with the first of the tendrils that struck. The rows of others that were arcing forward slowed before reeling back. The waterline from the edge of the wall along their platform slowly frosted over and slight crystals floated out toward the creature.

The creature's gaping mouth stayed open, but its neck and head slunk back slightly while it appraised the whitening water.

Simon clutched his forearm with his free hand, feeling the energy taking its toll to sustain the spell. Its power continued to grow and freeze the waters. The nearest tendrils became stuck in the ice, which then crept up their lengths and became completely frozen. He grimaced. *This is infinity. This is my power that I can do. So I have to!*

He felt the weakness in his muscles return and he fell back to his knees. Simon kept his arm held up to sustain the magic funneling from him.

The creature's various remaining tendrils that had sequestered to the far side of the room had no more space to go. The waterline receded and transformed into ice that caked the creature's scales. Its head wriggled violently, cracks forming in the ice where its neck protruded from the base of the former water. But still the ice progressed no matter how violently it managed to break free of it.

It roared, another deafening sound that violently shook the room. The sound alone was enough to break away pieces of ice clinging to its neck and several of its tendrils.

*No!* Simon winced, his body temperature rising. He refused to let it free itself. But his skin was clammy. Dull aches cascaded across his body like a fever. His vision wavered. *No...*

With his eyes drooping, he kept his arm elevated to sustain the spell.

Masaka darted across the iced over water and clamped her hands on the creature's dome and jaw. She grunted and forced its mouth shut, cutting off the scream.

Finally, frost coated over its mouth, nose, eyes, and entire head.

A brief silence ensued while Masaka breathed in and out heavily. She then inhaled sharply and tore the creature's head from its body. The frost lightly encroaching along her fingers also broke. She let go and kicked its head which collided and shattered into pieces against a wall.

Masaka hunched over with her hands on her knees. She turned finally to look back at Simon with a smile.

Simon weakly smiled back, and then fainted.

# Chapter 18: Replica

High Cleric Montel looked up from his broad desk. The room he occupied was unlike the rest of his basilica, housing tools for pragmatic rather than ecclesial use; shelves lined two opposing walls, all carrying bins with vials, droppers, stoppers, filters, and more; the wall behind his desk displayed ink-blotched aqueous diagrams and models and the like; and the front of the room where High Cleric Catalina entered held a watercolor painting depicting the glorified image of Goddess Toive above the door. "Catalina," he said, sweeping an arm over vials strewn atop his desk as a means to indicate he was too preoccupied to give a warmer welcome.

Catalina moved to the other side of his desk without shutting the door, her deep blue robes ruffling around her ankles. "The instruments you made that were used to detect changes in the dungeon have gone off."

"And?" Montel prompted, plucking up a vial and emptying a blue-tinted liquid from it into a bin on the edge of his desk that held more of the same liquid.

"The tenth floor has been breached."

Montel's eyes momentarily flicked up from scrutinizing the droplets remaining on the interior of his vial before placing it in another bin for similarly used vials. "Have you told Aldana and Thian?"

"No, I came to you first."

Montel shrugged. "I'm not nearly as interested in someone else who has an affinity for water like you all."

"You're the one who designed the instruments!" Catalina said incredulously.

"You designed the spell for the waterfall," he replied without a change in his casual tone. "As well as Aldana and Thian for the creatures. You all wanted a test to find more like us, I couldn't say no to helping."

Catalina sighed, propping herself on both hands to lean over the desk. "You went through all the trouble just to help?"

He shrugged again. "I also wanted to protect the treasures we've accumulated as best as I could. Whoever managed to get that far, they've earned it."

"That's it?" She stared at him. "You don't care to know who?"

"I'll leave that to you three," he said, picking up another vial for study. "The dungeon has one entrance and it'll take some time for them to climb back up. Meanwhile you can notify the others."

Catalina groaned and pushed away from the desk. "You're no fun."

The clinking of Montel's vials sounded in reply.

\*\*\*

Simon's eyelids flew open but he stayed on his back.

"Simon!"

Simon winced in surprise at the relief in Dulon's voice. He winced again with slight pain when the man rapped knuckles against his chest.

"You said you'd follow after me, you filthy liar!"

Rubbing the sore spot on his chest, he sat himself up and looked around at the empty cots lying about the ninth floor nearby the stairs leading down.

"Everyone else's moved on to scout," Dulon answered before Simon could ask. "I stayed back. Figured it wasn't right for the one who solved the tenth floor to not be there."

Simon blinked a few times before registering that Dulon was referring to him. "Masaka did—"

"I hate ill-timed modesty," Dulon growled. "She's already told the rest of us how you helped take down the chimera. Apparently the other ones were just parts of the big one you fought with her. I don't get it, but it had to do with the magic they possessed. Luckily you froze it so it couldn't regenerate or reform again."

Simon kept silent for a second, then smiled. *He's warmed up a bit to me, I guess.* "So it worked?"

Dulon nodded. "Congratulations on passing out naturally from exhaustion. Many mages do after using up most or all of their sakti, but I didn't expect you'd be one of them."

"I don't think anyone thought I'd be capable of much," Simon said.

"Well, even I thought you were capable of passing out." Dulon cracked a grin and added, "Given your previous run-ins with trouble, I mean."

Simon flexed his fingers. "So I finally found the limit of my magic," he said softly. "It's not quite infinite."

"Masaka noticed your magic was regenerating the same the entire time. It was, she said, the type of spell you cast that continuously used up what you regenerated until it got to the point the spell needed more sakti than what you could regenerate in time." Dulon glanced down the single corridor leading to and from the Waymakers' makeshift camp before looking sideways at Simon. "Who taught you about catalyst spells?"

"Um. Oh. Perish gave me some advice about spells not necessarily needing vast amounts of sakti to be strong. That's how I broke the waterfall." Simon awkwardly glanced around. "What's a catalyst spell?"

"It's what you did. Without actively casting more magic, the mage feeds the initial spell with their sakti to have it continuously build up doing whatever it does. Most mages use it for drastic measures or as a last-ditch effort since it drains sakti quickly."

Footsteps echoing up the stairs alerted them to the return of the other Waymakers. "Simon!" Perish and Masaka called in unison when they had climbed the stairs, both racing over.

Simon yelped when Masaka plucked him from the ground and spun him through the air in a circle around her. He landed awkwardly before sinking into the fluffs of Perish's gown when she hugged him with Masaka. He blushed but let it happen (he also figured he couldn't escape Masaka's strength even if he tried). "Is everything all right?" he asked before they let him go and the others in the guild walked over.

"It's wonderful!" Perish enthused. "It turned out there was no eleventh floor! Behind the waterfall was a vault the entire time!"

"A vault?" Simon echoed with unmitigated desire. "What was in it?"

"Lots of things!" Masaka said. "Such as a few swords!" She gestured to Frisk who was adjusting a scabbard strapped to his back with a sword's ornate hilt sticking out from the top. "We won't have to buy a new one for a while," she said keenly. "I hope. There were also *a lot* of magic items that'll be useful for the guild."

Simon raised his eyebrows at the guild master muttering something about funds under her breath. "Is everything going to be sold?"

"No way!" Dulon objected, standing up. "There has to be something worth keeping other than swords!"

"Indeed!" Masaka smirked at Simon and folded her arms. "As a reward and in honor of being the one to get us to the end of the dungeon, you'll get to be the first to choose any one of three magical items!"

Simon's heartbeat picked up. *Three magical items… This is what I've wanted!* "Where are they?" he asked excitedly, glancing from one Waymaker's face to another. "What are they?"

Perish procured a glittering metal bracelet with a series of blue gems embedded in a crisscrossing pattern all over. "This is an amplifier. Wearing it increases your magic in a number of ways."

Simon felt his fingers quivering. *Would this allow me to join Verlangen?* "Can I test it?" he asked.

"You don't have to decide what to choose immediately," she replied with a smile, handing it over.

Simon appraised the lovely gems. *Sapphires are fitting for a water affinity.* He shrugged. *Or maybe they aren't, but I think they are.* He slipped his hand through the metal bracelet and stilled, assessing how it felt. It felt cool, but he wasn't sure whether there was something more he should feel.

"Hm," Masaka said.

"What is it?" Simon turned his arm over, wondering whether he was using it right.

"I was wondering about your power. This confirms it: even an amplifier can't increase your magic."

Simon felt like he'd been slapped. "…No. It can't not increase… Not absolutely can't, right?"

Masaka and Perish shared a careful look before the former said, "Check out these other two." She held out a large perfectly round stone of pure blue that captivated Simon's attention enough to almost make him forget his disappointment. "This is a vessel. It's like a… What would you call it, Perish?"

"It's like a portable store for magic," Perish said. "This one is sort of different from others I've seen. I'm not sure what about it is different, exactly."

Masaka offered the stone. Simon reached out slowly, then paused. "What's the last item?" Simon asked, withdrawing his hand to reluctantly (and spitefully) slip the bracelet off and hand it back to Perish.

Kairi stepped closer and showed a slightly curved piece of silver metal no larger than one of her palms.

Simon gave it a cursory look before looking back at Masaka, feeling his dejection rise. He swallowed. "What's that?" His voice was strained from holding back exasperation.

"Well, that's simple. That's a, well…" She glanced over to Perish who jumped in.

"An occluder. It looks like it can be worn so it's more like an eyepatch, but more than covering one eye it's meant to increase your magic similarly like the amplifier. It's called a pact."

Simon hesitated, keeping from letting his hope rise again. "Can I try it?"

"I… wouldn't recommend it."

Simon clenched his hands into fists. "Why?"

"It's different from an amplifier. It's more like a tradeoff where you sacrifice something to increase your magic. The benefits are more drastic, but there's no telling what you'd lose if you put it on."

"Why?" Simon surprised himself as the anger bubbled forth suddenly and could be plainly heard in his voice. He reined himself in. *Why am I so angry? I want to get into Verlangen... Why do I really want to go there? I learned I have magic, that should've been good enough...* "Why offer it if it's dangerous?"

Perish hesitated before answering. "It was one of the few magical items in the vault. They truly are rare, and it's rarer to find one that'll work for you."

*No. I didn't just want to have magic. I wanted to be... special.* His anger turned to embarrassment at his own childishness. *But what does being special mean, anyway? I was reborn in this world, isn't that special enough?* He wanted to tell himself yes, but somehow he didn't truly believe it. His anger returned, but he'd turned it inward. *How selfish am I?*

"You can still try it, if you really want to. It's possible that whatever you lose would only be gone while you wear it, but... There are some that are permanent. Honestly, I'm surprised such an item is in the High Clerics' dungeon."

*It could break whatever curse or whatever I have that makes my sakti so restricted.* He slowly reached a hand out.

"Simon."

He froze, still unused to hearing Masaka say his name.

"It's fun to be strong, but it's not when you have to use strength."

He blinked. He wanted to ask what she meant, but felt he sort of got it. His hand inched closer toward the occluder. Then he extended his hand and grasped the vessel in Masaka's hand. "I'll go with this."

Audible breaths released from the other Waymakers. Simon looked around, realizing how stupid he must've looked almost throwing a fit about not getting a reward he wanted. *They must think I'm ungrateful...*

A force expanded from the stone he held, causing Masaka to let go and fall backward. Everyone else fell to the ground as well as the air itself shook. Similar waves of force expanded intermittently from the vessel. Simon felt its pulses, but he alone remained standing, otherwise unaffected.

Light illuminated from within the stone and a beautiful pattern like waves shimmered within. It was like watching the surface of water lit by the sun while being submerged beneath the ocean. And then the stone morphed, its surface becoming softer and springy as it sagged somewhat around Simon's fingers.

Simon let go and the amorphous blue thing itself expanded with no more of the waves of force. Before his eyes it grew upward, tall, just as tall as him. Limbs formed; arms and legs like his. Feet became more distinct, followed by toes. Hands likewise with fingers. A head rose from shoulders, followed by a neck wedged between. Etches appeared where eyes should be, and then two nearly blinding blue-white ovals opened up in its face while it lacked any other facial feature.

Taking a step back, Simon dumbly stared at it.

The blue-white light of its eyes dampened a bit before their angles sharpened as if focusing on Simon. Suddenly a mouth was etched under a nose, and it opened. "New user registered. Awakening nearing completion."

*It spoke.* Simon continued staring as the surface of the stone-turned-humanoid began shifting colors from blue to tan, like the color of his skin. Soon what stood before him was… him.

A replica.

## Chapter 19: Conquerors

High Cleric Catalina stood flanked by a portion of her clergy outside Narumont Dungeon's entrance. High Clerics Aldana and Thian were gathered beside her with their respective clergies as well, all waiting for the ones who had conquered their dungeon.

"Is it true?" The question was repeated in murmurs from civilians gathered nearby who gave the High Clerics some space out of reverence. The question was followed by other repeated words.

"…conquered."

"…dungeon was conquered."

"It's been conquered…"

"Narumont Dungeon…"

Catalina wanted to beat them all over the head with a knight's club. *No crap it's been conquered, why else would we be here?* She angrily set her gaze on the ground where Montel should've been standing. He'd remained uninterested even when the other two tried coaxing him away from his lab. His instruments kept track of the whereabouts of those within the dungeon who were soon expected to return to the surface. There were apparently a lot of them, likely one of the many guilds of Narumont. While they were mainly focused on the one with an affinity for water, she was also interested in which guild it was.

"They're here!"

Her head shot up. Whoever had called it must've had an eagle's eye or was watching from the upper floors of the buildings across from the dungeon. The entrance remained vacant for several seconds before people rose from the dim entrance. The first of them she didn't recognize, but soon a woman of average height in blue-black nun's attire caught her attention. She and the other High Clerics converged on the guild master.

In response a burly man and taller woman in an extravagant gown stepped between them. The High Clerics stopped short. "Hello, Masaka," Catalina said, appraising the two who'd gotten in her way.

"Of all the guilds, I didn't expect the Waymakers to be the ones to conquer our dungeon," Thian mused.

"Dulon, Perish, it's all right." Masaka put a hand on their shoulders and lightly guided them to either side before she stepped closer. Her eyes flicked between each of them. "I didn't expect a welcome party."

Several among the clergies stifled gasps and murmurs.

"Such insolence…"

"Brash ne'er-do-wells…"

"Uncouth…"

Catalina cleared her throat while she noted the tattered and worn clothes of each Waymaker, including Masaka, signifying the struggles they endured. "No matter. You've conquered the dungeon—*our* dungeon, and so will be known as its conquerors." She tilted her head, and one among her clergy in finer dresswear came forward holding a teal rod. She held out a hand and her tome appeared, its pages rifling from one binding to the other before closing itself. Taking the rod from the clergyman, she lifted both and waited.

Masaka shuffled her feet before kneeling and bowing her head. Dulon and Perish glanced at each other before doing the same, and the rest of the guild members followed suit. Everyone hushed, and in the next few moments not even their breaths or the sounds of nature were heard.

"In my name, Catalina, one of the High Clerics and Numen, I anoint you and your guild with the titles of…" She placed an end of the rod on Masaka's left shoulder while at the same time resting her tome atop a spot on Masaka's head. "…Conqueror. You may rise."

Masaka stood almost before the words had left Catalina's mouth. Catalina had disappeared the book and the clergyman had snatched up the rod to quickly retreat as if letting it touch the guild master any more would make it unclean. The other Waymakers took a bit more time standing. "Well, that was nice. I'd like to stick around, but all that conquering was tiring."

"Just a moment," Catalina said over more tacit objections from the clergies. "I—we wanted to meet the one who bested the final floor. The one with an affinity for water."

Masaka's eyes narrowed. "Hm." Seconds went by as Catalina, Thian, and Aldana waited expectantly. Finally Masaka smirked. " 'Course you can meet him. Simon! Get up here."

The Waymakers shuffled around as someone not as tall as the rest moved up. Then an adolescent boy stepped around Perish and hesitantly stood a foot back behind Masaka.

Catalina raised her eyebrows.

"Him?" Thian said.

"We all can vouch for him," Masaka said. "And you know I've got discerning eyes."

Catalina nodded but said, "I'd still like to see his tome."

"What makes you think he has one?"

Catalina's gaze crept from the boy's to meet Masaka's, conveying a silent threat. "Intuition. May I?" Her stride suddenly carrying her immediately in front of the boy startled him and he stepped back. She held out her hands expectantly.

The boy looked back at Perish, then forward at Masaka. Neither moved. He shivered, then nodded. "*Koota.*" His tome appeared and he haltingly turned it around and offered it to Catalina.

She picked it up and flipped open its front bindings. The image there was both unimpressive and intriguing. "It's true," she said quietly, the volume enough for both Thian and Aldana to hear. "His tome depicts the circle of Toive, denoting him having an affinity for water." She closed the tome, startling the boy again. "Simon, was it? I heard from one of the faculty of Verlangen Seminary that an applicant with a similar name had an affinity for water. Sinom." She handed him back the tome and stepped away, smiling sarcastically. "What a coincidence. Congratulations on conquering the dungeon, and at such a young age. I hope the experience was worthwhile."

Masaka barked out a laugh, this time startling the High Clerics and several of the Waymakers. "That and the treasure! Come on, everyone! Back to the guild house!"

The civilians who didn't know the Waymakers' reputation and hadn't heard the affronts to the High Clerics gave a few rounds of cheers. Perish walked ahead of the other guild members to interact with the crowds. She twirled, her gown sparkling in the sunlight, beaming at the praise. Catalina gestured with her head for Thian and Aldana to walk with her, their respective clergies forming a bubble separating them from the rest of the street as they went.

"You didn't bother looking at that kid's spells," Thian said ruefully.

"I didn't need to. I already knew him from the list of failed applicants this year at Verlangen. He doesn't have the sakti to perform god-tier spells, let alone high-tier ones."

"And his tome's image?" Aldana questioned. "What did it show?"

"Two small circles," Catalina replied. "Each aligned with one another and no bigger than the tip of my thumb. That was all."

"Seriously?" The disappointment was clear in her voice. She straightened when Catalina gave her a glare of warning. "I'm not actually questioning you. But how did they manage to conquer the dungeon?"

"Masaka and a few more of them are quite strong," Thian put in as their progression shifted down another street. "There are a number of ways without necessarily needing an affinity for water. But all are unlikely to have not left them with a casualty if not serious injuries. I'd have liked to question them further."

"They were already on guard," Catalina said. "Any number of lies could've been easily told. No, the open street isn't the place for interrogation." She glanced back, a restless habit mostly to spot tailers but in the moment was also to get another glimpse of the Waymakers. "We can call a summons anytime, or visit their guild house. In fact, I plan to."

\*\*\*

Simon settled into the comfort of his upper story room within the Waymaker Guild, lying on his back and sinking slightly into his bed. The blinds of his window filtered in a waning light telling him the time was nearing night. A knock pulled his attention from the window to the door. Masaka pushed her way inside without waiting for him to open it, her eyes glittering behind the horse mask she wore again.

Simon sat up quickly and straightened his clothes. "Um. Hi! What are you doing?"

"I'm here to chat about our little agreement," she said mischievously. She shut the door and paced to stand in front of him.

Simon's mind was spent and he couldn't recall what she was talking about. "What agreement?"

"The agreement that if you helped us get past the tenth floor I'd see about getting you into Verlangen."

Simon's eyes widened. "Oh!" Excitement bubbled forth, but guilt with the way he acted soured it. "I, uh... I didn't mean to seem ungrateful before. In the dungeon, I mean."

Masaka waved her hand. "Kids are prone to things like that."

*Oh. Okay.* It annoyed him that she treated it like a temper tantrum, but he let it go, figuring he deserved it somewhat.

"The High Clerics are bound to come knocking sooner or later," Masaka continued. "They're undoubtedly curious about you. When they do I can see about holding up my end of the agreement. No promises that they'll do anything, though."

Simon shrugged. "That's fine."

Masaka paused. "It is?"

"Well... the reason I was upset before was because I wanted to be strong. I mean, strong*er*. But I sort of get that I've already done things only strength can't pull off. And... if I can't get stronger, at least I can do that."

Masaka was silent for a moment, Simon guessing she was smiling beneath her mask. "Look at you, getting suddenly mature. At least wait for your birthday before doing that. Aren't you ten?"

"*Thirteen*," he groused.

"Right, right. By the way, Kairi took the occluder with the pact while Perish took the bracelet. It's what they wanted so I didn't go against them. How's your..." She trailed off as Simon withdrew the blue orb from his pocket that was now the size of a marble. "...vessel?"

Simon placed it on the bed beside him and the stone quickly expanded, going through the motions of the way it had first morphed into him in a series of watery transformations only more quickly and without the physical blowback. The replica of Simon sat beside him and looked back at him, mimicking his posture and expression. Simon frowned, and so did the replica. "It's—I mean, you're really alive, right?"

The replica nodded.

"It's a spirit, all right," Masaka commented. "Never would've believed they existed."

"I exist," the replica said in Simon's voice.

"Yeah, I believe it *now*." Masaka shook her head. "Anyway, regardless of the spirit, I think you made the right choice. Vessels can be extremely useful."

Simon turned his head, as did the replica, both looking at Masaka. "I'm not sure," Simon said. "I was mostly annoyed with my other options being useless to me since I'm apparently limited, but a vessel that can store magic seems more useful for people who run out of sakti."

"You're still capable of running out of sakti," Masaka said. "But… well, I'll let you figure out the possibilities of what you could do." She turned and walked to the door. Looking back over her shoulder, she shuddered. "Could you—not you, the spirit—could you at least look at me with a different expression?"

"Okay." The replica opened its mouth and kept it open as if it were in perpetual surprise.

Masaka nodded. "Great. Thanks." She left the room.

## Chapter 20: Back to School

The door to the Waymaker Guild dully shut behind Catalina. The interior of the guild house held a simple lounge with sparse chairs and tables. It was dark and vacant, the only light creeping down stairs aligned with a wall at the back. The sky, shrouded in clouds on her way there, covered any stars that could've been seen on a clear night.

"Hello again." A lit match held by Masaka appeared in the dark. She lowered it to a candle resting atop the table she sat at.

Catalina, who had leaned back in surprise at the guild master waiting in the dark, moved to take the opposite seat. "It's rather dead. Most guilds party through the night after a successful mission."

"Celebration can wait," Masaka said. "There's nothing that can beat the comfort of a bed after being without one for a while."

Catalina nodded, then noticed the match in Masaka's hand hadn't been snuffed. Her eyes widened as the guild master unflinchingly let the flame lick her fingertips. Swallowing, Catalina made her own hands into fists in a sympathetic response. "Are you going to put that out?"

"It'll put itself out," Masaka said.

Straightening her robes, Catalina nodded again. "I understand you were expecting me…" The fire between Masaka's fingers subsided while Masaka kept her eyes locked on Catalina's. *She really is a different person in private.*

"It's nice to have followers."

Catalina started. "Pardon?"

"There's strength in numbers. And authority."

Another nod. Catalina knew Masaka couldn't read thoughts the way she could discern magic in people, but the guild master's uncanny awareness made it a suspected possibility. "I take it you didn't appreciate our interaction earlier."

Masaka blinked for the first time, the corners of her mouth crinkling. "No, I appreciated the ceremony. You made it quick and easy."

"Then—"

"How strong are you when there's no one around?" Masaka's smile had vanished. "When there's no one to be impressed by a title?"

Catalina found herself swallowing again, her mouth dry. "Be careful with what you imply, Masaka. Rules will remain upheld so long as society exists."

Masaka finally withdrew her hand from the table and wiped remnant ashes from it. "Of course. I know I'll be punished if I say I'd beat one of the High Clerics in a fight when no one's around. I know I'll be sentenced to death if I *did* beat one of the High Clerics."

"*Masaka…*"

"But rules and punishments aren't concurrent. In she space between them, anything could happen. Horrifying, isn't it?"

*She's too much of a street-mind.* "Masaka," Catalina repeated, "I didn't come here to threaten you."

"No, you already did that," Masaka replied. "You're here for him."

*So that's what she's being protective of.* "I wanted to confirm some things. He was the one who broke the seal on the tenth floor?"

"He was," Masaka said.

Catalina leaned forward, resting her forearms on the table. "How?"

"A catalyst spell, or so I'm told."

She shook her head. "His capacity would've been spent the moment he cast it."

Masaka's eyes glittered in the flickering candlelight. "He has this quirky ability to regain magic quickly."

Catalina waited for the guild master to say more. When she didn't Catalina asked, "How quickly?"

"Mmmm... pretty quickly. Like, *whoosh*-quick." Masaka moved a hand horizontally through the air, causing the candle fire to dance rapidly.

Sighing, Catalina sat back. *It's possible they fed him their own sakti to sustain the spell.* "Do you see potential in him?"

Masaka folded an arm over her chest and cupped her chin with her other arm. "I think he's someone worth testing."

"Testing?"

"He wants to go to Verlangen Seminary."

Catalina caught the polite change in the other woman's tone and volume. *She's asking me to do something about it.* "He was rejected."

"Transfers are able to be given throughout the year. It's only been a month."

"You haven't attended such schools so I understand why you wouldn't know," Catalina said, feeling herself get somewhat more comfortable as the control of the conversation shifted. "Even a few weeks would be difficult to catch up on. However," she added before Masaka could speak, "at the end of the quarter it'd be doable. In another month."

Masaka kept quiet for several seconds. "I can pay for his tuition."

Catalina tilted her head. "You'd do that?"

She shrugged. "It's what he wants."

"Ah. Right." Catalina was familiar with the Waymaker credo. She pushed back the legs of her chair and stood. "Conquering a dungeon is reason enough to push through a transfer application, however unusual. But, there'll be another round of tests. He can expect the same from when he first applied." *This'll more than make up for whatever she holds against me. And it'll be useful to have her in my debt. And it'll help with observation of the boy.*

Masaka stood also and nodded. "Thanks. I'll let him know."

Taking the hint, Catalina walked back along the darkened floor and out the door.

\*\*\*

Students roved along the grassy grounds of Verlangen. Avril beamed at the many students who flashed her grins and called her name in greeting. It'd been only two months, but she'd quickly become a favorite among the student body to both students and faculty. Her popularity was matched by her academic performance, and with her end-of-the-quarter exam scores posted she'd all but been cemented as the top student among the underclassmen. All she needed was more time at the academy—yes, more time for her name to sink in and be prevalently known. She was still only a first year, after all. Still, she felt giddy walking back across the grass that'd quickly become home to her, back to the classes she missed despite the minimal three-day break between quarters.

"Avril!" a male student, Pintel, brushed by her shoulder and smiled back at her. "Ready for another quarter?"

She smiled back, patting down her snowy bangs. "Of course I am!"

Two more students playfully bumped into Pintel and fell into step with Avril. "Did you study all break?" Linda's light voice asked.

"What's there to study when you're as good as Avril?" Marilyn said.

Avril laughed. Calls of awe and surprise echoed across the fields and students turned their attention to a canopy set up beside a corner of the massive seminary building. "What's going on over there?" she asked.

Around her, without answering, students changed course from the front doors to take a look for themselves. Pintel shrugged and moved ahead of her.

Slightly annoyed at the lack of response, she followed near the building's high and imperious stone walls. Between the various students she made out a lone training dummy standing a ways away from the canopy. Murmurs from students became more and more incessant the closer she got. A voice from a faculty she recognized rose above them.

"The crystal next, if you would."

"What's Pheona doing?" she muttered behind Linda and Marilyn who were stuck at the back of a row of students looking on. An answer, if there was any, was drowned out by another round of awed murmurs. Her annoyance building, she left her friends to step onto a small lip elevated above the ground that adorned the perimeter of the building. She looked over everyone's shoulders and heads to see Pheona taking an aquamarine divining crystal from a boy.

"The ink next, please." Professor Pheona watched intently as the boy dipped his index finger into an inkpot before placing it onto some parchment.

*He looks familiar,* Avril thought while assessing the situation. *Is he a new applicant? A transfer student?*

Pheona snatched up the page to read the number that displayed there. She flipped it over and weighed it down with the inkpot, too quickly for the onlookers to see. "I don't believe it," she said, then pointed to the training dummy. "Attack the dummy with your magic. This is your final test."

The blue color of the crystal sent a slight shock down Avril's body as she recalled the face of the boy during her entrance tests who'd allegedly had an affinity for water. *It's him! What's his name?*

The boy stepped to the edge of the shade the canopy provided and extended an arm out toward the dummy.

Avril scanned the ground around him, noticing there were no provided materials for him to work with like there'd been when they'd all applied together. *What's he doing back? Does he seriously hope to get in now? There's no way, with what little he could do even with provided water—*

A torrent of water shot out from his palm like a whirlpool, expanding into a cone that engulfed the dummy twenty feet away. The current carried on further beyond the dummy, only letting up roughly halfway across the field.

When the water subsided into the grass the dummy reemerged, toppled and broken into several pieces.

*WHAT?*

The students around Avril clapped while Pheona stonily gaped at the semi-drenched field.

"That… will do," Pheona said finally. "Come with me."

The boy silently followed Pheona who parted the crowd and headed for the front doors to the academy.

Students from the crowd broke apart while following as well but at a respectful distance. Avril glanced back at the paper under the inkpot under the canopy. *What was that? Where did that come from?* She nonchalantly stepped off the building's lip and strolled to the table. Moving the inkpot, she flipped the paper over and read the number. *1000.* "That's not much," she muttered to herself, placing the paper back down. "It's less than half of my sakti."

"Are you interested in him?" Pintel's voice startled Avril and she spotted him standing a few feet away.

"Not really," Avril said, straightening herself. "He's decent, at least." *Were these tests a fluke? Or were his previous tests a fluke?*

"An affinity for water's rare," Pintel said with interest.

*I know.*

"Whoever he is, he seems like he'd be worth checking out. Well, I'm gonna head to my classroom. Don't be late to yours on the first day back!"

Avril frowned, standing still for a moment. She then silently walked toward the front doors with everyone else.

\*\*\*

"What's taking him so long?" Pheona tapped her foot while she waited outside the men's restroom. Straggling students gave her a wide berth as they passed in the hall on their way to their classes. "Another minute and I'm coming in there!" she called, causing the few in the hall to race off before she could get them in trouble.

Quick footsteps echoed, followed by Simon racing out. "Sorry! I'm done." He patted at a lapel on his new school uniform.

"Admiring yourself in the mirror?" One corner of her mouth quirked upwards before she continued leading him along the first floor of Verlangen Seminary.

"No," Simon rushed to explain even though he knew she was teasing him, "I'm just glad I got in! I mean, grateful. To you, for giving me the tome."

"You should show your gratitude to your guild master," Pheona replied, clearing her throat and turning down an adjacent hall to take him closer to the heart of the school. "The next time you see her, that is. There won't be a holiday until the end of the quarter."

Simon breathlessly nodded. The almond stonework of every hall was smooth, curving gently where the walls met the floor and ceiling. Only the outer halls bore windows. "I won't have to make up work for the quarter I missed?"

"No, you'll be taking the introductory course as if you were starting the school year. It's a quarter-long class offered every quarter when necessary, whether it's for transfer students, new applicants, or remedial for students who struggled with it."

Simon found it hard to believe students would struggle with an introductory class that only lasted a quarter of the school year.

"It'll cover the basics of what you'll need to know while attending here," Pheona continued, adjusting a decorative fern whose limbs had bowed outward toward the center of the hall as she went. "Locations of classes, dorm rooms, and other amenities. The history of the school and Toiveism. The basics of magic, of course. And your curriculum, which won't just be the one introductory class. You'll be starting Spell Composition and Practice I with the other first-years."

Simon swallowed. *The others had a full quarter to focus only on the introductory class, then. I'll have to work hard just to keep up.* He prepared himself when Pheona gripped a protruding metal handle fitted with a wood door and swept into a classroom. He followed her inside and froze when he saw other students. There were three of them, all already sitting in a row of four chairs and desks facing the front of the room.

"Take a seat, Simon," Pheona instructed as she took up a position at the head of the room.

Simon raced to the empty seat by the girl he'd long sparred with from the knight academy. *"Lumi?"* he whispered while settling down. Her uniform red bangs before her longer shoulder-length hair complemented her navy blue school uniform. She looked good in it, but it was confusing Simon's image of her after getting used to seeing her only in knight armor.

"A quick roll call before we begin," Pheona said loudly. "Simon, you're here. Lumi, you're here. And both Davids are here."

Simon looked around Lumi's head at the two boys with dubiously shaved haircuts. He didn't have to guess they were remedial students.

"I'll be in charge of you for a bit before you'll join up with the rest of your cohort," Pheona continued. "They'll be going through ice breakers, anyway. First, I want you all to know where this class is as you'll be coming back here after SCP I." She pushed her glasses up the crook of her nose and pulled sheets of paper from a long desk near her. "Take these maps with you and use them as much as you need. Your primary class will be lasting for most of the day from morning to a little after noon. This intro class will be from then on to early evening, and some days will be like today with this intro class being held briefly before your SCP class."

Simon took the map she provided for him and mentally noted a scribbled star over a box marking the room they were currently in within the much larger square outlining the academy. SCP I was scribbled over another box by the front doors to the academy, which would be easy enough to remember. He folded the map and put it within his uniform coat to then focus on the rest of Pheona's instructions.

Shortly they were all out the door and moving on to their respective Spell Composition and Practice classes. The two Davids went a different way than Simon and Lumi, Simon figuring they had a different teacher or were being truants. "Lumi," Simon finally got to ask, "What are you doing here?"

"I transferred here," she said simply as they walked.

"Yeah, okay, but aren't you, like, a knight?"

"I *am* a knight." She shrugged away Simon's next question before he asked it. "I can also use magic. The two aren't mutually exclusive."

*I know that.* Simon remained quiet, knowing the term from his past life but trying to process it fully. "I didn't know you had magic. I mean, you never *used* any when we sparred."

"It's a temporary transfer," Lumi added in her usual serious voice. They moved down another hall. "After the quarter I'll be going back to the academy. If you're staying here for more than a year you may see me next year. This is supplementary to becoming a knight. A high ranking one."

Simon was impressed by her dedication to knighthood. *Knights don't necessarily not have magic, but people tend to become knights when they discover they can't be mages.* "Do you want to become a captain?"

"A Toive Knight. It's not what I want. It's what I must do."

"A Toive Knight," Simon repeated uncertainly.

"I forgot you're not from here. They're magic knights, considered to be appointed by the Goddess herself."

"So… They're a pretty big deal." Simon quieted again when they passed the front doors of the academy and found the door of their classroom. Questions about her affinity and reasons for keeping it to herself scattered as he gripped the doorknob. *I'm going to learn more magic…* *Cool!*

## Chapter 21: Higher Learning

"Joining us are two new students," Professor Hane said, beckoning Lumi and Simon into the class.

*He oversaw my divining and field tests when I first applied.* Simon felt the eyes of the students glom onto him more than Lumi, but he mostly kept his focus on the white-haired girl he remembered from his first application. *Avril.* She was sitting in the front of a series of chair-desks lined in rows.

"Good to see you again," Hane said softly while gesturing to two seats toward the back of the room.

Simon could only nod at the teacher under the pressure of everyone's gaze. *I thought I'd seen her watching me—or rather the replica, Sim, while I snuck into the school.* He patted the lapel over the inner pocket of his uniform holding his vessel containing the spirit in marble form. A subtle vibration emanated over his chest in response. He walked down an outer aisle to avoid going by Avril. He reconvened with Lumi in the back two seats and they quietly settled down as Hane gathered the class's attention.

"So," Hane addressed everyone. "Spell Composition and Practice I. For the new ones and those who don't remember, spells cannot be cast without sakti." He turned and slapped a hand against a wide blank blackboard taking up the majority of the front wall of the room. "That much is common knowledge and sense. Sakti is what unifies mages no matter their affinity and capacity. What is sakti?" He quieted, looking expectantly around the room.

Several students raised their hands. Avril of all people was called on. "Sakti is spiritual force, or energy."

"Yes, very good," Hane said. He withdrew a piece of chalk from his pants pocket (explaining the white powder marks against the deep blue of his own attire) and began drawing shapes as he talked. "That's the theoretical understanding of sakti. The more practical understanding of sakti is that it is magic manifested. As you'll come to learn about this class, theory and practice will go hand-in-hand." The tapping of the chalk on the board ceased and he turned from the various four-sided shapes. "Does anyone know why I drew a bunch of quadrilaterals?"

Having no clue, Simon glanced around and a familiar feeling of anxiety arose when no one raised their hands. Pangs of annoyance drew his hands closed every time his eyes made their way to Avril.

"Maybe a better question," Hane said, "Do any of these shapes seem familiar to you?"

Avril raised her hand. When the professor nodded at her she said, "The shapes are like the image at the front of a tome."

Hane pointed at her and nodded. "Yes, exactly! Tomes are a wonderful tool that exemplify the bridge between theory and practice. They are, once bound to a mage, a literal manifestation of one's magic—which then provides more ways of the practice of magic, but I'm getting ahead of myself. What we call an 'image,' what's at the front of a bound tome, starts as a shape." Tapping a square he'd drawn, he pointed at a student sitting in the front row next to Avril. "Marilyn, would you mind if I used your tome for reference?"

*Why not use his own?* Simon thought.

Marilyn silently obliged, conjuring her tome out of thin air and handing it over to Hane.

Hane pocketed the chalk, wiping the residue off on the side of his pants, and held open the first page of

Marilyn's tome. "These shapes are what are essential in the manifestation of magic. Put another way, they are the composition of magic. Your magic, in particular." His finger traced a similar square written into the tome's page alongside several other squares.

*Her image is a lot more intricate and defined than mine.* Simon recalled Pheona telling him the image would develop as his magic developed back when she gave him his tome. *Maybe Hane's tome is too intricate with many shapes which wouldn't make it a good example.*

"This shape is the metaphorical representation of one's magic, as well as the very real manifestation of one's magic. It is the shape of your magic." Hane closed the tome and handed it back to Marilyn. "You might not have consciously realized it, or maybe you discovered it, when practicing spells how much shapes shape your magic." Hane connected two fingers of each of his hands, index to index and middle to middle, forming a square. He lifted his hands up to his eyes to peer through the square at the class. "*Smog.*"

The air throughout the classroom became opaque and filled with a foul smell causing the students to cough. It was so clouded Simon couldn't see the back of the student sitting directly in front of him. Suddenly loud bangs echoed along one side of the class and the air quickly filtered out the windows.

Hane's figure reappeared, walking from the windows back to the front of the room. "In case you didn't know it before, my magic is related to smoke, and that's my affinity. Can anyone tell me what I just did?" Three girls in the front row, including Avril and Marilyn, raised their hands. "Linda?"

"The shape you created made your magic stronger?"

"Yes!" Hane smacked his palm against the blackboard for emphasis. "Physically creating the shape of your magic yourself enhances the magic you practice. This will be what we're going to be doing today, in practice. Everyone, get out your tomes."

The sound of a series of tomes settling atop the desks percussed across the room, followed by the flapping of pages. Simon looked down at the first page of his tome with the two circles forming the sign of infinity.

"I've already demonstrated how to form a square with my hands," Hane said. "I want you all to figure out how else you can form different shapes. With your hands only, please."

Simon slowly glanced at Lumi to his right and another student to his left. He lightly connected one thumb to his index finger. *It's not perfect since my knuckles are angled. But the rough shape of a circle is there.* He did the same with his other hand and brought them together awkwardly. He pressed the nails of both his indexes together. *I guess that's more or less the shape?* He glanced again at Lumi and the other student's tomes to judge the images they had. *Theirs are also more detailed. It seems impossible to make entire images out of one's hands. But maybe that's the point of Hane's lesson, it's that the shapes are what's fundamental to the magic.*

"That looks good," Hane commented. He'd been observing and commenting on the other student's shapes as he walked down the aisle before stopping beside Simon and Lumi's desks. "Mind if I use your tome for another example once everyone's finished?"

Simon dumbly nodded, not giving it much thought until after Hane had taken it back to the front of the room. A few minutes later Hane cleared his throat to regather everyone's attention.

"Moving back away from the practical side of magic, I'd like to discuss some more about these shapes. Here I have Simon's tome which features the image of two circles. This is a rarity, as most images have angled shapes."

Muttering sounded across the class.

"Circles?"

"They're so small."

"I can't really see them."

"Is his magic that weak?"

"But you saw what he did this morning."

"The massive wave?"

Hane cleared his throat again to silence everyone. "A circle has always been known to represent an affinity for water. It's unique in itself, as all other shapes don't directly represent one kind of affinity. As you witnessed when I performed my magic, I've an affinity for smoke that is enhanced by the shape of a square. But Marilyn's tome also has the shape of the square, as do many others in this class I reckon. Marilyn, your affinity is metal, correct?"

"Yes," Marilyn said.

"So, many of us have the same shapes within our images within our tome. What is the reason for this inconsistency in what the shapes represent?" He paused before a smile lit upon his face. "That's where an interesting lapse in theory lies. It is not entirely without precedent and explanation, however, as the circle is considered sacred and representative of the Goddess Toive's power. It's possible that this explanation is enough to describe the shape of the circle. But, while this is a seminary, it does not mean we will be entirely satisfied with belief alone. This class in particular will be focused on experiment. Testing theory, as it were."

Simon nodded along with the other students. The lesson had already given him so much, but getting the attention of everyone wasn't exactly what he wanted also.

"One final thing before we do actual practice now that we have our physical representation of our shapes," Hane said. "We all more or less know that sakti isn't limitless. We all have varying degrees of it, and when some or all of it is depleted it must regenerate. The shape of one's magic also represents the flow of this regeneration. A circle like these are without edges—they're *smooth*. While I do not know all that Simon is capable of, I've witnessed each of the four High Clerics who have the same affinity for water practice spells. They all have a significantly shorter time to wait for their sakti to replenish than everyone else I know. Including me." He smiled again to himself and traced a square on the blackboard. "I believe the phrase 'cut corners' is somewhat apt here, without the negative connotation. The fewer angles there are, the quicker one's sakti regenerates." He paused, nodding at Avril who'd raised her hand. "Yes, Avril?"

"Not all shapes are angled," she said. "What about shapes that are curved but aren't circles?"

"That's a good question. Many shapes aren't perfectly angled, while many can be. And while none are as perfectly smooth as a circle, it is believed that smooth angles also represent faster regeneration rates. A squircle, for instance, would be among the shapes representing the fastest regeneration rates of sakti, it being a tossup with a triangle. For those interested in language, 'squircle' is a portmanteau—a blending of two meanings—of the words 'square' and 'circle.' And that'll be your last and only tangent lesson for the day. Let's get to practice, shall we?"

# Chapter 22: Sparring and Popularity

In a way, Simon had missed the normality of classes. Sure, he now had two separate experiences with learning the Brullian common tongue (or English in his previous life), numeracy (the same as arithmetic in his previous life), and history (given the same name as in his previous life, but with entirely different events). But his memories of leaving the fields to get classwork done and his parents scolding him later for shirking his responsibilities (but still doing his share of work for him) were fond. Many of his learning habits were consistent both times, no matter if it was skipping out on sowing crops or doing laundry. *I wonder how Mom, Luke, and Bear are doing in my old world.*

The window frame he was looking out from rattled as a light wind blew against it. It'd been some time since he reminisced, and he figured the empty grass grounds of the school conjured such thoughts. Not one student milled about. Then again, his dorm room faced the school's backside which had no paths and was space used mainly for practical purposes for classes or extracurriculars. The neatly trimmed grass stretched all the way up to an auburn stone wall separating the grounds from the rest of the city. Angled tiles of rooves could be seen poking above it, which were roughly at eye level with Simon. His room was on the second floor, so he could possibly see further on the higher floors. *I guess longing is lifelong.* His fingers clenched as his thoughts turned to the vulnerability of his life. *Both lives...*

He turned when the door of his room opened and his roommate entered.

"Hey," Pintel said, patting down a lock of lightly curled brown-yellow hair that had fallen across his face. "Looking out the window again? Are you looking for something in particular?"

"No," Simon said. "Well, maybe. It's been a week and I haven't seen anyone trimming the grass."

Pintel laughed and opened the door wider, gesturing for Simon to exit. "I, myself, have never thought about that, but I imagine it's trimmed in the early early morning while everyone's asleep. Then again, you grew up on a farm and would be up at a similar time, so maybe not?"

Simon shook his head and took the other boy's signal to leave the room and follow him down the dorm quarters to a stairway leading to the first floor. "I don't wake up that early. I haven't kept to that schedule in a while."

"I'm excited," Pintel said. "Since the time you arrived you haven't shown off your power. I think you've been holding out on me!"

Simon smiled lightly as they took the smooth stone stairs down. "Eh…" The truth was consistent with what Pintel thought, but the reasons were messy. On one hand, he didn't want to raise suspicion about his spirit Sim who'd taken the application tests for him if he performed magic himself. On the same hand, he didn't want to become more of a target of interest. More than he already was. Students talked with him often, mostly about themselves since they came from noble families while his country life background was uninteresting (or too poor for them). And he guessed they talked with him because of his power. Every so often they'd ask the same question about it: "How strong are you?" It was the one question he didn't want to answer, and it made him self-critical every time he heard it. *Oh, yeah, I have 10 sakti. Isn't that crazy?* His smile changed into a grimace as he pictured the looks of disdain on his classmates' faces. *'10? What a wasted opportunity on such a rare affinity!'*

*On the other hand,* Simon counter-thought as he stepped down and continued following Pintel toward a sparring hall in the back of the building. More students in his class, including those in the other SCP I class, were heading that way. *On the other hand, performing some magic would break the tension a bit. I do want to show off a bit... just a bit.*

"We only had sparring sessions twice last quarter," Pintel said, lowering his voice while in the company of other passing students. It wasn't entirely necessary as they all were caught up in their own conversations.

"They're really just practice, right?"

Pintel looked over at him ruefully. "Beasts may've been the largest threat where you grew up. But here in the city, people are the largest threat."

*It makes sense, I guess. It's still nerve-wracking fighting other people.* Simon set his shoulders. *But compared to Dulon, other students aren't nearly as threatening. Except for maybe Lumi.* The corridor ended at the open door of the sparring hall. Inside, the hall was large enough for three separate mats. Three professors, Pheona of his introductory class, Hane of his SCP I class, and Stephen for the other SCP I class, stood by each mat. They'd be the referees.

Simon went to stand with his classmates by Hane's mat.

"Good luck!" Pintel murmured before moving around students to talk with Avril.

Simon thought it was strange Pintel had been so friendly with him. *Not terribly strange, given we're roommates. Him being friends with Avril also isn't strange since everyone seems to be friends with her.* But of course, Simon still distrusted his friendliness. It could be genuine, but that didn't matter. Avril already proved the danger of trusting too easily. Simon spotted Lumi standing nearby and edged closer toward her. *In a way, Lumi's blunt but honest nature made her more worth trusting.* "Hey."

"Hey," Lumi greeted. She didn't say anything more, turning to appraise the other students.

*Right. I should be considering the other students' affinities and thinking of how to deal with them.* He judged the size of the mats as well. *We can't use anything that'd break the room, which leaves fewer options for earth magic. I can't very well flood the place, either. But we're not looking to obliterate our opponents the same way students did to practice dummies during the entrance tests.*

"Good evening, everyone!" Pheona called. Students quieted and she continued: "Matchups have already been decided and the sparring will begin shortly, but first to remind everyone of the rules and safety. The aim of sparring is to incapacitate your opponent or force them to give up. As you are all first years, this means nothing that would render your opponent unconscious or cause a greater injury than a bruise. In case a major injury does happen, the medical room is just outside and a few doors down. Leaving the mat is an automatic forfeit. Falling on your front or back is an automatic forfeit." Pheona paused, glancing at the other two professors. "That is all."

Simon patted his uniform jacket pocket, wondering if he would've preferred Sim to do his sparring match for him as well. Three pairs of students were called out, none involving Simon or anyone he knew well. He politely took a step back to allow space around Hane's mat and thought to himself while the ones who would spar prepared to begin. *All affinities have poor matchups even among the strict elements. I can't think of many for water, though metal wouldn't be great.* He glanced at Marilyn momentarily before refocusing on the students who'd begun to clash, both with clubs of rock they'd each created for themselves. *Rock... Avril has an affinity for earth magic, as well as wind magic. Could she have more? She didn't show it during the entrance test, so probably not.*

A student's rock club was knocked out of his hand and he fell backward.

"And done!" Hane called. Both students left the mat, the loser frowning and the winner smiling. "Lumi and Marilyn, you're next!"

Simon nodded encouragingly at Lumi as she stepped onto one side of the mat to face the other girl. *I haven't actually gotten to see her use magic. She told me it was friction magic, but I don't really know what that means.*

Hane called for them to begin. Marilyn procured a metal rod from her uniform and magically reshaped it into similar form as the previous rock clubs but much smoother and rounded.

*She didn't create it. Come to think of it, the previous students didn't create their rocks either. Is Creation a unique spell?* Simon continued to ponder other possible types of limitations of magic while the girls squared off. *Am I an idiot for not simply carrying water with me before I could create it myself?*

Lumi slid her left foot forward and to the left in a slight curve, then her right foot backward and to the right, taking up a wide sideways stance.

*Interesting. Usually she attacks first.*

Marilyn advanced with her metal bar already on the backswing.

*She's lifting it pretty high. She can't be going for more than a glancing blow, otherwise she'd be at risk of inflicting a serious injury.*

Marilyn's bar swung forward toward Lumi's shoulder and neck.

Lumi pivoted on her back foot to take up the same stance only with her right foot leading. She brought the back of a hand up to collide with the bar as it swung down. The bar stuck fast, almost freezing mid-swing as if it'd hit its intended target.

Marilyn kept control of her balance and tugged the metal bar back. But the bar didn't move.

Lumi's hand deftly twisted to grip the bar and yank it from the other girl's hand. She tossed it in a spin and caught it before swinging it fast back at Marilyn.

Marilyn yelped and stepped out of the way in time for the bar to swoosh horizontally where her body had been.

*Friction… So the things she touches she can change to either slide or stick.* Simon watched, impressed by how the knight used it to her advantage to make the spar more of a physical battle than magic.

Marilyn pulled out another piece of metal from her uniform, followed up by another to hold in each of her hands. The metal shifted and expanded into wider pieces she clumsily used to block another of Lumi's swings as she backed further along the mat.

Lumi continued to outdo her opponent in physical technique, overpowering with just the single metal bar. Soon enough Marilyn had been forced off the mat and Hane had called an end to the fight.

"Done! Next up is Avril and Simon."

Students from the other mats turned away from the ongoing matches and watched as Simon and Avril took to their mat. For Simon's part, his brain had partially shut off out of surprise and nervousness. He only unconsciously noticed everyone but the other referees and students mid-spar turn their attention to him. His thoughts finally caught up with him when Hane announced the start of the spar. Somehow he'd moved to take up his place on the mat and his body was already tensed in a stance.

Simon's eyes narrowed at Avril who sent out a gust of wind from an arm she flung out toward him.

*Creation. Rime.* Water proliferated around the soles of his shoes and promptly solidified, sticking him to the mat. It quickly climbed up to his ankles before the harsh wind blew across him. It did not knock him back or down.

Avril frowned and withdrew her hand. She touched her thumbs and index fingers together in the shape of a triangle.

Simon sensed the strength of the wind that she'd built from the center of her shape before it rushed at him. It would surely bruise him if taken directly. His magic stirred with his thoughts, and water flowed upward from the mat into a makeshift wall. It crystallized just as the wind arrived. But it shattered.

Simon noticed the direction of the wind hadn't only grown in strength but also was more controlled and directed. It tunneled through the wall of ice low to the mat before curving upward to strike Simon's stomach. It lifted him off the ground and he was flying backward through the air.

The end of the mat passed at the bottom of his vision before his body turned to parallel the floor. He watched the crisscrossing pattern of the stonework of the ceiling slide by as he flew. *I'm not done.*

Simon felt wet coils grip his ankles and his backward progression and descent stilled. He unbent his knees, bringing himself back upright. He looked down at the snakelike waterways extending from the two imprints of ice on the mat where he'd been standing. They traveled through the air and wrapped firmly around his low legs. Holding his arms out to give himself balance, he willed the waterways to drag him back firmly onto the mat.

The moment he touched down students cheered, but he didn't pause to take it in.

Avril had created a sort of shield of rock and, though transparent, the shifting of air formed a kind of sword similar to the way Kairi used her affinity. She ran at him.

Simon noticed that where she stepped down wasn't directly on the mat but other loose piles of rock she gathered, and he instantly judged he couldn't trip her. *I guess I've been wanting to use this spell with the concept of infinity.*

The water encircling his ankles broke and thinned, trickling over the mat. He circled his fingers as he'd learned to in class and pressed them together. Meanwhile, Avril was closing in dangerously fast.

*"Swell."*

Defying the speed of everyone and the rest of the room, a droplet picked itself up from the retreating water along the mat and hovered in midair just ahead of where Simon's fingers connected. Its surface undulated, rippling in a rapid expansion. Quickly the single drop became a swirling cycle like a horizontal whirlpool. It grew large enough to more than triple Simon's size.

On the other side of the swell, time had passed only enough for Avril to blink.

The water erupted away from Simon in a spinning concave wave. Its outside engulfed Avril before its center reached her, and her body spun before becoming obscured in the torrent.

The loud crashing and spray forced many to shield and avert their eyes while the wave carried clear past the end of the mat.

Simon cut off the stream of sakti he'd been feeding the spell and let the wave subside. Water fell to the stone floor, washing over and away from Avril who lay on her back. She blinked away the water, her breathing rapid from shock.

A second passed and then Hane called, "And done!" He gave Simon a wary look, then a nod, and announced, "Pintel and Linda, you're next!"

Simon snapped out of whatever trance had taken over him when the spar began. His hands shook and his breathing became unsteady. He gathered the water to dissipate as quickly as he could while exiting the mat. He saw the faces of the other students looking at him with a mix of awe and respect. At least, he hoped.

## Chapter 23: Popularity and Prestige

"And done!" Hane announced the end of the next match. "We'll go on break for several minutes!"

"Simon!" Pintel pushed through the crowd of students that glommed around Simon who struggled making his way out of the sparring room. He forced himself onto Simon's right side while Lumi appeared alongside his left. Together they hooked their arms around his and helped him forward, almost lifting him as they left the room.

"You beat Avril!"

"Who is that kid?"

"He transferred here a week ago!"

"He has a water affinity!"

Simon shook his arms to silently signal for the two half-walking and half-carrying him along to let him walk on his own. "Let's go to the stables," he murmured.

"O—kay," Pintel said. "You know that everyone's going to want to talk to you at some point?"

Simon continued to lead the way at a brisk pace until they'd gotten clear of the other students and found the quaint thatched door fairly close by their SCP I class. The stables occupied the corner of the building's first floor, a 'room' in the sense it held a floor, walls, and ceiling; its outer wall, which was really a series of wood-and-stone panels, facing the school's frontside could be shifted with a sliding mechanism that allowed each to roll back and forth. Simon went along the room's length to a point roughly halfway along before gripping one of the panels and sliding it aside.

The horse opposite the open panel neighed expectantly. The animals knew when someone opened the way across from them they'd get to go outside. Simon shook his head at the horse in apology for getting its hopes up and sat at a nearby stool set up beside a metal scraper to clean out horse hooves.

"Is something wrong?" Pintel asked. Lumi remained quiet, both of them standing on the other side of the setting sun's rays shining through the opening.

Simon touched the front of his lapel to feel the small bump of his vessel. "Avril isn't going to like this."

Pintel laughed lightly. "That's… true, no one likes to lose. To tell you the truth, though, she hasn't really liked you in the first place."

*I know that.* His fists clenched and he shook his head. "I can tell."

"What would you have done differently?" Lumi asked. "Would you lose on purpose?"

"No."

"Then there's no problem," Lumi said.

"No—just because I won doesn't mean nothing's wrong."

Lumi shrugged. "If Avril doesn't like you, that's her problem."

"I wish it were that easy." Some things he wished he'd forgotten from his past life taught him that it never was. *It was merely 'teasing' masked by resentment of a 'friend' that pushed me into the manhole.* Simon watched crowds filter along the faraway thoroughfare traveling deeper into the main city. From the look of it, the evening bustle after a day's work was beginning. "Can I tell you a secret?"

"Yes," Lumi said.

Pintel glanced between them uncertainly. They looked back at him and waited. He shrugged. "You can, but I don't know if I can keep it. If it's about Avril, just know I'm still friends with her."

"That doesn't really matter." Simon let out a quiet breath. "Before I say it, do either of you believe I belong at this school?"

"Why wouldn't you?" Lumi answered shortly.

"I don't get the question," Pintel said. "You got in, and you've been doing fine. More than that, given your latest performance in sparring."

"Mostly true," Simon said. "But it wasn't exactly me that got in." His hand retreated under his coat jacket to pull out the marble of his vessel and then held it out to let it reflect a bright blue in the direct rays.

"What's that?" Pintel asked.

Lumi leaned in closer, her bangs hovering just above her penetrating gaze. "A vessel. I've seen them in some of the gear our captains use at the knight academy. That gear is strictly for use of the Toive Knights." She straightened up. "You think you cheated by using a magical item?"

Simon ran his thumb along the marble and then dropped it. The orb liquified in a watery *pop*, its surface swirling wider and wider rapidly. In a few seconds Sim stood in the light.

"Whoa," Lumi murmured and took a step back, her hand instinctively reaching for the sword at her waist that wasn't there.

Pintel's head swiveled at Simon and Sim. "Two Simons? Or—one real and one fake?"

"Both real," Simon explained. "I'm Simon. This is Sim. He's a spirit that occupies my vessel."

Lumi paled and quickly knelt. "Forgive me."

"A spirit!?" Pintel stayed standing, but frozen. His voice quivered. "N-named Sim?"

"I named him that a little after we met," Simon said, leaving off the part about a certain video game from another world being the inspiration for it. He raised his eyebrows at Lumi. "Why are you kneeling?"

"Why aren't you?" she replied, keeping her head bowed and eyes on the floor.

"I don't quite get it," Pintel said, his voice more controlled. "You've been carrying a vessel with a spirit? Or are the spirit and vessel the same thing?"

Sim turned to Simon who nodded. The spirit turned to the other two and explained. "At first I was housed in the vessel. A powerful and clever man put me there and did experiments until I became the vessel, and the vessel became me. Now I'm simply both, able to change form from one to another."

"Surely your real form isn't Simon, though?"

Lumi's arm snapped out to slap Pintel's calf.

"That was simply another design of the one who merged me and the vessel," Sim said, appearing to not care about either's behavior. "I was designed the same way tomes work, being bound to a mage. Only, unlike tomes which can be bound to any mage, I could only be bound to one with a water affinity."

Lumi's head shot up and she glared at Simon. "What?"

"Be calm," Sim said.

Lumi's eyes softened and she lowered her gaze again. "Apologies."

"It's fine. My circumstances before becoming a vessel are trivial. I was simply bored and decided to let someone capable of giving me some change do as he wanted."

"You chose this?"

Sim nodded.

"Why are you acting so respectful?" Simon asked.

Pintel stopped rubbing his calf to put an arm on Lumi's shoulder before she could launch herself at Simon. "He grew up without magic."

Lumi huffed and shook his arm off while she stood. "Spirits are sacred beings, but surely you should know that much. They are like what magic is to us, the manifestation of our sakti. Only, they are the manifestations of the *gods'* magic."

Simon looked at Sim curiously. "You never mentioned that."

"Your introduction class hasn't gotten to that tidbit of history I guess," Pintel said. "Spirits are also thought to aid the gods' work, including magic. So, you're—Sim is a water spirit?"

"Yes," Sim replied.

"I still don't get how you met," Pintel said, gesturing to both Simon and Sim.

"It was in the Narumont Dungeon," Simon said.

Pintel tilted his head. "That dungeon was conquered by the Waymaker Guild, wasn't it?"

Lumi sighed. "Of course, Masaka would be crazy enough to give you a vessel with a spirit."

Pintel did a double take. "Wait, you're part of the Waymakers? You never said that!" Then he paled and took a step back. "You conquered the dungeon?"

"I'm sort of glad identities weren't given out," Simon said.

Lumi gasped. "If Sim was in that dungeon, the one who merged him with the vessel must have been one of the High Clerics!"

Sim dipped his head silently.

"But why would they—?"

"It wasn't sacrilegious," Sim said. "I'll ask you not to press further."

She clenched her jaw and nodded.

"Right," Simon said. "Now that we're up to speed, I wanted to ask again if you think I still belong here."

Pintel looked to still be in a daze as he stared at Sim. Lumi folded her arms. "Sim took the last practical test for you?"

"Yeah."

"What he did was within your power to do, so I don't see why you shouldn't be here. But I also don't see why you had a *spirit* take your test for you."

"The first time I applied they measured my total sakti," Simon said. "Pheona and the other professors administering the test placed a lot of importance on the fact I have such a small amount."

Pintel snapped out of his daze. "Avril mentioned that. She said your ability was only capable of bubbling water before." He tapped the topside of his foot on the ground guiltily. "I also heard she… teased you…"

Simon's face flushed, but he nodded. Ever since the spar with her his heart had been beating quickly. Before he'd attributed it to fear, but now… He glanced down at his hands that had become fists.

"I don't agree with what she did," Pintel went on.

"What did she do?" Lumi asked.

Simon didn't say anything.

Pintel then asked, "What *is* your total sakti?"

Simon sighed again. "10."

"*10!?*" Pintel and Lumi exclaimed in unison.

"Still think I belong here?"

Pintel struggled to speak. "But—how did you—during the sparring?"

"Was that Sim as well?" Lumi asked.

"Regeneration," Simon said. "I can regenerate sakti near-instantly, or infinitely. That combined with a catalyst spell can rapidly increase the power of a weak spell to make it much stronger."

Lumi frowned. "What's a catalyst spell?"

"That's something taught in a later SCP class," Pintel said. "It makes sense you'd know some things if you're part of a magic and adventuring guild. And I guess it's no wonder you're strong if you conquered a dungeon."

Simon looked at both of them. "You're more interested in the catalyst spell than the fact I can regenerate sakti quickly."

Pintel glanced at the horse in its pen that had huffed out after apparently realizing it wouldn't be untethered. "I mean, that's impressive, but that's expected of those with a water affinity. We learned that in our first SCP class regarding shapes."

"Oh. Yeah, I guess. So, yeah, that's what I did during sparring to replicate what Sim did during the entrance application, only since he has 1000 sakti he just used a more powerful water spell."

"Right…" Pintel slowly looked at Sim. "You know, I don't think I can keep all this secret from Avril."

"It's fine if she knows," Simon said. "It'd probably give her peace of mind knowing it wasn't a fluke. Not that she deserves it," he added quietly. "Just don't go telling everyone everything. I don't know what the professors will do if they found out."

"There's no need to worry about that."

Simon paled and leapt up from the stool. He hadn't heard the woman enter the stable, nor had he noticed her move to stand surreptitiously behind a nearby wall penning in a horse. None of the horses indicated she'd been there.

Lumi and Pintel turned and backed up to stand beside Simon, Sim remaining in place without reacting.

The woman stepped into the sun's rays and patted Sim on the shoulder. "Good to see you again."

Lumi gasped. "You're—"

"One of the High Clerics," Pintel breathed, now taking his turn to kneel.

"You're getting along?" the woman asked Sim.

"Catalina," Sim said. "You look different without your clergy."

Catalina's smile tightened, her incisors pressing against her lower lip. "It's been quite a few years. Then again, that's nothing for a spirit." She looked at Simon.

"Don't worry. The school won't care about the details of your entrance exam, nor about anything else."

Simon didn't know what to think of her. All he felt was doubt. "Why won't they care?"

"Because it's not their place to care," Catalina replied. "It's mine."

"Why are you here?" Simon asked. He felt Lumi nudge his back in warning.

"I grew tired of waiting for you to notice me observing you."

Simon now felt violated in some way, his face flushing. "You were observing me? How long?"

"A while. You're pretty popular. Your popularity will only grow from here on."

"What are you talking about?"

"Power has that effect on people." Catalina dropped her smile and let her hand fall from Sim's shoulder. "Maybe you don't realize it yet, but since you're a Waymaker here's something you might understand: I want to see what you do with your power."

*She's saying she's going to continue observing me?*

"Don't worry about her, Simon." Sim said. "She's the same as the one who merged me with the vessel when it comes to curiosity."

"Don't lump me in with Montel," Catalina said derisively.

Sim's calm, quiet look continued to face Catalina unwaveringly. "The way I see it, you're similar. The way he tests things is like the way you test people."

It unnerved Simon how casually Sim addressed the High Cleric. Then again, he was a spirit.

"No matter," Catalina said. "Now that I know the secret behind your power, I have something to work with. Continue learning, I'll be around." Her eyes shone brightly in the sun before darkening as she stepped back out of the rays and then away along the stable.

"Great." Simon slowly sank back onto the stool. "Now I have to worry about Avril and a High Cleric."

"Not just them," Pintel muttered, rising slowly. "There's the rest of the school. She's right about you gaining popularity, regardless of any secrets."

The nearby horse neighed and huffed.

## Chapter 24: A Rare Creature

"Our relationships with our sister nations have been peaceful since before I was born," Pheona said, thumbing through an open history book at the front of the introductory class consisting of Simon, Lumi, and the two Davids. She then flipped it closed with a satisfying *thump* and deftly wrote upon the blackboard with chalk. "And relations with others have been peaceable."

The David nearest Simon raised a freckled hand. Without waiting to be called on he asked, "What's the difference between peaceful and peaceable?"

"One means without conflict, the other means inclined to peace," Pheona replied without stopping her chalk-writing.

The other David raised his tanned hand. "So our 'peaceable' relations aren't without conflict?"

"Sometimes." Pheona finished writing up the names of five different neighboring nations and circled the 'peaceful' ones and drew a diamond around the 'peaceable' ones. "More often than international conflict is domestic, or the relations between cities. We'll talk more about this tomorrow, for today focus on memorizing these nations and the type of relationship Storfron has with each."

"What cities does Narumont have conflict with?" the freckled David asked.

"Salama, for one." Pheona put down her chalk loudly enough to signal for both Davids to cease the questions. "As eager as you are to get into our next lesson, I must end here and release you for your SCP classes. There is going to be a project assigned at the week's end."

Simon looked at Lumi who remained as serious as ever.

"The project," Pheona continued, "is essentially your choice. You will give a written report or presentation about any subject due in two weeks."

Simon raised his hand and waited for Pheona to gesture at him. "We can write or present on anything? And it doesn't have to be both?"

"Verlangen compiles a list of events going on over the upcoming weeks to give students ideas. Anything from attending theater performances to traveling. And yes, you either write or present about it, all that matters is the information on what you choose is conveyed well and includes some reflection of its importance."

"How important is the project?" Simon asked.

Pheona's lips quirked up. "Let's just say every student of every class of every year from those recently entered and those soon to be graduating is given this assignment."

*Then it's important.* Simon nodded and stood with the other three students to head for the door.

***

"Simon!"

Simon's head swiveled in all directions at the familiar voice. He saw the woman rushing toward him from behind in a flurry of blue-and-green lace ballooning from her dress. "Perish?"

Perish's fluffy dress almost enveloped Simon whole when she hugged him, then he was released the next second as she looked intently at his face. "How are your classes?"

"F-fine," Simon said, blushing lightly while aware that Lumi and Pintel along with other students finished with their SCP class were watching. "Why are you here?"

"Masaka sent me to check in on you. And I know this time of year is when students are given a project, so I wanted to offer a hand! How are classes? Are you settling in?"

"I've settled in," Simon said quickly. Other students had the decency to move on while Lumi and Pintel hovered nearby. "Um, these are my classmates. Lumi and Pintel."

"Surely we're more than classmates!" Pintel said. He waved at Perish while Lumi simply nodded.

*Tentative friends, then,* Simon internally amended. "The school just let you in?"

"I'm an alumnus, so of course they did!" Perish waved and bowed extravagantly to Pintel and Lumi. She then turned to other students slower to walk by and smiled and waved at them. The students looked unsure but politely did the same back before moving on.

"So… you wanted to offer a hand?"

"Yes! There was a new job posted in the guild hall about—! Actually, it may even be listed in the school's project. Is that it that you're carrying?"

Simon glanced down at the sheet of paper in his hand. "Yeah… What—?"

Perish snatched it from him and she looked over it quickly. "Ah! Here it is!"

Moving to look, he read the listing aloud. "*Rare creature sighted in Jordun Flatlands*. So?"

"*So!?*" Perish pressed the sheet back into Simon's hands. "Rare creatures are hardly ever seen outside of dungeons! For one to be roaming the world isn't just rare, it's *important*!"

"Actually," Simon said, "I was thinking of attending a theater performance. I still have money saved from the dungeon. There was one called *The Rivalry of Elements* that looked like it would be useful for my introductory—"

"No!"

Simon blinked. "What?"

"No!" Perish repeated. "This is a once in a lifetime opportunity! This is a chance for fame and fortune! Plus, none of the other Waymakers wanted to go with me, so that leaves even more for us!"

Simon recalled her motives back in the Narumont dungeon. "So you don't just want to offer me a hand."

"There's that," Perish said breezily, "But that's just how desire is. You never want anything without an idea of gaining anything. What about you two?" She turned to Pintel and Lumi. "Do either of you want to hunt a rare creature?"

"It sounds exciting," Pintel said haltingly. "But the creature isn't described. How will we know what we're hunting?"

"I happen to have more information about that," Perish said with a hint of smugness. She folded her arms and lowered her eyelids. "Others will need to reach out to guilds to get this kind of info. If you want to join, you'll be a step ahead."

"I'm not sure," Pintel said. "The Flatlands are a neutral area. My mother and older brother were traveling there and had a run-in with the Salama Knights."

Perish waved her hand dismissively in the air. "If you're traveling with me, we can say you're with the Waymaker Guild. We don't represent Narumont, so there won't be need for political conflict. Two steps ahead!"

"I don't know."

"Hmph! If you don't know what you want, I won't bother asking." Perish turned to Lumi expectantly.

Lumi raised her eyebrows slightly. "Yeah, I'll go."

Simon and Pintel said, "What?" in unison.

"Great!" Perish said. "Now you have to go, Simon." She took Simon's arm as well as Lumi's and led them down along the corridor.

"Hold on," Simon muttered, looking back at Pintel. The boy simply smiled and shrugged, then walked the other way. "Ugh, fine." He turned back and was surprised to see Lumi allowing herself to be led by the woman. "You said this was listed as a job in the guild. How much money is being offered for the creature?"

"One-hundred."

Simon's mind stuttered as it ran the number back. "Gold?"

"Yup."

"For one creature?"

"Yup."

"Okay." Simon wriggled his arm until Perish let go and he continued to walk alongside her toward the school's entrance. *Two weeks dedicated to this project and in which classes are off.* They left the building and continued on along the grassy grounds. They were clear, likely all the other students still deciding what they were going to do and those who had decided were likely still packing. "What is this creature?"

"It's…" Perish cast around to make certain no one was near. "…a horse."

The excitement of all the amazing possibilities of creatures diminished while Simon's practical mind worked. *Whoever posted the job would probably either work with the stables or be a zookeeper. It could also be one of the upper-class nobles looking to increase their reputation.* "A horse would normally be easy to catch, compared to other things. Since it wasn't caught immediately or shortly after its sighting, I imagine there's something more to it."

"There is. But I want to see your faces when we find it. We'll need our own horses before we go, and lots of food."

"Two-weeks-worth? How will we carry—?" He cut himself off when he saw the stark black bag Perish procured from a fold in her dress. "Oh. We'll have to thank Lenard."

***

The next day they were miles northeast of Narumont scouring the flatlands on horseback. Lumi rode exceptionally well, even better than Perish. Simon for his part grew up in the countryside and was used to riding, but he was by no means an expert. Between the three of them, he was still the least experienced.

The quiet rustling of the long grass being stirred by their horses accompanied the steady headwind blowing over them. Hoofbeats thudded continuously like the pattern of rainfall.

"There's a river ahead!" Perish called, Simon barely catching her voice on the wind.

He spotted flecks of blue filtering between the grass some ways ahead and angled his horse to turn while slowing. The three slowed together until they trotted beside the trickling river.

"Let's give the horses a rest."

Moments later they'd tied the three horses' reins together (a learned sign from being trained that the horses 'couldn't' wander despite having nothing sturdy enough to really tie them in place) and they looked across the wide fields.

"Should we have hired a tracker?" Simon asked, spotting nothing to indicate any horses had been there other than the trail their three horses left behind that disrupted the otherwise straight grass.

"Jordun is expansive," Lumi said.

"We can cover it in a few days' time," Perish said. "By then, if we haven't found any sign of the horse, we can retrace our way in a looser formation. Then…" She trailed off as hoofbeats sounded across the river.

The three of them turned and saw a horse speed by along the opposite bank of the river. Its pine green coat glistened in the sun before becoming obscured by the tall grass and lengthening distance.

"Is that it?" Simon asked.

"Hah!" Perish cried out suddenly, running off along their side of the river.

Simon and Lumi shrugged at each other and ran to catch up. Perish was fast despite wearing her flowery gown, but the horse's speed almost doubled the pace of their horses when they were galloping. "We can't catch up with it!" Simon called. "Not on foot!"

Perish's dress swayed forward and back as she halted, her breathing heavy. "We wouldn't be able to catch it if we tried to chase it on horseback." Her breathing steadied just as Simon and Lumi reached her and she marched back to where their horses continued to drink from the river.

"How are we going to capture it?" Simon reversed direction to follow her. Lumi remained back, silently watching the fleck of green become inscrutable on the horizon.

"I'm not sure yet," Perish replied. "But that was it."

"What was it?" Lumi said, having silently returned. Simon guessed her quiet, practiced steps were thanks to her training as a knight.

"That was an Akhal-Teke, wasn't it?"

Perish was preparing to answer when she turned on Simon open-mouthed. "How did you know?"

Simon held up his hands and took a step back from her. "They're wild in the area close to my home."

Perish drew in a long breath and sighed, apparently disappointed it wasn't a surprise she got to explain. "I guess you'd know it if you've seen one before."

"Saying its name doesn't really tell me anything," Lumi commented.

"Right!" Perish blurted before Simon could say more. "They're a breed of horse with a unique metallic-like coat. What makes them desired is that they've got high endurance and can travel for weeks without rest or water. They're one of the rare creatures that can use magic, but not all of them. Like chimeras," she added with a nod to Simon.

"Chimeras?" Lumi questioned. She shook her head a second later. "Must be another dungeon thing, never mind."

"When was it first spotted?" Simon asked.

"The job was posted a few days ago, so probably a week," Perish said.

Simon looked the river up and down, recalling what he studied of the area. *This is the only river running through Jordun. It flows from Rivermouth Dungeon and out of the forest into these flatlands. The next closest available sources of water would be in Narumont or Salama which would be too populated and scare the horse away.* "We could wait for it to stop and drink."

"Didn't she just say it can go for weeks without water?" Lumi said.

"And the river is too long for us to keep watch over it all," Perish said. "I like where you were going with that, but it's too uncertain. The likely reason it hasn't been caught yet is because it's almost always moving."

"Then we'd have to know which direction it was going, get there before it, and intercept it." Lumi shook her head. "Intercepting it while it's running at that speed is one thing, but I don't know how we could predict where it'll go next."

Simon looked up and down the river with a frown while the other two thought aloud. *If it's galloping so much, how could it not need water sooner than a few weeks? No creature could last a few days without it, so what makes that horse different? What is its magic?*

"Finding where it eats might work," Perish said.

Lumi shook her head. "I don't know about Akhal-Teke, but most horses could eat anything out here." She glanced at the fields of grass stretching everywhere on either side of the river.

"I think we're discounting the river too easily," Simon spoke up.

The tightness that'd pulled at Lumi's face relaxed and she turned away from Perish. "What are you thinking?"

Simon took a few seconds to piece together his idea. "I tried to sneak up on one when I was younger because I liked the shine of its coat. I was clumsy and every time I got sort of close the horse would move away. I gave up being sneaky and tried to run after it, and it simply trotted just a bit faster than me to always keep away. Then I knew it was too smart and I totally gave up trying to get one."

Perish shrugged. "So what?"

"*So*," he continued, "I think this horse knows it's being chased. Not just by us. That's why it's running."

Lumi hesitated before asking, "You're saying it's pointless to chase it?"

"Probably," Simon said. "I mean, if Masaka were here she might have the strength to catch it."

"We're not getting her help," Perish said plainly.

*She really wants the glory of catching it herself,* Simon thought. "I don't think we would be able to catch it regardless. I think the horse wants us to try to chase it."

"It wants us to chase it?" Lumi asked.

"Yeah. It's like what you told me about attrition that one time we were sparring at the knight academy."

Lumi's eyes lit up and for a moment she smiled. "It knows it can tire anyone out if it keeps moving."

"Both physically and mentally," Simon said. He pointed the direction the river flowed from. "It knows it has time to drink because it gives itself that time by always being ahead. But if we limit where it can drink, we'll force it to come to us."

Perish gasped. "If we cut off the river, that'd disrupt the wildlife and travelers!"

"Not greatly," Simon replied. "The alternative is burning the fields." He gave both of them a slow look before laughing lightly. "I'm joking."

"I hope," Perish said. "That'd just cause the horse to run off somewhere else in the world. If we dam up the river it'll just be for a week, maybe less if we're lucky, for it to come to us. That's all the time you have for your assignment, anyway."

"We could get in trouble with either city," Lumi said.

Simon's smile dipped. "Yeah, that could happen… But it's neutral area, so that should help a bit, right?"

Perish shook her head and shrugged. "Maybe, or maybe not. But it sounds like the best plan we have, and I like it. Let's go to the forest's edge and see what we can do."

## Chapter 25: Condense/Diffuse

The three sat side-by-side under one of the many trees marking the border between the forest and Jordun Flatlands. Condensation came out in puffs with each of their breaths. It was late and the night sky was mostly barren except for a scattering of stars. Simon straightened his back along the trunk to soothe a mounting ache.

"Stay focused," Lumi murmured, her eyes staring ahead at the expanse of tall grass.

Simon nodded, returning to a semi-hunched position. The nearby river sloshed as it pooled for some ways along the flatlands. He had cast a similar spell in the Narumont Dungeon to turn back the flow of the waterfall, but the effort here was significantly less. Lumi and Perish helped by raising the riverbed for roughly a mile so that the land was even more true to its name (Perish with a bassy song of magic that commanded the ground to move, Lumi with her bare hands coupled with friction magic). With his hybrid spell's help, a small lake had formed, its surface several inches below the tops of the blades of grass. Looking out over it in the shadowy night, it appeared ominous how the minimal light glinted off its dark and shifting surface. The grass blades, too, moving with the meager flow of water seemed off.

"There." The back of Lumi's hand brushed Simon and she pointed at a spot in the distance where the grass was obscured. Sure enough, at the edge of where the water ended the large dark form of a horse materialized. Its long neck inclined to drink from the unnatural lake.

"Simon," Perish said, an abridged instruction to continue their plan. She stood fast and quietly stepped down to wade through the water while Lumi went further out to follow the edge of the pooling lake.

Simon stopped feeding his catalyst spell to redirect the river and turned his focus to drawing the far waterline back. He connected his thumb to his index finger and whispered, "*Move*."

Standing up as well, he began wading into the water and away from the tree line. The shadow of the horse didn't move for a bit, though the effects of his spells were usually slow to build. *Unless I need to drastically move the water, but I don't want to scare the horse.* He continued concentrating on feeding the spell his regenerating sakti while sneaking forward.

The subtle sound of his wading remained consistent with the wider water's movement. He stilled when the form of the horse shifted, moving toward him and Perish. He silently breathed out and continued his approach. *Good, the spell's working and the water is receding our way.* Ahead of him Perish crouched lower, getting even more of her dress wet. She appeared unperturbed, her hands held in front of her as she lightly brushed the tall grass out of her way.

They were several yards from the horse before they confirmed it was the massive teal-coated Akhal-Teke. The horse, too, had noticed the two wading in the water towards it. The horse let out a huff, its hooves quietly thumping as it reared back.

"Hah!" Lumi cried, suddenly behind it. Her call startled the horse and caused it to rapidly shuffle forward and to the side, splashing into the water.

Simon broke the circle his right hand's thumb and index finger made and he felt his spell stop. He connected the same fingers on his left hand and said, *"Rime!"* A chill spread in the water ahead and Perish stood up with a gasp.

"Cold!" she said.

Ignoring her, he connected his middle, ring, and pinky fingers to the same thumb and silently repeated the spell another three times.

Perish leapt out of the water, emitting a clear and high note piercing the quiet night. She hovered in the air and then spun as her voice warbled, water spiraling off her.

The horse that galloped further into the water and was angling to run back into the dry flatlands halted. Around its legs the water froze solid.

Simon climbed up onto the frosted surface that ended just before him. The grass caught in the frozen water tickled his ankles as he walked nearer the stuck horse.

Perish cut off her brief song and touched back down, Lumi stepping onto the ice layer to join them. Suddenly a torrential wind blew over them. Lumi, reacting faster and with a trained reflex, kept herself supported while sliding slightly along the ice. Perish was pushed to a crouch, and Simon fell over completely.

He cushioned his fall with an outstretched arm, then quickly pushed himself up. The wind was gone as fast as it came. "What was that?" he asked.

The horse let out a cry, its body shifting wildly to try to break from the frozen water without success.

Simon looked around before noticing both Perish and Lumi facing the same way. He followed their gaze to a slender form further off in the dry tall grass. Long strands of bright white hair stirred in a breeze as the person drew closer. He recognized the girl, his thoughts unable to make sense of it. "What are you doing, Avril?"

The air around her danced and her fanning hair rose and fell in an eerie way as if she were underwater.

"Simon, the horse!" Perish said. "We'll handle her!" She yelped and darted away as a streak of wind tore a line in the grass in its path. The trail of wind ended several feet along the frozen surface of the lake, a sharp cut in the ice marking where it ended.

Simon shook his head, then another sharp *crack* echoed along the lake as more ice broke. He whirled and saw the Akhal-Teke leap free of the frost as lights flashed across its body. Arcs of light rebounded up and down its light green color, casting an ethereal aura with the way the glow reflected off the horse's metallic coat.

Simon felt the blood drain even more from his face as the green-white light sparked down the creature's legs. The ice around its hooves singed and cracked, instantly evaporating whatever water was within inches of it. The night was no longer quiet but filled with the combined echoes of crashing wind behind him and the crackling of electricity wreathing the horse ahead of him. *She didn't tell me the horse used lightning!* he thought desperately just as the horse charged him.

***

Perish sidestepped a gust that blew by, then ducked low under another that cut the heads off the tall grass. The tips of the grass tickled her face as they fell on her. She kept low, narrowing her eyes at the girl that appeared to be creating her own personal climate in a limited radius.

Lumi raced through the grass, a sword in her hand. She slashed, but her swing quickly turned into a desperate attempt to keep from losing hold of her sword when her hand entered the space where the wind whipped wildly around Avril. She drew back, tightening her grip.

Perish sang a quick note changing the decibel from loud to soft. Her voice altered the impact of Avril's next attack, a wind that blew over Lumi harmlessly. "She's just attacking us," Perish commented as Lumi backed further away. "What did you do?"

Lumi raised her eyebrows, affronted. "I didn't do anything to her!"

"She's attacking us," Perish repeated.

Lumi dodged two gusts that tore up more lines in the grass. "I know! All that happened was that she and Simon dueled!"

Perish opened her mouth, a look of knowing on her face. "Students were pretty competitive while I attended."

Lumi ran to Avril's side, hoping to split her attention. "This goes beyond competitive!" she called as she lunged toward Avril.

Perish hummed a song of protection as the magic knight plunged her sword into Avril's personal storm. Avril had to dodge this time, but Lumi wasn't strong enough to follow up with another attack. The wind acted against every one of the knight's movements. Lumi ran out and some distance away again.

Perish sang, *"Can you interrupt her magic for a second?"* The magic she laced into the words was only meant to carry them safely to Lumi's ears, but she doubted it mattered with Avril's wind whipping away the noise immediately around herself.

Lumi stood on the opposite side of Avril. Perish saw the girl nod, then charge Avril.

Perish sensed the barrier encircling Avril expand; no, only several points shot outward like tendrils toward Lumi. The wind whipped into Lumi, but slid off her like it was nothing. Lumi raced closer, approaching the barrier and Avril within.

Avril fully turned toward Lumi and directed the wind around her to drive all at once at the other girl.

Perish smirked and halted her singing to ask, "Is Simon better than you?"

Lumi was forced a bit back by the buffet of wind before her friction magic held her fast and the wind subsided.

Avril whirled, her face contorted with anger. "No!"

Perish sang a high and loud note the same moment Avril spoke, her voice mixing with and repurposing the younger girl's. A new barrier sprang up around Avril, this one still and echoing. Perish let her note trail off while its echo remained wavering in the barrier holding Avril in place.

"What did you do!?" Avril exclaimed even more angrily. Her fingers, hands, and arms were forced motionless at her sides while she stood still.

"Stick in school and you'll find out," Perish replied, turning to see how Simon was doing. "Oh, no."

***

*You can call me out at any time*, Sim's voice resonated in Simon's head.

Simon ducked left and away from a bolt of lighting that struck the unfrozen water of the lake behind him. The water didn't erupt or show much reaction beyond being slightly disturbed. The Akhal-Teke, apparently angered and keen on fighting rather than running, continued pounding away along the leftover patches of ice and melting them away. *There are some things I have to learn to do myself!* Simon communicated back to the spirit, then thought to himself *Should I run?*

While the horse hadn't fully charged him yet, he didn't want to provoke it into running after him. But if he remained close, he wouldn't have the time to react to another lightning attack. *Can water be a barrier? All I remember from science is it being a conductor.*

*Water would provide some resistance* came Sim. *Pure water more so.*

*No time!* Simon barely lifted his hand to cast Creation before a flash erupted from one of the horse's stomping front hooves and shot at him. A thin film of water materialized in its trajectory. The marble-sized water pooled only a bit wider midair before the lightning surged through it and struck Simon's extended hand.

Simon cried out as his fingers burned and a shock traveled up his arm. He clutched his index and middle finger with his other hand and ran sideways. He quickly pressed the hurt fingers into a patch of ice while hammering a fist up his arm to test his sense of touch.

*It worked. I can tell because you aren't dead.*

Simon refrained from sarcastically thanking the spirit for the notice. "Another," Simon said to himself. "*Creation.*"

Water pooled slowly in the air between him and the horse galloping in circles. The body of water got larger to the size of a disc before spreading more rapidly.

The horse neighed and another bolt shot out from a hoof as it slammed into the ground. The lightning surged into the hovering water, but this time not through. The crystal water shimmered with dazzling muted sparks before it altogether seemed to collapse on itself and disappear.

Something uncomfortable shifted within Simon's mind. No, it wasn't in his mind, it was Sim.

*What did you just do?*

*Huh?* Simon didn't have time to address the serious tone of the spirit's voice in his head. *"Creation."* Another ball of water thinned and expanded in the air between him and the horse. Simon planted his feet, directing the water through the air to remain between them.

The Akhal-Teke let out a cry, rearing back and slamming both its hooves on the ground.

Two cracks echoed as the lightning bolts flung out to hit the disc of water. The first hit the water dead center and both the water and lightning dissipated the same way as before. The second bolt went lower and struck the ground next to Simon's feet.

He jumped, a delayed reaction. It put him off balance and unready when the horse charged him after the second lightning bolt landed. He felt the sparks splash out from the horse's hooves mere feet away before its torso slammed into him.

The air left his lungs. His arms wildly flung out as the world keeled sideways. Somehow he managed to brace his fall. His hearing seemed to have been sucked away like his air by the blow. In a daze, he stayed propped on his elbows coughing while looking down his body. The cloth of his school uniform was singed down the front. As the air painfully returned to his chest his thoughts became clearer. *I should be dead.*

"Hyah!" A man's cry cut through the daze and snapped his hearing back into focus.

Simon lifted his head and saw someone swinging a sword and keeping the Akhal-Teke at bay, lightning continuing to course across its body and down its legs. The man wore a leather bandolier. He had a familiar wiry and tall build. His movements were fluid as he avoided the hooves and accompanying lightning bolts that flew out.

"Haha! I could dance with you for days, hahaha!" The man sounded joyful in the chaos of loud cracks and thuds.

Simon finally placed where he remembered the man from. *What's the knight Wild Fox doing here?* He noticed that the crashing sounds of wind had ceased and looked for Perish and Lumi. He relaxed slightly when he saw them standing unharmed by Avril whose body seemed strained in place.

"Oof!" Fox's sword clanged against the horse's aggressively striking hooves. Sparks singed against his hand and he exchanged the sword to his other hand. "Maybe not for days. Any of you care to help?"

Simon pushed himself off the ground, feeling burns under the spots his clothes were singed. His lower arms also ached from hitting the ground.

*Do that thing again* came Sim.

Simon shook his arms out of exasperation and to ease the pain. *Do* what *again?*

*Make the lightning go away.*

He lifted his hand over his head and silently cast another spell creating water. He released it and the water overhead poured over him, stinging and soothing his burn wounds. Simon then created more, using his go-to catalyst spell to increase the amount exponentially. The water rapidly expanded, taller and wider than him, Fox, and the horse. With his singed index finger, he pointed and the water surged forward.

It dunked over Fox who yelled in surprise. Like a waterfall, or rather a tidal wave, the water continued past the knight to engulf the horse. The flashes and sparks of white and blue winked out. The muted form of the horse struggled before falling sideways, pushed over by the water.

Simon released the spell and the water subsided to join the muddy ground of the field around them.

*Why didn't you do that sooner?*

*Because,* Simon thought in annoyance, *I didn't know if it'd make the lightning go everywhere and shock me!* He let out a breath, then flew into a fit of coughs.

"Are you all right?" Perish called.

Simon shook his head, then raised his hand to give her a thumbs-up. Damp leather squelched along the ground as Fox moved nearer him. In the time Simon spent recovering a bit the knight had bound the horse's hooves with rope to prevent it from standing back up.

"That was a fine job, kid. Don't appreciate getting me wet, though."

Simon stood upright in time for the knight to strike his stomach and knock the air out of him again. Simon fell backward, too surprised to do anything. He heard Perish call out something in warning. His eyes looked sideways at her to see Avril's body relax, and then a blast of wind strike both Perish and Lumi down.

"W-wait," Simon moaned, seeing a platoon of knights advancing on them from the shadowy night.

"Salama will be taking care of you from here," Fox stated, kneeling over Simon.

Simon watched the knight's fist rise and strike his head before he lost consciousness.

## Chapter 26: On the Edge of Life

The god's outline silhouetted in the spiraling multicolored dust was twirling when an air of uncertainty crept into her domain. She stopped spinning and placed her invisible hands on her invisible hips. "What are you doing back here, Doubt?"

The other god detached from the outskirts of the void and shambled slowly toward Desire. "You seem to be in a good mood."

"Why wouldn't I be when my subjects are following what they want?"

Doubt's chuckle resembled the intermittent crackles and singes of firewood. "Not everyone can get what they want."

Desire's form held still and silent for a long moment, the only sound being the pattering of dust on the translucent floor and both of them. "You're unusually talkative. But, like usual, you don't get what makes desire good."

Doubt let out a coo that was more like her usual way of communicating. She stopped shambling a few feet away from the exasperated form of Desire. "Not understanding is in my nature," she rasped before her voice cleared. "Who are you to say what is good?"

Desire tapped a finger to her chin. "I'm a god, for one thing."

"Yes, I almost forgot." Doubt cackled like a crone, her hunched shoulders roiling. "As am I. And I think giving hope to those in a hopeless situation isn't good."

"And it's good to give doubt to those in a hopeful situation?"

Doubt sneered before her face settled into a thin smile. "Let's not fight. I can settle with you giving direction, however aimless." A coo interspersed her talking as Desire let out a groan of disapproval. "And I give rationality."

"However defeating," Desire added.

Doubt shrugged.

"You haven't answered my question."

Glancing down, Doubt said, "How is Simon doing?"

"He's doing perfectly fine!"

"It looks like he's in a prison."

"It's just a bit of piffle! He's on his way to—" Desire's voice cut off with a sharp cry and her form staggered. The dust swirled around her faster, their glistening surfaces brightening around her body.

Doubt, unmoving, lowered her head to stare down. "He's… Oh." Her faded eyes returned to the other god's form that had fallen to the floor. "It seems I was right to doubt you."

The dust around Desire was now shining harshly as she clawed at the ground. She screamed.

*** 

Simon lay in a cot that occupied the entirety of a dingy cell barred on all sides. A door clanged open, causing him to waken and lift his head despite its throbbing. Lumi was already sitting cross-legged and upright in an adjacent cell while Perish lay prone like Simon in the second adjacent cell. The older woman was muttering profanities under her breath.

Groaning, Simon sat himself up and faced the entourage of guards surrounding an important-looking man approaching down a hall from one side of the row of cells. He spotted another trio of guards paralleling them on the opposite side. They both stopped beside Lumi's cell.

The man lifted his hand and gripped one of the bars. His skin was coarse and tan all the way up to the silk sleeves of his long brown shirt. Flourishing orange designs laced up the sleeves and ended beneath a tan-brown waistcoat. Both their tight fits signified the muscles underneath.

Lumi wordlessly stood without using her arms.

The man gestured, and one of his nearby guards handed him a sword. "You are a Narumont Knight." His plain, unassuming voice wasn't asking.

"Why did you imprison us?" Perish spoke up. "Valen."

"You three were responsible for damming the Jordun River."

"I told you we were doing a job."

"Neither Narumont nor Salama gave sanction."

Simon looked back and forth at the man—Valen—
and Perish. "You know him?" he asked her quietly.

Perish blew out air to send a strand of hair away
from her face. "I make it a habit to know those more
famous than me."

Valen let go of the bar and sidled to Simon's cell.
His brown eyes looked Simon up and down. "I don't
recognize anything about you."

Perish sat up quickly. "You know who I am, then?"

"A Waymaker," Valen said dismissively without
looking away from Simon. "A troublemaker."

Perish groaned and lay back down. "It's in neutral
territory. And, the river should be back to normal by now.
Can you let us out, already? If it hasn't, we can go back and
fix it."

"Who are you?" Valen asked Simon.

By this point Simon had gathered the gist of what
had happened, from Fox and Avril betraying them to take
the horse for themselves (given they weren't in cells like

them) to the reason they'd been imprisoned. "Why do you care?"

"Should I care?" The man's voice remained unassuming while his eyebrows raised with interest.

Simon didn't know how to answer. "I'm Simon. A student at Verlangen Seminary."

Something changed in the surrounding guards' expressions. Valen's eyebrows relaxed. "You're a mage like the songstress."

"We all are," Lumi said.

Valen glanced at Lumi. "What did you use to dam the river?"

Simon wanted to squirm when the man's eyes returned to hold his gaze. "I—"

"Magic," Perish said quickly.

"I'm asking about a particular spell or spells." Valen's eyebrows lifted again. When Simon, Perish, and Lumi didn't add anything he said, "A secret, then. One important enough to withhold from one of the eleven Numen."

Simon felt Sim actually squirm in his mind.

*I have to go.*

*What? Why?*

No response came.

Simon quickly swept the confused look from his face when Valen moved closer to the bars of his cell.

"Are you unfamiliar with them?" Valen questioned. "Four are the leaders of your city. Perhaps you know them better as the High Clerics."

"I know of them," Simon said haltingly, recalling the name for them while studying to get into Verlangen.

Valen tilted his head. "Perhaps I should release you all. It is just a river." He stepped backward. "Simon, was it? Since you're a student at Verlangen Seminary, could you tell me what other names Goddess Toive goes by?"

Simon blinked. "There aren't any, other than Desire—"

Valen drew out Lumi's sword and made two horizontal slashes. A section of the bars of Simon's cell clanged on the ground.

"Huh—?"

Valen was in Simon's cell and holding him in the air.

Simon stared at the man, in fear and awe at his strength to hold him up with one hand. A sharpening ache in his abdomen pulled his attention. Simon looked down to see Lumi's sword imbedded there. *I'm... Oh.*

Pale firelight flickered around the blade and a slick, wet sound emanated as it slid back out of his body.

Simon clutched the steadily dampening wound in his stomach. The ground rose up to meet him and he lay there with his head down on the cot. His body uncontrollably shook.

*It's cold.*

His trembling fingers reached partway up to his face. His vision blurred as he took in the red caking his hand.

*I don't want to die...*

His fingers found their way back to his stomach as his shivers became less intense. Someone was shouting nearby. Another was crying. It sounded like a woman.

*...Oh. This is a familiar feeling.*

He died.

\*\*\*

Perish's shouts were harsh and quick, her voice slurring together a song of healing and protection when Valen stepped back through the bars and away from Simon's body.

*"From divinity, there is no greater blessing than Toive's! May Her will flow through you and bring you peace; and may She wash away those that which snuffs Her will..."*

A faint light outlined Simon's body. Lumi's fists and feet pounded the bars between her cell and his.

Valen stepped over to Perish's cell, raising the sword.

*"...and be REPELLED!"* Perish's voice changed to a full scream.

The prison vibrated. Both teams of guards in either hall along the cells were flung back towards the entry door. Valen sunk the sword into the concrete floor and remained rooted in place. Smoke emanated from the spot the blade stuck in. His jaw was clenched as the force rolled over him.

Valen's other hand effortlessly curled up, a ball of fire forming above his palm.

"*Be repelled, be repelled, be repelled!*" Perish ceaselessly cried.

Valen's hand became stuck half-raised. His lips were pulled back and his teeth gritted. The fire in his palm dimmed before it grew and expanded to the size of his hand. As it did the heat all around the interior rose drastically and smoke began to rise from all corners of the room.

"*Be repelled, be repelled—be repelled! Be—*" Perish was forced to cough as smoke entered her lungs.

Valen's fiery hand lunged and melted the bars in one motion. He'd let go of the sword and now held up the woman by her throat with the same hand.

Perish choked, her hands grasping around his unwavering grip. The pressure in the room dissipated, along with the heat.

"Let her go!" Lumi shouted. "We have no association with the Goddess, we're only students!"

"You are," Valen replied calmly. "Perish is a Waymaker, and they're not associated with Toive either."

"So let us GO!"

"I will. But, Perish, you also didn't have to bring Toive up in that spell."

Perish gagged, feeling the pressure on her neck release enough for her to breathe and speak. "...You didn't... have to stab him... either."

Valen shook his head. "We all worship our own gods, us city folk. But one such as he, I could not permit to go."

Perish coughed. "...Toive..."

Valen's eyebrows lifted.

"...*take you.*"

Valen's body ripped away from her and he screamed.

Perish fell to the floor and gasped for more air. She took hold of the man's severed limb and tossed it to the other side of her cell.

Shouts from the guards that had recovered echoed along the prison and the rattling of mail and plate surged toward her.

Perish's eyes darted around, confirming that Valen had disappeared. Her glistening eyes found Lumi who stared in shock back at her. She looked down at Simon's unmoving body. *"And take us."*

The guards went quiet when the three prisoners vanished.

## Chapter 27: A Quiet Wrath

Fox shook the thick leather reins snugly fitted to the Akhal-Teke. Their length was already discolored and emitting a faintly charred smell.

"You didn't get them custom fit?" Avril asked, annoyance clear in her tone. She snatched the reins when he let go as the horse snuffed out threateningly.

"Not all of us are blessed with rich parents," Fox sneered. He jumped when three bodies thudded against the grass ahead of them.

The horse snorted again, and Avril hissed. "What are they doing back here?"

Fox's lips curled as he took in the state of the three. "Teleportation… I've not seen that before." His eyes held on the older woman with the fancy dress lying unconscious over the boy. "It must've been the singer's magic. Looks like it took a lot out of her." He eyed the unconscious boy. "The water-user…"

The lone conscious one of the three scrambled on her arms and legs to check on Perish and Simon. Lumi pulled off her red headband, her medium-length hair falling across her face as she pressed the cloth over a wound in Simon's chest.

"…He's dead. Unfortunate." Fox heard the horse neigh unusually far and turned to see Avril riding atop it away across the flatlands and back towards Narumont. "What about my money?" he called angrily.

"You'll get it!" Avril called back.

Fox gritted his teeth. "That's the last job I do for the nobles," he muttered. He turned back to the girl. "You. The young knight, we have an unfinished fight."

Lumi rasped out an impatient breath. "Come on…" She moved Perish to lie beside the boy.

Fox tilted his head at the slight glow surrounding Simon's body. "I don't know what you're trying to do, but that boy's dead. Wait a minute, where's your sword?"

Lumi stilled, her hands stained with red seeping through her headband over Simon's chest. "What are you talking about?" she murmured.

"Where's your sword?" Fox asked again, scanning the otherwise barren field.

"Why do you care about my sword and not *him*?"

Fox folded his arms, reappraising the body. "Some things are beyond repair. Ruminating on them gets you nowhere."

"Leave me alone."

"I'm afraid I can't." Fox flicked his sword out of his scabbard with one hand and fully drew it with the other. "I've been strung along by a schoolgirl and need to vent somehow."

Lumi's head remained still, hung over Simon's body. "Leave me alone."

"Then I'll kill the woman." He paced over to Perish's body. He raised his sword and stabbed down. Metal sunk into flesh.

\*\*\*

Dawn light crept across the building tops by the time Avril returned to her estate. She kept the horse's lightning at bay, thinning the air around its head every time it tried to buck her off or the faint smell of burning reached her nose. She rode the horse through an open gate, two guards closing it behind her in synchrony. The lonely hooves clomped along the rock way up to the front doors where her parents waited.

"I have it," she stated, climbing off the horse and landing on the ground. Her parents approached her, both their hands formally clasped together.

"It seems that way," her mother responded.

The horse reared back.

Avril's eyes narrowed and her hands formed a triangle. The air dissipated around the horse and it collapsed weakly.

Her father tutted. "It's still wild."

Avril's jaw tightened as her mother cupped her chin with a hand. "I can train it."

"No," her father replied. "I will." He looped the reins in one hand and guided the horse that was too weak to protest.

Avril stared ahead without moving. Her mother's fingers rose partway up her cheeks, then dug in hard.

"Where is the knight?"

Avril struggled to keep her eyes set while they watered in pain. "I lost him, like you told me to."

Her mother's nails dug in further. A crescent cut formed under her mother's thumbnail. "I told you to get rid of him."

Avril held her tongue.

"Did you not kill him?"

"H-he—" Avril cut herself off before she could let any trace of a whimper escape her lips. "—he got distracted. Others from the school were there looking for the horse."

Her mother's grip loosened. "What happened to the others?"

"I—I don't know. One looked to be dead and another unconscious!" she rushed to say.

Her mother tilted her head. "Dead and unconscious? What happened to them?"

"I turned them over to the Salama Knights. I left Fox and the rest there." Avril knew not to specify further.

Her mother released her face and calmly wiped away drops of blood from her thumb. "I suppose that's good enough." Her hand moved to lightly touch upon Avril's waist. "You will have breakfast with us today."

Nodding, Avril waited for her mother to withdraw within the estate before finally moving. She wordlessly entered the double doors and followed a path through finely furnished rooms, past several servants doing some morning dusting and guarding the building. She kept her vision set, knowing all too well the pained expressions they all regarded her with in passing. The pale white-pink door of her room cropped up along a hall and she hurried inside.

The door clicked shut behind her and her body sagged. Short, intermittent pants escaped her mouth. Her racing heart unsteadily grew calmer. She pushed herself from the door and moved to her wood bureau beside a vanity. She withdrew a morning blouse to change into and lightly pulled her previous grass-stained one off her body.

She held up the green-and-blue blouse between her and the mirror, momentarily spotting a dark mark along her pale body. She lightly ran her fingers over the scar on her waist her mother had touched. Shuddering, she quickly put the blouse on and went to find matching pants and shoes.

\*\*\*

Fox grunted. His sword had clipped off the woman's clothes and plunged into the ground, unbalancing him. "Wh—"

Something warm passed by his lips and he licked them. It tasted coppery.

Lumi withdrew her hand that had pressed within the inside of his shirt and against the inner chainmail he wore. Her other hand pressed against Perish's dress. There was a faint cut that barely breached the second layer in the fabric of the woman's dress marking where his sword had gone.

He coughed and felt more warmth along his chest. It also felt like his ribs had slammed into rock. He achily wiped the blood from his lips. "What happened?"

Lumi's hand gripped a piece of clumped up dirt and lightly tossed it toward his face.

Knowing he could easily sidestep, Fox instead caught the dirt with his free hand. Except the dirt slid from his grasp and fell to the floor. He looked at it in confusion. The moment he did, Lumi leapt.

She grabbed the sword by the sharp end with both her hands and tugged. It slipped from his fingers easily.

"What the—?" Fox staggered back, both in surprise and pain spiking around his upper body. His eyes narrowed at the lack of marks left behind on the girl's hands when she turned it over to grip the hilt. Cleverness and rapid analysis of situations earned him part of his nickname, and he could guess what kind of trick she pulled. "You've got magic as well?"

Lumi swung the sword vertically, nicking one of his upper arms.

Fox swore and more purposefully moved backward. "What you touch becomes slippery or firm. I won't get close to you again."

Lumi glanced back, aware she was being led further away from Simon and Perish. She stepped back. Fox didn't hesitate, advancing.

She swung the sword again in warning. "Leave me alone."

Fox smiled. "I want my sword back."

"You're not getting it back."

Fox looked past Lumi at the two bodies. "You might have a problem saving them."

"You already said he was dead," Lumi struggled to say the last word.

"He might not be."

"Don't try to trick me. Leave me alone."

"You don't have much time, if he's alive." Fox's smile faded at the feral look she gave.

"Then stay."

"Hm?" Fox questioned.

"You can stay. We can wait for Perish to wake."

Fox clenched his fists. Lowering himself, he prepared to attack. Then he relaxed and stood up, patting his torso where the chainmail had dug into his skin and coughed. "I'll cut my losses." Turning, he gave a backhanded wave and walked off.

***

It was nearing afternoon when Perish woke. She lifted herself, stray dirt falling from her crinkled dress. She sat by the Jordun river as it trickled by, back in its normal flow. Lumi was kneeling quietly beside it and wringing out a red headband. "Simon," Perish rasped, looking wildly around. She spotted his body on the other side of Lumi.

"Has he woken yet?" Her voice was hoarse as she scrambled up and swept over to them.

Lumi looped the headband over her head and pulled it to rest around her neck. She looked quietly up at Perish and shook her head.

Perish knelt by him where he lay, his eyes closed. She moved one hand to check for breath from his mouth, the other hand to check for breath from his chest. Nothing. "My spell's still working," Perish stated, gesturing at the faint light still surrounding Simon.

"It is," Lumi said weakly. "...He isn't."

Perish stared at the girl. She started, as if realizing something. She withdrew her hands from Simon's body and stood. "I'll take him back to Masaka. Our guild leader can heal him, if nothing else can."

Lumi failed to speak, looking helplessly at Simon. She could say he hadn't moved since he was stabbed by Valen. She could say that Fox knew from a glance he was dead.

A sudden flash of light reflected from the river, forcing both of them to cover their eyes. The light disappeared the next second and they saw Simon standing upright in the river.

"Sim—!" Perish cut herself off, looking at Simon's body still at her feet.

"It's Sim," Sim said. He waded out of the river and stood over Simon.

"Where were you?" Lumi asked, her tone conflicted between respect and scorn.

"That man. Valen. He was bad news, so I fled."

"You left Simon to die!?" Perish's hoarse voice shook.

Sim shook his head. "He could sense spirits. He's devoutly opposed to the Goddess, so if he sensed me he would've killed me and Simon on the spot."

"He *did* kill Simon on the spot!" Perish opened her mouth, a quiet horror as she processed her own words. "We have to take him to Narumont. Now!"

Lumi held up a hand. "You're a spirit. Can you sense him? His spirit?" she asked.

Sim's mouth twisted into a frown as he hesitated. He then knelt and touched Simon's forehead. A moment passed. He shook his head. "He is gone."

## Chapter 28: A Stately Secession

The following week saw many visitors arrive and depart The Waymaker Guild. The first were the High Clerics themselves, dumbfounded by the news at their rising prodigy's demise. Perish remained in her room, only talking when they forced their entry to demand answers. Masaka broke the news to fellow Waymakers one-on-one. Most took it lightly. They didn't know the boy Simon for long, but they valued his contribution to conquering the Narumont Dungeon. Among those who were apparently affected were Kairi and Dulon. Masaka, for her part, remained the stalwart guild master. She made sure everyone in the guild was busy with some job or another while more visitors came. Toward the middle of the week Simon's parents arrived to collect his body. She consoled them as best she could.

"Were you there?" Simon's father asked, stone-faced as he turned from the wagon where Simon's body lay.

"I wasn't," Masaka said stiffly. "But I know the details from those who were."

"How?" He'd asked the question many times to the courier and his wife before they arrived in Narumont, and still several more to Masaka after they'd arrived.

"It was over in an instant," Masaka said once more. She thought that much was some small comfort, over the unprompted attack of the Numen that had killed their son. She wanted to tell them more than what the High Clerics ordered to disclose to the public. But it was a state secret.

Simon's parents left shortly after, the wagon trundling down the road on their way out of the city and back to the countryside. Members of other guilds visited the rest of the week to pay their respects. Masaka greeted and thanked them. Perish remained in her room. At the end of the week the High Clerics returned, looking slightly less dumbfounded but vastly more frazzled.

"There is an arranged assembly that will be happening on this week's final day," High Cleric Catalina murmured, sitting in the same seat the night she'd visited to glean more information about the boy from Masaka. "Regarding the… incident. Both Narumont and Salama officials have been ordered to attend. The king himself will be attending."

"The king," Masaka repeated quietly. She, too, sat in the same seat across from Catalina. The three other High Clerics stood around their table within the guild house.

"Will you take that mask off?" High Cleric Aldana asked.

Masaka's eyes silently held on the tall, slender woman.

"It is a bit hard to hear you," High Cleric Montel commented.

High Cleric Thian placed his palms on the table to lean on. "It is also a bit hard to take you seriously."

Masaka slowly lifted a hand to rest on the bottom edge of the horse mask's snout. After a pause she took it off and lightly placed it on the table. She continued to silently watch each of the four in turn, patiently waiting for them to continue with their reason for the visit.

Thian removed his hands and stood up, averting his gaze. Aldana shuffled her feet and folded her arms. Montel looked down to play with the lapel on his austere blue cardigan, and Catalina glanced away. None commented on the faint tear marks on the guild master's face.

"As you know, aside from us four, the guild masters are the officials of Narumont," Catalina finally continued. "Due to your association with Simon, you will also likely be asked to testify."

"Like a trial?"

"An inquisition."

Masaka's hands clenched. "And who will be acting as Inquisitor?"

"Valen." Catalina stood up an instant before the table ruptured and fell apart under Masaka's fist. Splinters filtered through the air as the horse mask clattered to the ground in the heap, a crack running from its right cheek to its eye.

"Like hell," Masaka said.

"The king appointed him himself," Catalina replied with her hands raised in a shrug. "I hate to say it, but Salama is a step ahead of us here. They've likely been in contact before the incident in Jordun."

"They're using the incident as an excuse to strongarm us," Thian put in. "Most likely."

"They're likely wanting control of Narumont and to finally and decisively put their god above our own," Montel added.

"That incident likely happened because they revile Goddess Toive," Aldana said.

"Likely," Masaka repeated. "It's all true, isn't it?"

The High Clerics looked amongst each other. Catalina shrugged with her hands again. "As politicians, we can't commit to an opinion."

"It was murder."

Masaka recognized the voice and remained facing the High Clerics as they all turned to watch Perish slowly descend the steps from the second floor. She wore a dull white dress as extravagant as a nightgown.

"What you're describing is murder," Perish said in a monotone, her bare feet stepping up beside Masaka's chair just before the heap of wood and splinters.

Montel tutted while the other three High Clerics gave ambiguous head movements. "We're hoping to argue that to be the case," Catalina said. "But it'll take a lot to convince an audience that isn't impartial. We'll need you there as well."

"Politics and gods," Masaka muttered, then said more loudly, "What does the opinion of a murderer matter? Changing Valen's mind is pointless."

"It matters when the murderer is the inquisitor," Montel said lightly, averting his gaze from the anger emanating from Masaka.

"But you're right," Catalina said. "We're not exactly aiming to change Inquisitor Valen's mind. Those who appointed him the position, namely King Dormond and his advisors, are our best bet to convince."

"What do we do?" Perish asked.

Catalina leaned sideways and gestured at the back wall with the counter and sink where a flier rested. "Gather as much evidence as you can. You still have the job posting for the Akhal-Teke?"

Perish nodded.

"And the knight girl," Catalina continued. "She was also a witness. We've already contacted Wild Fox who may be crucial as a neutral party since he's a knight of the countryside. The Estamon family, too, we've contacted, though we don't know how forthcoming they'll be."

Masaka shook her head at Fox's name then tilted her head. "The family with the girl who goes to Verlangen?"

"Avril," Perish said. "She was there too. Lumi said she fled with the…" She trailed off, her eyes darkening.

"Yes, her," Aldana said. "Gather what more you can. We can only guess what Inquisitor Valen and Salama will argue to get what they likely want."

Their meeting lasted a few more minutes with the High Clerics suggesting the formalities and approach to the upcoming assembly. After they left, Perish turned to Masaka. "This is a state affair for frauds," she said plainly.

"Yes," Masaka said. She stood up from her chair, nudging a piece of broken wood with her shoe. "It's not going to go the way we want."

"What do we want?" Perish asked.

Masaka turned, her face stony. She gently brushed away a tear that silently trailed along the other woman's cheek, then rubbed her own. "I know what I want, but it's something I can't have."

Perish nodded, knowing her thoughts on Simon matched the guild master's.

"But I can have the next best thing." Masaka's tone became low and serious. "He's going to be at this so-called assembly. Perish, do you remember the one and only rule of being a Waymaker?"

Perish hesitated. "Never back down from what you want."

"Good." Masaka dropped to the floor and spun her body, her foot crashing through the wooden heap. She kicked the horse mask which flew out from the mass and shattered against the wall. "I'm going to kill Valen."

\*\*\*

The assembly hall was circular like an indoor colosseum. A wide dais centered the room with rows of chairs facing it from all sides. Bright blue banners on one side fell from buttresses high above, the section denoting Narumont's representatives. On the other side, orange banners fell sporting Salama's city color. Light filtered from high windows past the banners.

Pillars rose from floor to ceiling in the walkways between the chairs where most had already been seated. At the halfway point between Narumont and Salama on one side an imperious and walled-off area sequestered the king himself and his advisors. Opposite him was Inquisitor Valen standing resolutely on an elevated platform overlooking the dais.

Proceedings were already underway by the time Masaka and Perish entered the assembly hall. She glanced around at other guild masters, some she recognized and others she didn't, and found her seat at the frontmost section by the round dais. The knight girl, Lumi, stood alone on the dais looking straight ahead at the pale stonework making up the platform beneath Valen.

Valen cleared his throat and spoke. "If you will, repeat your story so that I may formally pose it to the assembly."

Masaka sat, staring long at the man. He was muscular, as imposing as the regal seating and presence of the king in a way. Like Perish had told her, one of his arms was gone. Perhaps she could use magic to return it to him before tearing it off again.

"As a group, I alongside two Waymakers went to the Jordun Flatlands to track and capture an Akhal-Teke that had a bounty on it. We were assailed and captured by the Salama Knights who then imprisoned us and killed Simon, one of the two Waymakers."

"Assailed," Masaka repeated under her breath. "The girl can play well here."

"Was it not your actions that disrupted the Jordun river's flow and threatened both wildlife, crops, and water access for people?" Valen questioned.

A chair sliding against wood resounded lightly as Catalina, in royal blue robes, stood amongst the three other seated High Clerics. "As Inquisitor for this assembly, you may not give arguments for any sides. We are currently hearing from one side and their evidence and have yet to address different perspectives and evidence that you seem to already hold yourself."

"I was there," Valen said dismissively without looking away from Lumi who continued to stare at the stone platform below him.

"Your perspective and any such information privy to yourself is null and void as the acting Inquisitor,"

Catalina replied tamely. "As is your station as Salama's Chief Warden. Should you wish to give input, you may step down as Inquisitor and we may all recess as we wait for a new Inquisitor to be appointed."

Valen glanced once at Catalina before returning his focus to Lumi. "No need. That is all you will say on the matter?"

Lumi nodded. "Yes."

"Then return to your seat."

She obeyed, moving down one of the walkways further up and melding with the rest of the attendees. Perish tapped Masaka's shoulder and whispered in her ear. "She didn't mention who killed Simon."

"It'd give Valen an excuse to give his perspective," Masaka murmured back, her eyes finally drawn from the Inquisitor to Catalina who was still standing.

"Who is Narumont's next witness?" Valen asked.

"Perish Song," Catalina called.

Perish stiffened.

"Just make it hard for them," Masaka murmured.

Perish nodded before standing and moving to the dais. Before she could take up position in its middle Valen asked his first question.

"What evidence and information do you have to say on the matter of Simon Maanvi and the Jordun Flatlands?"

Perish stood still, watching the Inquisitor for a moment. She hadn't known Simon's last name and it felt wrong to hear it first from his murderer. She brushed her flowing blue gown down, the same she had worn when traveling to the Rivermouth Dungeon with Simon. "I was the one who told Simon and Lumi of the job to find and capture the Akhal-Teke. I'm one of the two Waymakers Lumi mentioned, Simon being the other. We went to the Jordun Flatlands to search for the horse. When we found it, we were assailed by the Salama Knights who then captured us, imprisoned us, and killed Simon."

"Is that all?"

Perish paused, glancing back at Masaka. "For now."

"For now?" Valen asked. "Are you withholding information?"

"Why do you ask?" Perish countered, her eyes meeting his.

"Of both witnesses so far, neither have disclosed the identity of who killed Simon Maanvi. Do you know the identity of the person who killed him?"

Perish didn't look away. "I do."

Masaka's hands tightened, knowing the next question the Inquisitor had been leading up to.

Valen leaned forward. "Who was it?"

"We were held captive by the Salama Knights in one of their prisons," Perish said. "The identity of the one who killed Simon is among the representatives of Salama, as he, Lumi, and I were under their authority while captive. Things got out of hand…" Her eyes slowly fell to the empty sleeve on the inquisitor's side. "I encourage you to inquire one of them, Inquisitor."

Valen stayed quiet for a few seconds, then smirked. "You aren't in a position to omit information in this assembly, Perish Song."

"No, I do not have that luxury as you do, Inquisitor."

Valen stepped forward on his elevated platform. "Who killed Simon?"

A chair scraped the floor. "The witness has answered this question already, Inquisitor Valen," Catalina's voice resounded. "I'll ask for the assembly's approval to move forward to the next witness. We'll have time to address key details in the follow-up."

Heads turned to the king and his advisors in their sequestered seating. The plump king looked both ways before nodding, additional creases forming on his skin below his chin.

Another chair scraped and a man in royal orange robes amongst Salama's representatives spoke. "We move to amend our compensatory charges in the matter of Simon Maanvi and the Jordun Flatlands."

Valen met the king's eyes, waiting until the king nodded again. "Piones Sylvester, please state the amendments to your charges."

The man looked directly at the king before speaking. "Upon favorable decision of this matter, I formally request the secession of Salama city from the kingdom."

## Chapter 29: Murderer

The king remained seated while his advisors stood and shouted. Murmurs of confusion and worry roiled across the Narumont representatives while Salama's patiently waited for the uproar to cease. Perish turned in a circle before leaving the dais, figuring it wasn't her place to say or do anything more. She sat beside Masaka who had merely raised her eyebrows while her serpent-like focus remained on Valen.

Valen pounded his fist on his platform's railing once. The loud sound shocked everyone momentarily before one of the king's advisors shouted again. "You're requesting treason!"

"The qualms between your cities is being addressed here!" another advisor shouted. "Seceding the kingdom would be blaming it, and the king, for your actions!"

Valen slammed his fist again, this time the sound silencing everyone. "With respect to King Dormond and his advisors, it is within the Inquisitor's power, as appointed by the king, to adjudicate charges and formal decision on the presented matter."

"Why, you little snake—!" The advisor gasped when the king held out his arm and rose. The plump man adjusted his royal black fur-lined coat resting over his pronounced torso fitted in a lacy purple buttoned shirt.

"I appointed you Inquisitor at your request to ensure justice in the ongoing conflict between Salama and Narumont," King Dormond's deep, throaty voice resounded. "Do you wish to take advantage of my good faith?"

Valen considered the king for a moment.

"Speak quickly," a male advisor said. The king clapped his hands this time, the sound lackluster compared to Valen's. Still, guards that had been making themselves discreet around the perimeter of the hall uniformly stepped in front of every exit in pairs. The doors at the end of each walkway shut behind them and the guards placed their hands on the hilts of their various weapons from swords to axes and lances in preparation. The Narumont representatives murmured with worry and concern while Salama's representatives silently glanced around the room.

"Let's not rush to chaos," Valen said finally. "Treason is not the aim of our assembly today. This is a stately matter, as you said, Advisor Lonov."

"Wha—!"

"Piones," Valen interrupted the advisor, causing him to splutter. The Inquisitor turned to the Salama representative and said, "What reasons do you have to request Salama's secession from the kingdom?"

Piones bowed his head slightly. "Unchecked discord has been longstanding between our cities. The Salama Knights have been treated inhospitably by Narumont's denizens in every visit and matter requiring interaction, and when their knights and denizens visit our humble city they still yet treat the city and us, *its* denizens, inhospitably. Narumont's repeated frivolous activity affecting our way of life, this matter we are assembled for today being only the most recent among many, has time and again been ignored by both Narumont's leaders and our kingdom's. That is why we wish to peaceably secede."

"These are grand accusations which may easily be spoken but difficultly evidenced," Catalina said, standing opposite Piones and looking across the hall at him.

Valen said, "As Inquisitor, I accept the stated reasons and approve the request to change Salama's compensatory charges in the matter of Simon Maanvi and the Jordun Flatlands."

Piones nodded and sat back down while the king and his advisors broke out into objections.

"I do not," the king's voice echoed over the others, a hand clenched against his chest. Scrapes of metal weaponry unsheathing resonated around the hall.

"Do you wish to annul this assembly?" Valen asked. The simple manner in his tone emphasized he wasn't merely asking. Everyone knew his position as Inquisitor designated him to be the one to ask, yet they also knew his position as a Warden of Salama. He stood on the center platform but his side was with Salama.

Everyone knew and understood, except King Dormond, unfortunately. "I do," he said. A barbed wood-and-pine spear appeared in his hand. He moved uncharacteristically fast for his body mass, his arm powerfully arcing back and rocketing forward as he threw the spear.

The birch spear grew leaves and petals as its tipped head spiraled straight at Valen's torso. Wood creaked as the hall became infested with the king's nature magic, roots unfurling from narrow crevices between pillars, ceilings, and floors. Vines fell across the high windows and darkened the room while wood overtook the fine stonework of the surrounding walls. The spear tip sunk into the slight cavity of Valen's chest and the Inquisitor staggered a step back.

Valen's body went still a moment, then his arm lifted to grip the length of the gnarled spear. Smoke rose from the wood as he pulled it away from him, revealing he had not been impaled as the spear tip was actually missing—disintegrated. The rest of the spear disappeared in a flash of short-lived fire, and Valen's eyes narrowed at the king.

The advisors stepped ahead of the king and began sending out their own magic, a variety of elemental projectiles.

Valen almost rhythmically dodged some and blocked others, his one hand rapidly grasping balls of metal, rock, and fire. Whatever the element, each dissipated within his grasp in a puff of smoke.

The representatives of Narumont and Salama largely hesitated, others looking on in shock, and few moving to intervene however they could.

The temperature in the hall rose and white fires engulfed the king's nature magic. Walls of wood and foliage became walls of flames, and Valen flourished a sword in the center of the haze and heat. He pointed it at the king and bowed his head in a final act of respect.

On the ground by the dais Masaka stood along with Perish. "Now?" Perish asked worriedly.

Masaka nodded, eyes stuck on Valen. The Inquisitor tossed his sword up and it moved in an arc through the air. Fire and smoke billowed into it as if sucked into the blade.

Valen clicked his fingers and pointed at the king. The sword shivered once in response and flew like an arrow straight between the advisors and at the king.

At the same moment Masaka tapped her foot and a weight pressed down on everyone. Those who were still sitting struggled to remain upright while those who were standing were all but forced to their knees. The king, forced by the weight, escaped death while the sword drew a gash through his clothes and shoulder before plunging into his seat behind him.

The next second a high, clear note sung out and the flames along the walls went out at the same time; the light from the windows high above also went out.

In the sudden dark that surprised and blinded everyone came shouts and screams. They were accompanied by the noise of weapons restlessly clattering from the guards who scrambled in the dark down the walkways.

Light returned in moments, revealing the mess of guards stumbling along the ground around the circular dais and wider hall. The chaos took a turn as eyes registered the scene. Atop the platform was Valen, lying still on his stomach. His face was turned to the side, eyes blankly staring. Blood trailed from his mouth and pooled on the platform. There was a gash straight through his chest. He was dead.

The king's advisors made cries of horror that joined the cries from Narumont and Salama representatives. Opposite the Inquisitor was the king, lying flat on his back. The only part of him that moved was the blood escaping the flesh wound in his shoulder. He was otherwise intact. But he was dead.

"He's dead!" Advisor Lonov shrieked. "The king is dead!"

"Valen's dead!" Piones roared, having leapt to inspect the Inquisitor's body.

On the ground, Perish looked at Masaka, her eyebrows raised worriedly. "Did you get him?" she whispered.

Masaka slowly looked back at Perish, wide-eyed. "No," she said. "I didn't."

*** 

The High Clerics of Narumont quickly rounded up the guards and stationed them at the exits while the king's advisors were relocated to the center dais. Salama's acting leader Piones stood alongside them, gazing up somberly at the platform Valen's body still lay on.

"No one is leaving," Piones called.

"No one is leaving," Catalina echoed, moving with the other three High Clerics to the center dais. "Everyone return to your seats while we… deliberate."

Masaka glanced around, coming to her senses. She sat back down, clenching and unclenching her hands.

"What happened?" Perish whispered, taking her own seat beside the guild master.

"I don't know," Masaka whispered back. "Everyone should've been stunned during the blackout."

"Won't the High Clerics suspect you? They know your magic enough to—"

"They might, but it was chaos." Masaka glanced back and forth from Valen's body to the secluded seating where a cover had been pulled over the king's body. "Did you see anything?"

Perish shook her head. "Darkening everything doesn't let me still see."

An outburst from the group gathered on the center dais interrupted them. "You're still bringing that matter up?" Piones roared.

Catalina cleared her throat, then spoke for everyone to listen. "We have three crimes on our hands." She looked at the king's advisors first. "One: King Dormond has been murdered." She turned slowly to address Salama's seated representatives. "Two: Inquisitor and Chief Warden Valen has been murdered." She stopped turning when she faced Narumont. "And three: Simon Maanvi has been murdered."

"The matter of Simon is no longer—"

"It remains the matter of our assembly here," Catalina stated. "In addition to this new matter."

Piones folded his arms. "We refuse to accept your version and your authority of the matter of Simon—"

"If we're to resolve anything here, I suggest we be upfront, Piones." Catalina gave him a long look. "Simon was murdered. With pretenses gone, I can say that it was none other than Chief Warden Valen that had killed him. Do you deny it?"

Piones's face contorted as his mouth opened and closed. His eyes darted from Catalina to the three other High Clerics and then to the king's advisors. Whether he thought better of worsening Salama's position with the kingdom or obstructing the current matter of Valen's own murder, he relented. "Valen murdered Simon."

A brief moment of silence passed in which Catalina gave the others meaningful looks before saying, "We can start investigating what happened here by working backwards. The king and warden died at the same time, though Valen was noticed last. What did you see first, Piones?"

"When the room lit back up, I saw only him lying dead as he is now. The rest of the room was in chaos and I couldn't discern any single person, but I did not see anyone approach or retreat from where Valen was."

"Neither did I," Catalina said. "As for the king, his advisors were surrounding him." She eyed the advisors. "Did any of you see anything?"

"No," the advisors murmured.

Thian cleared his throat. "If I may suggest so, we should determine the individuals whose magic shut out the light."

"I don't know if we can ascertain that," Catalina said. Her gaze shifted from the advisors to Masaka and Perish who were unabashedly eavesdropping while the rest of the hall's occupants discussed between themselves. She raised an eyebrow at Masaka who subtly shook her head in turn. "With so much magic being used at once, I doubt they will be forthcoming."

"Not necessarily," Thian said. "We can take stock of the most apparent types of magic and deduce—"

"Both the king and warden were stabbed through the chest?" Catalina asked.

Thian frowned as an advisor said, "Yes, but none of us carry weapons, save for the guards."

"The guards," Catalina repeated, gesturing the attention of those on the dais toward the knights stationed around the perimeter of the hall. "Let's have them approach the dais one by one. We," she nodded at each of the High Clerics, "can ascertain whose weapon has been used. If there's residual blood on a blade even if the killer wiped it, we'll find it."

Piones nodded and together with the king's advisors called out orders for the attendees to remain seated while the guards lined up in each aisle.

Masaka shifted her elbow to allow the knights space to walk up to the impromptu gathering of authorities (and avoid their chainmail armor from knocking into her). "Looks like they're narrowing the culprits," she murmured to Perish.

Perish folded her arms in her lap. "Did you sense or feel anything? When you had everyone's bodies locked down?"

"I mainly had Valen's body locked down. Until he died, obviously. I sensed him being pierced by something sharp, so checking the guards' weapons first seems obvious and practical."

"Magic could cause the same wounds," Perish commented.

"I didn't sense magic in particular harming Valen. As for the king... I'm not sure, I wasn't focused on him." Masaka observed the High Clerics take a sword from each of the knights in turn and hover a hand along the blade. Once finished with their inspection, the knights walked back up the narrow space left by the still waiting guards in the aisles. "I'm not clued in to today's politics. Who'd want to kill the king?"

Perish shrugged. "Whoever it is, Salama's assembly would be at the top of the list given their announcement of secession. The king's advisors were the closest to him to potentially do it without being seen... though I don't imagine anyone would want to make such an accusation."

"If no one does, I will," Masaka said. She hesitated as another round of guards' swords were appraised before the guards retreated up the aisles. She then gasped loudly, sprang up, and whapped Perish's shoulder with the back of a hand. "The advisors were closest to kill the king!?"

"Accusations and questioning will be held shortly," Catalina's unamused voice rang over the ripple of murmurs around the hall. "Please refrain from any further outbursts for the time being."

Masaka sat back down casually and folded her arms while ignoring the glares from the advisors standing along the dais. "That should ease people into the possibility," Masaka muttered to Perish. They both sat in wait as the remainder of the knights continued coming and going amidst the High Clerics' inspections. The last of the knights returned to take up position along the walls of the hall and there was a pause while those on the dais discussed.

Finally, Catalina announced, "After deliberating, we've concluded that none of the knights are responsible for what happened here today—however, we know both the king and warden were killed with a piercing weapon or spell."

"It's Narumont!" a member of Salama's seated assembly called. "They obviously killed Valen!"

"Obviously?" Catalina asked.

"They're the only ones here with a clear motive: revenge!"

Piones pursed his lips while the High Clerics and advisors considered this.

Masaka loudly cleared her throat and stood back up. "Did you all forget the king's advisors were the most upset when Piones announced Salama's secession, and it was the king himself who attacked first?"

The advisors shared grimaces before one of them spoke up. "While we would have pleasurably meted out punishment for Valen and Salama's insubordination, it was not any of us who killed him. And if it were, we'd be declaring having done it on the same grounds of insubordination."

"Maybe, maybe not." Masaka eyed the advisor. "All we really have is your word."

"All you have is anyone's word," the advisor retorted. "Whose side are you on, anyway?"

"Huh? Sides? What do sides matter when people are dead?"

Piones rolled his eyes and stepped up to the edge of the dais in front of Masaka. "Don't act righteous. You would've killed Valen for revenge yourself."

Masaka gave a cold grin. "I would've."

"See? A confession!"

"If that's a confession, then the advisors confessed as well," Masaka said.

"There are motives more obvious than others as we all know," Catalina interrupted. "Perhaps if we start with those who had a connection with the warden prior to this hearing."

"I have an idea," Masaka called. "It concerns both a motive and a means. There is still someone who was involved during the events leading up to Simon's murder who has not taken the dais."

Catalina pinched the bridge of her nose quickly enough it could have been passed off as scratching an itch. "We've questioned Lumi, Perish, and all of Salama's guards from that day. If you're referring to Valen, we can't very—"

"I'm talking about the Wild Fox."

Catalina closed her mouth and glanced at the end of a row of Narumot's assembly. "Fox," she stated plainly, then turned to face him. "You weren't among the guards who had their weapons inspected."

"No, ma'am," the tall and slender man grumbled. "I was told to sit and wait during this farce."

"You don't have to wait anymore." Catalina beckoned him over. The knight crankily stood up and paced the few steps down the aisle to the dais. He leapt nimbly up and unsheathed the sword strung at his waist in a flash. The metal shrilly rang for half a second. He pushed it at Catalina.

"Go on, then."

Masaka watched quietly while Catalina tentatively ran her hands over the sword. She felt Perish tug on her sleeve as the High Cleric rose and gasped. They could see flecks of red recede from a sharp edge of the sword and gravitate toward Catalina's outstretched hands. Catalina's face fell as she stared at Fox.

The knight licked his lips, shifted his feet, and appraised the blood that had come off his sword. "Huh. I don't remember killing anyone recently."

Piones whistled and several guards lining the hall advanced up the aisles towards Fox.

"Now hold on a minute. Why would I kill Valen? I mean, I'm wild, but I'm not as unhinged as he is to go and kill—okay, just hold *on*!" Fox spun around Catalina and leapt up onto the platform where Valen's body lay before anyone could react. He lowered his sword with the wound in the warden's chest. "Look, you idiots! My sword is twice the length of this cut!"

The guards making their way down the aisles froze while Catalina alongside the other High Clerics and advisors observed the difference between Fox's sword and Valen's wound. "That's troubling," Catalina muttered, shaking her head. "The fact you forgot what you used your sword for, and that you're not responsible for Valen's death," she clarified.

"But what about the king's wound? Compare the sword to that!" The advisors murmured agreement and Fox sighed. He leapt back down from the platform and obligingly moved to where the king still lay within the imperious sequestered area between both Narumont and Salama's assemblies.

"Hmm," Fox commented maneuvering his sword close to the king's chest wound. "This looks about the same size as my blade…"

The Narumont representative sitting beside where Fox had been seated groaned and shouted, "Oh, for god's— Wild Fox couldn't have done it because he was complaining to me during the entire commotion!"

"Very well," Catalina said, clapping her hands. "It seems, while Wild Fox had means, he lacked a motive and opportunity."

"Great," Piones said sarcastically, glaring briefly at Masaka as if to silently and sarcastically thank her as well.

"There's one other knight here whose sword hasn't been inspected." The sudden clang of Fox's sword returning to its sheathe caused many in the hall to jolt in their seats. He smirked, head lolling sideways as he gazed over the Narumont members. "She's someone who also happens to have a slim sword."

Masaka paled and turned toward the spot Fox's eyes gazed at and saw Lumi slowly rise. The young knight now wore the sword in a sheath along her hip, having left it at her seat when giving her perspective earlier.

"We have our next accused," Catalina stated. She beckoned Lumi expectantly.

Lumi hesitated before resting a hand on the sword's hilt and slowly drawing it out. A quiet hiss emanated in the brief silence. The slick, red-tinged blade gleamed in the open for all to see. Conglomerated drops towards its tip dripped onto the ground.

Gasps and outcries roiled from both sides of the hall. Catalina's hands dropped to her sides as she frowned solemnly. Beside her on the dais Piones barely audibly let out noises of relief and satisfaction. She snapped her fingers and the closest guard along the aisle beside Lumi took hold of the girl's sword arm. "Lumi Valse, you will be taken into confinement for the murder of Valen Castille."

Lumi defiantly stilled her arm from the guard's attempts to pull her from the Narumont assembly. "I would like to contest this so-called crime," Lumi called. She glared at the guard pulling on her arm; he stilled in response while keeping his hand clenched tight so as to prevent her from suddenly moving.

Piones let out a short, humorless laugh. "Which part? The fact your sword matches the size of Valen's mortal wound, or the fact your sword currently has blood on it?"

"The murder part," Lumi said.

"You actually expect us to—?"

"She may speak her defense," Catalina interrupted. "We are all already gathered here."

Lumi waited a moment before continuing. "I was raised as a knight by my father. He taught me a code of honor, the honor of old that has since been watered down by legislative jargon and that the knighthood now only follows as guidelines in favor of holding fast to new politics." Her voice shook slightly, but she controlled her breathing. "New laws that have the credibility of honor without being bound by its method or rules. New laws that cleverly cite morals while making immorality admissible. You say that I murdered Valen, but I didn't murder him."

Exhales of disbelief sounded among the crowd, but no one interjected.

"I did not murder him," she repeated. "Murder is unlawful. I *killed* him."

"That," Catalina said slowly, "is a confession."

"Indeed," Piones said, the relief plain on his face as control of the situation was growing. "No matter how you dress it up, you're responsible."

"Valen murdered Simon!" Lumi said loudly, her eyebrows lowering. "When one murders, he cedes his right to life. When you hunt, it's not only others' lives that are at stake. You also put your life at stake."

"Rubbish!" Piones called, gesturing for the guards to continue taking Lumi away. "You stabbed him while everyone was blind in the dark. That's not honor!"

Lumi narrowed her gaze at Piones. "He stabbed Simon while he was imprisoned and helpless in a cell. An eye for an eye." Lumi's arm jerked back, slipping through the guard's hand. The guard cried out as her sword followed through, nicking his fingers. She stomped on both of his feet and the guard then found himself uncontrollably sliding down the aisle.

More guards followed the outskirts of the room toward the aisle Lumi retreated up and away from the dais. Her sword darted either way at outstretched hands, warding off those in the crowd attempting to restrain her.

"I have a confession!" Avril shouted above the rising commotion. The High Clerics and advisors faltered before they could begin pursuing Lumi. "I killed King Dormond!"

The guards ready to attack Lumi turned their full attention to Avril whose parents were furiously trying to force her back into her seat.

"I killed King Dormond, and my parents ordered me to do it!"

Piones looked back and forth between Avril and Lumi. "What the—!?"

"Seize them!" an advisor shouted, pointing at Avril.

"Seize them all!"

Lumi pushed past the guards before they recovered. She parried a guard by a door and slipped out, slamming the door shut behind her. The guard cursed and the echoes of him banging on the door that refused to budge added to the shouts of Avril's parents.

"This is absurd! Avril, what are you talking about!?"

"We didn't order anything!"

Avril fell backwards and away from her parents, shrieking. "They ordered me, they forced me to, they told me to kill the king to add conflict between Narumont and Salama, so I *did*!"

"I guess this hearing is concluded," Masaka said quietly to Perish while Avril and her parents were detained by both guards and officials of either assembly. She looked meaningfully at Perish and then at the door Lumi left through. "We have work to do."

## Chapter 30: Reformation

"My lord!" Instructor Lochley jiggled the knob to the eldest prince's chamber door twice for formality before letting himself in. "A courier—" he rushed before Prince Michael could question his intrusion, "—a courier returned in haste from Narumont. My lord, I—this is difficult to say, but his majesty—at the hearing between Narumont and Salama your father was killed."

Prince Michael stayed seated at his study desk, the arm he had rested on its top to prop up his head lowering slowly.

"Equerries have gathered in Mason Study to review the documents of the hearing, but what is known is the daughter of a noble family in Narumont was the one who did it." Instructor Lochley took a breath, eyes darting around the plush matted floor and hardwood walls as if trying to ground his racing mind with the upkeep and order of the simple furnishings.

"A Narumont family." Prince Michael finally spoke, his words low and monotone.

"Yes, my—your majesty."

The prince's hand clenched atop the desk. *That's how it is.*

"The girl claimed to have been coerced by her parents to do it. She has marks on her body consistent with her claims; abuse, it seems. At the same time, a young Narumont knight also killed the acting inquisitor of the hearing and Salama's Chief Warden Valen."

Prince Michael blinked. His gaze he had fixed to his instructor fell to his hand on his desk that had begun trailing the sculpted woodwork along its edges. *Father carved this himself to smooth out the edges and prevent me from seriously injuring myself... How long ago was it when it was at my head level? I was prone to running into things.* "Two assassinations at the same time," he commented in the same low tone.

Instructor Lochley hesitated. "Oddly enough, they were not coordinated. According to Narumont's High Clerics the knight had acted alone in vengeance, and they were unaware of the noble family's plot."

"I tried to warn him," Prince Michael said. "I suspected foul play when Salama called upon Father to settle the matter. It was the first time real blood had been shed in these cities' conflict. I had a feeling Salama would pull something… But it seems I was worried about the wrong people."

"You weren't entirely wrong, your majesty. During the hearing Salama announced their intention to secede. That was when… things fell apart."

Prince Michael stopped tracing the smooth woodwork of the desk and stared at the wall. "This rivalry they have… they can settle it."

"Settle it?"

"They can settle it themselves. They started the conflict, they will be the ones to end it. I don't care how it resolves, as long as they let it be finished."

"You mean Narumont and Salama? What if they don't?"

"I won't let this country get sucked into their affairs. We've already wasted its greatest asset."

Instructor Lochley stopped himself from nodding as the gesture would be pointless with Prince Michael not looking at him. "I was worried you would seek revenge."

"I don't know if I won't," the prince replied. "Not until I know more from the others about what happened.

But, for now…" He stood up and turned from the wall to look at Instructor Lochley. "I hereby order all unaffiliated with either city to withdraw. Take this decree to the other Numen. Station available knights along all routes to and from both Narumont and Salama. Both cities will henceforth, indefinitely, not be recognized as part of the kingdom."

"You realize they hold some of the highest power and authority?"

"They are merely a strong couple limbs," Prince Michael said. "The kingdom remains with its head. Should worse come to worse, we can manage without them. The country's border with the Remote Expanse is a greater concern. As for the noble girl… have her brought here."

Instructor Lochley nodded. "Yes, your majesty."

Prince Michael forced himself to hold his instructor's gaze before the man turned and exited. He knew he was expected to follow, to join the equerries in the study. But he waited for the door to close. He gave himself one last moment of selfishness.

He closed his eyes. He breathed in. He sighed.

Then he opened his eyes and lightly tapped the back of his hand against the smooth woodwork of the desk a final time before moving to the door. He was no longer the prince. He was the king.

\*\*\*

Masaka eyed the Waymakers sternly from the banister at the top of the stairs. They had gathered in the main lounge of their guild and awaited her pronouncement of the assembly's outcome. She noted Procel was the only one missing.

"Well, what happened?" Dulon asked impatiently, seated amongst the others around the tables.

"A lot." Masaka tutted, then drew in a breath. "The guilds of Narumont are being hired to go to war with Salama." She observed as Dulon's face went through a series of phases like the phases of the sun across the span of a day only in a few moments. "Yes, we've been enlisted by the High Clerics to go to war as well."

"What? Why?"

"Two members of Narumont's assembly went and killed Salama's chief warden as well as our fine country's king. They acted independently, but there is no room for negotiations with blood being spilt."

"But there was room for negotiations when Simon was killed?" Dulon's fists visibly shook.

"We all know certain matters aren't going to be adequately addressed the way we want. It's why many of us joined this guild, I hope."

"So, now what? We have to go to war?"

"Legally, yes," Masaka drawled. "But there are many ways of participating in a war. We've already been compensated with money, yet we have little reason to join this fight…"

"We don't?" Lenard asked slowly, his head remaining facedown beside the bottom step of the stairs. "The people from Salama killed Simon."

"*Valen* killed Simon. And then Lumi, Simon's friend who is also a knight, killed Valen."

The Waymakers murmured, most uttering compliments to the knight.

Frisk materialized sitting on a tabletop and raised his hand. "We'll either be killed or seriously punished if we lose this war... right?"

"Right, we have some reason to join this fight. But that's not what we're going to do, at least not until it's absolutely necessary. We're only a minor guild, and we're considered a black chamelion amongst the other guilds. The war is currently Narumont's number 1 priority, but the High Clerics have also made locating and arresting Lumi a priority."

The Waymakers made murmurs of discontent and understanding. "She's technically the reason for the war," the unusually somber Barto said.

"All it was was revenge," Lenard's slightly muffled voice echoed from the bottom stair step.

Frisk reappeared and poked Barto, then ducked away from the man attempting to grab him. Frisk stumbled and was caught by Kairi who was standing by a wall. She kept hold of him while saying, "She's going to be the scapegoat, then."

Dulon gruffly cleared his throat before addressing Masaka. "You're saying we'll be making finding Lumi our own priority. What happens to her when she's found?"

"*If* she's found, she's to face public execution," Masaka said plainly. She again eyed each Waymaker in turn. "Narumont has been good enough to us to allow us a place to live. It also hasn't been that good to us, another reason many of us joined this guild. Our objective, if you want it, is to find Lumi and hide her. Protect her, until negotiations are back on the table. Until we can assure she'll be granted amnesty. So, that leaves the question: do you want to help Lumi?"

Dulon pounded a table and stood up. "She did what any of us would've done if given the chance. I'm in."

Masaka lifted and lowered her hands in exasperation. "I was *going* to kill Valen myself..."

Perish stood up behind Dulon and nodded. "I couldn't protect Simon. I *will* protect her."

Several Waymakers whooped and Barto let out a laugh, one of his first in a while.

Masaka grinned and nodded. "All right, then—" The front door of the Waymaker Guild opening drew everyone's attention to the man who entered. "Procel. You're back."

The slender man wearily met the pairs of eyes as he nudged the door closed with the back of his foot. He blinked and shook his head to cause his semi-long bangs to sway out of his face.

"Where've you been?" Kairi asked as he steadily paced by her toward the guild master.

He halted at the base of the stairs, his feet digging into Lenard somewhat. "I finished what you sent me to do."

Masaka's grin widened. "Good."

"What did you send him to do?" Dulon asked.

Procel remained silent, facing Masaka.

"Might as well fill them in," Masaka said. "It's related to our overall objective."

Procel momentarily lowered his chin, then turned to the rest of the guild. "Well…"

\*\*\*

Toive Knights rode their horses briskly up the thoroughfare. A shadow flitted a street over in pursuit. The horses' breaths measuredly pushed out as they progressed every block.

"Steady," the captain of the knights ordered as they neared the end of the thoroughfare where a grand cathedral rested, one of four across the city. The knights silently eased their horses' paces until fully stopping at the wide steps leading up to the building's front doors. They dismounted and three followed the captain up the steps while a fourth tied the horses' reins together before assuming a stance of attention.

The shadow detached from a nearby alley and purposefully paced toward the lone knight while the others entered the cathedral. The knight broke his stance and faltered when the man placed a firm hand on the knight's chainmail-clad shoulder. Procel drew close to murmur in the knight's ear, "Any news of the girl knight?"

The knight's eyes cleared and his face relaxed as Procel withdrew his hand to stand a couple feet away. "There is news. Captain Kirsten is in a debriefing with the High Clerics."

Procel raised his eyebrows and glanced up at the pristine cathedral steps. "They're all gathered there?"

"They will be discussing the ongoing war effort for some time. Concerned citizens will be informed eventually."

Procel nodded and fixed his gaze on the Toive Knight. "I'm a part of a guild."

The knight shifted his stance. "Apologies. I should have guessed from the way you carry yourself, Mr…"

"Procel," he supplied, continuing to hold the knight's gaze.

"Procel. What guild are you part of?"

Procel stared at the knight quietly.

"…Mr. Procel?"

"The Waymaker Guild," he said after another moment without breaking eye contact.

"Oh. Them. Well, all guilds will be notified in due time, so I must ask you to wait until then."

"The girl," Procel said.

"Right. You will hear news of Lumi Valse soon."

"The girl. The girl knight. Lumi. Lumi. Lumi Valse."

The knight frowned.

Procel clapped his hands loudly, causing the knight to flinch and break eye contact. He then grabbed the knight's hand and shook it. "Thank you for serving our city!" he said brightly, grinning.

The knight blinked and smiled. "No problem! Stay safe, Mr…" The knight faltered, taking a moment to think.

"I'd like to take a moment to pray. Good day!" Procel let go of his hand and retreated up the steps of the cathedral. The knight shrugged and resumed his stance.

Upon opening one of the two large oak doors Procel received a blast of chilly and vaporized air. He gently shut the door behind him as his body shivered and adjusted to the cold emanating from the running water filling elegantly carved canals and waterfalls flowing between altars and pews. He took practiced steps along the main aisle leading to the largest altar lying beneath a stone bust of Goddess Toive. The waterways were arranged to visually signal for entrants to move at a certain pace before stepping over them. None of the devotees in their various blue garbs kneeling by the side altars or sitting in the pews paid his progression any mind.

*Lumi.* The thought summoned memories not of his own but of the Toive Knight. *She fled the hearing and briefly went to the knight academy before fleeing Narumont. Where she went...* Procel sighed when he found the knight held no memory of where exactly she had gone. They did, at least, point him in the direction of Captain Kirsten who was apparently privy to the information.

Halfway through his progression along the grand hall he turned to exit into a staging room where deep pools of water cycled the former room's waterways. A member of the clergy based on her more regal blue robes straightened up from a kneeling position by a pool and appraised him. "Who are—"

*No one,* Procel implanted the thought in her mind as he walked through and on to the next room. His mouth twitched as a new memory of filtration systems snagged his own thoughts. The next room was a waiting area with many chairs lining every wall and only breaking at the door he entered through and the door across the way. It was vacant, but he knew the very next one wouldn't be. He braced himself as he briskly walked the room's length and gripped the door handle. He pulled the door open.

"Salam—" Captain Kirsten interrupted himself and turned his head to face Procel. He alone sat on a cushioned sofa that faced a matching sofa where three of the four High Clerics sat. The fourth, High Cleric Montel, stood facing away from the center of the room and swirled the contents of a small vial around with a hand by shaking it. The three Toive Knights aligned behind Captain Kirsten placed their hands on the hilts of their swords and advanced on Procel.

High Cleric Catalina's eyes narrowed at Procel. "You—"

"You know where Lumi Valse is going," Procel said loudly. "Lumi Valse left Narumont and you know where she is heading. The girl knight who killed Valen Castille. Lumi."

He backstepped and shut the door in front of him, then turned and briskly walked back past the waiting room and staging room. Memories surged forth and he had to force his back upright to keep from buckling. *Lumi Valse was excommunicated from the Narumont Knights. She packed her things and left before the order for her arrest went out. Ow, my head.*

Procel rushed out into the main hall, narrowly avoiding sticking a foot into a waterway. He straightened his steps and hurried toward the large oak doors of the cathedral. Pain lanced across his head and he staggered. He subtly transformed the motion into stepping out of the main aisle and sitting down onto a vacant pew. He knew he could take his time as he'd made sure the High Clerics and Toive Knights wouldn't remember him intruding. He lowered his head and closed his eyes, pressing both hands over his scrunched face.

*The girl knight who killed Valen. One of the Toive Knights saw her on her way out of Narumont. He pursued her, caught her, but she resisted and got away. Before she did, she mentioned where she was going.*

"Nngh," Procel mumbled, rubbing his temples and lowering his head further until it was barely above his knees. *The Cursed Lands. The Remote Expanse. She said she was going there.*

The pain subsided and he sat back slowly, opening his eyes. Muted light trickled through the high clerestory windows and reflected from the shifting streams along the hall. It had been a while since he used his magic on several people at once. *What did I lose in return?*

He did a mental inventory of the memories he never wanted to lose. *I am Procel. Parsha was my mother. I am a summoner. Masaka took me in. Lime was my first pet. Hay was the first gift I ever got. I like the smell of lavender…*

He lowered his hands from his face, his fingers slightly wet. *Someone gave me lavender once. Someone… important.* He wiped the teardrops from his hands on his pants and shook his head. *That's the last time I overuse my magic. I'll give Masaka what she wants, then leave before I'm asked for another favor.*

Procel stood and returned to the main aisle to make his way out. *The Cursed Lands in the Remote Expanse.*

## Chapter 31: The Forge of Curses

A faded sign nailed to a short post beneath a decaying beech tree welcomed them to the Cursed Lands: *Walker, there is no path; the path is made by walking.*

A yellow-orange haze blanketed the landscape stretching on for miles ahead of them. The Waymakers stood before the dry plains, adjusting their hold of their horses' reins and taking note of the transition between the semi-lush grass to the barrenness before them that marked the end of the known country.

"Hey, that's perfect for us!" Masaka said cheerily, rapping a knuckle on the sign. A brief wind tilted the thin branches of the tree, momentarily easing the heat pressing from all around them.

"None of us are trackers," Lenard said. His nose and forehead looked worn from having been pressed against flat surfaces. "How will we find Lumi?"

"The obvious way she'd go is that way." Masaka pointed straight ahead from where the back of the sign faced. Far along the plains, so far it looked hazy enough to be a mirage, mountains cropped up on the horizon.

"Great. Let's go." Dulon took a step forward and felt his body seize up.

"Hold your horses," Masaka ordered. She glanced at the horses each Waymaker held by the reins then shook her head. "I mean, let go of your horses. We're not taking them any further."

Several Waymakers laughed, at first lightly, and then their laughs tapered off with uncertainty. The pressure on his body eased and Dulon rolled his shoulders. "Geez, you didn't have to force me to stop."

Masaka shrugged. "We'll do as the sign says. We walk." She gestured and called out directions, the Waymakers moving as instructed. In a short while they had unbuckled their necessary belongings from the horses and sent them off to either wander back to civilization or graze in the wilds. "I'll take a few people straight ahead. Dulon, you head a group over that way give or take thirty meters. Perish, you do the same on my other side. Keep flanked by me and don't break formation unless something happens."

"What could happen?" Frisk asked, appearing beside Dulon and tugging at the large man's sleeve playfully.

"We're venturing into unknown land," Masaka said. "From the few who briefly ventured into the Remote Expanse, it's rumored to not be normal."

"That's vague," Dulon muttered, then added, "But that's also pretty much all I've heard of it, too."

"It isn't when you think about it. What we take for normal, we can expect not to happen here." Masaka raised her hands and wriggled her fingers in front of her face. "Magic is not exactly normal. It's suggested the creatures and the very land in the Remote Expanse are magic."

"How is that any different from a dungeon?" Bartol asked.

"Dungeons are made by men," Masaka said. She lifted a foot and lightly placed it onto the auburn ground just past the tree. "Of course, the rumors of abnormal magic happening are mostly around the Cursed Lands. It's also rumored the curse is that there is no magic and not even your own magic works should you venture there."

Several Waymakers shuddered. "Why would Lumi go there?" Perish asked.

Masaka shrugged again. Her eyes met each of the Waymakers in turn. Several lowered their gaze while others shifted their feet. Everyone, save for Procel, had come. *I hate to ask favors of him, knowing the sacrifice. I'll have to properly thank him for everything next time I see him.* She sensed their hesitation. "I'll ask one last time: are you in?"

No one spoke up either way. A bright laugh tumbled from Perish's mouth, startling the other guild members. "I remember you asking me that before," she said. "I was barely out of childhood then."

"Your wardrobe was as flashy as it is today."

Perish's smile faded, her lips settling over her teeth. "It was the first encouragement I received."

Masaka regarded the other Waymakers whose hesitation betrayed by their muscle tension turned to a relaxed curiosity. *Only a few've heard her story.*

"I didn't like to sing before. But at first I did. My parents initially took it as a phase, something every girl obsessed with. It wasn't until later I learned they'd named me from the cries I made when I was born, because it was what they felt would happen to them when they heard me. Still, they put up with it when I sang a rendition of a concert or traveling songstress I got to see. After a year they shunned my singing, finally telling me to shut up and that my voice was grating. Then came my teen years and they discovered my affinity was based in my voice; they were indignant. Unable to bear hearing me so much as speak, they sent me to the seminary, the same one as Simon… My whole matriculation was paid for up front. They told me to graduate and leave. They didn't want me to come back. I followed what they wanted me to do for a couple years. But I knew I couldn't go further with school. The way students narrowed their eyes when I spoke, and the way they frowned, I knew they were troubled listening to me the same as them. I didn't sing my entire time there. So, I didn't exactly graduate, but I did what my parents wanted and left."

Perish glanced around at the Waymakers before continuing on. "I didn't know you then, but before you asked I'd already made my answer. I left the school and Narumont to sing on my own or to anyone who'd listen in the wild. Which wasn't anyone for a while, since I only sang to practice with my affinity as well as get better. Birds and other wildlife listened, and for their part they didn't flee in terror. From the few years of study in the seminary and on my own I became confident enough to sing somewhere marginally closer to civilization and danger.

That's how Masaka stumbled upon me singing in the Rivermouth Dungeon."

Bartol alongside a few other Waymakers chuckled.

"I wanted to hear someone—anyone praise me. So, when you asked if I was in to join your guild, after being the first person to confront me when I sang, *of course* I was."

Smiling, Masaka gestured at the unknown lands behind her. "I can't promise any praise from this. What we're doing is traitorous."

"There won't be much of that going around regardless, during wartime. Still, even in such times I can get a compliment here and there from one of you." Her smile returned, and she nodded. The gesture seemed to speak for everyone as they squared their shoulders and looked ahead. She unclasped the metal band she'd been rewarded from the Narumont Dungeon and reclasped it around her left wrist, experimentally turning her hand in circles while the amplifier rolled with her movement. Kairi withdrew and tied a band of silver metal—the occluder, also rewarded from the dungeon—behind her head, lifting her hair up and over to cover the loop. The girl blinked several times, her right eye obscured behind its jagged edges that lightly clawed her upper cheek.

If Masaka didn't know any better, she would've thought Perish laced magic into her words to build their confidence. "We make for the mountains," she stated. "Go." She turned and began walking into the unknown.

Lenard and Kairi fell in step behind her. Frisk went with a group of five more to follow Perish, Bartol going with another group of five to follow Dulon. Dried and dying tufts wavered from the air disturbed by their footfalls as they progressed across the plains. They were few and far between, most of the ground even after whatever plant life had lived there gave way to dirt and earth.

Masaka wrapped the sleeves of her nun's habit around either arm to remain tight rather than hang loose. Soon the two groups flanked her at an appropriate distance and they each headed straight.

"Where do the Cursed Lands actually begin?" Kairi asked some time after the silence set in. It had become apparent the distance between them and the mountains would not appear to be closing for a while.

"I'm not sure," Masaka replied. "The only real structure to its name are those mountains. Kairi, take the lead and cast a low-level wind spell every twenty paces. We can test if something is off about magic here."

Without raising her arms, Kairi held open her palms and sent a strong breeze to wash over the trio. It warded off the humidity for a good minute before heat settled back in. "Sorry," she muttered, tapping the back of her fingers on her occluder covering her right eye. "I've not practiced much with this thing on."

They walked on. Her subsequent spells, while lasting, were lighter in force. Several times more she sent her wind magic out to cool them off before something else shifted in the air. The very space around them seemed to ripple like it had turned to cloth. Then the other groups disappeared and they were alone on the plains.

"Where'd they go?" Lenard said sharply, his eyes darting as he turned in a circle.

"They're still there," Masaka said slowly. "Something is blocking them from view, but I can still sense them." She glanced both ways then said, "We continue on."

Kairi and Lenard hesitantly moved to keep up. After several paces the two groups reappeared. Neither looked to have changed or be in distress. Another several paces and Kairi sent out a light breeze of magic.

The air rippled again and the other groups again disappeared.

"We continue on," Masaka repeated. "Kairi, don't cast any more spells until I tell you to."

"O-okay."

They moved on in silence. Dulon and Perish showed up once more, Masaka noting their heads turning toward them with likely confusion. She gestured for them to keep going. They walked for several minutes until Masaka said, "Kairi, cast a spell."

Kairi did as told, opening her palms up and letting a gentle wind blow over them. The ground shook slightly, followed by the air rippling around them, and the two groups disappeared.

Masaka held up her hand for them to stop walking. She quietly pointed in the direction of where Dulon's group would have been and slowly reached out her hand. Lenard and Kairi watched as her hand stopped midair, apparently touching something. The air rippled again and Masaka's hand was shoved back.

Masaka took a couple steps back before catching herself and freezing in place. She turned her head sideways in the direction of where Perish's group would be. She bent down and picked up a handful of dirt. She tossed it outward. The dirt stopped at a point in the air and appeared to filter around a surface.

"Is the environment changing?" Kairi asked quietly, starting to reach her hand out.

"Don't move," Masaka ordered.

Kairi stilled.

"When I say 'go,' run." Masaka didn't wait for the others to acknowledge the command. She reared her hand back, formed a fist, and punched the air. The eastern atmosphere roiled as Masaka spun and hammered the air in the other direction. To both sides the air shifted as if changing into different textures. "GO!"

Masaka took off and was shortly followed by the other two. The ground had started to shake again as two massive forms faded into focus. A pronged leg jutted sharply from the ground and into their path. Masaka performed a sweeping kick that knocked it away. The masses turned, what once looked to be transparent air now opaque outlines of creatures.

A huge reptilian head resting its chin on the ground came into view as they ran on, a dark pupil at the center of a rounded eye. Its lattice-like skin shifted into an offset orange that stood out from the surrounding haze and dirt.

Pushing past both creatures, Dulon and Perish's group came back into view. Masaka looked behind. Her eyes widened. She twisted and tucked both Kairi and Lenard under her arms and jumped.

Pink flesh extended out from a creature's mouth and shot underneath their feet. Lenard let out a cry of surprise and revulsion as the tongue slapped into the dirt before sliding back toward the creature.

"What are they!?" Kairi asked when they landed and Masaka let go and pushed them to continue running.

"Those—" Masaka checked back to make sure the second creature's head wasn't facing them or trying to pursue them. "—are chameleons. Massive ones."

"Ka-*me*-leons? Not ka-meh-*lie*-ons?"

"They're the normal breed," she said while panting. "Except they're huge." She saw Dulon and Perish rushing their respective groups in her direction. She waved fervently. "Don't use magic! Just run!"

Both leaders nodded and they angled themselves straight ahead again.

Masaka panted harder as she looked over her shoulder. Neither of the chameleons gave chase, remaining stony and still as their skin rippled back into an uncanny resemblance of the surrounding landscape. "Okay," Masaka breathed then came to a halt, putting her hands on her knees and catching her breath.

"Are you okay?" Kairi asked, slowing to a walk and putting Masaka between her and the now invisible chameleons.

"I'm—fine—*gah*—it's hard to run in this outfit without using body magic."

"So magic is what drew them to us?" Lenard stated. "That's… treacherous. They could've eaten us and we wouldn't have seen it coming."

Kairi involuntarily shivered. "I thought chameleons were an extinct breed? And they were smaller?"

The guild leader waved a hand through the air. "That's how—they were before—they were domesticated. But these are like behemoths."

"We could just walk into one randomly out here," Lenard said.

"Maybe. Hah." Regaining her breath, Masaka stood upright then continued to walk, patting Kairi on the shoulder as she passed the girl. "They seem unlikely to attack unless we're using magic, so let's try to refrain from doing that until we need to."

Kairi shook her head and moved to follow beside Lenard. "I hope that's *all* this place has as a threat."

The air ahead of them shimmered.

Kairi sucked in a breath. "God *damn* it!"

Steam rose from the ground, distorting the mountains in the distance. They all could feel a searing heat emanating ahead. Suddenly the ground beneath them shifted and dipped. None could catch their footing as the angle grew sharper. All three of them tumbled down into the dark and the sky shut out.

There wasn't time to slow themselves as the ground quickly leveled out and let them slide to a halt on their stomachs and backs. Groans echoed from further away, along with the stark cursing of Dulon.

"Did everyone fall down here?" Masaka called. She was the first up. "Dulon!"

"Here!"

"Perish!"

"I'm here!"

Masaka continued to call out the Waymakers' names. One by one they all reconvened where she and Kairi and Lenard had fallen. "We're all here," she said finally. "Good. Now, does anyone know where here is?"

"Underground," Kairi said decisively, running the back of her fingers against the sharp edges of her eyepatch.

"That's not vague at all," Masaka replied slowly.

"There's light coming off a few walls," Lenard said. Sure enough, the minimal area they could see was thanks to partly jagged and partly rounded walls forming what looked like a tunnel in a cave. From within the walls a faint orange glow emanated.

Frisk appeared by one of them and ran the back of his hand along its surface. He winced and pulled his hand back. "They're hot. Are these manmade?"

"The ground looked like it was steaming before we fell down," Kairi said.

"And ground doesn't normally return back to its original position like a lid," Lenard, the expert of containers, said. "Were they pitfalls we fell in?"

Masaka shook her head and unfurled the sleeves of her nun's habit. "You're right. The ground seemed to move back in place like it was part of a mechanism."

Perish hummed a melancholic refrain softly, and the frills of her sundress glowed bright until it cast a sharp, tolerable light. Her final note trailed off and she looked at Masaka. "Why would there be a manmade underground structure in the unknown Cursed Lands of the Remote Expanse?"

"Maybe they aren't manmade," Masaka said.

"What does that mean?"

Kairi inhaled sharply. "You don't mean…?"

Frisk appeared next to her and smiled wide. "Aliens?"

"Quit using your obscuring magic and scurrying around," Masaka said with annoyance. "You can still draw the chameleons to us."

"That's what they were?" Dulon asked.

"Forget about them," Masaka said with a sigh. "And about aliens. This place exists, so let's go and see what it is." She marched ahead, the footfalls of the others tagging along behind her echoing quietly around the apparent cave. The walls randomly curved back and forth. No paths branched out offering other options. Perish's illuminated form lit the way some distance ahead where the walls shifted in a slanted direction. Masaka noted that the area they had fallen into was the most open, almost as if it were intentionally some sort of entrance or start to this underground place.

Around a curving corner the walls suddenly angled inward to form a narrow passage that led straight to a square metal door with an iron handle. Masaka stilled, and the others behind her did the same. The door was the only thing not glowing with the ethereal orange light, save for the floor and ceiling. It waited somewhat ominously, a dark spot between the walls.

"Single-file," Masaka said calmly, continuing down the narrow way. She stopped at the door and waited for the others to organize themselves. She peered closer at writing etched into the metal.

"*You who enter take up the burden of learning*

*What would yet be known but for time turning;*

*A plan rests here for wonders and their reverses*

*You are welcome to the Forge of Curses.*"

Masaka looked down and noted the settled dust and dirt on the ground had been sifted to the side. She knelt and brushed her hand along it.

"What does any of that mean?" Dulon asked. "Other than what the name of this place is."

Masaka stood up and turned to face the single-file line of Waymakers. "We'll see," she said loudly before giving a thumbs up. "But there's two pieces of good news I do know. This door has been opened recently, which means Lumi has been here."

"Do you know for certain it was her?" Perish asked amidst a few of the Waymakers audibly celebrating with expectations to be back in Narumont soon.

"It's most likely," Masaka replied. "The other piece of good news is that this is the entrance to a dungeon."

## Chapter 32: Of Men and Other

"How do you figure this is a dungeon?" Kairi paced in a circle around the guild leader as the others filed into the first room past the door. Its floor and ceiling were flat. The continuously glowing walls were also flat, running in straight lines and forming the room in a stretched, symmetrical quadrilateral shape.

"For starters, it's underground," Masaka said. She tousled the hair of Frisk who'd cloaked himself again in his peculiar magic to not be visible and tried to skirt by her without being noticed. "It's also not naturally formed by the environment. It's also got a cryptic challenge for anyone who enters. It's also—"

"Got magical creatures guarding it," Dulon said as he pushed his broad shoulders through the slim frame of the entry door.

"The giant chameleons weren't part of this dungeon, were they?" Kairi asked.

"No," Masaka said, "The magical creatures are coming into this room now."

On the other side of the room where a subsequent metal door was implanted in the paralleling wall, dusty figures somewhat resembling ghosts filed in. The door itself was shut, giving the beings even more of a ghostly presence. They aligned themselves opposite the Waymakers as they in turn filed in. Masaka's eyes darted along the dust clinging to the creature's bodies. When the last of the Waymakers entered she let out a laugh. There were 17 wraiths matching the 17 among the guild.

"These aren't shadow wraiths, are they?" Kairi murmured as she stopped pacing, a tremor in her voice.

"Not at all," Masaka said, gesturing to the wraith-like creature standing still opposite her. "These are mimics. This room must have some sort of check that copies the people who enter it." The mimic opposite her lacked defined features, but it was roughly her height and build. So notably, too, did Dulon and Perish's counterparts, the mimics having broad and poofy forms respectively.

"What do we do, then?" Lenard said. "Do we fight them?"

No one had to answer. The mimics surged forward at once, advancing on their matching member of the Waymakers.

Frisk let out a cry of surprise as his mimic appeared in front of him and sent out a flying kick. He was knocked back into the arms of those behind him.

Wind whipped along the room and buffeted Kairi, the force buckling her legs as she fell to the ground.

"They can use our magic, too!" Masaka yelled. She blocked her mimic's elbow strike, and then blocked its following knee strike. "You, on the other hand," she said calmly to the mimic while blocking a palm strike, "can't quite copy my magic, can you?"

She caught her mimic by the arm on its next swing and lifted the mimic off the ground in a single hand. "My magic is body magic. Unfortunately for you, you don't have bodies." The cloud of dust sifting along the mimic's arm let out an audible *crack* as Masaka's hand broke through the form.

Masaka's hand clenched all the way shut, tearing off the mimic's arm which in turn caused the mimic to fall back to the ground. She sent her own foot out in a roundhouse kick that obliterated the rest of the mimic. Another audible *crack* echoed as the mimic dematerialized.

Wasting no time, she whirled and caught the neck of Frisk's mimic which had been magically cloaked by her back. Once again, her hand ripped through the mimic and caused it to disappear completely.

"Whoa," Frisk said, his voice breathy from the initial surprise. "You really... killed that mimic."

"I've wanted to strangle you countless times," Masaka said. "But really, an enemy version of you would cause the most problems, so I felt it necessary to get rid of first."

Frisk made an unconvinced sound before disappearing himself, Masaka partly keeping track of him with her body magic while focusing the rest of her body magic on strengthening the Waymakers and also deciding which mimic to deal with next. She spotted Lenard desperately throwing punches at his corresponding mimic and approached him.

Lenard's left fist flew out and seemingly disappeared altogether when the mimic lifted its hands and held out something that looked like a bag. "It's countering all of my moves!" he said desperately as Masaka neared. He withdrew his arm, his fist reappearing.

"You have no moves," Masaka said.

"What do you call *this* then?" He attempted to do a front kick but the mimic lowered its hands and his foot disappeared into the mimic's bag.

"It's trapping your limbs in a separate space, mimicking your containment magic," she said. While the mimic continued to hold Lenard's foot in its own makeshift bag, she swept its legs out from underneath it.

The mimic fell, it also tugging Lenard to the ground whose foot remained stuck in a different space.

"Remove your foot, otherwise when I kill it its magic will remove it for you." Masaka raised her leg and waited a beat before bringing her own foot down in an axe kick.

Lenard yelped and tucked his legs close to his body, his foot reappearing just as Masaka destroyed the mimic.

The initial din of the fight had waned somewhat as most of the Waymakers had dealt with their respective mimics and had similarly moved on to help others take down the rest.

Masaka nodded to herself and ceased the magic she was expending to support the others as the final mimics *cracked* and disappeared into nothing. "Regroup and prepare to move into the next room," she called.

"Hold on!" Perish half-sang and half-called. She moved between the others and stopped short of the guild leader. "*Why* is there a dungeon in the Cursed Lands? This place is meant to be remote and unknown!"

Masaka thought for a moment and shrugged. "I guess the obvious reason is there were people who were here once, and now they're not."

"You mean a past civilization?"

"Maybe," Masaka said and shrugged again. "Maybe they died out. Maybe they moved north to the known country and this place was forgotten about."

"Hold on," Kairi said, swiping down wrinkles in her shirt and pants left from the rough winds she'd fought. "There was that thing written on the entrance. It addressed people entering and said they'd learn something that was lost in time, or something."

"Right. That's the thing, if this place was forgotten about, then who retained the knowledge of it being here and it being forgotten to be able to write that message for us?"

Kairi shook her head. "Are you saying people who built this place, or at least know about it, are alive?"

Masaka also shook her head. "I doubt it. Those who create dungeons may make them secret as a means of hiding whatever treasure they want to stay hidden, but the message in the entryway literally welcomed us. Whoever made this dungeon would've not exactly kept it secret."

"They still could've," Kairi said, though her words were slow with doubt.

"It would've been a hard secret to keep, even then. Maybe it's a testament to how unconquerable this dungeon is and everyone who discovered it died."

"But... did Lumi know this was here?"

The Waymakers shifted uneasily. Dulon cleared his throat. "If that's the case, we should find Lumi fast."

"Catch your breaths for a moment longer," Masaka said. "It's good to think this place over before rushing further in. I don't think it would remain secret as those who spread the rumors about the Cursed Lands would surely have told people a dungeon of all things was here. Guilds pay exorbitantly for information on dungeons, especially for a discovery of one."

"So what does any of it mean?" Kairi asked. "If no one is alive who knows about it—except for us and hopefully Lumi right now—who would have written the message on the entrance?"

"Those who made it," Masaka said cryptically.

Perish groaned. "But you said those who made it wouldn't be alive, so they couldn't know whatever secrets or 'wonders' here would be forgotten to have written that message."

Bartol brushed past the other Waymakers to stand beside Masaka. "You've been hinting at something since we first started our journey." He pointed one of his pinky fingers at her and narrowed his eyes. "Before we entered the Remote Expanse, I asked you how it was any different than a dungeon given it was said to have magical creatures and territory. You said dungeons are made by men. Then after we fell down here you suggested this place wasn't manmade. So who, do *you* think, made this place?"

Masaka hesitated, glancing down at her clothes. "I guess I chose the right outfit," she commented.

The Waymakers stared at her.

"Huh?"

"What?"

"I thought you put random clothes on because you wanted to, like that dumb horse mask."

Masaka tutted, then waved a hand to silence them. "I mean they're fitting, for what I'm about to say. My theory about this place? It's partly manmade, and partly not."

"Well, then, what's responsible for the other part?"

"Ahem." Masaka clasped her hands in front of her and straightened her posture. "Perish, back me up here." She then started to sing a pitchy cadence that vaguely resembled the unaccompanied sacred songs in churches.

Perish looked around her, then folded her arms and kept quiet.

Masaka let a final low note hang in the air before saying, "You didn't back me up!"

"Nope," Perish agreed.

"What the hell was that?" Dulon asked gruffly.

Bartol alone chortled.

Masaka cleared her throat. "Guess I won't do that again. What I'm saying is the opposite—it was divine intervention!"

The Waymakers fell silent as they processed what she meant.

"Gods?" Kairi stated. "Gods made this place?"

"Maybe," Masaka said, suddenly casual again. "I hardly believed in them before, so what do I know? Now, are you all ready to continue on?"

"Pffft," Dulon muttered, moving to the next door. He opened it and a blast of warm, salty vapor engulfed him. He braced himself against the sudden breeze and held a hand over his face to protect his eyes.

Alongside the changed atmosphere that rushed over the rest of those waiting in the mimic room came a cacophony of waterfalls. The rugged breeze relented somewhat and Dulon took several steps into the next room before stopping and letting his hand drop to his side.

Masaka moved through the door and slowly paced around him to take in the next room. It could hardly be called a room. The space was vast, and if not for the continuing orange glow of the walls that stretched wide, low, and far she wouldn't have believed it was inside or underground.

The rest of the Waymakers stepped onto the landing just past the door. Imperial stone stairs branched to their right and left while a banister at the edge of the platform cordoned off a stark plunge into an abyss. Intersecting pathways of the same smooth stonework wove in an orderly manner across the massive underground area. It was hardly a room, nor area. It was a domain—no, a region. A wide, open-air region.

Masaka gaped at the varying heights of the architecture that navigated a multitude of waterfalls that came from seemingly nowhere, or at least unknown or impossible to see places above. Their platform was nearer the ceiling, as the stairs largely descended throughout the vast space. The waterfalls fell continuously on standalone columns of some kind. The columns were discrete, cropping up from the faraway abyss between the stairs, bridges, and platforms. They were pounded relentlessly by water, yet somehow had not eroded even an inch. The columns' tops were squared off, almost like platforms of their own. A salty spray wafted outward from where the water collided, gradually dissipating around the room.

"This is like the 10<sup>th</sup> floor of Narumont's dungeon," Dulon murmured. "Only bigger. And not really like that at all."

## Chapter 33: The Way is Made

"How is this anything like a forge?" Perish grumbled. She rubbed her arms as if to prevent the vapor damaging the sleeves of her dress.

"It's warm at least," Masaka said. "And the walls are hot, as Frisk discovered." She continued appraising the vast area, taking note of how the waterfalls striking the various columns somewhat resembled hammers striking anvils. She rubbed her eyes and felt the magic within her gather to them. Her vision sharpened as she scrutinized the faraway architecture along the edges of the area. "There don't seem to be any other doors leading out of here," she said slowly. Her eyes caught movement along one of the bridges. She smiled. "I found Lumi."

The Waymakers gathered to the banister and looked in the direction she pointed. Knowing it would be impossible for them to actually see Lumi from that distance, Masaka turned and said, "Follow me." She took the right stairway down, her eyes already picking out the quickest route to where the young knight was headed along the elevated labyrinthine walkways. As she descended loud slams briefly interrupted the steady flowing of the nearby waterfalls. She kept her focus on not slipping on the slick steps while glancing at sudden strong currents in an adjacent waterfall that caused another slam when it impacted the column.

Spray wavered in the air before coalescing into the form of another mimic. A few others floated through the air away from the waterfalls and columns in the direction of the Waymakers.

"More mimics!" she called and hurried her pace down the steps. She made it to the next level's platform that branched out into two bridges crossing a sizable distance toward the far wall and the right wall. Many more bridges connected along the way, and some led to stairs that either descended further or ascended to the top level they had just been on.

A slew of more water slamming the nearby pillars caught her attention and she noticed that each slam was timed with when a Waymaker crossed by a waterfall. Each slam sent out more sprays of water that formed into yet more wraiths.

*They look like they're coming from the waterfalls. Each one we pass by will likely create more.* She moved ahead down the bridge approaching the faraway right wall, noting that while there was another mob of mimics matching their number of Waymakers, they weren't all humanoid and moved through the air not very quickly.

"Where are they coming from?" Dulon asked.

As they passed by another nearby waterfall two more slams echoed and a pair of wraiths in the form of reasonably-sized chameleon-shaped mimics crawled through the air toward them.

Masaka halted herself and pummeled both chameleons as their translucent forms surged at her. They dissipated in another spray of vapor. "Everyone!" she yelled. "Split up and pace yourselves! No more than three people per path! If we all go the same way at once we'll have mobs overwhelm us!"

"Where are they coming from!?" Perish both sang and shouted as she touched down on the platform and split off to head down the bridge approaching the faraway opposite wall.

"They're being created by the waterfalls! It's the forge, apparently!" Masaka picked up into a light jog as Dulon followed behind her, who in turn was followed by

Frisk. The subsequent mimic that formed once Frisk passed the previous waterfall took the shape of a house-sized guppy.

"How are the waterfalls creating them?" Dulon asked. He shouted as the massive fish swam and rammed into him. He took the blow in stride, grabbing the guppy's pointed snout in both hands and letting Masaka use her body magic to strengthen herself and deliver a killing blow.

The guppy splattered into water that drenched them all. "They must respond to our presence," Masaka said. She turned and beckoned the two to continue while holding up a hand for the others further down the path to have them pause. "Don't rush!" she called back, then said to Dulon and Frisk, "We'll take three at a time. The water or columns or both must have some sort of magic that's creating them. But I don't know how they can create something autonomous."

They approached the next waterfall that fell very close to the banister of a joint bridge. Masaka dismissed the path, continuing on the bridge running toward the right wall that was still something like a mirage in the distance.

The waterfall didn't emit resounding crashes this time.

"It seems there's a certain perimeter around the columns that can trigger it," Masaka said as they neared another column that was closer and adjacent to the path they jogged along.

This waterfall churned out a trio of crashes as they passed by. The vapor solidified into three distinct forms that raced through the air, encircling them. The mimics were three horses, their hooved legs rising and falling in succession as they ran.

One mimic let out a very loud neigh. Two pinpricks on its face where its eyes would be sparked and lightning shot out.

Masaka sidestepped the bolt that cracked into the floor of the bridge. She gaped as the debris from the impact reassembled itself into a smooth surface. She gritted her teeth and focused on the horses circling them, their hooves continuing to touch on an invisible ground as well as the bridge ahead and behind them. "This place is wild."

The other horses' eyes glowed and more lightning struck the bridge.

"Ow!" Frisk cried as an electric current happened to zigzag between droplets along the bridge and his bare shin.

"Get behind me!" Dulon put himself in front of the boy as another lightning bolt singed the air and hit his stomach. He grunted, but remained standing. "They're keeping their distance," he growled, making himself as wide a target as possible to block any other lightning.

"My reach is only as far as my body," Masaka replied, taking a similar defensive stance on the other side. She felt Frisk's magic spring to life and sensed him invisibly move out from between them and ahead of her to the spot on the bridge the horse mimics ran across every time they circled back.

A quiet hiss of metal sounded above the ever-pounding water of the waterfalls. Then a horse cried out as it passed the bridge, its front and left leg dissipating into water that fell away. The rest of the horse shortly dissipated. The other two wraiths, unaware, followed their same path in a circle to also then have their legs cut off. Frisk reappeared, his sword in hand.

"Good work, Frisk," Masaka said. Before she went to move on, she peered closely at the nearby column that had created the three mimics. She noticed similar etchings of words like the message on the door leading into the dungeon. "*Behold, here, the curses They forge unto Their world.*"

"Who's 'they'?" Frisk asked.

"Who cares?" Dulon replied, pointing ahead. "There's a stairway close to the end of the bridge that'll take us down to a lower level. It runs far and doesn't pass by many waterfalls."

Masaka shook her head and followed them. A final waterfall along their bridge posed the last challenge, but they dispatched the three created bird-mimics with ease. Many more minutes passed as they finally approached the right wall that loomed ahead. She hesitated at the top of the stairs while the other two continued down, noting more etchings in a dark spot that appeared to be metal implanted in the wall right above where the bridge ran to a dead end. "*They called them curses, but what was a curse they later called magic.*" She frowned at the letters holding a more refined penmanship than the writing on the column.

"Come on!" Dulon called to her.

She turned and descended the steps. These stairs took them two levels down. She jogged behind Dulon and Frisk while observing other Waymakers scattered along platforms and bridges some distance away on various other levels. She let out a sigh of relief knowing they were holding their own, for now.

"Here comes another!" Dulon said as they approached the nearer of the two columns adjacent to their bridge. They passed it, and the water surged in the telltale three crashes.

A bird, a fish, and a lizard of normal sizes sprang forth and attacked. Masaka let her magic flow into the bodies of Dulon and Frisk, strengthening their muscles. While she let them punch and swing at the mimics, she read yet more etchings in the column. "*Behold, here, the curses They forge unto Their world.*"

"It's the same thing!" Dulon remarked after the three mimics dispersed into vapor and then nothing.

"Is it a riddle?" Frisk asked.

"It's a lesson," Masaka said. She inhaled slowly, gathering the magic within her to fill her lungs. Then, she bellowed: "WAYMAKERS! READ THE WRITING ON THE COLUMNS YOU CROSS!"

Dulon and Frisk clutched their ears as her voice carried harshly above the crashes of the waterfalls and far across the expanse.

"All right, let's go on," she said, taking the lead. She spotted Lumi still in the distance but getting closer; her form turned in their direction after having heard her shouting. Another several minutes later they crossed the second waterfall and defeated a trio of fruit-sized ants. She read aloud the writing on the column, "*From none living, living They forge.*"

"That's different, but I still don't care," Dulon said.

Masaka kept quiet as they continued on. When their bridge forked, they took the left path heading back away from the right wall. She glanced up at a bridge crossing ahead and overhead. Lumi was following it and would be crossing their path shortly. No other waterfalls or columns lay adjacent their path.

She picked up into a sprint. She made good time, much faster than Dulon and Frisk due to having not fed them her magic. She skidded to a halt underneath Lumi's bridge and cupped her hands over her mouth. "Lumi! Jump down here!"

Lumi, wearing her full knight armor of chainmail and heaume, looked down. Her face was hidden behind the metal helm, but Masaka could hear the incredulity in her voice as she shouted back, "No! I'm not jumping that distance! And why are you all here?"

"I'll catch you!" Masaka called, beckoning invitingly.

"No!"

Masaka bent down, feeling her magic surge into her legs and feet, then jumped high. Her head just leveled out with the upper bridge. Her hands shot out and caught the banister, and she pulled herself onto the bridge beside Lumi. "Did you forget what I could do when I fought Fox?"

"No," Lumi's muffled voice said more calmly.

"Good. Then let's go." Masaka swept Lumi's legs out from under her with an arm, putting the girl in a bridal hold. Ignoring Lumi's spluttering defiance, she leapt back over the banister to fall onto the lower bridge in front of Dulon and Frisk. Her feet landed firmly and hard, her legs taking and dispersing the impact.

"Holy—!" Lumi pulled herself out of Masaka's hold and took off her heaume, her hair in disarray and red headband encircling her neck. "Why are you all here?" she asked again.

"Because we wanted to be here," Masaka said. "You're here. We can talk all about the state of Narumont and Salama later, but first we should leave."

Lumi backed away, shaking her head. "I'm not going back yet. They'll kill me if I do."

"We know," Dulon growled.

Lumi's hand instinctively reached for the slim sword at her hip.

Frisk raised his own sword defensively.

"We're not here to fight you," Masaka said. "And we don't have to go back to the city. But… do you really want to stay here?"

"I don't *want* to stay here," Lumi said angrily. "But you've realized this is a dungeon, right?"

Masaka glanced around at the various scattered waterfalls and pathways then back at her and nodded.

"This being here and no one knowing about it is odd enough. I've not been in dungeons before, but they're meant to have treasure. Right?"

Masaka looked at Dulon and Frisk. "Yes, they're typically built to store precious things. I didn't take you for a treasure hunter. But you didn't know about this place?" When Lumi shook her head she asked, "Are you here because you think there'll be something that will help protect you?"

"Maybe." Lumi looked around, eyeing the other Waymakers still heading along the various paths and fighting wraiths. "If there is any treasure, I do know where it'll be."

Masaka's body straightened, her mood shifting. "Oh? You do know about this place?"

Lumi shrugged, then pointed. Masaka turned and followed the invisible line between Lumi's finger and what seemed to be the center of the massive airway labyrinth. There, a lone column larger than the others and rising only up to the lowest level of the paths was buffeted by several smaller waterfalls. A single path among the multitude of intersecting bridges met the column.

"There?" Masaka mused. "I don't see any passage to a lower floor or anything between the waterfalls or in the column."

"As far as I know, this is the entirety of the dungeon," Lumi said. "It's all this room."

Masaka slowly looked at Lumi. "Well, I'm not really sure about there being treasure. Going by how all these waterfalls react to us, getting close to that column would spring a bunch more wraiths."

"I've read several of the columns already," Lumi said. "The writing seems to refer to gods. And what the columns make are 'curses,' or the magic of gods."

"I knew it was divine intervention," Masaka murmured proudly. "But, that's something. Actual evidence of gods, I mean."

"Why are you so smug when you didn't believe in them in the first place?" Dulon asked.

"It means I have something other than myself to blame for my hardships," Masaka said. "Anyway, a plaque on a wall said 'curses' are actually magic. If this place is really where magic from gods is, why call it a curse?"

"The writing on the columns is different from the writing on the walls," Lumi said. "Someone different wrote each. The writing on the columns always refers to 'They' or 'Them,' which I think is referring to gods. The writing on the columns always refers to some other 'they' or 'them' and isn't capitalizing the words. The wall-writing also is more clean as if written more recently and by someone with more knowledge."

"Someone," Masaka offered, "like a god?"

"Maybe. At least, if the writing on the columns is referring to gods, the writing on the walls that is somewhat in response to the other writing would make sense to come from gods."

They stood in relative silence as they thought it over. Frisk said, "Before we regroup with the others, I'd like it known that I still don't believe in gods."

"It *is* a leap to believe," Masaka agreed. "Magic is inexplicable, but it's something most of us have. Who's to say this place isn't the design of other people with extraordinary magic, or maybe the land itself having magic?"

Dulon huffed. "So you don't believe in gods?"

"Well…" She glanced at Lumi, then at the large column in the center of the massive area. "No magic I know can create such creatures. The writing referred to them as alive. Are they?"

Lumi shook her head. "I don't know." Her face paled and her body became taut as some thought hit her. "I noticed the wraith-like things become more defined the longer I was unable to defeat them. They were losing their translucence and kept more to the bridges. Could it be possible this forge creates life?"

"Okay," Masaka said, nodding. "Okay. Whoa."

"What?" Frisk asked. "Wait, seriously? This place creates life?"

"And it's called The Forge of Curses?" Dulon added. "And it's in a place called The Cursed Lands, within a place called The Remote Expanse? Why would life be cursed, and why would a place life is made be mostly barren and uninhabited?"

"Maybe magic was a foreign concept to whoever built this place," Masaka said. "And maybe life created by unnatural means, like magic, would be considered cursed.

A column did say, '*From none living, living They forge.*' Life that comes from other life is natural, but here…"

Dulon shrugged. "If gods are real, wouldn't it be moot since all life would then be attributed to gods?"

"That would, again, mean that maybe magic was a foreign concept to the… past civilization that built this place. I can hardly fault them. I mean, if taking a stroll through here creates random life just like that, this place could cause chaos."

"Plus everything created here attacks you," Lumi said.

"Mmmm. So, what would be the benefit of going to the largest column here that creates life?" Her eyes bore into Lumi's, forcing the knight to look away.

"I…"

Understanding washed across Dulon's face, followed by sorrow. "Ah."

Frisk looked at them all. "What?"

Masaka considered the girl with a look of sympathy. "You want to see if this place can resurrect Simon."

The knight remained quiet. Nearby, Waymakers on the same level but on a parallel bridge called to them.

"We found her, so what do we do now?"

A rumbling shook the entire area for a brief moment. Masaka looked up, her eyes widening. Before she could so much as blink, a wave of water reaching from one corner of wall and ceiling to another fell. It engulfed everything and everyone, sending them tumbling off their bridges, stairs, or platforms.

Wherever she looked there were no pockets of air, the water unyielding and pulling her down. She could sense the others being dragged in a swirling motion, their bodies drawing closer to hers. A long shadow formed below her and a lone bridge came into view as she descended. She bumped into it, the water pressing down on her. She forced her head up to see that the water that filled the entire area was receding. The water level lowered as the other Waymakers moved clockwise in a whirlpool.

When the water level went by her and she could suck in another breath of air, she forced herself to her feet and gathered her bearings. Where the water had dropped them all off was the bridge leading to the large column near the bottom of the expansive area. Though, after the sudden downpour of water, none of the waterfalls had returned. It was silent.

Perish sat up and groaned as she began to wring out pockets of water in her dress.

Lumi dumped out the water from her heaume she had somehow kept hold of during the torrent.

Soon the other Waymakers were groaning themselves as they stood up. "Do we have to climb all the way back up now?" Kairi asked dejectedly.

Masaka sighed. "At least the waterfalls have stopped."

Lumi walked along the bridge toward the column.

Dulon snapped his fingers. "Hey, where are you going?"

Lumi waved a hand over her shoulder dismissively, looking up as she neared the large vacant column. It being so close to the floor of the whole area it looked more like a stout platform. There was a small space between the column and bridge. Lumi stepped over it and continued to the center of the column while looking up.

The Waymakers gave Masaka a myriad of looks. She shook her head and watched Lumi slowly pace across the flat column.

Lumi stared straight up and stopped when she reached the center of the column. Something touched the top of her head. She took a step back. She held out her hand, palm up. Several seconds went by. Then, another droplet bounced off her hand. More seconds went by. Then, another. Three seconds elapsed before the next. Then two seconds. Soon, the drops had turned into a trickle.

Lumi took more steps back, letting the trickle that slowly turned into a stream fall onto the column's surface. Her heels touched the edge of the column and she stopped.

The stream shifted into a cascade, and then a full-on waterfall. It splashed over her, but she didn't get off the column.

"Lumi, something is going to come out of there!" Masaka warned.

The waterfall emitted a series of harsh crashes. Another sudden wave, this time condensed to the column, fell and sent out a massive spray in all directions. With it, the waterfall ceased.

Lumi uncovered her face, having kept her footing.

Masaka also uncovered her face and looked past Lumi at a pool of water that remained condensed at the center of the column. It was roiling, not forming into any distinct shape or form.

The Waymakers readied themselves as they watched the pool of water slowly expand upward. Bubbles surged up and out from its center, causing it to emit little puffs of air when each reached its surface. Finally, the puddle took form and lost its translucency. The bubbles that popped all across its surface diminished. It stopped roiling.

The puddle's color turned from azure to a dark blue, then an unnatural pink, then red, then tan. Limbs extended outward. Four of them, humanoid. The distinct shape of a head cropped up along the puddle's top. Its features became more defined. It was definitely a person.

Masaka stepped forward to join Lumi on the edge of the column, then froze. She sensed something. All the other wraiths she'd fought before had no bodies, and so she couldn't fully sense them save for their magic. But...

This...

The puddle hardened, no longer wavering at all. The tan surface became more colored, more complex. Features continued to become defined along the body, short cropped strands of hair deepening into a brown. Nostrils and lips took shape. Ears, eyelashes, hands, feet, and nails.

The torso and legs of the form became uneven like a sheet of cloth gathering wrinkles. Then, distinct clothes covered the tannish body of the person. A quaint farmer's tunic and travel pants.

Lumi let out a gasp, taking a step forward. She took another step before stopping herself. "…Sim?"

The puddle-now-person taking on the resemblance of the water spirit and Simon opened its eyes and blinked.

"Is it a mimic of Simon?" Perish asked angrily, remaining on the bridge with the others. "Is this why this place is called cursed?"

"Sim?" Lumi asked again.

It blinked, its eyes unsteadily shifting from Perish to Lumi.

Masaka stepped beside Lumi, putting a hand on her shoulder.

Lumi glanced down at the guild master's hand, eyebrows lowering in question at how it trembled.

"Simon?"

He blinked, a slow smile lifting his mouth. "I made it."

## Chapter 34: Of Gods and Other

Doubt looked upon her fellow goddess that lay quietly on the translucent floor. The multicolored dust kissing Desire's invisible form moved slower than usual. "I had my doubts, but I didn't think they'd be actualized so soon." Doubt emitted a laugh like a fat crow. "Don't be so down."

Desire uttered something incomprehensible as she shifted onto her knees, head bent down and facing the endless darkness beyond the floor.

"At least don't be so down, literally," Doubt went on. "Or are you actually in pain?" She glanced down, following the other goddess's invisible gaze in the direction of the faraway world. "Simon is just one among many others who never got the chance to fulfill what he wanted. Not just many others, everyone, really—but that's beside the point, I guess. Sure, he was short-lived. But that's life."

"Leave me alone," Desire murmured quietly.

Doubt, for once, straightened her crooked back. She'd had her rivalry with the Goddess of Desire plenty of times. Every time she reveled in the other's rampant machinations being nipped in the bud by a cold dose of realism. Still, it was fleeting, more barmecide than anything. She more so longed for the other goddess to quash her hopes so that they wouldn't continuously be stampeded. She would never admit it, but she really wanted Desire to protect herself from such unnecessary pain.

Letting out more of a whimper than a coo, Doubt nodded, her form hunching back into the usual position. She turned and trepidatiously walked away.

The subtle sifting of dust picking up pricked her ears. Doubt turned, eyeing the other goddess's form that had visibly tensed up and drawn closer to the floor. Desire's head was face-to-face with the barrier separating their realm from the other. It wasn't the posture of despair or defeat. It was doubt.

Doubt fully turned at the outskirts of the other goddess's domain and watched uncertainly.

Flecks of dust speckled the floor underneath Desire's hands.

Doubt's mouth quirked downward. The dust wasn't on their side of the barrier. It was pattering from the living's realm. She unsteadily walked back toward Desire, watching the widely distributed dust from far off thin into a stream that then sifted against the barrier in the same way of an hourglass. "What is that?"

The stream of sand jerked as if magnetized to a different spot on the barrier. It moved from falling just beneath Desire's hands and began falling underneath Doubt's feet.

Doubt opened her mouth to repeat the question. "What—?"

All at once the dust permeated through the barrier and erupted around Doubt. A translucent fist caught the underside of Doubt's chin, causing the goddess's feet to lift off the floor and fall backward.

Doubt landed on her back, wide-eyed and clutching her jaw. Her bones creaked and cracked as she stood back up. Silently, she watched the boy who died stand up from a crouching position.

Simon unclenched his hand and looked down at it curiously. The dust that he had materialized from left to join up with the dust spiraling around Desire who was no longer lying down.

"I told you to leave me alone," Desire said, her voice grim yet regaining its pleasant hum.

"What is he doing here?" Doubt asked.

Simon turned to look at Desire. "What *am* I doing here?" He then turned back. "And who are you?"

Doubt cooed, her sardonic smile returning to her face as she held her jaw. "You punch what you don't know?"

"I just had the desire to punch you," Simon said, his feet shifting awkwardly. "Are you in pain?"

"Pain?" Doubt let go of her jaw. "There's a difference between shock and pain. Pain isn't a factor here, as that's for the living to suffer."

"The living?" Simon's face paled as memories returned to him. "I was stabbed! Am I no longer alive?"

"You're here with us, aren't you?" Doubt said.

"He shouldn't be here with us." The serious low voice was followed by the imposing and stern form of a man in a suit advancing on Desire. "What did you do?"

"Easy, Terminus," Desire said, her arms folded.

The God of Boundaries didn't let up, his bunched fists swaying as he swiftly approached her.

Simon felt a strange tugging sensation and he stepped into Terminus's path.

"Out of my—"

Simon's fist moved of its own accord. He struck Terminus in the chin and sent him sprawling onto his back just as Doubt had.

Simon reopened his hand and stared at it. "I'm not meaning to hit anyone, I—just somehow felt like it for a moment."

Terminus lifted his head off the floor, his pitch black eyes boring into Simon's. "Impudence." He unnaturally rose from the floor without pushing himself and lay a hand on Simon's shoulder. "Bend."

Simon's knees buckled as he felt an indomitable force course through his bones, causing him to kneel.

Terminus lightly hopped straight over Simon as if the boy were no more than a pothole and continued up to Desire. "You've gone too far, Desire."

Desire remained unmoving, the dust outlining her invisible crossed arms over her chest.

Terminus stuck a finger in her face. "What you've done to him is—"

"My business," Desire retorted. "You speak of impudence, yet both of you waltz into my domain whenever you like to lecture me."

"Meddling *directly* with the Living Realm is never our business! Him being here again as he is means you did something. What did you do?"

Desire's featureless face appeared to examine the finger he kept pointed at her. "I gave him just a fraction of myself."

"You *what*!?" Doubt and Terminus said simultaneously.

"Haven't you wondered what it's like?" Desire asked. "To live and feel pain? Joy? I have, so I figured why not try it?"

Terminus withdrew his finger and pinched the bridge of his nose. "Do I need to ask why you would go and do that?"

Desire laughed, the dust trickling over her momentarily outlining the semblance of a smile on her otherwise invisible face.

Terminus sighed. "You've gone too far," he repeated, then placed a hand on her shoulder. He froze, feeling a hand on his own shoulder and turned his head.

Simon was standing behind him, gripping the fabric of his suit jacket. Then he hoisted Terminus above his head and flung the god through the air in the direction of Doubt.

Doubt unsteadily stepped out of the way as Terminus crashed to the floor.

"What am I doing?" Simon asked uncertainly.

"What you want," Desire said. "Which is, to be alive again. This invisible floor beneath us, it's a barrier between what we humbly call our realm and the Living Realm. That man you just tossed happens to be the God of Boundaries, as in the one who created this barrier."

"I didn't know that," Simon said dumbly.

"Yes, but I did. That fraction of myself I lent to you is still with you, at least some of it. I'll be taking it back."

Simon took a step back. "What will happen to me?"

"Nothing," Desire said. "As Doubt said, pain is neither here nor there," she pointed at Terminus who again unnaturally got to his feet. "But it is there." Her finger dropped to point beneath their feet.

Simon shuddered as some dust detached from his skin and joined the flourishing breeze of it surrounding Desire. "So I'm not alive. And none of you are? Then what am I?"

"You just *are*," Terminus growled as he paced back to the two.

"Not gods like us," Doubt added creakily, "but you *are*."

Simon edged away from the stern suited god. "I don't exactly want to fight you…"

Terminus continued to approach. "Throw me twice…"

"A fight is no good here," Doubt agreed.

Desire regarded the other goddess with a tilted head, then addressed Terminus. "He just died, Terminus. Again. You can give him some slack."

"Pain is no factor here," Terminus breathed. "You just are. That doesn't mean there can be no consequences. I can make it so you are *not*."

The dust around Desire expanded furiously into a rising tornado. Her voice echoed serenely, yet fiercely. "You seem to have forgotten where you are, Terminus."

Terminus halted, holding out his hand palm out. The dust flurry spiraled without hitting him, warded off by an invisible square of space around his form.

Simon covered his eyes protectively, watching the gods face off. His feelings were conflicted, and he was uncertain if they were being influenced by the beings here who were apparently gods.

"Just a moment." A voice that belonged to none of the gods gathered there reverberated. The spiraling dust sprinkled down as if reacting to the sound waves, meekly returning to sift around Desire's form.

Simon looked at each of the gods curiously. Doubt was no longer smirking. Terminus's arm had dropped. Both of them shared a wide-eyed expression. Desire was motionless, her dust moving clockwise around her at a snail's pace.

"I'm interested in fights, particularly between you two."

Simon blinked and suddenly a tall, blond-haired man had appeared, resting his head in the crook of Desire's left shoulder and neck as he looked at Terminus. The man, the one who apparently had spoken, wore tan shorts and a shirt.

"Before that, let's figure out what to do with this Simon."

"Another god?" Simon asked himself quietly.

"Name's Ohn. Nice to meet you." Ohn lifted his head, faced Simon, and winked. The man instantaneously stood beside the boy, patting him on the head. "I decide what is and what isn't. I'm fine explaining more if you'd like, but whatever happens here should you return to the Living Realm or find the end of your existence, you will forget."

"I—well—" Simon stuttered, noting the submissive behavior of the other gods as he thought over the vast implications of a power that determined… existence from nonexistence. "Do gods have a hierarchy?"

Ohn laughed. "Why, of course! Surely you know that much with the way you tossed around old Terminus here with just a fraction of Desire's power."

Simon swallowed, then nodded. "I… guess. So Desire is a more powerful god than the god of boundaries?"

"Largely, yes," Ohn agreed. "As paradoxical as it is, some things are bound only by themselves. And hierarchies can change and be more complex than simply 'more' or 'less,' 'better' or 'worse.' For me, they simply are what they are, as I deem them! Haha!" His laugh more faintly echoed as he reappeared beside Doubt to lean an elbow casually on her shoulder. "You didn't live long enough to learn of infinite regress, but all you really need to know to understand is that every thing depends on another thing. As one human put it, it's turtles all the way down, baby! Or up, if you're looking at the higher order."

Simon again shifted his feet awkwardly. "O…kay."

"Ohn…" Terminus said slowly.

"You'll get your fight!" Ohn assured him, now standing in front of the suited god and straightening his button-up shirt. "Since this is Desire's domain and she's the one graciously giving us direction for our feelings, I'll let her decide what to do with Simon." He turned, a hint of seriousness slightly dimming the remaining smile on his face as he eyed Desire.

Desire mimicked Simon's shifting, then refolded her arms. "I think Simon should decide."

Simon hesitated. "Well…" He looked at Desire. *Could I ask to go back to my former life?* "Is… my family all right?"

There was a moment where Desire didn't move and all there was was the quiet shifting of sand. "Your mother and brother on Earth, after you died. They mourn, but they are also at peace." Dust sparkled another outline of an upturned mouth on her face. "And so is Bear."

"A nice, caring kid," Ohn mused. "Tell you what, if you want to live again I'll spare you some memories of here! Existential ponderings, my treat."

Nodding, Simon knew what he wanted. "I want the same thing. As the previous time, I mean. I want to live again. But," he rushed to say, "not starting out as a baby. I still want to be me, as I was. A Waymaker."

Ohn clapped his hands. "So it is!"

Simon could only let out a short cry as he crashed back through the floor.

## Chapter 35: Pond Theory

Simon looked at the Waymakers staring at him worriedly. He then looked up and around at the labyrinth of elevated bridges and stairs intersecting everywhere. Far off in every direction were mesmerizing red-orange-yellow lights wavering along what seemed to be walls. "Is this underground? Where am I?"

"Simon?" Masaka asked for a third time, her hand gripping Lumi's plated shoulder and holding her back.

"Yes, I'm Simon," Simon said as he turned in a circle to confirm the walls weren't really moving and were in fact glowing. "And you're Masaka, and Lumi, and... why are you all gathered here? Were you expecting me?"

Masaka shared a look with the other Waymakers while Lumi continued trying to push forward.

"Are you really Simon, or another curse?" Dulon asked.

"Curse?" Simon lowered his eyelids at the man. "Another one? What are you talking about?"

"*If* you're Simon," Perish said, stepping off the near bridge where the other Waymakers waited and on to the strange circular platform Simon was in the center of, "what's my favorite color?"

"Uh." Simon's eyes screwed up. "How should I know? You never told me." His eyes widened at Frisk appearing in front of him, holding a sword ready to strike. "Frisk? You still have your sword?"

Frisk lowered his poised arm, his mouth open. "You know I'm always losing one!"

Simon looked at the others slowly. "Yes. I also already demonstrated I know your names. So do you still think I'm a curse or whatever?"

Masaka let go of Lumi to cover her face. Lumi rushed forward and hugged Simon firmly.

Simon felt the cool, hard metal of the mail outfit she wore dig into him. He tried to push her away but couldn't due to the girl's strength. "Um. Hi, Lumi. I know I died shortly, but—" He cut himself off when Lumi pulled away sharply to look at him, her eyes wild.

"Shortly? You've been dead for weeks!"

"Weeks!?" Simon was about to ask more before Masaka clapped her hands loudly.

"Let's catch each other up on the way out of this place. It's eerie without the waterfalls running." She turned and gestured for the Waymakers still on the bridge to turn and start moving.

Lumi let go of Simon quickly, her eyes darting around as she brushed off residual water droplets from her armor. "I'd like to ask you where your sense of time came from while... well, dead, but we can start explaining where this is." Lumi walked beside Simon at the tail-end of the Waymakers as they made their way up a series of paths that progressively took them to higher levels, filling him in on the Forge of Curses and the trials along the way. Perish and Masaka explained further about their own experiences and reasons for pursuing Lumi there, along with all the events following Simon's supposed death at Salama's hands. Frisk added some unnecessary details of how his toilet in the guild worked inconsistently.

"Interesting," Simon said finally, thinking over all the information. "I appreciate all of you willing to kill for me. And you apparently actually killing someone for me."

Lumi smiled with mild embarrassment.

"But it's hard to believe Narumont is at war with Salama… *and* the king was killed, because of me."

"That part doesn't have anything to do with you," Masaka said. "We don't actually know what Avril was thinking when she killed Dormond. But, upstarts like her and Lumi would be welcome in our guild if they're unwelcome everywhere else."

"*That's* hard to believe," Perish said incredulously, repeating Simon's words. "You've been resurrected and *that's* hard to believe. We saw your body carried off by your parents, you know."

Simon nodded, seeing her point. "Ah. Huh. I hope they buried me, otherwise they'd freak out about my body being gone…"

"Okay," Lumi said impatiently, "tell us about all that, then. You materialized here out of water, a 'curse' created by gods that somehow built this place. How *are* you alive?"

Simon recalled the interaction with Ohn and the other gods of other distinct concepts. "I think it's pretty much what you already know. Gods returned me here after I died."

The three stared at him. "Gods," Lumi said. "You saw them? Like, actual gods?"

"From what I remember," he said. "They were like people, except one who was invisible and outlined in dust."

"Dust?" Masaka questioned.

"What they looked like isn't important," Simon continued. "They went by names. One was called Terminus. Another was called Doubt. And another was Desire. And also Ohn. The last one was the one who sent me back here."

"Gods, plural," Perish said thoughtfully. "And one named Desire. That has to be the Goddess of Desire, Goddess Toive, that Narumont worships."

"I've never heard of the others," Masaka said.

"Isn't this kind of crazy?" Frisk asked. "If gods are real, what does that mean for us?"

Simon's mouth quirked up as he started up another flight of stairs. "Existential ponderings…"

"What was that?"

Simon dropped the smile. "Uh. Well, I don't think it means as much as you think."

Lumi frowned. "What does *that* mean?"

"I mean, knowing about gods doesn't change anything… Right?"

Masaka nodded. "Correct, young one."

It was Simon's turn to frown. "Young one?"

"You were virtually reborn, so technically you're less than a day old now. I can call you 'kid' again."

"Please don't."

Smirking, she nodded again. "Simon is correct. Knowing things differently doesn't change things as they are. Things simply continue as they are, the only difference being our better knowing of them."

"There's also a theory," Simon said. He felt stupid bringing up an idea he knew little about, but it being a concept in his first life and not this second—or third—life meant it could be new to them. "A philosophical one, about existence." They reached the top of the stairs and turned down a bridge that brought them closer to a massive glowing wall. Still a couple levels up was a door. "One of the gods referenced it. 'Turtles all the way down.' It's an idea for what upholds the world. If something supports the world, something else has to support that thing, and that thing has to be supported by another thing, and so on. So, the world could be supported on the back of a turtle, which would be on top of a bunch of turtles. It doesn't have to be turtles, the theory just poses the idea ridiculously like that."

"A philosophical theory?" Perish mused. "That's interesting. I never heard of such a theory when I went to Verlangen."

"Really? I guess it must've been something the gods put in my head. I can't really remember where it came from." Simon shrugged, internally restraining the impulse to mention a completely different world where he lived a completely different life. *I'm not totally lying.*

"Infinite turtles," Masaka said. "Very interesting. I don't know if the gods are truthful or a bunch of quacks."

"They could be both!" Frisk said.

"It's not a good idea to badmouth gods," Lumi said. "Whether or not you believe they're real."

"Simon inexplicably being alive and here is enough for me to believe in them," Masaka replied.

"Magic was enough for me to believe in them," Lumi said.

"So they're real," Frisk continued, "and so insulting them is bad. That means *something* for us."

Simon considered it. "I don't think so, really. I guess it can affect how you'll live your life, but is that really gonna be different?"

"We can hold morning and evening prayers," Perish said jokingly.

"Ohn sort of hinted at the hierarchy of gods, other than the turtle thing. It sounds more or less like how it is here, there being people of different professions, classes, and strengths."

The others considered Simon quietly as they made it to the next level in the elevated labyrinth.

"There's that saying about being a big fish in a small pond. It's like we're in a pond, and the gods are in a lake or ocean. And maybe their ocean is just another pond relative to a larger ocean."

"Whatever the pool, you can only do what you can do when you can do it. That's about enough philosophizing for me for the rest of my life," Masaka said with a yawn. "Now that you're alive again and we sort of get why, let's strategize what to do next."

Simon was suddenly caught in the fluffs of Perish's dress when she hugged him. "Well... I need to see my parents," Simon said slowly after Perish let go. He continued walking, feeling his cheeks heat up.

"Right, gotta give them time to freak out and everything. Will you be coming back to Narumont?"

Simon frowned. "What do you mean?"

Masaka looked at him seriously. "Do you want to return to Narumont?"

"Of course I—"

"You first set off to see if you could use magic," Masaka interrupted. "Which you can. You also wanted to learn enough to be able to use magic effectively. Which you can. Do you really want to go back to Narumont when you've already accomplished your goal?"

Simon was at a loss for words. Sure, he wanted what she said he had, and getting that would more than suffice the rest of his life. *I could return home and live a good life. But*... But he remembered the anger of having his life cut short. Not just once, but twice. *Both times, somebody was responsible. I won't get the chance to take it out on them myself. But*... He then realized what she was doing. "Do you really think I'm not greedier than that?" he asked with annoyance. "If you're trying to protect me by sending me off before the war, forget it."

She smirked, then shrugged. "As long as you know the drawbacks of what you want. War is serious, and your life isn't something that can be refunded."

"Of course I know that," Simon muttered, though half-wondered if he would start to believe he could come back yet again if he died. "Is there a way to stop the war before it happens?"

Masaka sighed. "I doubt it. Salama will be even more furious to find out you're alive after Lumi's revenge kill."

"I don't know anything about the history between the cities," Simon said. "If the war is unstoppable, what would end the war after it's started?"

"Two obvious options," Masaka said, raising both her pointer fingers as they began climbing the last flight of stairs to the level with the door leading out of the labyrinth. "Narumont wins and becomes sovereign of the two cities, or Salama wins and becomes sovereign of the two cities. The manner of how either is sovereign would vary, but we can more or less assume what authority Salama would enforce on Narumont."

"What's that?" Simon asked.

"The same authority and reason Valen had when he killed you. Devout loyalty to the god they respect, forsaking anything else."

Simon considered how such restrictive beliefs played out on Earth as well as how they would mesh with the Waymaker Guild's way of life. "Which god do they worship, by the way?"

"I never bothered to know," Masaka said dryly.

"God Rajaa," Perish supplied.

"Mmm."

"Hold on," Simon said when they reached the last level. "Goddess Toive goes by Desire, what's the other name for Rajaa?"

"That would be Terminus," Perish said.

Simon froze. The others noticed and stopped walking while the rest of the Waymakers continued ahead. "Those two? Could their actions in… heaven or wherever also affect us?"

"What do you mean?" Masaka asked, stepping closer.

"When I was with them, I sort of pissed off Terminus. He and Desire also seemed at odds and were going to fight."

"Could be coincidence," Masaka said breezily, walking on. "Based off what you said, they can't—or at least, they aren't supposed to directly be involved with our little pond."

"Still…" Simon moved to follow, shortly accompanied by the others. "People or the world could be influenced by the gods. If so, Salama wouldn't want to just win but possibly also kill everyone. With me being public enemy number one."

"I think I still hold that title," Lumi said.

Masaka grinned. "Then that's another possibility. Salama wins and kills everyone, especially you two. All the more reason you might want to avoid this war."

"If I do and they win, then what? They could be emboldened to go and strongarm and terrorize smaller towns like my own, and I'd end up getting killed anyway. I didn't come back twice to be meek."

"Spoken like a true Waymaker," Masaka said. She tilted her head and eyed him up and down. "Twice?"

Simon blinked. "Oops."

# Chapter 36: Recoup

"I'm going to be okay," Simon said, backing out the door. He felt the coolness of the outside air replace the toasty atmosphere set by the hearth within his home.

His father put a hand on his mother's shoulder, stilling her protest. "He's alive," he murmured in her ear.

"Yes, but—letting him go again so quickly is just—"

"That's what children do," his voice said soothingly. "They grow up and leave, but they do come back eventually."

"Not from death—!"

Simon suppressed a smile and eased the door half-closed. "I won't die again," he said. "Not for a long time, anyway."

His father smiled in return and surreptitiously waved him off behind his mother's back.

Closing the door, Simon shivered and trekked away from the farmhouse to the trio of horses grazing beside Perish and Lumi.

"They took it well?" Perish asked when he came within speaking distance.

"Well enough, same as you more or less." Simon unfettered the reins to loosen his horse. Hoisting himself up and atop the horse, he looked back at the warmly lit home. "I would've liked to stay until morning. Just to assure them I wasn't a ghost or something."

"They won't come after you? They know the war that's going on?"

"They heard about it a week after that hearing you both attended." Simon tore his gaze from the house and fixed it on the nearby road stretching out before them. Lumi and Perish got on their horses and together they started to ride. As the steady chill of the air washed over them he said, "I wish I'd been there to see it. Kind of like seeing how people would act at your own funeral. Seeing the people of Salama upset would've also been fun." The road curved around an incline, the raised land belonging to oat crops that were still green. On the other side of the road was a wide expanse of barley also too young to be harvested. He noticed Lumi shiver and shift to lean down and be more protected by her horse's head from the headwind.

"There's already been so much talk about death and we haven't heard any news of how the war is going yet," Lumi said. "I'm kind of sick of it already."

"Strange, coming from a knight," Perish commented. "A knight who killed a Numen. But, you are still young."

Simon hadn't given it much thought until then, how she was around his age and had actually killed someone. *An* important *someone.* "Would you have killed Valen if you knew I'd come back to life?"

Lumi remained silent, her face staring straight ahead. After some time in which Simon began to believe she hadn't heard him she answered. "Yes, I would have."

Simon nodded, mainly to himself since the constant up-and-down shifting as the horses trotted masked most movement. He was happy by her response, but also confused about her answer as well as his own question. "Why?"

Her eyes glinted in the moonlight when she looked at him. "Because your life means something."

"Oh. Right." He felt his face redden as thoughts of how stupid he was for not knowing something as obvious as that raced through his head.

"Also, I don't know if you realized it yet, but I'm just as devoted to Goddess Toive as Salama is to Rajaa. Not enough to murder a heretic on the spot, mind you. But anyone tarnishing what has been blessed by the Goddess would cross my blade eventually."

Simon let her words sink in. *What has been blessed by Toive…* "Oh, that's why! *I* have been blessed with a water affinity. So to you, I'm something sacred."

Perish let out an audible groan over the horses' hooves clomping the packed ground and Simon gave her a confused look.

"I don't think you're sacred!" Lumi protested.

Simon's head snapped to the other side to give the girl a different confused look. The sharpness in her voice surprised him. "Huh?"

"Well, not *just* sacred," Lumi mumbled.

Simon didn't quite hear her and said, "Huh?" again.

"Never mind!"

He turned back to Perish who shook her head solemnly. With both traveling companions not clarifying, he was left to be confused for the next league in silence. "It's weird," Simon said finally after the curvature of the long road had straightened and there was a long stretch of path before them.

Lumi and Perish glanced at him without saying anything.

"You want to be a Toive Knight, but the knighthood you're devoted to is out to capture you and sentence you to death."

She shifted in her saddle. "Why is that weird?"

"I mean, to you you've avenged my death. But to them, and Narumont at large, you've done a crime. Why is there such a difference in your beliefs compared to theirs?"

"Interpretations of teachings are always splintered."

"But your father taught you. Was he a Toive Knight?"

Lumi turned her head, hiding her face. "You remembered that. Yes, he taught me what I now believe." She turned back to continue looking ahead. "Toive is a kind god. Where more common beliefs differ from me and my father's beliefs is how that kindness is practiced. To tolerate an enemy is 'kindness.' " She gestured quotes with her fingers. "That 'kindness' is how Narumont has addressed many conflicts. In some cases it makes sense, and in others… like your case, Simon, it's idiocy."

Simon shivered at the vehemence in her last word.

"It's like going to sleep while there's an intruder in your home holding a knife over his head. I honestly wouldn't care if it were just someone else in their own home and they chose to fall asleep knowing full well of the danger, I'd let nature take its course, but if they also had kids in the home…"

"That's awful," Simon said.

"I *know*. That's the point. What *I* believe to be kind is holding your own. You don't do nothing about the danger because it would be 'unkind' to *them*. Kindness applies to yourself as well. If you are wronged, it's unkind to you to ignore it. You take care of it, and, that way, danger is put in check, and not only are you safer, but so are others. That's what being a knight means."

Simon shifted his hands, lightly patting the short brown fuzz of his horse as its muscles worked. "So Narumont sees your actions as unkind, and therefore deserving of punishment."

"There's plenty of political nuances contributing to what they think makes me deserving of punishment," Lumi said dismissively. "That, coupled with their beliefs, is what makes things different between where I stand and Narumont."

"Are—are we actually on Narumont's side in this war?" Simon asked.

"No side is perfect," Perish said, reminding him of her presence. "In a perfect world, we'd have our own, imperfect side. Hmm. That things aren't perfect could be evidence the gods aren't perfect."

Simon laughed, startling himself.

"There you go. The dead boy laughs. But spare your energy for the rest of the road, we're going to meet back up with Masaka in another few days or so. She should have come up with a plan by then."

*\*\*\**

"Plan?" Masaka repeated Simon's question back to him. "Oh yeah, sure. We're going to go into the city and beat everyone up."

Simon, Perish, and Lumi gaped at the guild master. Perish spoke first, saying, "You had the better portion of a week to plan, and that's it?"

"Simple plans are good plans," Masaka said simply.

"Half-baked ones aren't," Lumi commented.

Masaka silently whistled. "The girl has a mouth!"

"We're talking about Narumont, right?" Simon asked. "Not Salama?"

"That's right!" Masaka lifted her leg to rest on a half-buried rock on a hill overlooking the city. On the more gently sloped side of the hill behind them the other Waymakers were doing their own things in a temporary camp. She pointed her arm straight at the lights shining their way in the late evening darkness, completing her majestic pose of an adventurer targeting her next quarry. "The war has already begun, and it looks like Salama wants to end it fast. They've sent three entire guilds out to break apart the defenses." Her arm moved slightly to indicate Narumont's walls facing the Jordun Flatlands. Portions of the tops of the walls were broken or missing but their bases remained otherwise intact. "Repairs are slow, but the damage would've been far worse if the High Clerics didn't mitigate the attacks. If not for them, the city would've already been taken. But, all three attacking guilds were instead routed, most captured while several ran off."

Simon slowly watched Masaka gesture to the four grand cathedrals for each High Cleric as she talked. When she finished, he said, "Great. Why are we attacking our allies?"

"Because I realized when people are pressured, they're more inclined to act."

"I don't follow," Lumi said, sitting herself down on the short, cluttered tufted grass carefully, still in her chainmail.

"If we beat everyone up, they're likely to go along with what we want."

"So we're making demands by power of threat," Perish mused slowly. "Demanding them to... to do what? What do we want?"

"Well, first of all, to absolve Lumi," Masaka replied, dropping her hand to now rest on her hip. "That's the first order of business. After that, if we can get that, we'll have to see."

"You really didn't think of what we'll do after?" Lumi asked incredulously.

"*I* did, but that's nothing to worry your little head about right now," Masaka said. "You should be appreciative! We went out of our way to the Cursed Lands to save you, now you're our top priority to continue saving."

Simon heard Lumi grumble something in the realm of not wanting to be saved. He coughed then said, "I still don't know why we're attacking our allies."

Masaka looked at him thoughtfully. "Let's put it this way. If you're attacked by one enemy, you only have to focus on that one enemy. If you're attacked by two enemies, your focus is split. And if you discover one of your allies is an enemy, you become even more frazzled."

"I get the pressure thing," Simon said impatiently with a nod. "I don't get *why* we pressure Narumont in this way. It seems unnecessary and risky."

"Narumont is one of a few peculiar cities where healing damage to people takes less time than damage to things. If we were to destroy a wall or building, we'd be causing more pressure but the damage would harm ourselves when we re-ally with Narumont to fight Salama. I as well as the High Clerics can take care of people easy with our affinities."

"Sure, but what if they just beat us up? Not to downplay what we can all do, but we're just one guild."

"Okay, maybe I exaggerated," Masaka said. "We're not beating *everyone* up, just the High Clerics."

"What!?" Simon, Perish, and Lumi said in unison.

It was Masaka's turn to gape at each of them. "You doubt we can do it?"

"They're—the—High Clerics—!" Lumi spluttered.

"Fighting four of the eleven Numen is worse than fighting all of Narumont's forces combined," Perish muttered. "Lumi was lucky to take out Valen amidst chaos, but…"

Simon reeled, his thoughts more so processing the fact they were attacking the leaders of a war rather than considering their actual power. "Didn't you take Valen's arm off?"

Perish shook her head. "That was lucky, too. I can only do something like that in close proximity to them, and it takes a lot of energy to do."

"Pffft." Masaka waved her hand dismissively. "We're not relying on luck. We're going to fight them head-on. I've already sent Frisk off to notify the High Clerics."

"You—what—!?" Perish now spluttered.

"I couldn't send Procel. I've asked him for too much and his magic takes a lot out of him. Don't worry, Frisk is only delivering messages for the clerics to meet us on the Verlangen grounds."

Perish gathered herself, her expression grave as she took a step and brought her face inches from Masaka's. "Why the hell... would you choose to fight Numen... at a school?"

Masaka took a beat to consider the seriousness of the other woman before laughing. "It's technically by a school."

Perish grabbed Masaka's shoulders and shook her while Masaka's laughter grew maniacal. "This is the most ridiculously rambunctious, worm-shit, pathetically planned, stunningly stupid, lousy, critter-crap, piece-of-piss, stupidly stunning…"

## Chapter 37: Pressure

"…dumbshit, gormless, god-damned, damn-damned, twit-twatted, rot-brained, *zero*—"

"Enough of that, we're here," Masaka interrupted Perish's ramblings as they stepped off the thoroughfare and onto the fields surrounding Verlangen Seminary. They moved further forward before stopping and looking around. The high, suspended waxing moon lacked only slivers of itself around the edges, a near-perfect circle.

Bartol sauntered ahead of them a couple paces while gazing across the open area, shading his eyes. "We can get attacked from any direction here." He halted and turned to the two women, his teeth glinting in the moonlight. They knew him to be a goof, but the smile coupled with his obscured eyes unnerved them slightly.

"We're not going to be attacked on sight," Masaka said. "Unless Frisk slipped up and said too much." They each turned their backs to each other, facing a different direction to prevent being snuck up on.

"Is it really wise to leave the other Waymakers behind?" Perish asked, seemingly past her anger.

"There'd be heavy suspicion if *all* of us showed up in the dead of night outside a school." Masaka glanced at the other two, nodding to herself. "Us three is all we need." She caught the faint sound of chainmail and lowered her eyelids. "Lumi…"

The young knight detached from the shadow of the nearest building along the thoroughfare, her heaume covering her head.

"You weren't supposed to follow us."

"If there's going to be fighting on my account, I'll be a part of it," the girl said defiantly. She folded her arms, the only bodily indication of her opinion of Masaka's disapproving stare. "Where's Simon?"

"Lumi Valse."

Before any of them could react to the newcomer's voice, Lumi felt the soles in her shoes dampen. She let out a cry as her feet yanked out from under her. Her body slid painfully along the grass before coming to a stop at the feet of High Cleric Catalina, flanked by High Clerics Aldana, Montel, and Thian who now stood at the end of the thoroughfare. Each wore pristine blue regalia from head-to-toe, loose in places to be considered formal for a ceremony but fitted enough to also be considered battle-ready. A trail of water receded from Lumi's shoes, converging into a marble-sized sphere that balanced on Catalina's raised index finger.

"You've managed to find the wayward knight. Is this why you called us all here so late?"

Perish cursed under her breath and silently stepped next to Masaka's left while Bartol stepped to her right. Masaka masked her gritted teeth with a grin. "That's right."

Catalina clapped her hands slowly, the marble of water retaining its shape as it moved along with her finger. "You did well in finding her. With the way you insisted on the Waymakers tracking her down yourselves, I suspected ulterior motives. Thian also doubted you'd be forthcoming in returning her, but it seems we were wrong."

Thian frowned and shook his head. With a swirl of his own hand, water streamed from a medium-sized barrel attached to his back by a strap. The water quickly engulfed Lumi up to her neck and froze over as a slab of ice.

Lumi's head turned both ways, her heaume impotently thudding against the ground. Her upset grunts could be heard behind the mail covering.

The High Clerics turned and began walking away, the ice slab sliding autonomously alongside Thian.

"You're not gonna ask where we found her?" Masaka said.

The High Clerics stopped and turned. Catalina said, "The girl can tell us before we execute her. You all should get rest. We've received intel there will be another attack in the—" Catalina's eyes bulged as a wave of pressure caused her and the other High Clerics to seize up.

The four recovered quickly, though the unnatural pressure also didn't linger. Catalina's eyes narrowed as she turned fully to face Masaka. "What are you doing, Masaka?"

"I was hoping to have a little chat," Masaka said, her grin faded but not completely gone. Wisps of clouds gently blanketed the moon, dimming the light around them. "It's not like it'll rain."

The other High Clerics turned before cringing as another wave of pressure convulsed their bodies. They straightened, their hands coiled. "I take it my former doubts were correct?" Catalina said coldly.

Masaka made a fist and clasped it with her other hand. Perish and Bartol responded to the light slapping sound by getting into fighting stances.

Lumi's encased body began to slowly slide back over the grass away from the High Clerics. Thian pointed a hand at her, causing the slab of ice to go still. "What happened to having a chat?" he said, his voice low and fierce.

Masaka shook her head. "We can chat with our fists."

A tense, quiet moment elapsed with the seven faced off with each other, all poised and ready to attack.

Thian shifted first, but not to fight. He looked down in confusion as Lumi's body started to continue slowly moving away again on its own. He effortfully brought both his arms out, commanding the ice slab to stay still.

It did not.

Lumi slid faster until she reached the pace of a horse's gallop. She careened past Masaka, Perish, and Bartol and off toward the large school building at the center of the fields.

"Thian," Catalina said quietly, "What was that?"

"I don't know," he replied. The High Clerics noted the three Waymakers also turning in interest to watch the ice-encased Lumi near Verlangen Seminary and jolt to the side. Lumi let out a distant, startled cry as the bright and cold blue slab slid left and then jolt again to move out of sight behind a corner wall.

Masaka glanced both ways at Perish and Bartol and shrugged before turning back to face the High Clerics.

"Interesting," Montel mused, clasping his hands together. Around him the air appeared to shimmer as mist formed. The slack of his sleeves ruffled with a growing breeze that stirred the mist in a circle around him. "I'm something of a specialist with flurries, but I did not sense any such magic being performed. And Thian being a specialist with frost and not knowing what happened, it's a wonder what force took Lumi away."

"You did it somehow, didn't you?" Catalina asked Masaka.

Masaka shook her head. "My powers only strengthen or weaken the body; I can't force them to move on their own."

Aldana clapped her hands. "Enough!"

Montel tilted his head, then unclasped his hands slowly and the building flurry expanded. It encircled the High Clerics, then continued to grow. Within, the wind began to whip across their clothes.

"Easy, Montel!" Catalina called.

Montel's eyes widened with surprise, reversing course and bringing his hands back together.

The flurry grew stronger.

The High Clerics shared looks of confusion while protecting their faces. The flurry engulfed the Waymakers and sent chills across all of them.

"It's getting hard to see anything!" Bartol said, rubbing his arms.

All at once the flurry dissipated and the seven were left standing in the clear night albeit with mildly damper clothes. The four High Clerics had hold of each others' hands to concertedly get rid of the spell.

They all blinked uncertainly, then noticed an eighth person standing between them. Simon looked at each of the High Clerics in turn.

The High Clerics started, letting go of each other. "I see," Catalina said. "You were using your spirit, Sim, to mess with our spells."

The boy silently stooped and slammed a palm into the grass. All at once, the flurry reignited, even more furious than the one before, alongside a wave erupting from the grass and consumed them all. Both the High Clerics and Waymakers were torn off the ground, carried upon water and wind.

***

Bartol blinked repeatedly. The world had gone white for a couple moments before he ended up in a far quadrant of the Verlangen Seminary grounds. Several paces away was Thian, having washed up nearby as well. Far off in another quadrant he could see the telltale nun's habit marking Masaka who stood nearby another High Cleric with the beautiful blue outfit. In another quadrant was the figure of Perish alongside another High Cleric. "Ohhh," Bartol said to himself. "So this was the plan."

Thian grimaced at him. "Whatever your antics are, if you want to fight us individually, then I'll oblige," he growled. He pumped his fists sequentially, water rapidly rushing out from the barrel on his back and forming icicles like the head of a spear around each.

Bartol backed up a few paces, wary of the wickedly sharp ice Thian jabbed in his direction. "Quick on the draw!" he exclaimed, narrowly dodging a jab to his lower stomach.

Thian then simply grunted before launching his arm at Bartol's face.

"Whoa!" Bartol didn't move in time, and the ice struck his cheek with a soft *mush*. "Ow-ow-wow..."

Thian withdrew his hand.

Bartol touched his unpenetrated cheek gingerly and shivered. "That's cold! Are you trying to kill me?"

Thian lifted his eyebrows and angled his arm around to look at the makeshift spearhead over his right fist. The tip was gone, or rather no longer sharp and instead caved inward. He now held a makeshift glove of ice.

Bartol winced as Thian's left fist launched faster than he could react, stabbing his chest over his lungs.

Again, Thian withdrew his arm and maneuvered his weaponized ice to note how its sharpness had receded into a blunt block of ice.

"That's cold!" Bartol said again, swiping away remnant frost clinging to his shirt.

"Why aren't you hurt?" Thian muttered. More water coiled around his shoulders and arms and condensed at the tops of his fists, reforming sharp edges.

"You're trying to kill me!" Bartol continued to back away, but was unable to get fully out of range of Thian's arms.

Two more mushy sounds emanated as the ice connected with Bartol's arm and stomach. The Waymaker stumbled back and fell down clumsily to then awkwardly crawl backwards. Thian looked down to again see he was left with two blocks of ice over his hands. He groaned with frustration, unclenching his hands. The ice around them cracked loudly and became individual floating daggers. He pushed at them violently and they whizzed directly at Bartol.

Bartol pushed himself to the side to avoid a few sharp icicles while a series of others pelted him up and down his body. "Eeee!" The ice daggers seemed to refuse to cut him, instead blunting themselves and falling harmlessly to the ground in imperfect, translucent balls.

"Why aren't you hurt!?" Thian asked angrily. The ice around Bartol's body quivered, floating up and flying back to hover around Thian in the air.

"I'm uncomfortable!" Bartol said indignantly. He stopped crawling backwards and gave Thian a look of reproach. "You can't hurt me. Whatever you throw at me will become soft."

Thian thought quickly. His grimace transformed to a smirk when he arrived at another means of subduing the Waymaker. "I can't hurt you, can I?" His fingers curled as the sharp icicles unfroze, becoming small individual pools of water. The water then connected together to form a long stream that continued extending from the barrel on his back. The stream followed along his body until it coiled his right hand like a rope. The far end of the stream zigzagged through the air and wrapped itself around Bartol's left ankle. "I may not have enough water to encase you like Lumi, but I *can* hurt you!"

Bartol blinked a few times as the water began to tug him toward the High Cleric. His mouth quirked up slowly, morphing into a grin as giggles bubbled from him.

***

"Leave them be for now," Masaka told Simon, beckoning him away from Lumi and the escalating profanities leaving Perish's mouth.

"...inane, crap-bucket, asinine, sodded..."

Perish's words faded away finally as they came to a secluded flat part of the incline along the cliff's edge overlooking Narumont. Masaka stopped and turned, putting a hand on both Simon's shoulders. "There's more to the plan, and it will hinge on you."

Simon anxiously shifted his feet. "Me?" he questioned.

"As you can tell from Perish's reaction over there, the High Clerics will be no joke. You saw what they could do in their dungeon, and now we'll be facing them head-on."

"What can I do?"

Masaka smiled, hearing a subtle tremor in his voice. "You only need to do what you can. For starters, you're going to go alone to Verlangen Seminary ahead of us."

Simon paled.

"Relax. No one in Narumont really knows who you are. The only people who know what you look like are us Waymakers and the High Clerics, and we won't be convening for some time. As for your teachers and classmates who might notice you in the school, just pretend you're Sim—Catalina would have told others about the spirit. It'd be best if they didn't notice you, but that might not be possible."

"I forgot to ask about Sim," Simon said as color slowly returned to his face. "He's still around?"

"Ah… Well, yes, but—What happened was, after you died, he vanished. Perish personally checked your room in the school and found him returned to the form of the vessel in which we originally found him when we conquered the Narumont dungeon. He's safe in your room still, and he's the reason you're going to go to Verlangen Seminary."

Simon nodded. "You want me to get Sim to help fight the High Clerics?"

"Yep, exactly. Together you can cause a lot of confusion, especially while they think you're dead."

Simon nodded again, though chewed the inside of his mouth. "You really want my help in fighting them?"

"I don't think we can fight them without you," Masaka said.

Simon rocked back at the sincerity in her voice. "I can sort of guess what you want me to do," he said tentatively. "But what exactly do you want me to do?"

"All five of you have an affinity for water, which means you all work with the same element. But each of the High Clerics specializes in a particular application of water that isn't the same. Thian specifically uses it to create frost which none of the others can do, except Montel. Aldana uses condensation which is tantamount to spontaneously creating water, which none of the others can do, except Montel. Catalina uses it to scald, which is somewhat like the opposite of what Thian does. And Montel does what could be considered a mix of the other three, but with the terrifying control of water in gas and solid states that in turn controls the air."

Simon gave her a long, silent look after she finished explaining the High Clerics' abilities. "Isn't that everything I can do? Well, except for controlling the air?"

"Why, yes, Simon, you can do all of that," Masaka said mischievously. "Isn't that something?"

"But I'm not nearly as powerful or experienced as them. What does being able to do what they can do do for me?"

"Many things," Masaka said. "You're not wrong that between you and them it's unbalanced, something like a bug fighting a bird. The thing is, you can do all that they can do, only less powerfully, but also more than what they can do." She pointed a thumb back at Narumont. "You know that trick you did to revert the waterfall in the dungeon? Doing a version of that is going to be key to how you fight them. Take out your tome."

Simon tilted his head, but obliged. "*Koota.*" The tome materialized midair between them and Masaka caught it deftly with a hand.

She flipped it open to the first of the blank pages and turned it to face Simon. "What you have done already is more of a technique than a spell, but it's still called a catalyst spell. In addition to that, you can do an actual spell. I use it every time I use my magic."

"You do?" Simon asked, surprised.

She nodded. "Surprisingly, I'm not powerful enough to control people's movements whenever I please. I can affect people's bodies, but that doesn't mean it will affect them. People have a natural resistance to such magic that directly interacts with them. People with active magic have an even greater defense mechanism. As much as I'd like to force the High Clerics to seize up and be incapacitated, it won't work. But, there's a spell I've learned to use by necessity to make my magic work at all."

"How did you learn this was a spell without a tome?" Simon asked.

"Trial and error, until Perish was kind enough to let me reference a tome for the first time. And then I learned it's a spell just about everyone has. Except you right now," she added, shaking the blank pages of his tome at him. "The spell is simple: you take control of another person's spell."

Simon's thoughts raced back to the moment in the dungeon he worked through what Perish had taught him about spells and his working analogy between magic and computing. *Spells are like data. The type and degree of spells are like 'data entry' while the complexity of spells is like 'command entry.' Taking control of another person's spell would be like...* "Override," he murmured.

Masaka blinked. "Huh?"

Simon shook his head, then gaped at the first blank page she held out towards him. Letters spontaneously wrote themselves across the page, detailing the spell Masaka had described and Simon conceived in his head.

*Override 10*

*Alters the type, degree, or complexity of another spell.*

Masaka noticed Simon's eyes darting back and forth and turned the tome back around to see. "Aha! You've got the... spell?" Her words rose in pitch as she read the page. "Override sounds like it's political. Others' tomes have variations of the spell name like 'Overturn,' 'Counter,' or 'Alter.' The name that I personally use is 'Subjugate.' "

"It's a word from my previous life that pretty much means the same thing," Simon said quickly. "With this spell, you're saying I stand a chance against the High Clerics?"

Masaka looked up from the tome slowly. "Maybe."

***

Simon felt his back bump against the perimeter wall of the seminary grounds. He had drawn Montel as far away from the other High Clerics as he could, both to prevent double-teaming and to keep his identity unknown for as long as possible.

"You're acting timid for a spirit," Montel mused. He held his hands upward. His fingers curled rhythmically, mimicking a pattern of ripples as the air around him glazed with frost. "I never was able to fully summon you from the vessel myself. I assumed I wasn't strong enough, but when I learned that boy had done it I figured I missed something else. Should I assume I'm stronger than you?"

Simon palmed the wall behind him, feeling loose dust cling to his hands. "Yes."

Montel chuckled as the flurry around him intensified. "That wasn't a sincere question. I really shouldn't assume anything." He grimaced when the flurry's intensity reversed. "Your counterspells are quite a nuisance. I can't seem to get control of them after…"

Simon waited and watched as Montel's curling fingers slowed to a stop over a couple seconds.

"…a bit of… time." Montel dropped his arms to his sides and narrowed his eyes. "You're alive. How?"

Simon shivered. "What gave me away?"

"The record of your magic is kept by the High Clerics. I, myself, went back to Narumont Dungeon to assess how the spell on the waterfall was broken. Your magic is gradual and builds momentum. Now, how are you alive?"

"Would you believe me if I said a god helped?"

Montel's eyes narrowed further as he took a beat to think. "If you're suggesting Goddess Toive is responsible, you may be subject to punishment for blasphemy."

"Even if it's true?" Simon asked while sweat gathered around his hands and caused more dust to cling to him.

"What's true is hard to determine at the moment," Montel said slowly. All at once his eyes opened up and his posture straightened. "Alive or not, you attacked the High Clerics. Punishment is due." He stomped a foot and water gushed from the surrounding grass which withered immediately. Directing it with his index fingers, the water rushed at Simon from all sides.

Simon slammed his hands against the wall behind him and a sound like two balloons exploding echoed. With the dust and sweat as axes, more water built upon itself and propelled outward from his spot against the wall.

Both torrents collided and appeared to cancel each other out as the water scattered harmlessly in various directions.

*It collected just in time*, Simon thought. *If he uses more sudden and powerful spells I won't be able to keep up.*

Montel unclenched his hands from pointing and then clapped them together. The air seemed to crack like glass, only the accompanying brittle sound was much weightier. The lines of ice that had materialized instantaneously zigzagged in jagged patterns. Again, with a point from Montel, the ice converged on Simon like an avalanche.

Simon's hands instinctively formed circles as he frantically chanted, "Override, override, *override!*" Ice glanced off across several points of his body. The flurry-turned-cascade *crunched* back in on itself like a riptide, sending flakes scattering everywhere.

Montel stilled, eyes dropping to the small circles Simon formed with his fingers, and smirked. "I'd almost forgotten the basics." He curled his own pointed finger back to touch his thumb. The moment they touched the surrounding air shattered and *crunched* again. "I heard your sakti was nigh-limitless. I want to find that limit, even if it kills you."

Something of a fog in his mind descended. "Even if it kills me?"

"Too soon?" Montel asked. His smile broke when he registered the far-off and dazed gaze Simon looked at him with.

"There is a place where lost souls go."

Montel curled his other fingers into individual circles, the surrounding flurry spiking in force. "What?"

"In time you will see that place, and the beings that inhabit it."

Montel hesitantly moved his foot back, then returned it. "What are you talking about?"

Simon's thoughts unclouded and began to chant his override spell. His voice echoed the chant as he continued to ward off the roiling frost storm pushing towards him. Even while preoccupied with overriding the High Cleric's magic he could tell his successive spells weren't keeping up with each time the man tapped his fingers together in makeshift circles and another staggering flurry arose. The first one had only pricked his skin, but each subsequent storm cut deeper and in a growing number of places along his body. *I... need... momentum...*

*And space.*

"Sorry, Masaka," Simon whispered. He pushed off the wall and ran headfirst into the next storm Montel conjured. He began weaving "Creation" into his "Override" chant. Though even more ice cut his skin and clothes, simply moving away from the wall reduced the intensity of the storm that was converging on the point he had been standing in.

He neared the obscured figure of Montel who held out his hands which created a protective wall of ice. Simon ran by without trying to break through it, his feet sloshing in a growing stream of water that followed beneath him.

Montel spun, directing another onslaught of frost storms at the boy. "Running?" he muttered to himself before following in pursuit.

The puddle rippling along the ground underneath Simon continued to grow. Simon's chant now no longer sought to keep Montel's storms in check. "Swell. Swell. *Swell.*" When facing Avril in the student duel it had taken only one word, but he could not muster the sheer concentration to make a drop of water a wave while being outpaced by the High Cleric.

Simon's feet sank into a pool that then swept him forward towards the corner of the grounds where Masaka and Catalina faced off.

The two were locked in a hand-to-hand fight with the guild master pummeling a darting ball of steaming water that Catalina seemingly danced to manipulate. They broke focus when the sounds of rushing water and the cacophonous storm were upon them.

Catalina's face blanched before she covered her head, the steaming ball of water responding by fanning out and surrounding her before the wave and frost hit. Masaka grimaced and simply braced herself as Simon's wave submerged her.

Simon continued to control the wave to keep himself afloat and flow along the grounds around toward the other corner where Bartol and Thian fought. Simon also continued to chant "Swell." The wave was now at the same height as Verlangen's second floor.

The current suddenly slowed and Simon found himself falling. He caught himself with the water that remained beneath him and touched back down onto the flooded grass. The chill of Montel's flurry nipped at him again.

"What are you doing, Simon?" Masaka called, ringing out damp spots of her nun's habit.

*He overrode my own spell!* Simon clenched his teeth, his eyes darting around the receding wave that would soon disperse into the field. *I can build water up in a succession of spells, but he can undo it all with just one!* He glanced up at the darkened, impenetrable sky past the roof of Verlangen Seminary. *I need to do more!*

"*Create, bubbles,*" Simon chanted under his breath as he continued running towards Bartol and Thian. "*Create, bubble, bubbles. Swell. Swell. Move.*" The dispersing pool across the grounds shifted. The water consolidated in several points and began to hover in the air above the grass.

Bartol laughed maniacally as Thian tugged a makeshift rope of ice tied around the Waymaker's ankle. The rope looked to keep loosening and unsuccessfully dragging Bartol only a few inches with each tug.

Simon ignored the sight as he raced by, focusing on the globules that continued to expand in the air behind him. Without looking he felt as well as heard several explode from a sudden expanding pressure. "*Create, bubble, create, bubble, move!*" He panted, feeling mild pressure on his mind while trying to simultaneously direct all the spells.

Several levitating globules that formed before him exploded in brief splashes. "*Move,*" he breathed. The deformed water that started to fall reversed course and flew upward before disappearing. "*Create, bubble, swell, create, move…*" More and more his words tumbled to keep pace with his thoughts in managing the spells.

All across the grounds the hovering and expanding bubbles splashed from Montel countering each of the individual spells Simon cast. And still, the High Cleric gained on Simon with his ongoing snowstorm. Knifelike shards coursed through the air, embedding themselves in the grass dangerously close to Simon's heels. Something tipped him off that the shards would have hit him but a force shifted them off course. His eyes caught a figure in an upper floor window looking down on the grounds. *Sim's helping where he can.*

"*Swell, swell, swell.*" Simon briefly stopped chanting aloud and glanced around at the remaining water that had not yet sloshed away from the wave he had created or had recently fallen from the last of his creation and bubble spells. He skidded to a halt some distance from Perish and Aldana, barely registering the fourth High Cleric confining the songstress in her own large bubble of water that was both condensing and expanding. Perish's melodic voice was muted but still audible as her magic pushed back against Aldana's.

"*Override, override, override!*" Simon faced the flurry and focused solely on taking over and redirecting the brunt of the storm as Montel ran towards him. The swirling frost whipped upward and away into the night like a funnel.

The High Cleric was almost upon him when the strength of Simon's redirection couldn't keep up with the storm's strength.

More splinters of frost cut across his clothes and bit into his skin. "That's enough!" he called, raising his hands high into the air.

Though Montel stopped a couple paces from him, the storm raged on. "You're surrendering?" The High Cleric tensed when Simon's splayed fingers retracted and the boy pointed with both hands upward. His mouth half-opening indicated that he understood.

In a few seconds the flurry wound down, revealing the decimated fields that were left behind. Masaka and Bartol had both stopped fighting Thian and Catalina, all four readjusting to no longer having to protect themselves from the wind and frost.

"What's happening?" Thian called while he and the others made their way towards Montel and Simon.

"Tell them to stop," Montel said stonily when they were all close enough, gesturing to Aldana still fighting with Perish.

"Why are you pointing like that?" Bartol asked Simon between leftover fits of giggles.

"I have to keep it controlled," Simon said.

Bartol and Masaka looked at each other, then up. "It?" Masaka questioned, staring up at the dark sky.

"It…" Thian and Catalina mimicked Montel's open-mouthed reaction. Catalina cupped her hands around her mouth and called, "Aldana! Stop!"

The swirling bubble surrounding Perish burst and trickled across the ground. Perish's singing stopped and though the two were some distance away, they both seemed to also understand as they looked up, noticing the moon no longer visible in the sky.

"It can't be that big, can it?" Masaka asked. She then called to Perish, "Lighten things up!"

Perish sung out a long note, and an ethereal light streamed from the top of her head and up. The light glistened against a dark, translucent surface just above the top of the school building. A few straggling 'bubbles' floated up and melded with the giant mass. Perish's voice wavered, and the light moved to follow the outlined surface. The surface shifted minutely as the light uncovered more and more of its length. It continued on past the perimeter of the school grounds before the light became too faint to follow it across the city.

They all looked down at Simon who was sweating. "Simon…"

"Just tell them the deal already before I lose control!" he said.

Masaka flashed a grin, then addressed the High Clerics. "We'd like amnesty given to all Waymakers, and Lumi, for everything that's happened up to now. We'd like it in writing."

Catalina looked dryly at the guild master. "Is that all you want?"

"Just that, as quickly as you can before it's more than this school that suffers water damage."

Catalina shot Thian a dark look. He flinched and then took off in a run before ice coated his shoes and he skated swiftly off the grounds and out of sight.

Masaka rubbed Simon's shoulders, easing some of the tension and stress he had built up. "You can do quite a lot when you put your mind to it." She looked sideways at Catalina. "I told you we weren't going to get rained on."

The High Cleric sighed. "This was your plan from the beginning. But why?"

Masaka lifted her eyebrows. "Because we can."

## Chapter 38: Waymaker

Simon sat on the end of a marble pew within one of the grand cathedrals while Masaka and Perish huddled over a wide, imperious lectern towards the back of the building opposite the High Clerics. His muscles had been tense for what seemed like hours while he disciplined himself to maintain the mass of water hovering over Narumont.

"Hurry it up," Masaka snapped, glancing back at Simon.

"Saying that won't make things go any quicker," Catalina responded. Her hand flourished a reed pen across amnesty documents. Every now and then each of the other three High Clerics brought their own pens in to quickly scrawl their names.

Simon barely registered their ensuing arguments over bylaws and wider legalities. He gazed out a clerestory window set high in the closest wall, watching the undulating underside of the water. It really must have been hours due to early morning light illuminating the water in its entirety. It was massive, on scale with a lake. If not for it being blue, it could've been mistaken for a cloud shrouding the city.

"And... done!" Catalina dropped the pen on the lectern and stared expectantly at Simon. The others shortly turned their attention to him as well.

He shivered. They waited.

"Is it going away?" Thian asked, looking back and forth between Simon and the floating lake looming over the city.

"I don't know a spell that gets rid of water," Simon said tenuously.

"Oh, for—" Catalina cut herself off with a huff. "*We*'ll go do something about it. Just... keep holding it up there for now." She nodded at Thian, Montel, and Aldana and they swept down the middle aisle between the pews to the front exit.

Taking the papers, Perish followed Masaka to the pew Simon sat on and folded her arms over her still slightly damp dress. "It's been a long couple of days. To think this all happened because we hunted a horse."

"What's going to happen with the war?" Simon asked, shivering again.

"Don't strain yourself... more than you have to," Masaka said. "And don't worry about the war. The adults will take care of it."

Simon narrowed his eyes at her. "I thought you were done treating me like a kid."

"When you learn how to put away your magic I will," she teased. "But I'm serious about the war stuff. You may have already helped by showing Salama this floating mass of water that could flood a city." Simon let out a sigh. Masaka quickly caught on it wasn't out of frustration but relief. She looked up through the windows to see small streams of water funneling from the larger lake. Other portions of the lake appeared to steam and dissipate, while yet more portions frosted over and broke away into clouds of flakes.

Simon gradually and visibly relaxed as the size of the floating lake decreased. "Steam and snow," he said to himself. "Those would be cool spells to learn."

The front doors of the cathedral creaked as they opened and Lumi, wearing her heaume as ever, walked in with Bartol. "Is it done?" she asked.

"You're no longer a wanted girl!" Masaka said brightly. "Speaking of," she added, "there is still a wanted girl. You both went to Verlangen Seminary with Avril?"

Lumi stopped at the pew just behind Simon's and nodded. "She killed King Dormond. What about her?"

"You," Masaka started to say, then turned to Simon. "*Both* of you will be her escort. She is due to be sentenced in the capital along with her family."

With more of his focus available to be angry, Simon shook his head. "No."

Masaka and Perish shared a look with each other. Perish said, "I know she attacked us and is partly responsible for your... second death, but—"

"I don't hold *that* against her," Simon said stiffly. *Although, I do.* "She's a snake."

Lumi's face clouded. "Because she killed someone while no one was aware?"

Simon glanced back at her, then shook his head. "No, she—did something else when we first met. It's nothing."

"You say it's nothing, but also it's something," Masaka mused, then shrugged. "Well, snake or not, does she deserve execution?"

"She killed the king," Simon said. "Sounds like something is deserved."

"Okay," Masaka said. "Do you know why she killed the king?"

Simon clenched his hands, though the effort was weak after having been tensed up for so long. "Do you?"

"No."

"Why should I care? And why do you want us to be an escort for her?"

"Because you two were at the heart of the fiasco and are now exonerated," Masaka said. "It would potentially be hypocritical if you don't think she should be exonerated as well."

Simon sighed, now with both frustration and relief as the last of the water outside was dispersed. "Even if she has an excuse like Lumi, how would either of us change what her sentence is? She killed *the king*."

"I'm not asking you to save her," Masaka said simply. "I'm asking you to do what you can."

"What if I don't want to?"

Shrugging again, Masaka finally sat in the pew ahead of him and faced away. "Then that is your way to make."

He felt a new wave of tiredness wash over him. Unable to think of anything else to express his anger, Simon dazedly stood up and walked toward the exit. Lumi hesitantly followed while Bartol stayed with Perish and Masaka.

"You're not going to argue with him?" Bartol murmured so Simon couldn't hear.

"I'd be pushing what I want onto him," Masaka said with her own sigh. Despite the wrinkles on her forehead, she smiled. "Besides, I trust he knows what he wants. And, he now has the power to choose it."

Simon hesitated at the doors. Lumi moved ahead to push them open for him. He tilted his head at her in thanks and walked into the growing sunlight. There he met with Sim in his replica form. They embraced for a moment, Sim's eyes glittering as they looked back at Masaka. When they let go the spirit handed him something. Simon looked down and absently took it. The corners of his face lifted, and together they walked on, him holding a birch bowl.

# Epilogue

"Why are we doing this?" Simon asked again. He sat in the back of a covered wagon opposite Lumi as it trundled down a smooth road leading out of Narumont.

"You know why," Lumi said. Her heaume was off. "You decided to."

"Yes, but... can't I be unreasonable sometimes?"

Procel shifted beside Simon, his head lightly resting on an interior bow that held up the cover shielding the inside of the wagon from the sun. His eyelids drooped, a slight glimmer hinting that they weren't totally closed.

Simon grunted annoyance, searching for other ways to vent. "Why are you doing this?"

"I'm curious to see why Avril really did kill the king," Lumi said. "She sort of helped me escape from the hearing when she announced what she did and distracted everyone."

"And you?" Simon turned to Procel.

"I was told to take care of you," Procel replied softly.

"And you just do what you're told?"

"Not usually." He rolled his neck and sat forward. "I'm going to monitor the road." He stood, keeping himself hunched as he stepped out of the front of the wagon to the driver's perch.

Simon went quiet, watching the inner cover flap after it fell back and obscured the outside for some time.

"Are you okay?" Lumi asked.

"Just wondering when we'll catch up with Avril," Simon said. He winced at saying her name.

"You really don't like her," Lumi observed.

"I don't have a reason to like her yet."

"I don't really blame her for all that happened," Lumi said. "I obviously don't like her," she added quickly when Simon frowned. "Still, it is odd Masaka wanted me to go along. I'm not a Waymaker."

Simon blinked. "Who's Masaka?"

Lumi smiled, tugging at her hairband she wore around her neck. "You're joking. Or are you mad at her?"

Procel's head poked back through the cover flap at the front of the wagon. "We're nearing the next town Avril is staying in. We should go over preparations before we… engage with her and her family."

Simon sighed for what may have evenly matched the number of times he asked why they were doing any of this. He felt the wagon slow to a halt before ducking out the back flap of the wagon. The dry sunlight temporarily blinded him and he cast out a hand to shield his eyes. The road behind them stretched on along flat farmlands without another town in sight. Leaning to peer around the side of the wagon, he saw the road continue around a mile toward the outskirts of buildings marking the town.

Straightening back up, he reached for the sky to stretch his back. The aches of prolonged uncomfortable stillness eased. "I figured it would take longer," he said as Lumi leapt out from the back of the wagon next to him. "Or that Avril would already be in the capital by now. Hasn't it been a few months since that hearing?"

"The son of Dormond, the new king, deferred the sentencing what with the conflict between the cities being ongoing," Procel said, jumping down from the driver's perch and experimentally walking to stretch his legs.

"Hold the preparations," Lumi said, sidling away from the wagon. "I'm going to relieve myself. Give me a bit." She turned and walked purposefully toward a break in the crops a ways off where plants grew and stepped off the road to disappear in the foliage.

"Hey, Procel," Simon said distractedly.

"Hm?"

"Who's Masaka?"

Procel looked at him slowly. Then he shrugged. "I don't know."

*The story will continue in the second and final book: Summoner.*

# Simon's Tome

## Koota / Poista (10)

Summons and dismisses this tome.

*Bubble (10)*

*Creates a single bubble from an available water source.*

Bubbles (10)

Creates a short stream of bubbles from an available water source.

Swell (10)

Adds a fraction of the water from an available water source to the water source.

Creation (10)


Creates water.

Rime (10)

Turns water from an available water source into frost.

Move (10)


Manipulates water in a given direction.

Override (10)


Alters the type, degree, or complexity of another spell.

Riptide (10)

Creates an opposing water current within a dominant current.

# Acknowledgements

This book would not exist without paper (or digital technology as the case may be).

I thank Pat Oey, for unpaid editing as well as countless other things both remembered and forgotten. I also thank family, for being there regardless of whether I want or need you there.

I'd be remiss to not extend further thanks to readers for also existing. Without you, this book would not have been read.

# About the Author

Torion holds a B.A. in Creative Writing and Psychology and an M.S. in Psychology. He has had short stories featured in *Galaxy's Edge Magazine, Cohesion Press,* and *NonBinary Review.* He dedicates his free time toward writing and critiquing speculative fiction both personally and in separate writing groups; he also likes to play volleyball. Torion has published several novels, including *Not James, Vespertine Blue,* and *The Disgraced Mage.* You can find latest news about him at his website torion.us.